DARK SPACE VI: ARMAGEDDON

(3rd Edition)
by Jasper T. Scott

http://www.JasperTscott.com
@JasperTscott

Front Cover design by Thien A.K.A "ShooKooBoo"
Back Cover design by Justin Adams
http://www.variastudios.com/

TABLE OF CONTENTS

ACKNOWLEDGEMENTS

Six books in three years. It's been a wild ride. In that time you, the readers, have bought over 250,000 books, and I couldn't be more thankful. Whether you write a review, buy a book, help edit an advance reader copy, or all of the above, you've all made this an incredible journey, one I hope to continue on with you for many years to come.

As always I have to thank my wife and stepson for this book, because they had to put up with my obsessive working habits!

I also owe a big thanks to my editor, Aaron, who managed to get this manuscript back to me in record time, and my cover designer, Thien, who came through at the last minute with an exceptional cover.

And finally, thanks to all of my beta readers, without whom, this 1st Edition would be a mess of missing words, muddled prose, and cockamamy (that's right, cockamamy) mistakes. In particular, I'd like to thank, Bill Schmidt, Clair Gassoway, Daniel Eloff, Dani J. Caile, Dave Cantrell, Dwight, Gregor, Gary Watts, Gary Wilson, H. Huyler, Ian Seccombe, Indra Johnson, Jim Meinen, Michael Madsen, Peter Hughes, Rob Dobozy, Rafael Gutierrez, Rod Gotty, Shane Haylock, Sandra Roan, and Wade Whitaker. You guys made editing this book a whole lot easier!

Thank you, all of you!

To those who dare,
And to those who dream.
To everyone who's stronger than they seem.
"Believe in me /
I know you've waited for so long /
Believe in me /
Sometimes the weak become the strong"
—STAIND, *Believe*

DRAMATIS PERSONAE

Ortane Family
Ethan Ortane
Alara Ortane
Trinity Ortane
Atton Ortane / Darin Thardris

Heston Family
Strategian Hoff Heston
Destra Heston (clone)
Atta Heston (clone)

Avilonians
Valari Thardris / Neona Markonis
Grand Overseer Vladin Thardris / Omnius
Strategian Galan Rovik
Jena Faros
Lena Faros
>	**Nulls**
>	Farah Hale
>	Ceyla Corbin

Human Refugees
Destra Heston (original)
Atta Heston (original)
>	**The Rictans**
>	Rictan One Sergeant Cavanaugh - Deceased
>	Rictan Two Lieutenant "Magnum"
>	Rictan Three "Hop"
>	Rictan Four "Rockhead"
>	Rictan Five "Streak"
>	Rictan Six "Blades"
>	Rictan Seven "Carnage"

Rictan Eight - Deceased

Gors
Torv
Matriarch Shara
General Raka

Sythians
Shallah "The Supreme One"
Queen Tavia
Lady Kala
High Lord Kaon
High Lord Shondar
High Lord Worval
High Lord Rossk
High Lord Thorian
High Lord Quaris

Drones
Drone 767 / Bretton Hale
Drone 999 "Triple Nine" / Lena Faros

Others
Captain Marla Picara
Therius "The Redemptor"

PART ONE: THE SHADOW OF DEATH

—The Year 11 AE (After Exodus to Dark Space) Twelve Years Since the Original Sythian Invasion—

"There He will remove the cloud of gloom, the shadow of death that hangs over His people."
—The Etherian Codices

CHAPTER 1

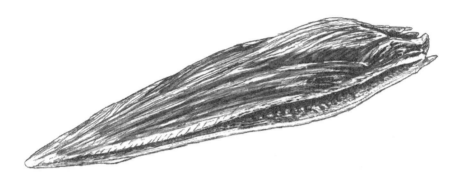

Destra Heston sat on a hard cot in her prison cell, staring at the cracks in the castcrete floor between her feet. She eyed one toe, which had begun to peek out through a hole in her left boot. That hole had been worn not from the month of being stranded in the frozen warrens of Noctune, but from the past five months of endlessly pacing around her cell.

It was hard to understand her captivity. After daring to explore the labyrinthine depths of Noctune and its ancient ruins, she and the other survivors from the expedition had stumbled into none other than the lord of all the Sythians, Shallah.

They'd all been promptly thrown into isolated jail cells, and since then the Sythians only came to give them food, water, and soap. Their captors never spoke, never lingered. They hadn't interrogated or executed any of the prisoners—at least not that she knew about. All she knew was the endless monotony of her cell.

From what little Shallah had divulged at the moment of their capture, Destra had realized that the Sythians were hiding from Omnius, the ruler of Avilon. That was a strange concept given that what she had learned of the Sythians was that they were impossibly numerous and they had invaded the Adventa galaxy to find new worlds to colonize. Was Omnius powerful enough to frighten a species whose warships numbered in the millions, and whose people numbered in the quadrillions?

Destra didn't know much about Omnius, but based on what she'd learned from Admiral Hale and the rest of the Avilonian rebels who had traveled with them on their fateful expedition to Noctune, he was a force to be reckoned with. Omnius was an artificial intelligence who had somehow managed to clone and resurrect everyone who had died during the Sythian invasion— including her husband Hoff.

That was probably the worst part of all, knowing that Hoff was alive, and that she was stuck on Noctune being held prisoner by Sythians, unlikely to ever see him again. Somehow she'd ended up on what was probably the wrong side of a civil war, a war against the ruler of the planet where her husband now lived.

Destra felt despair begin a slow march toward her heart, the one warm spot left in her body. Even here, in the heated confines of the Sythians' refuge, Noctune was freezing. Destra shivered violently, and something stirred in her lap.

Atta moaned softly and buried her face into the relative warmth of Destra's insulated pilot's suit. Destra reached out with a cracked and worn glove, and stroked the back of Atta's head, admiring her daughter's long, dark hair. Somehow it still looked lustrous and healthy. That was a good sign. It meant that the cold green mush they were given to eat every day must have sufficient nutrients in it to keep them healthy. Atta's cheeks were rosy and red, her small, button nose flushed pink at the tip from the cold. Destra supposed it was too much to ask the Sythians for a blanket. Not that she hadn't tried.

They were trying to drive her skriffy with isolation, but it wouldn't work. She still had Atta to talk to. Dear sweet Atta. Seven years ago she and Hoff had conceived her while stranded together on a world not unlike Noctune. Now she and Atta were back on another dark and frozen world. There was some irony in that.

Seven years...

No, that wasn't right. By now Atta had to be close to eight, but there was no way to know for sure. Destra's eyes burned with a sudden heat. She didn't even know when to celebrate Atta's birthday. A tear ran hot and wet down her cheek. Destra sniffled and laid her head back against the castcrete wall of her cell.

Thud.

She rocked her head back and forth, as if to deny the reality of their circumstances. A lump rose in her throat, and then the sobs came. She kept them muffled for Atta's sake.

Atta stirred once more, and Destra took a deep, shuddering breath. She forced it all down, kept it bottled in. She had to be strong. Had to show Atta that there was still hope, even if they didn't know exactly what they were hoping for.

Destra's despair retreated a step, and in its place came a creeping numbness that had nothing to do with the cold. She rolled her head to one side, her ear pressing up against the frozen wall of her cell, and she allowed her eyes to drift slowly shut. Her mind gave up the agony of consciousness. It was a sweet surrender of not-knowing and not-feeling.

And then the dreams came.

She saw herself sitting on the floor of her cell, mindlessly scraping away at it with some kind of stick that she'd found. Atta was nowhere to be seen, but perhaps she was asleep on the cot behind her.

Scrape. Scrape. Scrape.

Her stick broke. She stared at it in her callused and shaking hands. Dirty fingertips showed through holes in her gloves. The tool she'd been scraping the floor with was white and dirty, splintered on the end that she'd been scraping against the concrete. Then she saw it for what it was.

It was a femur—the longest and thickest bone in the human body. Destra recoiled from it, dropping the bone with a hollow-sounding clatter. She scuttled back into the farthest corner of her cell, terrified and sick with horror.

Scrape, scrape, scrape, came the echoes inside her head. Where had that bone come from? *Scrape. Scrape.* Where?

Scrape.

Where was Atta?

Suddenly she felt something sharp and protruding between her and the wall, something had been pushed into that shadowy corner, something that was not meant to be seen.

Destra felt around behind her. Her fingertips grazed more bones, and she screamed.

Her eyes popped open.

She blinked away a sudden rain of tears. The comforting weight in her lap where Atta had fallen asleep became suddenly horrifying. Destra couldn't bear to look, afraid that she might find a skeleton lying in her lap instead.

Scrape, scrape, scrape.

Destra screamed at the top of her lungs. Atta leapt up and fell over. Then she turned to her mother with a puzzled look.

"What's wrong, Mommy?"

Destra curled into a fetal position and shrank against the wall. Atta approached slowly. Destra hugged her knees to her chest and rocked back and forth, slowly shaking her head.

Scrape. Scrape. Scrape.

"It won't stop!" she said.

Atta touched her gently on one arm. "What won't stop?"

Destra rounded on her daughter, her eyes wild. "The sound! Don't you hear it?" Her voice cracked with the strain of shouting after untold months of aching silences when all that had been needed was a whisper. "You have to hear it! It isn't in my head. I'm *not* losing my mind. I'm not..."

Scrape. Scrape. Scrape.

Destra squeezed her eyes shut and pressed herself more firmly to the wall, but the noise only grew louder.

Scrape! Scrape! Scraaape!

Destra's eyes shot open, and she stood up. Her mind felt brittle, like an old rusty piece of metal bent back and forth too many times.

"I heard it..." Atta murmured.

Suddenly she noticed that Atta had gone completely still, her ear cocked toward the wall that Destra had been pressing herself against a moment ago. Then the noise came again, another long *scraaape!*

Suddenly a block of castcrete slid out of the wall and landed on their cot with a muffled *thud*. Then came a pitter patter of debris and a cloud of dust.

Destra stared into the hole, scarcely believing what she saw. Something within the hole coughed, and then a pair of slitted yellow eyes appeared, glinting in the gloom. As the dust cleared, a giant head appeared—a familiar skull-shaped head with corpse gray skin.

The being hissed at her and bared its dagger-like teeth.

"Torv?" Destra said, wondering if this was another dream.

More hissing.

She didn't have her translator anymore, so she had no idea what the Gor had said.

"How did you get here? Never mind. I can't understand you."

"He said he wanted to find a way out, not another box to live in," Atta said.

Destra turned to her daughter, blinking slowly, not understanding until she remembered that Atta, being a child, was more sensitive to the Gors' telepathy than human adults.

Torv hissed some more, and Atta translated. "He says that now the Sythians will find his tunnel and kill him."

Destra shook her head. "No, we'll hide it on our end, but you have to promise to take us with you when you find a real way out of here."

Hiss-sssss.

Atta flashed her mother a pretty smile. "He says he is happy to help, but first he must find Shara."

Destra nodded. "The matriarch..." Shara was the last female Gor, and the only hope for their species. "Tell him we'll do whatever we can to help."

"He says you can start by helping him fix the wall."

Destra hurried back to the cot and tried lifting the castcrete block from her cot. Her arms strained until it felt like they would snap, but the block was far too heavy for her. In the end it took all three of them to lift it. Torv helped with one muscular arm reaching out of his tunnel. He barely managed to pull his fingers out from under the block before it slid back into place.

Destra and Atta chewed soap and mixed it with dust to fill in the gaps in the wall. It was dirty work, and the taste of the soap nauseated her, but Destra couldn't help feeling elated. It felt good to finally be *doing* something. It felt even better to have hope. They weren't going to die in captivity after all.

They were going to escape.

CHAPTER 2

—One Month Later—

Farah Hale stood alone on the deck of the *Baroness*, an old venture-class cruiser. It came equipped with a cloaking shield, but that was the extent of its modernizations. It was a far cry from the warships that Farah had served on as a Peacekeeper in Omnius's fleet.

She sighed and splayed a hand against the cold transpiranium of the *Baroness's* main forward viewport, as if to narrow the intervening space between her and Bretton, wherever he was.

She'd done her best to keep sentiment out of it, to make a logical decision, but she knew that was impossible. Bretton was her uncle, yes, but he was also the man she had secretly loved since even before the Sythian invasion. There was so much to admire about him, so much to care for; it had been inevitable that she fall for her superior officer. The *uncle* part was the only reason she'd never done anything about it.

It had taken some convincing to get her bridge crew to agree with the rescue mission, but Bretton's ship, the *Tempest*, was quantum-refitted. That meant it could jump across thousands of light years in the blink of an eye, and it could communicate with equal ease. Finding that ship had been their incentive. The *Tempest* was too valuable to simply give up as lost. In spite of that, her XO, Deck Commander Tython, had shown early signs of resistance to the rescue mission, and the rest of the bridge crew hadn't been far behind.

Unlike the *Tempest,* Farah's ship did not have a quantum jump drive, and it would take six months just to reach Noctune. Making matters worse, they only had enough fuel for a one-way trip, which meant they'd be stranded in the Getties Cluster once they arrived.

There's a rule about rescues, Farah mused. *You don't dive in to save someone from drowning if you aren't strong enough to swim with them to shore.*

If they found the *Tempest* intact and used its quantum jump drives to get back to the Adventa Galaxy safely, then all would be well, but even Farah was realistic about the chances of that. If the *Tempest* could bring them home, wouldn't Bretton have used it to come back by now?

Adding to the multitude of reasons against a rescue mission was the fact that it wasn't just the skeleton crew of five bridge officers whose lives she risked. There were also the rest of the original crew of the *Baroness,* all of them survivors from Dark Space, all locked away in the ship's stasis rooms, and all ignorant of the fact that their vessel had been commandeered by a resistance movement from a planet called Avilon.

Put it all together, and going to Noctune seemed like a skriff's errand. Farah had heard the crew whispering behind her back, and she'd seen the tight-lipped smiles they gave her whenever she walked by. She'd known what they were thinking.

So one night, about a week after setting course for Noctune,

Farah had found herself alone on deck with Commander Tython, and she'd decided to do something about the looming threat of mutiny. She'd waited for just the right moment, and then she'd walked up behind Tython, drawn her sidearm, and pulled the trigger.

The rest of the crew had been fast asleep in their beds at the time, so she repeated the process, sneaking into one crewman's room after another until all five of them were incapacitated.

The weapon had been set to stun, of course. She wasn't a murderer. Once they were all unconscious, Farah had used a grav sled to carry them to a row of empty stasis tubes. Then, one by one, she'd wrestled them into position and activated the tubes with the auto-wake timer disabled. That done, she'd checked the rest of the crew's stasis tubes, just in case any of them accidentally woke up. She'd been surprised to find them all with the same settings. Clearly the former captain of the ship had been just as paranoid as her—and with good reason: from what she'd heard, he'd been killed during a mutiny.

But there was a price to pay for being so wise; Farah had spent the last six months in complete isolation. With no one to talk to, she'd begun talking to herself. She told herself it was to keep her vocal chords working, but the road to madness was littered with better rationalizations than that.

Skriffy as a space rat or not, her lonely mission was finally at an end. The *Baroness* was about to arrive at its destination.

Farah traced the bright, kaleidoscopic patterns of light that raged just beyond the bridge viewports. Legend had it that one could go skriffy just from staring out into those spinning strands of light for too long.

"I'm not that superstitious. Then again... I am talking to myself, aren't I?"

Farah wondered what she would find at Noctune after all

this time. Perhaps the *Tempest* had suffered some catastrophic failure of its jump drives and none of the crew were sufficiently knowledgeable to fix them. Or maybe Bretton had landed on Noctune with the Gors, and the Sythians had found and destroyed his ship in orbit, leaving him stranded on the Gors' icy home world.

A small voice in the back of her mind whispered to her about other, darker possibilities, but she refused to listen. She couldn't turn back now, so she had to leave room for hope to live and breathe inside her weary soul.

Not that she had a soul. Omnius had resurrected her and Bretton along with everyone else who had died during the Sythian invasion. They were immortals now; they didn't even age. Perhaps that was why she found it so hard to believe that Bretton was really dead. Death had long-since ceased to have any meaning for them.

An automated countdown began, and Farah shook herself out of her thoughts. She took the gangway back from the viewports and hurried down the stairs to the crew deck. Finding the nav station, she sat down and began configuring the displays in preparation for the reversion to real space.

The countdown reached zero, and a bright flash washed away the rainbow-colored swirls of SLS. As the brightness faded, it was reduced to a myriad of twinkling pinpricks—the flickering candles of the universe.

Farah held her breath and pulled up a star map. She'd set most of the ship's systems to auto, so by now the gravidar station must have finished a preliminary scan of the area.

The star map showed Noctune dead ahead, a few moons in orbit around it, and a small field of...

Farah shook her head and squinted at the map. Her heart was beating so hard she felt like it was about to explode. There was a small field of *debris* orbiting the planet.

Farah jumped up out of the nav station and ran over to gravidar to get a closer look at the debris. Optical scans revealed familiar components. In-depth scanning showed that the debris was mostly duranium. The clincher was what she saw when she switched back to an optical display and zoomed in on the largest piece of debris. Light amplification overlays revealed details that never should have been visible in the weak light of Noctune's sun. She saw a sheet of metal, curled and blackened at the edges. A trio of Imperial-white letters were emblazoned on one side — *EST*. If the other half of that hull fragment was spinning around out there somewhere, Farah was sure it would have read *TEMP*.

Farah sat back with an incredulous snort, her eyes busy filling with a suspicious warmth. "You selfish *kakard*, Bret. Six months and *this* is what I've got to show for it?" She shook her head. "No."

Bretton wasn't dead. She refused to believe it. She tried to calm herself, to remember that she'd already allowed for this possibility. Debris didn't mean that Bretton was dead. He might be frozen and half-starved to death somewhere on the surface of Noctune, but he was *not* dead.

Farah toggled the ship's scanners for an in-depth scan of the planet. It was only 60% complete by the time she thought to wonder about what had destroyed the *Tempest*.

Her thoughts went to the *Baroness's* cloaking shield, and she turned to look at the engineering station where she could activate that shield.

She may as well be cautious and keep a low profile. Rising from the gravidar station, she hurried over to engineering.

Just as she was about to sit down, a thunderous *boom* roared through the ship's sound in space simulator (SISS). Damage alarms screeched and alerts popped up all over the engineering station. Aft shields had dropped from blue to green.

Boom!

Another hit. This time the dorsal shields flickered into the green.

"Frek!" Farah queried the ship's computer to locate her attackers. She found them moments later—two Sythian cruisers racing up behind, and a massive battleship pacing her from below.

Farah's mind raced. She couldn't fight back without a bridge crew to man the control stations, and even then, she'd still be short the gunners and pilots she needed to put up a proper fight. Running was the only viable option, but fuel was far too low for that.

Boom! Boom! Boom!

The deck shuddered underfoot and acrid smoke began drifting through the bridge. The lights flickered out, and then the red glow of emergency lighting cast the bridge into a bloody gloom. Damage alerts flashed up all over the engineering console with a steady flood of information that any competent engineer would have forwarded to his repair crews by now. Except that she wasn't a ship's engineer, and she didn't have any repair crews.

Farah noticed that the ship's aft and dorsal shields were already in the yellow at 47% and 36% respectively. Her hands flew over the shield control board to equalize power by draining the shield arrays on the other sides of the ship. After that, she set shields to auto-equalize, and a dialog appeared at the bottom of the main display:

Shields Equalizing...

Then another flurry of attacks made those efforts useless, battering the ship's dorsal shields down into the red at just nine percent. The SISS filled the air with a continuous *roar* that made it hard to think. Farah was about to bark out an order for someone to turn down the volume, but then she remembered that she was the only one on deck, and she did it herself.

Suddenly, she saw the folly in betraying her crew before they could betray her. She'd made it to Noctune all right, but she wasn't about to make it any further.

Then a desperate idea occurred to her, and Farah's eyes darted to the comms station. She ran over and quickly hailed the battleship running below the *Baroness.* Her message was short, but to the point.

"We surrender!"

Farah wasn't expecting an answer, and even if she got one, she wasn't expecting any kind of mercy. The Sythians had systematically slaughtered humanity for more than a decade.

Then the comms board lit up with an incoming message and Farah's eyes grew round. She keyed the message for playback, and the ship's speakers crackled with an alien voice. It took a moment for her to focus on the speaker enough to pick out words, and it was another moment before she recognized those words. The alien *hissed* at her in *Versal,* not Sythian.

"Lower your shieldsss and prepare for boarding, humanss. Do not resist or you shall be killed."

Farah must have gaped at the display for fully half a minute before she thought to comply with that demand. By then the Sythians had lowered her shields for her, but she disabled them anyway. After that, it wasn't more than five minutes before dozens of shuttles began streaming from the Sythian warships and landing in the Baroness's hangar bays.

Steeling herself, Farah started up the stairs from the crew deck to the gangway leading off the bridge. On her way, she checked the charge on her sidearm and flicked the setting from stun to kill—just in case. Surrender did seem like the only option, but there was always the dubious alternative of going down in a blaze of glory.

Only one thing held her back. If the Sythians wanted to take her alive and her ship intact, then why hadn't they done the same with Bretton? Perhaps he'd fought to the bitter end, but he might also have abandoned his ship after setting it to self-destruct. Knowing him he'd rather blow it up than let the Sythians get their hands on quantum tech, and if he'd done that, then maybe he'd been captured, too.

See you soon, Bret, Farah thought as she walked off the bridge. The doors *swished* shut behind her with a resonant *boom,* as if to warn her that there was no going back now, but she was long past the point of no return.

All that was left was to follow through.

CHAPTER 3

Ethan Ortane watched as a pair of heavily-armed goons unloaded the cargo crate from the back of his air car. He didn't know their names, but that went with the territory. It wouldn't be wise to participate in a resistance movement against an AI as powerful as Omnius without some degree of anonymity.

Thick cords of muscle bulged as the goons carried the crate to their grav sled. Ethan mentally nicknamed them Tall Goon and Short Goon. Tall was in charge, and he had the devlin-may-care swagger to prove it. Red-glowing tattoos crawled down from tightly rolled shirt sleeves, and the man's shaven skull sported some ugly scars that looked like they'd been carved out in a knife fight. It was all too familiar. Ethan had been exiled to Dark Space for stim-running, and even after all these years it was still easy to recognize another runner.

Ethan suppressed a scowl and pasted a pretty smile on his face instead. Stim-running had cost him his family once. He couldn't allow it to happen again. Just because he didn't know what he was delivering didn't mean he couldn't guess. He was an express courier making small deliveries to suspicious-looking people in deserted alleys, and Admiral Vee paid him as much as *three* cab drivers to do it. He would know. He used to be a cab driver.

It was hard to argue with a job when that job was the only thing between his family and a life of poverty, but Ethan was an old veteran of short-term gain for long-term pain, and he wasn't a big believer in ignorance being bliss.

Besides, *Bliss* was exactly what he was worried about. It was the super drug behind half of the crime in the Null Zone, a performance-enhancing panacea to everyone's problems. Take it and suddenly you become smarter and stronger than all of your peers, but stop taking it long enough and the withdrawal symptoms would turn your brain to mush. Those unfortunates turned into the deranged masses of the city's lowest levels. *Psychos* they were called.

Ethan eyed Tall Goon and Short Goon as they deposited the crate on their grav sled with a grunt. Then Tall walked over to him and held out a *byte* reader. Ethan handed over the credit chip that Admiral Vee had given him for this run. Tall began configuring the reader, and Ethan took the opportunity to shuffle a few steps closer, until he could watch the transaction on the reader's display. He had just enough time to see a large number flash up on the display before Tall noticed him watching and turned the reader away.

Ethan gave an innocent smile and said, "Business must be good."

Tall grunted and handed the credit chip back. "Keep your nose where it belongs or I'll cut it off."

"Sure thing." Ethan watched as Tall Goon strode back to his grav sled while Short Goon scanned the misty gloom of their surroundings with one hand on the pulse rifle slung over his shoulder. "Pleasure doing business with you!" Ethan called out, but neither Tall nor Short Goon deigned to offer a reply. As soon as both of them had slunk into the shadows, Ethan allowed the scowl he'd been suppressing to fester on his lips.

Rounding his car to the driver's side, Ethan hopped in. The car recognized him immediately and powered up when he flicked the ignition. He hovered up half a dozen meters past barred and lifeless apartment windows and then gunned the throttle, eliciting a roar from the car's thrusters. Inertia slapped him back against his seat.

Ethan kept half an eye on the rear display as he climbed, watching as the slithering mist and skulking shadows of the surface were swallowed whole by overlapping golden halos of light, now pouring out in shimmering waves from the buildings rising to either side of him.

The higher you went in Avilon, the brighter and prettier things got. Climbing at a steep 45-degree angle, Ethan could even see a hazy slice of blue in the distance. Unfortunately, it wasn't the sky. It was the Styx, the planet-wide shield on level 50 designed to keep Nulls like him from poking their heads out into the paradisiacal upper cities. Anyone could live up there, but not everyone wanted to. In the Uppers Omnius ran nightly simulations to predict people's behavior and help them avoid making mistakes. Living in paradise meant a daily sacrifice of even the most basic freedoms, and on Avilon everyone had to choose: live free in the Null Zone with the crime, chaos, and poverty, or live with a nagging voice inside your head constantly telling you what not to do.

Ethan shuddered at the thought. He leveled out and joined the traffic on level 30. Up here the air was bright with city lights, and just five levels below, crowds of pedestrians walked the Null Zone's elevated streets. Ethan set course for Thardris Tower and let the car's autopilot manage his speed and heading for a while so that he could think.

Having completed yet another successful courier mission, on

his way to receive payment for another week's work, Ethan should have felt a sense of accomplishment, but instead all he felt was despair and apprehension.

The last time he'd been making such easy money he'd *known* what he was delivering. Somehow this time he'd agreed to a *don't ask, don't tell* policy for his cargo. Maybe it was because he had a lot further to fall on Avilon. Here, poverty wasn't just a matter of living with less. The lower levels of the city were deadly. Ethan still remembered how he'd had to escort his wife to and from work with one hand on his gun, the other squeezing the life out of hers. He wasn't about to subject Alara to that again.

As Ethan flew into Admiral Vee's private hangar, he tried to keep that in mind. Hovering down between the gleaming hulls of expensive-looking air cars, Ethan powered down and left the vehicle.

He spent a few minutes waiting outside, leaning against the midnight blue hull of his courier car before Admiral Vee came gliding across the glossy black floor of the hangar. She was dressed in a flowing yet figure-hugging red gown, transparent in so many places that Ethan didn't know where to put his eyes. Long, silken legs stole a glance from him without his permission, and then he resorted to staring at his feet.

"You're back early!" Vee said. The steady *clock clock clock* of tall heels striking the floor abruptly ceased, and Ethan noticed a pair of white feet appear right in front of his. She stood so close that her cloying scent almost suffocated him. The admiral's hand came to rest on his arm, just below the curve of his biceps, and he flinched at the touch.

Finally, he looked up, having chosen a wary frown as his greeting. She seemed amused that he was uncomfortable, which only annoyed him further. Ethan eyed her hand on his arm for a long, silent moment before reaching into his pocket and handing her the credit chip she'd given him earlier.

"I don't know if it's all there, since you didn't tell me how much our—" Ethan hesitated, searching for the right word. "—*supporters* were supposed to pay."

"Don't worry about it," Vee said. "What would be the point of them pledging their support only to withhold payment?"

Ethan smirked and gestured to Vee's luxurious hangar, with no less than ten expensive air cars landed there. "Maybe word has spread about your judicious use of their funding."

Vee laughed and flashed a grin. "Who says I'm using their money? Besides, we all have appearances to maintain. It's what we use to shield ourselves from the wrong kind of attention."

"Appearances lie. I prefer to shoot straight and live straighter. Speaking of which, I don't think you're being honest with me, Admiral."

Vee took a step back and withdrew her hand from his biceps to cross both arms over her chest. "Oh?"

Ethan nodded. "Your backers are criminals."

"Of course they are."

Ethan blinked. He'd been expecting a denial, an excuse or a justification—not a straight admission of the facts. He shook his head. "What do you mean *of course* they are?"

"So are you."

"I *was*. Not anymore."

"You're part of a resistance movement against the established government of the planet where you live. That's about as far outside of the law as you can get."

"You know what I meant."

"Ethan, when you're fighting against an all-seeing, all-knowing, god-like intelligence, who would you rather sign up for the cause—people who keep their noses clean and live ordinary lives, trying to stay safe and warm in their shells, or people who are used to living in the shadows? People who are actually good enough at hiding their affairs from prying eyes that they've become professional outlaws."

"You're saying that the ends justify the means, and the means are criminals."

"Until Omnius is defeated we don't have the luxury of being law-abiding citizens."

Ethan narrowed his eyes and Valari uncrossed her arms long enough to make a grab for his hand. He'd already tightened both of them into fists, but she seemed content to rub his whitened knuckles. As much as he hated to admit it, her logic made a lot of sense, but he wasn't ready to back down yet. "Vee, if I find out I'm being used as a mule to transport Bliss, I swear I'll—"

"What? Have a tantrum? At the risk of repeating myself, you can't stay above it all, Ethan. That said, I'll keep any shipments of Bliss for our other couriers. Satisfied?"

Ethan hesitated. "I have your word on that?"

"Of course." Vee withdrew her hand from his and produced a credit chip from the bosom of her gown. "Two thousand bytes. Not bad for a four day week."

Ethan snatched his credit chip from her and gave a curt nod. "Thanks. See you next week." He turned and crossed the hangar to his own air car, a modest AR12—a lease.

Admiral Vee's words found him before he could escape. "You can't fix your mistakes by painting your world in black and white, Ethan. There's a reason we see in color."

"Tell that to dogs! They seem to get by just fine, and they're probably the nicest creatures I've met."

A long silence followed while Ethan fumbled in his pockets for his car's ignition chip. He assumed Vee had left the hangar. Then a hand reached around and grabbed him below the waist.

She *squeezed,* and Ethan's breath caught in his throat. Every muscle in his body went rigid. Vee's violating touch was followed by a sibilant whisper in his ear. "Dogs also frek everything that moves. Is that a part of your moral code now, Ethan? Because if so..."

Ethan rounded on her, his nostrils flaring and chest heaving. He had to force himself to keep calm, but it took everything he had not to yell at her. He could handle this. It was just more of the same, and Vee couldn't force him to *do* anything.

"I've told you already—I'm married. *Happily* married. So knock it off, or I really will quit. Money isn't everything."

"No? But safety is, isn't it? In this crime-ridden city, your beautiful wife wouldn't last long if you had to go back to living below level ten. She might even make some interesting entertainment for a few lowlifes before she dies. Are you sure that's what you want?"

Ethan gritted his teeth and loomed toward her. "Are you threatening me?"

Suddenly the playful, sarcastic spark left Vee's turquoise eyes, and something ugly took its place. "No, I'm stating the facts. I pay you enough money to keep your family safe, while I pay the rest of my couriers half of what you get. You want to point fingers about misspending the Resistance's funding? You can start by pointing one at yourself. I'm doing *you* a favor, Ethan, not the other way around. Don't forget that."

"I won't sell my soul for you."

Valari gave a short yip of laughter. "You'll do whatever I say, or else all you'll have left is your soul, and considering souls don't exist, that's about as poor as you can get in this life."

Ethan scowled. "Just keep your hands to yourself, Vee," he said as he opened the car door and climbed in.

"Very well," Vee said. The playful spark was back.

Annoyed and speechless, Ethan slammed the door in her face and flicked the ignition. The car thrummed to life, and Admiral Vee took a few steps back. She stood waving at him while he gunned the car's grav lifts and ignited the thrusters to get away.

On the way home, the tail lights of other cars left a bloody trail between him and the witch's lair. Maybe dealing with the seedier side of Avilon in order to lead a resistance movement had left Admiral Vee jaded and cold, but he didn't have to follow her down that road.

It took him the better part of the drive home just to get his breathing under control. Ethan reached the apartment he shared with Alara in less than half an hour. Thankfully, they'd managed to move up from the rat hole they'd been renting on level nine of Sutterfold East to level twenty of Sutterfold West. It was more than twice as much per month, but thanks to the Resistance, Ethan could afford it now—even with Alara on maternity leave and looking after their newborn baby, Trinity.

Quitting was a bluff, and the admiral knew it. He had to Keep Alara and Trinity safe. They were everything to him. *Moving up in life is easy. Going back down is the hard part.*

Ethan pulled into the garage just below his apartment. The blue haze of static shields fizzed against his car as it slid inside; then the outer door of the garage began rolling down, and he killed the engine. The car's running lights snapped off and plunged him into a momentary darkness before the garage lights came on, swelling to a dim, soothing golden hue.

Ethan climbed out and made his way over to the steps. A shiny silver door at the top *swished* open, and Alara appeared in the opening, looking more beautiful than ever as the light turned the finer strands of her dark hair to liquid gold. Ethan smiled and Alara's cheeks dimpled as she matched that smile. In her arms she held a beauty to rival her own.

Trinity.

Ethan hurried up the steps.

"We missed you," Alara said as he drew near.

He reached the top of the stairs and lifted her chin for a kiss. Then he bent to drop another kiss on Trinity's nose. Bright violet eyes cracked open, followed by a baby squeal and a toothless grin. Ethan stroked her tiny hand as she kicked her feet with excitement. In that moment all of the day's worries seemed to melt away, and he sighed.

"I missed you two even more," he said, enfolding Alara in a one-armed hug.

She walked inside, and he followed. They made their way to the living room and sat down on the couch to watch a bright and sparkling view. Air cars raced soundlessly by their twentieth-floor window, casting fleeting shimmers of light against dark mirror-glazed office windows on the face of the building opposite theirs.

"How was your day?" Alara asked.

"Great," he lied.

"Payday today, wasn't it?"

"It was."

"And?"

"Two kilobytes."

Alara gasped. "That's even more than last week!"

"Depends on how many hours I work, how far I have to drive..." Ethan was at a loss to explain any better than that without also revealing what he was really doing.

"Why would Valari pay you so much to be a limo driver?"

Ethan shrugged. "I think it's a form of charity for her. She has so much money that she can afford it. That, and I guess she pays well to ensure loyalty and good service. We got lucky."

Alara took a deep breath and turned to look at him. "There's nothing else? No catch?"

Ethan furrowed his brow and played innocent. "Like what?"

"I don't know... like some reason why she might be paying you more than she should."

"I haven't noticed anything strange yet, but if I do, you'll be the first to know." Ethan felt a deadly weight settle on his shoulders with those lies, but lying was the only way to keep his job and protect his family. If Alara knew everything that went on in his job, she'd force him to quit, and then she'd go scratch Vee's eyes out for even daring to look at him.

Alara let out a breath and relaxed against his shoulder, getting comfortable. She rolled her head against a hard knot of muscle in the crook of his arm. "You're tense."

Ethan forced himself to relax. "Sorry. It was a tough day."

"I thought it was *Great?*" Alara shot him a suspicious look.

He replied with a cocky grin. "Payday's always great."

Alara snorted and subsided once more.

They passed a minute or two in silence before Trinity began making discontented noises and grabbing at the air, looking for something. It wasn't until Alara bared one of her swollen breasts that Ethan realized what that something was.

He watched as Alara fed their daughter. After a while both Alara and Trinity fell asleep, and Ethan smiled. A warmth of contentment spread through his chest. Seeing his family safe and at ease made everything else somehow worth it. He couldn't afford to jeopardize that.

No matter what.

CHAPTER 4

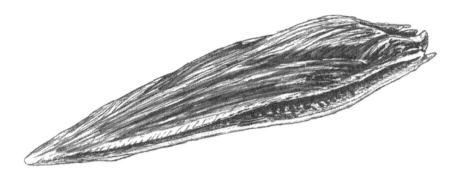

Farah awoke staring up at a dark castcrete ceiling. The last thing she remembered was Sythians in their glossy black armor storming the bridge of the *Baroness*, shooting at her with radiant blue fire.

She'd surrendered, and they'd taken her alive. But where was she now?

Disoriented, Farah sat up to see that she was inside of a small, windowless room with two cots, a wash basin, shower, toilet, and a heavy door with a suspicious-looking hatch at the bottom. Two people sat on one of the cots, staring down at her. It took Farah a moment to recognize their gaunt, dirty faces. One of them was a little girl, and Farah recalled that the other was her mother. Farah struggled to remember the woman's name...

Destra Heston. The little girl was harder to place. Both of them had gone with Bretton and the Gors to Noctune. *If they made it, then surely Bretton did, too!* she thought.

"You're alive!" was all Farah could think to say.

"So are you," Destra replied in a whisper of a voice. "We were beginning to wonder." Farah watched as the older woman crossed the space between them. "Who are you?" Destra asked, getting down on her haunches and meeting Farah at eye level.

"I'm Captain Farah Hale of the *Baroness*—" she said, rubbing a painful lump beneath her curly blond hair. She must have taken a bad fall when the Sythians shot her. "Or I was anyway," she amended. "Now I'm just Farah. The Sythians have my ship."

Destra's eyes widened. "I remember you... the admiral sent you back for us?"

An icy weight settled in Farah's gut. Her head felt suddenly airy and light. "The admiral didn't send me. I came looking for him. You mean he's not with you? Where is he?"

Destra shook her head. "I went with the Gors to the surface. The admiral stayed in orbit. We lost contact with the *Tempest*, and our shuttles on the surface were attacked while we were out exploring the planet. We assumed that maybe the admiral ran, but if he didn't send you..."

Farah shook her head. "He can't be dead," she said, suddenly fascinated by the hard-bitten stubs she called fingernails.

"Maybe he isn't," Destra replied.

But she knew better. She'd seen the debris in orbit. If he wasn't here as one of the Sythians' prisoners, then he wasn't anywhere.

"I came here looking for him," Farah explained. "I delivered my entire crew to the Sythians, thinking that he was still alive and that I could do something to help him if I came."

"I'm sorry," Destra replied, as if her apology could wipe Farah's conscience clean.

Suddenly she felt the full weight of her foolishness, and despair gripped her. "I shouldn't have come."

"You didn't find the admiral, but you did find us. We're alive, and we do need help."

Farah glanced up from her nails and saw kindly blue eyes looking back at her. "I'm a prisoner now, too," she said. "I can't help you."

"You couldn't have known you'd be captured."

"No, but I didn't have any grand plans for a rescue either. We didn't have enough fuel for a two-way trip."

"Mistakes always look worse in hindsight."

The older woman sat down beside her, and after a moment the little girl joined them on the floor, too. Farah looked from one to the other and saw two smiling faces. They were *happy* to see her. *Misery loves company*, she supposed.

"Don't worry, things will look better in the morning," Destra said.

"How can you even tell what time it is?" Farah asked.

"We're about to go to sleep," the little girl explained. "When we wake up, it will be morning."

"Yes," her mother agreed.

Farah's brow furrowed at that. "What do the Sythians want with us?" she asked.

Destra shook her head. "We don't know."

"It's been more than six months and you don't *know?*"

"They bring us food and a few supplies, but that's it. They never ask questions, and they don't give any answers."

"Then we're frekked! They want to see us rot in here. This must be our punishment for *our* war crimes—as if we ever killed any of *them!*"

"That's enough!" Destra said. "You're scaring Atta."

Farah noticed that the little girl's eyes were suddenly full of tears. She took a deep breath and shook her head. "Sorry. I came a long way for nothing, that's all."

"There's always hope."

"I spent six months thinking that. Now I'm not so sure."

Bretton is dead, a solemn voice whispered inside her head, and another wave of despair hit her, causing a painful lump to rise in her throat.

"Can you keep a secret?" Destra asked.

Farah shook her head. "Who am I going to tell?"

Then Destra smiled and leaned over to whisper in her ear. The woman's breath smelled like an open sewer, but her words were as sweet as any honey. "We have a tunnel."

"What? *How?*" Farah breathed, eyeing the solid castcrete walls of their cell.

Destra smiled, revealing yellow teeth. "They took the Gors prisoner, too, and they're not as easy to contain as we are."

Farah blinked and blinked again. Then something strange happened. In spite of everything—the crushing sadness from Bretton's passing, and the guilt she felt over her crew—Farah's lips stretched taut and she matched Destra's smile with one of her own. The grin on her lips felt manic, and it probably wouldn't last, but mania was still better than despair.

"There's always hope," Farah decided, nodding slowly.

* * *

Captain Marla Picara of the Resistance stood inside the echoing jump core of a derelict judgment-class cruiser. They'd managed to bring the ship's backup generator online, so at least they had light to see by.

The rest of Marla's crew were scattered around the core, using handheld scanners to image the different components so that they could disassemble a digital model before they disassembled the real jump core.

Sythians stood guard all around the circumference of the room, their glossy black armor making them look like diminutive Gors.

This was Marla and her crew's reward for surviving the battle in Dark Space—being forced to reverse-engineer quantum jump drives so that the Sythians could reach Avilon and finish what they'd started.

There was just one problem: only Omnius knew how quantum jump tech worked. The Sythians had spent enough time probing her mind to see that she wasn't on Omnius's side, that she was de-linked, and that one of her recent roles in the Resistance had been to help refit old human warships with quantum tech. But somehow the Sythians refused to believe that Marla had no idea how to make a quantum jump drive from scratch. The Resistance had smuggled the components for their jump drives off Avilon using a quantum junction that they'd stolen from Omnius. No one actually knew how to create those components.

Marla blew out a breath, and a nearby pair of Sythians turned toward the noise. They appeared to notice her idleness, so Marla smiled and took out her scanner.

It was time for her to look busy again.

She walked up to the component she was supposed to be imaging, absently wondering how long it would be before the Sythians realized that their prisoners had outlived their usefulness. She began scanning the giant silver rod coming down from the center of the dome-shaped core. As she did so, she saw that the internal structure of the rod was like that of a supercollider. It appeared to curve away from the aft of the ship, disappearing both above and below the jump core. Marla recalled seeing cylinders like this one in Avilonian ship schematics. They ran in rings through the drone decks that made up the insulating outer hulls of Peacekeeper ships. Marla studied the scan of the silver rod in the center of the jump core, wondering what purpose a supercollider might serve. Marla began to formulate a hypothesis, as if she'd known the answer all along.

The jump core used black holes generated by the particle accelerator to... do what exactly? Power the jump drive?

Her hypothesis ended there. It wasn't much to go on, but it was a start, and it might just be enough to keep her and her crew alive for a while longer. Marla whistled and waved her hand in the air to get her crew's attention. They came over in a hurry. "What is it?" her chief engineer asked, sounding painfully hopeful.

Marla turned to him with a smile. "I found something."

CHAPTER 5

Strategian Hoff Heston sat in his office on the second level of his apartment in Etheria. A wall of floor-to-ceiling windows running adjacent to his desk gave a sprawling view of pristine towers, shining bright and majestic in the fading light of the Celestial Wall overhead. That shield layer served as Etheria's sky, but it was also the highest level of segregation on Avilon. It separated Omnius's children from his chosen ones—the Celestials. Those white-robed men and women rarely ventured below Celesta, and it wasn't hard to understand why. Their city lay basked in *real* sunlight, with so many green, growing parks planted on its rooftops that from above it looked almost like the natural surface of Avilon.

Hoff sent a mental command to the room's control system via his augmented reality contacts, and the windows polarized until the only thing he could see was the holographic star map hovering above his desk.

Ever since the Sythians had defeated Omnius's Peacekeepers in Dark Space, Hoff had felt restless. Stargazing helped diminish that anxiety. For as long as he could remember, he'd been fighting the Sythians, and now Omnius had declared that *He* would defeat them with the help of the drone fleet and an army of self-replicating nanites. The Peacekeepers were grounded.

That was as frustrating as it was suspicious. Omnius had explained that the nanites were a last resort, far too deadly to risk bringing back to Avilon. In theory, the miniature machines wouldn't affect the ecosystems of the worlds they infected, killing only Sythians and Gors, and disassembling only their artificial creations. Yet that did nothing to limit the damage they would do to a world like Avilon that was almost entirely artificial. Worse yet, shared DNA between humans and Sythians left them at equal risk of extinction. So whoever or whatever delivered the nanites to their targets, they would not be returning to Avilon.

It wasn't the way he'd been trained to think of war, with torpedoes and beam weapons flashing bright against shields until hulls peeled open like mechanical flowers. Using a microscopic army to do all the work was somewhat less than satisfying, and not being able to watch the action was even worse. It was... *hollow*, Hoff decided. *A hollow victory.*

There came a knock at the door, and a wave of light invaded Hoff's sanctuary. He turned and saw his wife, Destra, standing in the open doorway.

"Atton is here," she said.

Hoff's dark eyebrows lifted. "He's early."

"He says he has an important announcement to make."

"Oh?"

"Dinner's about to be served, so we should go sit down."

Hoff nodded, turning off the star map and brightening the windows in his office with another mental command. His ARCs responded by minimizing the associated displays from his periphery until they were out of sight.

Hoff took Destra's hand on his way out and walked with her down the hall. The glossy white walls to either side of them came to an end as they reached a spiral staircase to the main floor. They descended the stairs into a bright, open-concept living area with another wall of floor-to-ceiling windows running along the breadth of it. Hoff saw his seven-year-old daughter, Atta, standing there, admiring the view with his elder stepson, Atton.

Hoff went to join them, and Destra let go of his hand, heading to the kitchen. Appetizing smells of roasted meat and vegetables wafted from that direction. Across the bar, Hoff saw the family drone, Ninety-nine, busy putting the final touches on their dinner. Skinny, silvery arms and the drone's red, cyclopean eye gave the family servant a forbidding look that didn't sit well with Hoff, but it wasn't as though they had other models to choose from, and they were lucky to even have a drone. Ever since Omnius had sent the drones away to fight the Sythians and to work on New Avilon, they'd become a much rarer sight.

Walking past a shiny black dining table, Hoff looked up to admire the crystal chandelier hanging above it. Prismatic shapes shattered the light, casting off sparkling rainbows in all directions. Hoff walked up beside his stepson, Atton, and nodded to the view. Gilded light poured from the Celestial Wall above, simulating a real sunset with a gradient of red and gold light. Just below that air traffic raced in orderly lines, the cars' hulls gleaming in the fading light. Looking down, Hoff saw several more levels of air traffic flowing like rivers against the distant blue haze of the Styx. They were over a hundred and eighty floors above the surface of Avilon.

"Nice view, isn't it?" Hoff said.

Atton turned to him with a wry grin. "Nice? This is as good as it gets."

Hoff nodded appreciatively. Soon the traffic would disappear entirely as light from the Celestial Wall dimmed to its natural blue haze and *Sync* approached. No one in Etheria needed to sleep after they'd been resurrected by Omnius, but they did need to Sync the data in their Lifelink implants with the databases in the Trees of Life.

Omnius used the data from their Lifelinks to predict any mistakes they might make in the coming day. Armed with that information, He told his children what to do to maintain their perfect world. But Sync was also necessary to create backups, just in case someone died too suddenly to transfer. Death was a rare event, however. The only Etherians who died were those who dared to venture into the crime-ridden chaos of the Null Zone. Most chose to avoid the danger entirely rather than risk going through the pain of death and the expense of resurrection.

"Your mother said you have an announcement to make?"

Atton turned to him with a cryptic smile. "Two announcements, actually, but they're related."

"He won't tell me anything," Atta pouted.

Hoff arched an eyebrow at her. "Kind of like how *you* won't tell your mother and I anything?"

"That's different. We're not supposed to talk about The Choosing."

Atta would be turning eight soon, and that meant she had to go through her Choosing Ceremony to decide whether to become a Null or to resurrect in a new, Immortal body and stay in Etheria with her family forever.

Hoff regarded Atta with a smile. She might not be allowed to say anything, but he already knew what she would choose. She wasn't foolish enough to become a Null. The prospect of going to a boarding school for years just so that she could *learn* how to scrape out a living in a world of crime and shadows wasn't appealing to most people, and Atta was too smart to fall for either the libertarian view that humans should be free, or the old Etherian view that there was a better life waiting beyond this one.

Hoff turned from Atta to face his son. "Back to your news— should I be breaking out a bottle of Avilon's finest?"

Atton grinned. "Mom already has."

"Dinner is served," a robotic voice said.

Hoff turned to see his wife and Ninety-nine come in from the kitchen carrying silver platters piled high with food. It was a feast.

Once they were all seated and Ninety-nine finished bustling around the table to pour wine, and red berry juice for Atta, Atton raised his glass from the foot of the table and clinked his fork against it to get their attention. Hoff eyed his stepson speculatively, waiting for the news.

"As you know, I've been working on special assignment in the Null Zone," Atton began.

Hoff nodded.

"What you don't know, is the reason for that assignment."

Ninety-nine momentarily blocked Atton from view as he leaned over the table to begin serving the food. Hoff watched the drone spoon out an extra helping of meat for Atton. Ninety-nine was trained to know their preferences.

Atton went on, "After we lost the battle in Dark Space, I came home feeling lost and wondering what to do with myself."

Hoff could relate to that. All of the Peacekeepers could.

"It occurred to me that the only reason I chose to become an Etherian was to join the Peacekeepers and fight the Sythians. After that was taken away from me, I found myself longing for the things I'd given up to be here."

"What things?" Destra asked quickly, defensively.

Hoff's brow furrowed and he, too, began wondering what Atton meant by that.

"Love, for one. I spent the night before The Choosing with a woman named Ceyla Corbin, a pilot from my old squadron. The next day she chose to become a Null, while I chose to go to Etheria."

Hoff began to suspect where this was going, but he didn't understand. Relationships between Nulls and Etherians never worked. Only Etherians were allowed to cross the Styx, and their visits were limited. People couldn't share a life together with a physical wall separating them.

Atton went on, "I begged Omnius to give me another chance, to help me convince Ceyla that I'm still the same person I was before the Choosing. She believes that we have a soul and that it passes on when we die, or in my case, transfers to the body of an immortal clone. Because of that, she told me even before I ascended that she wouldn't want to see me after I was resurrected. She'd already made up her mind that the real me would die during transfer, and all that would be left is a convincing copy. So, I made a deal with Omnius to win Ceyla's heart without her realizing who I am. In exchange, I've been working undercover in the Null Zone to help prevent an organized Null rebellion."

"Go on," Hoff said.

"Well, Ceyla and I have been dating for the past six months, and—"

"No," Destra said.

"Mom, just listen."

Destra shook her head. "You can't become a Null, Atton! For the love of a woman? What about us? What about Omnius? Etheria? Don't throw away an eternity in paradise for a love that you could just as easily find with someone else—someone from the Uppers!"

Hoff watched Atton's green eyes flash and his features

darken. "I've already made up my mind. Tomorrow, on our six-month anniversary, I'm going to ask Ceyla to marry me."

"I suppose you've come to ask for our blessing," Destra said, sounding equal parts hurt and angry.

"That would be nice to have, but no, I've come to share the good news with you, and to ask you all to come down and meet Ceyla in the Null Zone—assuming she agrees to marry me of course."

"Go down *there*?" Destra sounded frightened at the very thought of it.

"We'll meet somewhere safe," Atton said.

"There isn't anywhere safe! That's why we have a shield to keep them away from us!"

Hoff raised his hands for quiet. As he lowered them, he found Destra's knee under the table and he squeezed it just hard enough to convey a warning. "I'm curious, how did Omnius help you win this woman's heart without her realizing who you are?"

"That's the other surprise I came to share. Brace yourselves; this might come as a shock..."

Dinner sat steaming on their plates, rapidly cooling, but no one moved to touch their food. All eyes were on Atton, waiting for something unexpected to happen. Then, suddenly, Atton's features shimmered and morphed from the green eyes, dark hair, and oval face of the boy they knew, to the face of a complete stranger. Golden eyes replaced green; brown hair replaced black; and gaunt cheeks and sharply-defined features replaced his boyish good looks. Atton's new appearance was sinister, though Hoff supposed others might have said he looked *dangerous*.

Beside him, Destra gasped, but Hoff smiled with sudden understanding. "A bio-synthetic suit."

Atton nodded. "Yes." Even his voice was different. "Unfortunately, a bio-synthetic suit isn't enough to fool someone who lives with you. That degree of intimacy leaves considerable room for failure, and I couldn't afford for Ceyla to see through my disguise too soon."

"Atton, what did you *do?*" Destra asked, sounding horrified.

"The face you saw a moment ago, the face of Atton, was the one projected by the suit. This one is real. It's the face of Darin Thardris, the estranged grandson of Vladin Thardris."

"You transferred to *another* body?" Destra said.

"Can *I* do that?" Atta asked.

"No," Hoff replied, his eyes narrowing on his daughter. "You're already perfect the way you are." To Atton he said, "Have you thought about what will happen when Ceyla finds out who you *really* are and that you've been lying to her all this time?"

"I'm going to tell her tomorrow, before I propose. She'll either accept me for who I really am... or not."

"She might need some time to think about it," Hoff said.

"Probably, but I'm prepared to wait as long as she needs."

"She might also say no," he warned. "It's a big deception."

Atton appeared to consider that. "I lied to be with her, not to hurt her. She's smart enough to understand the difference."

Hoff sighed. Destra looked ready to say something more, but he squeezed her knee again. "Well, If you're sure, then we're sure, Atton. It might be premature to say, but—" Hoff raised his wine glass. "—congratulations." Everyone else raised their glass for the toast—everyone except for Destra.

"Thank you, Hoff. Mom? Are you okay?"

Hoff saw her staring out the windows at nothing in particular, her lips pressed into a stubborn line. He knew that look.

Atton frowned and rose from the table. "I think maybe I'd better come back another day."

"Destra, darling..." Hoff began.

Then she rose from the table, too, and rounded on her son. "You're a foolish, foolish boy! You expect me to be happy that you're leaving us? You won't even be able to visit us anymore!"

"Hopefully Ceyla will agree to ascend to Etheria, and then we'll all be together."

"Then why didn't she do so sooner? You said it yourself, she believes we have a *soul*, and that hasn't changed. Her beliefs will keep her where she is until she dies and leaves you a grieving widower." Atton looked uncertain. "Have you considered what you'll be giving up? Or the risk you'll be taking with your life? If you choose to go to the Null Zone now, you'll become a *target*. You won't age, and you don't look like them. You're too perfect. Right now it's suspicious, but once people get to know you, they'll realize you don't belong."

"I can look after myself."

"Let's suppose you can. And that Ceyla can, and that everything works out just fine. Twenty years from now she'll be looking old already, and you'll still be young and handsome. How do you think that ends up? It ends up with you looking after an old crone."

"Love goes beyond the surface," Atton insisted.

"But not beyond death! There's a reason marriage vows used to read *till death do us part*."

Atton smirked at that. "And now they read, *until this contract expires*. What does your marriage contract read, Mom? Ten years? Twenty? It's the same thing."

"That's none of your business, Atton. The point is, your marriage is doomed to failure one way or another, and in the meantime you'll run the very real risk that someone kills you out of spite. Omnius won't bring you back after that, not after you've chosen to become a Null and live apart from Him."

Atton threw his hands up. "Don't you think I already know all of that? Omnius has already tried to change my mind."

Destra snorted. "So why didn't you *listen?*"

Hoff rose from the table now, too. "I think we should all agree to discuss this at another time. Atton, I'll show you out. I'm sorry that your news wasn't the cause for celebration you thought it would be, but..." Hoff glanced at his wife, and she turned her scowl on him. "Your mother is right."

"Thank you!" she replied.

"But even though I don't agree with your decision I still support it. If it's what you really want, you have a right to make that choice. In fact, all of Avilon is built on that premise. The Null Zone wouldn't even exist if not for Omnius saying the exact same thing to all of us—that we are allowed to choose to go our own way, even if that way is dangerous. If He allows for us to live apart from Him, then we should allow for you to live apart from us. We'll visit you in the Null Zone. I can't promise that it will be very often, but you will still get to see us."

Atton nodded. "Thank you. Mom..."

Destra had her arms crossed over her chest, and she refused to reply.

"She'll come around." Hoff crossed from the head of the table to the foot and wrapped an arm around Atton's shoulders to guide him out. Once they reached the door and they had some privacy, Hoff whispered, "Be careful, Atton."

"I will. Dark Space wasn't safe either. I know how to look after myself."

Hoff frowned. "No, it's not that. It's Omnius."

"What do you mean?"

"He gives us a choice to live free as Nulls, but I'm pretty

sure he still has his ways of *influencing* people in the Null Zone. It's in his best interests for the place to look dangerous and oppressive from up here."

Atton cocked his head curiously, and Hoff couldn't help seeing the head of a stranger. *Darin Thardris.*

"You have proof of something?" Atton asked.

"Not everyone who lives in the Null Zone lives there because they believe we have a soul. Most of them just don't trust Omnius, and they want to be free to make their own choices. So why is it that none of them have thought to start cloning themselves and using Lifelinks to transfer to clones when they die? Or for that matter, why haven't the Nulls figured out how to engineer their DNA for immortality the way Omnius does with Etherians and Celestials?"

Atton shook his head. "All of that's against the law in the Null Zone. The government is too religious to support those kinds of measures."

"Exactly! But it's a democracy, isn't it? Try asking Nulls what they think of those laws, and you'll begin to wonder about a lot of things. Nulls aren't as free as they think they are. Do you remember the battle in Dark Space?"

"Yes."

"The Sythians shouldn't have been able to see us coming. We were cloaked, but somehow they had developed scanners that could penetrate our cloaking shields. I think Omnius *knew* they could see us, and he didn't tell us. I tried to warn the Grand Overseer that something was wrong with the way the Sythians were behaving, but he wouldn't listen. It was almost as though he wanted to shut me up."

Atton's glowing golden eyes seemed to flare suddenly brighter with Hoff's treasonous words. "You could get into a lot of trouble for telling me all of that. It's bad enough just to *think* it."

"I already am in trouble, Atton."

"Then telling me is making it worse."

"Don't worry about me. Worry about yourself. There are too many things on Avilon that don't make sense, and if you're going to live in the Null Zone, where Omnius has ways to conveniently silence dissenting voices, then you'd better have your eyes wide open."

"I appreciate the warning, but I think you're jumping at shadows. You should have more faith. You're a *strategian*. You should know better."

Hoff's lip twitched at the rebuke, and he sighed. "Maybe you're right. I hope you are. I'll have to repent of my doubts tonight. Forget I said anything."

Atton grabbed both his shoulders and squeezed. "I don't want you to get into any trouble on my account."

"Why are you in trouble, Dad?" a soft, girlish voice interrupted.

Hoff turned to see Atta hiding behind a plant in the far corner of the foyer. She'd heard everything. Hoff's eyes widened. "Atta! What are you doing here?"

"I—"

"Go to your room!"

Tears welled in Atta's eyes and she ran off.

"That was a bit harsh...." Atton said.

"She's about to go through The Choosing, Atton. I don't need her head filled full of doubts now."

"That's strange, because you just filled my head full of doubts."

"To keep you *away* from the Null Zone, not to drive you into it."

Atton shook his head, looking confused. "Good night, Hoff."

"Good night, Atton." *Be safe,* he thought, as he mentally triggered the door shut.

CHAPTER 6

Atton left his parents' apartment with a heavy heart and an empty stomach. His mother had taken the news worse than he'd expected, and his stepfather...

Somehow Hoff had taken it even worse than that. He'd acknowledged Atton's right to choose, but he had also taken a dangerous risk to warn him about Omnius. Atton had tried to stop Hoff, tried to dismiss his suspicions, but Atton had seen the truth shining in his stepfather's gray eyes. Doubts like his couldn't be dismissed.

The worst part was, Hoff was right. Omnius really *had* led his fleet into an ambush, and he'd even allowed the Sythians to attack Avilon before that. Admiral Vee had explained those betrayals at the same time that she'd explained the Resistance was actually run by Omnius as a safe way for the Nulls to oppose him, and as a way to justify supplying Bliss to the unsuspecting masses. The Resistance financed its operations with that performance-enhancing super drug, and Omnius used it to make the Null Zone worse than it should have been in order to accentuate the chaos caused by human freedom.

It was hard to wittingly take part in all of that, but Atton had made a deal. He'd said he would do *anything* for a chance to be with Ceyla again. Justifying his involvement was easier than he'd expected. For every one person hurt by Bliss, ten more stayed in Etheria because of it. Only complete skriffs would want to live in the Null Zone in spite of all its problems.

Atton reached Hoff's parking garage and climbed into his air car, a shiny black one-seater he'd nicknamed the *Black Arrow*. He fired up the engines and cruised out through the hazy blue wall of the garage's static shields. On his way out, he configured the autopilot to take him down to the Styx. It was time to return the *Black Arrow* to Admiral Vee's hangar and start making preparations for his proposal tomorrow.

The autopilot took him into a stream of vertical traffic, and Atton watched as the car dropped past bright and shining monoliths, rooftop parks and fountains, and safe, tree-lined streets elevated high above the Styx. Over a hundred levels blurred by before Atton actually reached the shield wall that separated Etheria from the Null Zone.

The lowest levels of Etheria were much darker due to their distance from the Celestial Wall. Down here buildings and streets still looked pleasant, but not quite as luxurious as those in the upper levels.

The car came to a stop just above the Styx, and then drone-fired grav guns seized his car, preventing him from going anywhere until both he and his vehicle had been scanned. Atton used his ARCs to mentally submit his credentials and his permit to enter the Null Zone. That done, he sat back and waited. The line ahead of him was short, a handful of cars at most, so it wouldn't take long. Going down was always faster than going up. Ascending from the Null Zone meant one had to Sync first, just in case contact with Nulls had caused changes in Omnius's behavioral predictions. Atton was one of the few people who knew that system was a ruse. Omnius said he didn't try to predict Nulls' behavior; he said he deactivated their Lifelink implants when they became Nulls, but it was all a lie to lull the Nulls into a false sense of security. De-linking was impossible, and there was no way to escape from Omnius. The need for Etherians to Sync upon returning home was just a formality to support the lie that the Null Zone was *free*.

Bright blue fans of light flickered through Atton's cockpit, and then the drones manning the grav guns at the border crossing moved his car down through a narrow opening in the Styx. That opening would be sealed completely when it came time for the Uppers to Sync.

Thanks to his special assignment in the Null Zone, Atton wasn't forced to Sync at the exact same time as everyone else in Etheria. Instead, his Sync occurred whenever he chose to go to sleep, just as it did for all the other Nulls, but without their knowledge.

As soon as Atton was on the other side of the Styx, his autopilot disengaged. Autopilots were mandatory in Etheria to prevent accidents, but in the Null Zone, hands-on flying was just another part of the chaos.

Atton grinned as he gunned the throttle and flipped the car up on its end to make a highly illegal U-turn through a narrow alley between two buildings. Bactcrete walls rushed by in a gray blur. His car's running lights flashed into apartment windows, startling residents as he streaked by. The acceleration pinned him to the back of his seat. Air roared around his canopy, causing subtle vibrations in the fuselage. Then he shot out the other side of the alley and into a yawning chasm between two long rows of buildings. In the Null Zone the danger was part of the thrill. *Nothing like the constant threat of death to make you appreciate life.*

Atton dove down into the stream of traffic on level 30 and

used air brakes to slow to a more law-abiding speed. The car's nav system automatically painted lines on his HUD to tell him where the lanes should be.

After half an hour of keeping within those lines and minding his distance from the cars in front of him, Thardris Tower appeared in the distance, a specter of black bactcrete and mirror-plated red windows. Atton took an up-ramp to depart from the main flow of traffic. He followed the simulated street to the level of Admiral Vee's penthouse. When he was still a few hundred meters from Vee's hangar, he submitted his clearance code to her security system. A green light turned on and glossy black doors parted, revealing a blue haze of static shields that kept pollution out and warm air in.

The shields sizzled as he slipped inside.

Once he'd landed in the hangar, Atton popped the car's canopy with a *hiss* of escaping air and went to announce himself at the admiral's front door. He used the vidcomm beside the door to call her. A moment later, Admiral Vee's voice bubbled out, sultry and smooth.

"I wasn't expecting you so soon, Atton."

"My visit with my family was cut short."

"I see. I'll be down in a moment."

It was more like five minutes that Atton waited, and by the time the door *swished* open, he wasn't in the best of moods.

"Would you like to come in? I haven't eaten dinner yet," Vee said, as if she somehow knew he hadn't had a chance to eat.

Atton was about to refuse when his stomach growled loud enough for both of them to hear. Vee smiled, and Atton nodded.

"Thank you."

The inside of the Resistance leader's penthouse apartment was lavish with plush white rugs, and a deep indigo floor that seemed to sparkle like a sea of diamonds in the room's recessed lighting.

"Let's go take a seat, shall we?" Valari said, taking him by the arm to lead him through a high-ceilinged foyer with winding stairs. She led him through the living room to a long, white dining table with seating for twelve. Above the table hung a strange light fixture that looked to Atton like a spider. Snaking black legs radiated from a central ball, and at the end of each leg, hovered a glowing orb of light that seemed to radiate from the air itself.

Admiral Vee took her seat at the head of the table, while Atton sat facing a high wall of windows. Those windows gave a startling view of the Null Zone with its shadowy towers and glowing rivers of air traffic. Dozens of stories below the apartment where they sat, lights from towers and traffic alike disappeared into a carpet of inky black mist that concealed the planetary surface. Atton spent a moment admiring the view before a sudden noise drew his attention. Two drones came *clanking* in from an adjoining room, pushing grav carts laden with food and drinks. One of the two drones began setting places around the table—*three* settings, one at each end of the table, and one for him.

"Are you expecting someone else?" Atton asked.

"She's expecting *me*," a deep, resonant voice replied.

Atton turned to see a familiar man come striding in from the foyer. That man was none other than Vladin Thardris, the Grand Overseer of Avilon. Atton hurried to his feet and raised one arm perpendicular from his body, palm angled up to the sky. "Hail Omnius," he said.

Vladin smiled, but did not return the greeting, a fact which Atton found to be unusually irreverent for Omnius's right-hand man. "Yes," was all he said as he sat down at the opposite end of the table from Admiral Vee.

Atton shook his head. "I'm not intruding on anything, am I?" Vee was short for *Valari*, her last name Thardris. She was the overseer's daughter.

"Of course not, Atton," Vee replied. "My father asked me to have you join us when you arrived. He wants to share something important with you."

Atton accepted that with a nod. "In that case, I'm honored."

One drone came to attend each of them personally, asking their preferences for dinner. Atton selected a choice cut of steak with sauteed vegetables and an expensive wine. The food was laid out promptly, and drinks were poured. Atton dug in greedily, determined not to miss his second dinner. Peripherally, he noted that while Valari had begun to eat, Vladin didn't even touch his food. Instead, he nodded to Atton and asked, "What do you know about Omnius?"

He finished chewing before he replied. "He's the ruler of Avilon and an artificial intelligence—our god for lack of a better description."

"Is He *your* god?" Valdin asked, arching an eyebrow at him.

Atton hesitated to reply. "The idea of a god or gods came about to explain where humans came from and why. Omnius didn't create us; we created him, so true deity is hard to attribute. But he is the most powerful being we are likely to ever encounter, so the attribution is fitting in that sense."

Vladin looked amused. "How did humans create Omnius?"

Atton recited a piece of Avilonian history. "Thousands of years ago an Avilonian named Neona Markonis hypothesized that the only way to create an intelligence superior to our own would be to somehow increase our own intelligence, so she networked thousands of people together, using digitized copies of their own minds."

Vladin nodded. "That's correct. And what happened to

Neona Markonis after that?"

Atton frowned and reached for his wine while he considered that. "No one knows."

"But she was Immortal."

"It was a long time ago. More than thirty thousand years. Neona could have chosen to die in that time."

"She could have, but she didn't," Vladin said. "She's still very much alive. In fact, she's eating dinner with us right now."

Wine burst from Atton's lips in a red mist. He turned to Admiral Vee, suddenly seeing her with new eyes. "What? *You're* Neona Markonis?"

She smiled. "Surprised?"

"How old *are* you?"

"Now, now, Atton, don't you know it's not polite to ask a woman her age?"

Atton shook his head, awed and frightened at the same time. There had to be a reason they were telling him this. When he turned back to Vladin, he saw the Overseer's eyes glowing brighter than before. As he watched, that brightness swelled, consuming Vladin's features. Atton winced and looked away, a sudden suspicion brewing inside his churning gut.

From within that blinding radiance, Vladin spoke, but his voice was different now. It rumbled like thunder, rattling the windows and making the floor tremble. "She created *me*, Atton. *I am Omnius.*"

Atton shook his head, dumbstruck. He forced himself to look up into the blinding light, and as he did so, both the light and the man he'd thought of as Vladin Thardris disappeared. Suddenly he understood why the overseer hadn't *hailed Omnius* when he'd arrived, and why he hadn't touched his food. Vladin was Omnius, and he'd never really been there. His presence had been nothing but a projection on Atton's ARCs.

Turning to Valari—*Neona,* Atton corrected—he worked some moisture into his mouth, and asked, "The Grand Overseer is Omnius?"

Neona inclined her head to him, still smiling. "You didn't really think Omnius would allow a *human* to rule Avilon?"

"Why? Why tell *me?*"

"Omnius wants you to join us, Atton," she replied.

"Us who? I thought I was already an Etherian."

"*Us* the people Omnius trusts enough to know the truth. His chosen people, Atton, the Celestials."

Atton's thoughts skipped to his girlfriend, Ceyla, hopefully soon to be his wife, and he shook his head, wondering how he could choose to become a Null now. They were offering him a place in Omnius's inner circle. A place of trust. How could he betray that trust by choosing to live apart from Omnius?

"Atton, you're a part of the Resistance. The Resistance operates inside the Null Zone, nowhere else. That means we'll need you down here for... well, as long as you'd like to stay, actually. Naturally you won't be subjected to living in the Null Zone's more dilapidated depths, and you will never die or age."

"What if people begin to suspect?"

"To suspect what? If you need to explain your immortality, you'll tell them that you're an Etherian who chose to become a Null. There are plenty of those down here. In fact, aren't you planning to tell your girlfriend exactly that?"

Atton felt his skin crawl with the realization of just how little of his life was actually private. "Yes."

"So tell her, and tell anyone else you trust enough to know. Tell everyone if you like; it doesn't really matter. The only secrets you need to keep are the ones that I or Omnius explicitly reveal to you."

Atton looked down at his food, desperate to escape Neona's

gaze. He stared at his plate with unseeing eyes. He held his knife and fork ready to cut another bite of steak, but his appetite was suddenly gone.

"Why me?" he asked.

"We saw how you responded to Strategian Heston's doubts. You could have told him the truth. Instead, you denied his suspicions."

"Because I don't want anything bad to happen to him."

"Exactly! That's why we keep the truth to ourselves, isn't it? To protect people." Atton looked up to meet Neona's gaze once more, and she went on, "Not everyone can handle the truth. We know it, but what does that gain us? It's a burden, not a blessing."

"So why burden *me?*" Atton asked, feeling suddenly numb. His gaze drifted out the windows into the glittering sea of lights below.

"Because you can take it," Neona said. "People like us have to bear the burdens that others can't. We have to use the wisdom and insight that the truth brings to guide everyone else. We are their guardians, Atton, and Omnius's truest servants."

"Celestials," Atton said.

"Yes."

Looking up once more, he asked, "So I'm a Celestial now?"

"Not yet, but someday you will be," Neona said.

Atton frowned, wondering if he had any choice in the matter. "What else am I going to learn?"

"A great many things, Atton. Among others, you're going to learn the real reason for The Choosing."

Atton blinked. "It's not to keep Etherians and Nulls separated?"

"Oh, it is, but not *just* that. Why do you think they need to be separated in the first place? That's the question you should be asking."

"Because Omnius doesn't predict and control what Nulls will do."

"But you know that he does. The Nulls aren't as free as they think."

"Then why?"

"All will be revealed in good time. For now, eat your food. You must still be hungry."

Atton nodded and made a show of pushing his food around on his plate. Why would Omnius need to separate the Nulls from Etherians and Celestials? Atton had a bad feeling that he wasn't going to like the answer to that question.

CHAPTER 7

Strategian Galan Rovik stepped out from under the quantum junction and straight into the high council chamber at the top of Omnius's Zenith Tower. Galan remembered this place well. Once, not so long ago, he'd sat on the council as an overseer himself.

That was before he'd allowed doubt to consume him and drive him into the Null Zone. Now he was back on the ascendant path, and already a strategian in the Peacekeepers.

Galan turned in a slow circle, looking around the council chamber. Avilon's overseers should have been there, floating on chairs all around the circumference of the room's transparent dome, but their chairs were all empty.

"Hello?" he called out.

No answer.

Galan looked up at the speaker's podium on the catwalk above the quantum junction in the center of the room. Even that was empty. His stomach churned with anxiety. It was a rare event for an Etherian to even be allowed up past the Celestial Wall, let alone to be summoned for an audience with the high council.

But the council wasn't there.

Galan tried to still his churning stomach by walking up to the edge of the dome and distracting himself with the view. It was breathtaking. The Zenith was the tallest structure on Avilon, reaching over three kilometers above even the lofty heights of the Celestial Wall. From that vantage point, Galan saw rooftop parks stretching out to the horizon in a lush green carpet, gilded by the light of the setting sun. Snaking blue rivers ran through the greenery, cascading from one level of the city to the next. Below even that, the shimmering blue grid of the Celestial Wall lay around the bases of the buildings, giving the impression that the city was submerged under water. Clouds shone in golden ribbons on the horizon. Towers of transpiranium rose against that, silhouetted and glittering in the fading light. Thin lines of traffic and bridges ran between, like silk spun from a giant spider.

Celesta was the most awe-inspiring city of Avilon. Unlike most of Etheria, which was crowded with closely-spaced skyscrapers, Celesta had plenty of wide open spaces, some of which were so wide and so open that completely natural and suburban settings could be simulated on the city's rooftops. Parts of Celesta boasted artificial mountains, and dense green forests—even lakes and beaches.

Galan waited for the purpose of his summons to be revealed. When nothing happened, he looked up through the top of the dome to stare at the eye of Omnius. It was an impossibly bright light projected half a dozen stories above his head between the twin spires at the pinnacle of the Zenith. The tinted transpiranium dome dulled that radiance just enough that he could stand to look at it, and when he squinted, a pattern emerged. It was the symbol of the Ascendancy, without the letter "*A*"—a spiral galaxy full of shining stars, and at the center lay what appeared to be an actual *eye,* burning bright and silver.

"Great is Omnius," Galan whispered.

"There's no need to whisper that, Galan."

He jumped with fright and turned to see Grand Overseer Vladin Thardris standing right behind him.

"Words of praise should be shouted from the rooftops," the grand overseer said.

He certainly looked grand. His flowing white Celestial robes appeared luminous, and his eyes were a bright and *flickering* silver in the light of his ARCs. "Master," Galan said, bowing his head.

"You are wondering why you've been summoned here."

Galan nodded, not yet daring to look up. He was also wondering how the overseer had appeared so suddenly and silently. Surely he would have heard the junction slam shut and then open again.

"Omnius has been watching you," Thardris went on. "He has seen your unwavering loyalty. You descended into darkness, and then you climbed triumphantly back into the light. This proves that the light is where you belong. By now you know that everything Omnius does, He does with love, and that all things—even suffering—are for the benefit of His children."

Galan nodded.

"Omnius has decided to make you a Celestial once more."

Galan looked up, his eyes wide. "I don't deserve such an honor, Master."

The overseer's smile grew wide, and his burning silver gaze became suddenly brighter. Then the *eye* of Omnius flared overhead, washing the entire dome in a blinding light. The Overseer replied, his lips moving to speak, but the thunderous voice of Omnius came out instead. "Before you are elevated, you must pass one final test. It is the test you ultimately failed the last time. The test of enlightenment."

Galan gaped at the overseer, his eyes burning with tears from the overpowering brightness in the room. He bowed his head to escape the blinding light, but even that didn't help, so he shut his eyes, making his blindness complete. In that moment, he had his first revelation.

There was no grand overseer of Avilon, only Omnius. Galan felt a giddy thrill of surprise. He had learned many things when he'd become a Celestial the first time, but even so, he'd never learned that the grand overseer was just a human avatar for Omnius. And as far as he knew, none of the other overseers knew that either.

Omnius continued, "As a Celestial, ascendance becomes synonymous with enlightenment. Only a Celestial's faith is strong enough to handle the burden of truth. Is your faith strong enough, Galan?"

He hesitated. Was Omnius *asking* him? Surely He already knew. He decided that the question was a courtesy.

"It is. I am ready."

"Good."

What came next wasn't words, but a pure stream of information, downloaded directly to his Lifelink and from there to his brain. Images flashed before his eyes in a dizzying stream of shapes and colors. Sensations came and went; tastes and smells flickered through his awareness. Voices alternately whispered and shouted, speaking too fast for him to hear, and yet somehow he understood it all. Galan's mind felt heavy and full, his brain bursting with information. He felt himself falling...

But the jarring impact never came. Instead, he settled gently to the floor, as if cradled by giant, invisible hands. Then the flood of information ceased, and he lay there gasping on the floor and gazing up through the domed ceiling of the council chamber. The blinding light pouring from the *eye* had dimmed to a more comfortable radiance. The grand overseer was nowhere to be seen, but Galan now knew that Vladin Thardris had never really been there at all. The grand overseer did exist as a physical being, but he rarely appeared in the flesh. He had too many different places that he needed to be, and Galan wasn't the only one who needed to be enlightened.

Now he knew everything. Along with the revelations, Omnius had supplied the reasons for what he had done, and Galan was surprised to find that he *understood*. Even the most shocking, most atrocious acts seemed justifiable.

Omnius had created the Sythians and caused the war, but he had also united humanity on Avilon because of it, and now they would never know the horrors of war ever again.

As for the Null Zone, Bliss, and the fake resistance, all of it was necessary to keep people from forgetting why they needed Omnius. No one was forced to live down there, so in a way, their suffering was their own fault. Further justifying it all was the fact that most Nulls eventually became Etherians anyway. Their experiences in the Null Zone only served to cement their loyalty to Omnius in the future. Galan knew that much firsthand.

But the most shocking revelation of all wasn't any of that, it was something that Galan never would have suspected. It was the real reason for The Choosing. Galan understood why it was best that people didn't know. The shock of finding out was so overpowering that he had trouble accepting the truth. Yet the very fact that Omnius had *allowed* him to know, suggested that he would come to grips with it all sooner or later.

"How could you?" he asked, staring open-mouthed up at the eye of Omnius, even as that eye glared down on him.

"How could I? I am God, Galan. I can do anything I want."

CHAPTER 8

ASCENDANCY

Atton kept a hand on his gun as he walked down Darwin Street on level ten to his and Ceyla's apartment in the East Grunge. The first ten levels of the city were considered a red zone. Crime was so bad down there that most enforcers refused to actively patrol, but Atton wasn't on patrol. He was walking home, and unbeknown to the sketchy-looking passersby, he had a ring in his pocket that was worth over four thousand bytes.

Hence the weapon he wore on his hip. Apart from that he relied on the fact that he, unlike the rest of the denizens of the Null Zone, was actually an immortal Peacekeeper from the uppers with a limitless supply of clones to draw on. If someone killed him, he'd be back again within the hour. Emboldened by that knowledge, Atton had taken to walking home at night rather than taking a taxi or bus directly to the relatively safer outer entrance of his apartment. Tonight, he really should have opted for a taxi, but he needed the time and the brisk air to help him compose his thoughts.

Flexing a gloved-hand around the butt of his plasma pistol, Atton eyed the shadows pooling around the bactcrete buttresses of the buildings to his right. Tonight the fog in the lower levels was thin and visibility was good, but there were still plenty of places for someone or *something* to hide. Between buttresses lay darkened shop windows aglow with the faint blue haze of active shields. To Atton's left, a line of trees and street lamps ran along the railings of the elevated street, and beyond that was a ten-floor drop through a slithering gray fog to the decaying surface of Avilon.

He shivered at the thought and went back to watching the shadows. He half-expected to see a Psycho come lunging out at him, drooling with hunger, eyes wide and bloodshot with Bliss-induced madness. But instead of bony, sub-human hands clawing out of the darkness, he heard the honeyed words of streetwalkers and stim-pushers reaching out to him from the light.

"Hey handsome, you looking for some company?" asked a young woman standing beneath the glaring yellow eye of a streetlight.

Atton turned to the sound of the woman's voice. Excessive makeup, a white trench coat, and red high heels left no doubt as to her profession. She flashed open her trench coat, revealing a lacy red pair of underwear and nothing else.

Then he passed under the streetlight and she noticed his eyes. They glowed gold in the light of his ARCs. The woman shut her trench coat quickly and shied away from him. Enforcers were among the only people in the Null Zone who wore augmented reality contacts. For everyone else they were simply too expensive.

"Sorry," the woman said quickly. "I didn't—"

"I'm off duty," Atton grumbled, putting her mind at ease. Not that he would have detained her if he had been on the job. Atton's cover for all the Bliss-running he did with the so-called Resistance, was that he was an undercover Enforcer investigating lower levels' crime rings.

In reality he was a part of those crime rings.

That irony became particularly clear when he walked by a burly-looking Bliss-pusher standing two streetlights down from the woman in the trench coat. Atton guessed he was probably the woman's handler.

"Care for a taste?" the man asked, holding out a vial of luminous red liquid. "First one's free," he said.

The cowled black robe Atton wore hid his glowing golden eyes. "No thanks," he replied, looking away quickly to avoid the pusher seeing his ARCs.

The stim-pusher wasn't taking no for an answer. He took a few hasty steps toward Atton, still holding out his vial. "Just take it home with ya. Think about it. Wouldn't have to walk down here anymore if ya had a better job. I can have it delivered straight to yur door."

This time the pusher got close enough to see Atton's glowing eyes. He swore and dropped his vial with a *clink* of transpiranium hitting bactcrete. The pusher's hand flew to his sidearm, but Atton waved him away before he could draw it.

"I didn't see anything," he said, patting his own sidearm as a warning. "Carry on."

The burly man nodded, looking hesitant, his hand still on his gun.

If that pusher knew who Atton really was, he would have been asking for Bliss rather than offering it.

Five minutes later, Atton reached the door to his apartment building. He hurried through the retinal and biometric scans, and then slipped inside the first door. It quickly slid shut behind him while a second set of scanners made sure that no unauthorized persons had slipped in behind him. Finally, the inner door gave a pleasant chime and *swished* open. Atton hurried to the bank of lift tubes at the end of the building's run-down foyer and rode the nearest one up to level fifteen. From there, Atton walked down the hall to apartment 15G and submitted to a final security scan. Another chime sounded, and the door slid open.

"Ceyla?" Atton called out as he walked inside. He noted the dim, sleep-cycle lighting in their apartment and he frowned. Had Ceyla forgotten their anniversary and gone to bed already?

The front door slid shut behind him, and Atton removed his black robe and hung it in the coat closet by the door. Before leaving the coat there, he remembered to remove the small blue velvet box from the robe's inner pocket. He slipped the box into his pants pocket and then turned to look for Ceyla.

The main living area was empty, but now Atton noticed the trail of rose petals leading through the living room to the bedroom. He smiled and kicked off his boots, hurrying to follow that trail.

Halfway there, he was ambushed by a shadowy figure and pushed roughly against the wall. Soft lips pressed greedily against his, and a sweet, familiar fragrance filled his nostrils, making his head swim with a pleasant buzz.

When Ceyla withdrew for air, Atton noticed that she wore nothing but a lacy red bra and panties. That brought to mind an unwanted image of the half-naked streetwalker. He pushed it aside with a shake of his head.

"Happy anniversary, Darin," Ceyla said, breathless.

Atton smiled, watching as Ceyla trailed her hands over his chest, quickly undoing buttons on his nanoweave-armored shirt. Once Ceyla finished with his shirt, she took a moment to appreciate her work and bit her bottom lip as her eyes flicked over the hard ridges of muscle running across his chest and abdomen. She began kissing his chest, trailing fire all the way down to his navel. She got down on her knees and reached for his belt, but Atton grabbed her hands to stop her there.

"Wait," he said.

She looked up at him, her big blue eyes suddenly full of concern. "What's wrong?"

Atton shook his head. "Nothing." He pulled Ceyla to her feet. "But I think I should be the one on my knees."

He dropped to one knee, and produced the blue velvet box from his pocket.

Ceyla gasped, and a sudden sheen of tears replaced the worry in her eyes.

Atton opened the box, revealing a diamond and platinum ring that he never should have been able to afford. It was too much to safely wear down here, but Atton held out hope that Ceyla wouldn't want to stay for much longer once he told her the truth.

Atton began steeling himself for exactly that as he put the words together inside his head. "Ceyla, I—"

"Yes!" She knocked him to the carpeted floor, and straddled him there, stealing his breath with more kisses. Again, she blazed a trail down his bare chest and stomach before reaching for his belt. This time she wouldn't take no for an answer, but Atton found himself unable to appreciate the moment.

After a while, she let him up and led him to the bedroom. He admired Ceyla's backside as she walked ahead of him, his pulse singing in his ears and his blood burning with desire. She had conveniently distracted him from the speech he'd planned to deliver. There would be a more appropriate time to tell her the truth.

Ceyla pushed him onto the bed, assaulting him with kisses and crawling on top of him with eager haste to finish what she'd started.

Later, as they lay naked and gasping beside one another,

enough clarity returned to Atton's mind for him to wonder at the wisdom of showing Ceyla the ring before he'd told her who she was really going to marry. Atton found the blue box on the night table and turned to Ceyla. She smiled, her cheeks flushed red from exertion, and her eyes bright with emotion. She held out her hand for him to put on the ring, and Atton didn't have the heart to hold back. He opened the box and slid the ring onto her finger.

"It's beautiful," she whispered. "Is it..."

"Real?" Atton nodded.

"How did you *afford* something like this?"

Atton took a breath. "I—"

Suddenly Ceyla gasped and sat up straighter. The sheets puddled in her lap, baring her breasts and distracting him once more.

"What is it?" he asked.

"I haven't even met your parents yet!"

"I haven't met yours either."

Another lie. Atton had been there when Ceyla had first come to Avilon and been reunited with her parents. She'd been orphaned during the Sythian invasion, and it had been more than ten years since she'd seen them. Unfortunately, her joy had lasted only as long as it took for her to realize that Omnius was a human creation, and that he'd resurrected everyone via physical rather than spiritual means.

"My parents are dead," Ceyla replied. Atton frowned. They weren't dead, but he supposed that to her, maybe they were. That didn't bode well for what he had to tell her.

"Well, my parents are also Etherians," Atton said, hoping to broach the topic with that admission. He had deliberately not talked about his parents before, hoping to avoid awkward conversations that might reveal who he really was.

"I guess that makes sense. Your last name is *Thardris,* after all."

Atton grimaced at the reminder of his lies. "Yeah."

"So who are they? You're not the overseer's son, but you must be related to him."

"He's my grandfather."

"Do you still see him?"

Atton shook his head.

Ceyla blew out a breath. "That's a relief."

"Why's that?"

"I don't trust Omnius, and I don't trust any of his puppets either. I wouldn't even want to be in the same room as the grand overseer."

Atton nodded and Ceyla snuggled closer to him. She laid her head on his chest and held out her hand to admire her ring. "We've just got each other. We're going to grow old together, Darin, and then one day, after a long and happy life, we're going to die and live together in a real paradise—in the real Etheria."

Those words sliced through the slender hope that Atton still clung to, dropping him into an abyss of guilt and despair. He had hoped that he could escape the Null Zone and his involvement with the Resistance, that he could convince Ceyla to join him in Etheria. Then there'd be no more need for him to lie.

"Don't you think it would be safer for us to raise children in Etheria?" Atton asked.

"Safer?" Ceyla snorted. "We'd die and wake up in the real Etheria, with Etherus asking us why we decided to kill ourselves."

Atton tried to wrap his head around Ceyla's thinking. "What if you're wrong? What if life goes on without a blip, and we're still the same people that we were before?"

"But we won't be."

"What if I could prove to you that people don't change after they're resurrected? In the Uppers we won't have to worry about the violence and crime. We'll be living in luxury, not poverty, and we won't even be allowed to make mistakes. It's a real utopia. How is that any different from the paradise you believe we'll go to when we die?"

Ceyla sat up and turned to him with a sharp look. "Where is all of this coming from, Darin?"

The truth sat on the tip of his tongue like a drop of acid, burning a hole. He was desperate to just spit it out, to tell her, and to the Netherworld with the consequences—except that he was living in the Netherworld, and he'd have to live with those consequences.

"Don't tell me you're actually one of them and you just came down here to get some excitement."

The look of wary judgement on her face gave Atton pause. He snorted and shook his head. "No."

"Because I fell in love with you knowing that you were different, that unlike half of the Nulls living down here, you're actually *real*."

"Of course I am!"

"Then don't throw that away. You can't get your soul back once it's gone."

Atton sighed, defeated. Not even Ceyla's love for him would be enough to overcome her prejudice against a man-made eternity ruled by an equally man-made god. "I'm sorry," he said. "It's just that with all the terrible things I see on the job, it's hard to imagine anything like that ever happening to you, or to one of our children someday."

Ceyla nodded, and some of the angry fire left her eyes. She rubbed his chest reassuringly. "I understand, but the solution isn't to run away and hide in the Uppers. That's what Omnius wants. We'd be falling right into his trap. Better to grow old and die than to live trapped inside a lie forever."

Atton felt those words stab through him like knives. Ceyla didn't realize she was talking about him. *Except that I won't have to live trapped inside my lies forever.* Ceyla talked about growing old together, but he was an *immortal*; he would never grow old and die, and someday Ceyla would wake up and realize that she had aged, but he still looked just as young as the day she'd met him. Atton's brow furrowed, and pressure began building inside of his head.

"What's wrong?" Ceyla asked, noticing the look on his face.

"Oh... I was just thinking about introducing you to my mother," he lied without thinking.

"Do you think she would come down to the Null Zone to see me?"

Atton's eyes drifted out of focus as he stared at the wall at the foot of the bed. "She won't have to. She lives on level 45 of Thardris Tower."

"She's a Null? I thought you said your parents were Etherians?"

Prickles of adrenaline stabbed Atton's fingertips as he got caught in his first lie. The irony was, with the exception of Ethan, his parents really were Etherians, but he could never introduce Ceyla to any of them without her realizing who he really was. She'd already met Ethan and Hoff, and she knew they were *Atton's* parents.

Thinking quickly, he turned to Ceyla. "My parents *are* Etherians. Valari is like a second mother to me, but she's actually my aunt. She took me in when I chose to become a Null."

Ceyla began nodding as if all of that made perfect sense. She lay her head back on his chest, her suspicions assuaged. "That was nice of her."

"Yes." Atton's smile tightened. "I'll talk to her. We'll have dinner sometime."

Ceyla covered a yawn with one hand. "Sounds great."

Atton's smile turned to a frown. Now he had to bring Valari Thardris into his lies. He supposed that was only fair, since she had brought him into her and Omnius's lies. But the problem was he didn't trust Valari, and now he needed her cooperation. That would only give her more leverage over him. Although, Atton supposed that didn't change anything. Valari already had all the leverage over him and anyone else that she would ever need—she was Omnius's creator—his *mother,* if that made any sense—and because of that, Atton suspected there was nothing she couldn't do, have done, or get away with. Whatever Valari wanted, she got.

He just hoped she didn't start wanting something that he couldn't offer.

CHAPTER 9

Galan Rovik lay staring up at the eye of Omnius through the domed ceiling of the high council chambers. Dazzling light beamed down on him, making him feel exposed and vulnerable. As he lay there, processing everything that he'd learned, he wondered how he could go on living. Omnius was right—the truth was a burden, and it was *heavy*.

A voice like thunder rolled through the chamber. The voice of Omnius. "Now you know everything. How do you feel?"

"Betrayed. I want to know *why*."

"You already know the answer. Not everyone can handle the truth, Galan, but you can. Arise, my child; you are stronger than you think."

Galan found himself rising from the floor, floating up and onto his feet, caught in a grav gun hidden somewhere within the room.

The grand overseer reappeared before him, materializing out of thin air. The man's sharply-angled face and flickering silver eyes made him look sinister now that Galan knew he was really Omnius.

"You have already begun to accept it," Omnius said, smiling and nodding.

"You didn't leave me any choice."

"You won't even try to resist me?"

"How can I? You already know what I'll do before I do it."

"So fear compels your loyalty."

"Did you expect otherwise?"

Omnius's smile grew. "You needn't be upset, Galan. Fear of God is the beginning of wisdom, and I have just made you wise."

Galan shook his head. "What are you going to do about the Sythians?"

"Come, and I'll show you." Omnius turned and preceded Galan up the stairs to the catwalk above the quantum junction. There, they walked up to a radiant white sphere sitting at waist height in the speaker's podium. Omnius placed his hands against the sphere, and the council chamber grew suddenly dark as the transparent dome overhead polarized. A holographic star map appeared hovering in the air, showing both the Adventa Galaxy and the neighboring Getties Cluster.

Omnius pointed to the nearest edge of the Getties, and the map zoomed in. Stars whirled by in a dazzling blur until one star system in particular came into focus. Galan recognized it almost immediately.

It was Noctune.

Omnius pointed to the planet by the same name. "Here, on the Gors' home world, below kilometers of ice, Shallah, the Supreme One, is hiding."

"How do you know?"

"My view of Noctune is clouded. The planet causes too much interference for me to see clearly beneath the surface, but I have an agent aboard Shallah's command ship. A human by the name of Lenon Donali."

"The Sythians trust a human aboard one of their ships?"

Omnius turned to Galan with a smile. "Why wouldn't they? He's their agent, too."

Galan shook his head, confused. "If Shallah is hiding on Noctune, then we should send a fleet and kill him before he leaves."

"No. Most of the Sythians' fleets are elsewhere, scattered across the Adventa Galaxy. Shallah is desperately trying to reverse-engineer quantum jump drives so that he can reach Avilon and attack us here, and I'm going to let him. He has a group of rebel Nulls that he captured during the battle for Dark Space. They're helping him to develop the quantum technology. He thinks those rebels have been de-linked, but just like Donali, they are still connected to me. Every breakthrough those Nulls have made was subtly fed to them by me. Rather than hunt the Sythians all over the known galaxies, I'm going to help them to come here so that I can defeat them in one decisive victory. All of Avilon will watch as the Sythians are defeated. Humanity will have its revenge for the invasion, and I will be the hero."

"Until they find out that you created the Sythians."

"They won't find out. Only my disciples get to know that."

"What if one of them talks?"

Omnius turned to Galan with a smile. "I would predict their betrayal and stop them before they could even speak."

Galan frowned. "If you can predict betrayal then how did Shallah betray you?"

"He is a collective intelligence. That made him smart enough to find a way. Once he realized that Sythia was really *New Avilon*, and that the paradise I had promised to the Sythians as a reward for their victory was not for them, but for the humans I had created them to despise and kill, Shallah turned against me."

"Where is New Avilon now?"

"Facets of it are scattered across the Getties dropping nanite bombs on every planet they can find. Given enough time, the nanites will erase all of the ruins that humanity left behind when they came to the Adventa galaxy. One day, when my people find the Getties empty, they'll remember the nanites wiped out the galaxy-spanning empire of Sythians, and that any archaeological remains of their past were naturally wiped out along with them."

Galan blew out a breath. If the Sythians, who were unpredictable and more powerful than humanity had ever been, couldn't defeat Omnius, then surely no one could. "Why tell me all of this?"

"You asked," Omnius said, "and I don't hide anything from my disciples."

Galan nodded, wondering what other burdens he would have to bear as Omnius's web of lies grew. He began to suspect that humans were Omnius's entertainment—his playthings—but if Omnius objected to that thought, he chose not to address it.

"I have an assignment for you," Omnius said. The star map hovering in the air disappeared and the inside of the council chamber brightened again.

"What is it, My Lord?"

"I want you to watch over another strategian—Hoff Heston."

Galan's brow furrowed at that. "So I won't be going to live in Celesta? I thought you made me a disciple already."

"I did, but before you come to live up here I want you to help guide another doubting soul along the ascendant path."

"What do you need me to do?"

"Answer his doubts, but not with the truth—not yet. Otherwise, just be ready to act when I tell you to."

"You're going to kill him."

"I don't *kill* people, Galan, I save them. You will help make Hoff's fall from grace more graceful, and one day he, too, will become one of my disciples."

"Very well," Galan replied, bowing his head. "It will be done."

"*My* will be done," Omnius replied just before he vanished again.

* * *

Shallah stood looming over the sensor operator's station on the bridge of his command ship, the *Asharn—Death-bringer* in Sythian. There'd been a transmission from an unknown vessel, lying cloaked at the edge of the star system. A *human* vessel. They'd requested to speak with the Sythians' leader.

Rather than risk speaking to them from within his sanctuary below the surface of Noctune, Shallah had made his way to the surface and flown up to his command ship to deal with the threat personally.

"There it is, Supreme One." The sensor operator pointed to a purple blip on the star map hovering above his control station.

Details about the ship appeared on one of the sensor operator's physical displays. The enemy contact was an unknown hull type, barely a hundred meters long.

"Let me see it," Shallah said.

A visual materialized on the main forward viewscreen. The ship looked ancient. It certainly wasn't any kind of threat.

"Why do you wait? Disable them. We find out what they want when they are at our mercy."

"Every time we draw near, they jump away and reappear in another part of the system."

"Then blanket space with fighters and hit them with SLS

— 82 —

disruptors when they get too close."

"We try that. They are not using SLS drives."

Shallah was taken aback by that. "You mean they're making *quantum* jumps? Why do you not tell me sooner? Omnius is here. We must evacuate!"

"Wait, My Lord. We are about to inform you when *this* appears, sitting on your command chair." The sensor operator handed him a flat silver disc.

Shallah turned it over and over in his hands. He was tired of asking questions. He closed his eyes and made a direct connection with the sensor operator's cerebral implant. Once the connection was established, he sifted through the operator's memories to obtain his answers directly.

The device he held was a holographic projector. The sensor operator had seen part of the recording, an image of a man sitting in Shallah's command chair. The man in the recording asked to see the Sythians' leader, and he said that the rest of his message would only play in that one's presence.

Shallah was confused. Why would Omnius send them this when he could have sent a bomb aboard instead?

"Are we still cloaked?" Shallah asked, opening his eyes and looking around quickly, searching both visually and via his remote link with the ship's scanners to see if there were any other foreign objects on board.

The engineering operator replied, "We are safely cloaked, My lord."

"You fool! Raise our shields immediately before they send us something more dangerous!"

"A thousand apologies, My Lord! It will be done!"

Shallah hissed with displeasure and turned and walked up to his command chair. He had acquired an intuitive grasp of how the disc-shaped device worked from what the sensor-operator knew about it. It would only play its recording from the command chair. Once he'd placed the device, Shallah stepped back and waited. A flicker of blue light scythed out from the device, scanning everyone in the immediate vicinity. A moment later, a man appeared sitting in Shallah's chair. He was an ordinary man, nothing remarkable about him. His features were marred with asymmetries and imperfections, meaning he wasn't one of Omnius's clones, unless the imperfections were deliberate.

"I am Therius the Redemptor, Commander of Etheria's Army." Shallah resisted the urge to reply. Surely the recording held no capacity for conversation. "I seek an alliance against Omnius. You will want to know what we have to offer, but you need look no further than the device sitting before you. You wish to reach Avilon, and we can help you get there. All we ask in return is that we fight our enemy together. As a token of our good faith, please accept this gift, and know that you can trust us."

The recording ended and the holographic projection of the man sitting in Shallah's command chair disappeared.

"What gift?" he wondered aloud.

Then a new hologram appeared, a static image. It was a schematic, a blueprint to build something. Looking at it more closely, Shallah realized what it was. Then another schematic appeared in its place, followed by another and another, until Shallah had seen more than a dozen, each one detailing how to create one component of a quantum jump drive. The schematics were annotated in Avilonian, not Sythian, but translating them wouldn't take long.

Shallah caught himself gaping at the holo projector. He wondered if it was possible for this to be a trap laid by Omnius.

Of course, it was possible, he decided, but he couldn't afford not to investigate further.

"Hail that vessel," he ordered.

"They are already hailing us, My Lord," the comms operator replied, speaking in strangely-accented Sythian. "They would like us to drop our shields so they can come aboard."

Shallah turned and nodded to his comms operator, the human traitor Commander Donali. At first Shallah hadn't trusted him, but over the years Donali had been nothing if not faithful to the Sythian cause. More importantly, brain scans showed he did not have a Lifelink implant to tie him back to Omnius. "Tell them that we will send out a shuttle and they can jump aboard that. No more than three of them. I won't risk lowering our shields. If possible, I would like to speak with this *Therius the Redemptor* in person."

A moment later, Donali replied, "They agree to our terms."

Shallah was surprised. That human was taking a big risk to come aboard under those circumstances. Perhaps he could be trusted after all.

"I shall be in my meditation room," he said. "Have them brought to me there."

"It will be done, My Lord," Donali replied.

To his engineering operator, Shallah said, "Have those schematics translated and analyzed. See if they offer a workable design for quantum jump drives."

"A design for... forgive me, did you say *quantum* jump drives, Supreme One?"

"Your ears do not fail you. Tell me what you can learn from these plans." Shallah gestured to the series of schematics still projected and playing on a loop above his command chair.

"Yes, My Lord," his chief engineer replied.

Shallah turned and left the bridge, feeling simultaneously hopeful and apprehensive. If Therius had been sent by Omnius, then nothing good would come from his arrival, but if Omnius were somehow unaware of the people that called themselves *Etheria's Army*, then this might just be what the Sythians needed to catch the old snake off guard.

CHAPTER 10

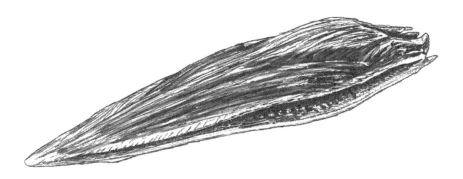

Shallah sat waiting in his meditation room aboard the *Asharn*. Here there were no distractions, nothing except for a single glossy black chair sitting on a pedestal. Stars sparkled all around. The ceiling and walls were dome-shaped and littered with holo projectors, giving a 360-degree view of space.

Shallah used this room, and others like it, to allow his mind to drift free of his physical form and connect with his greater self.

The minds of every Sythian under his command were stored aboard the *Asharn*, not for the purpose of resurrecting them in new bodies when their old ones died, but rather to join all of them together into a glorious whole. Shallah was that whole. He was the curator and director of the Sythians' collective intelligence, just as Omnius directed the human collective.

Information was exchanged seamlessly and between the individual cells inside Shallah's collective mind. He reveled in the feeling of oneness and empowerment that came from the collective. Shallah was connected to every system and every living Sythian aboard his ship. Through that connection he saw the shuttle bearing the human rebels land, and he read Donali's intent to inform him of their arrival even before he did so.

Shallah watched through the ship's sensors as a trio of humans walked through his ship, a dozen Sythians escorting them to his mediation room. That was his cue to return to the comparatively limited awareness of his physical body. The return to that body felt like waking up inside a coffin. Shallah blinked his large Sythian eyes and tried to ignore the feeling of claustrophobia. The impression of floating in the vastness of space created by the mediation room's holo projectors helped, but it wasn't nearly enough. The walls seemed infinitely far away, yet Shallah still felt them closing in; the stars were too heavy and too close, burning mere inches from his face.

Shallah worked to control his breathing, and a measure of calm returned. The rest of the Sythians had yet to learn the truth of their existence, so for the time being, Shallah was forced to exist in two places at once, but the part of him that was relegated to a physical body always resented it.

Shallah opened the door with a thought and watched as a dozen Sythians walked in pushing three human prisoners in front of them. They walked up to the foot of the throne. These three had already been thoroughly scanned. They bore no weapons, and they were not linked.

"Who are you, and where do you come from?" Shallah demanded, speaking in Versal rather than Sythian. He recognized the man in the center of the three from his pale blue eyes and dark brown skin. He was the one from the holo-recording—Therius, the so-called Redemptor. He and the other two men standing beside him wore Imperial Fleet uniforms, the colors faded with age. That suggested that they hailed from the original Imperium. Their Imperial rank insignia further supported that notion, but for one key difference. They all wore a silver six-sided star above their insignia. Shallah recognized it as the Star of Etherus. Those symbols had been found hanging on pendants around the neck vertebrae of fossilized skeletons throughout the Getties. Shallah's eyes narrowed as he considered what that might mean.

"You already know who I am," Therius replied. His pale blue eyes gleamed in the low light of the room, but they weren't aglow with ARCs. "As for where we come from, some of us escaped Avilon, while others were rescued."

"Rescued? Does Omnius know about that?"

"He doesn't even know we exist."

Shallah wasn't sure he should believe that. "How is it that you have access to quantum technology that only Omnius understands? If even *I* can't comprehend these technologies, how do you explain your knowledge of them?"

"Omnius did not develop quantum technologies; he *found* them and reverse-engineered them. The schematics we sent to you were originally recovered from the ruins of a world that is found here, in the Getties."

Shallah was taken aback by that. Apparently Omnius had still kept some secrets. "You have proof of thisss?" he hissed.

"I can take you there."

"Why should I trust you?"

Therius spread his hands. "I and the men who accompanied me are not linked. There is no way for Omnius to spy on you through us."

"You call yourselves Etheria's Army. I assume that name doesn't refer to the city of Etheria on Avilon."

"No."

"Then you mean Etheria in the religious sense. You believe in an afterlife."

Therius nodded.

Shallah grew uneasy, and his gaze returned to the six-sided stars on the humans' uniforms. He realized that he was dealing with a group of religious fanatics. These people embodied the sentiment that had caused not one, but two Great Wars between mortals and immortals. History seemed to be repeating itself now, circling back around for a third Great War.

"We are already developing quantum technologies. We don't need your help."

"The rebels helping you are still *linked*. Omnius *let* you capture them, so that he could use them to lure you into his trap. He *wants* you to develop quantum jump drives, but in his timing. And when you do, he expects you to use the technology to attack Avilon. He'll be waiting for you when you arrive."

Shallah sat back in his chair. "If that's true, then we should stay as far away from Avilon as we can."

"You can't hide forever."

"Perhaps not, but we cannot defeat Omnius by falling into his trap."

"You have a chance if you surprise him by attacking Avilon earlier than he expects."

Before Shallah could ask any further questions, news from the surface of Noctune intruded on his thoughts, fed to him through his collective awareness.

The prisoners had escaped.

That wouldn't have been a problem were it not for the fact that the human prisoners were all still linked to Omnius.

"You'll have to excuse me," he said. "Something important has come up. We will have to continue this discussion later."

"Something?" Therius asked.

"A group of human prisoners are trying to escape from Noctune. They are still linked to Omnius, and if they make it to the surface of the planet, Omnius will find out where we are hiding."

"Omnius already knows you are here," Therius replied.

Shallah's Sythian eyes narrowed swiftly. "If he knows we are here, then why hasn't he attacked us?"

"Because he's waiting for you to come out of hiding and attack *him* at Avilon, as I already mentioned."

"How do you know this?"

"You have a traitor in your midst. He is the one who communicated with us before we came aboard."

Shallah blinked. "Donali? How do you know he is a traitor?"

"We've been intercepting Lifelink transfers on Avilon. That is how we rescue people from the planet. We know what Omnius's people know, and they know a surprising amount."

"You cannot *intercept* quantum communications," Shallah replied. "The data is instantly *jumped* from one location to another."

"Instantly, yes, securely no. Omnius knows of the vulnerability, but he doesn't know about *us*. He thinks he is the only one who can manipulate the fabric of the universe."

"Telling me you have access to hidden knowledge that only you and Omnius share makes me even more suspicious."

Therius spread his hands. "But your suspicions are baseless."

"Perhaps. Again, why should I trust you?"

"You don't have a choice. I don't see anyone else here offering to share the secrets of the universe with you."

Shallah's gaze traveled over the Sythian guards in the room, wondering how much they had understood from the conversation going on around them. *Not much,* he decided. Most Sythians couldn't understand Versal without the aid of a translator.

Turning back to Therius, Shallah said, "I was going to attack

Avilon to get revenge on Omnius, not because I thought we could actually defeat him there. Our fleet is strong, but Omnius's fleet is far stronger. He has created a warship larger than anything ever built. It's made up of tens of thousands of city-sized warships called *Facets*. Together, they form a hollow 20-sided sphere—an Icosahedron. It's large enough to encompass entire planets and mine them to their cores, all the while collecting solar energy from nearby suns. Omnius calls his creation New Avilon. He used it to create my people, the Sythians, eleven years ago, and since then he has been creating more Facets. By now, New Avilon could have doubled in size."

Therius appeared unfazed by that information. "New Avilon has actually tripled in size, but construction of new Facets has stopped as the existing ones spread out through the Getties, seeding planets with nanites to wipe out any possible evidence of Omnius's lies. Even with an estimated quarter of a million Facets, seeding the galaxy will take a long time. The Getties is made up of more than a hundred million stars. We have observed that it takes an average of ten days for a Facet to seed a star system with nanites. That means Omnius will need roughly 11 years to seed every planet in every star system."

Suddenly Shallah understood. While spread out across the Getties, those Facets would be unable to jump home in time to defend Avilon. It would take days or possibly even weeks to calculate so many different jumps over such vast distances, and a lot could happen in that time.

"Then eleven years is how long we have to get to Avilon and destroy it," Shallah decided.

Therius shook his head. "Not destroy it. *Liberate* it."

"What? Why would we do that?"

Therius arched a dark eyebrow at him. "When I proposed that you ally with us against Omnius, I wasn't just talking about

Etheria's Army, I was talking about allying yourselves with all of *humanity*."

"Impossible. I would have to tell my people the truth in order to justify such an alliance."

"I'm surprised you haven't told them already. You're only helping Omnius by keeping what you know to yourself."

"The truth would demoralize my people."

"It will motivate them. You'd be surprised what people can do when they have nothing left to lose."

"What makes you think humanity will even want our help? We slaughtered them. They'll never join us."

"They will when we tell *them* the truth."

Shallah wasn't sure he liked the direction this was going. "Why should we help you set humanity free?" Shallah asked.

"Because you're going to need their help to defeat Omnius. Speaking of which, I'd like to meet these prisoners of yours. Avilon isn't defenseless, and we're going to need all the soldiers we can get if we're going to fight through Omnius's garrison of drones."

"The prisoners are linked. If you tell them what we're planning, Omnius will find out, too."

"We'll *de-link* them first."

"Lifelinks are like a cancer. Even if you cut them out, it just takes one stray nanite for them to grow back. If you are right about Donali and the Null Rebels being on Omnius's side, then that is only further proof that de-linking doesn't work. The only way to de-link someone is to kill them."

"Exactly," Therius said.

Shallah's eyes began to itch with frustration. "Very well. I will agree to this alliance, assuming you can show me proof to back up your claims."

"I can and I will."

"Good, and I will see if what you say about the traitor in our midst is true."

"You better hurry, before he tells Omnius we are here."

"I am already looking into the matter," Shallah said as he rose from his throne and walked past his new human allies.

* * *

Donali sat at the comm operator's station aboard the Asharn, thinking about the arrival of the mysterious human vessel. This was something his master should know about. Donali glanced around quickly, making sure that none of the Sythians were close enough to see. Then he began composing a message, in human Versal, not Sythian or Avilonian, just in case someone should happen to see what he was doing.

He wrote: *Unidentified human vessel arrives at Noctune. Ancient design. Possesses quantum jump technology. Captain of human ship claims to be Therius the Redemptor, Commander of Etheria's Army. Therius has sent schematics for quantum jump drives. Is seeking alliance with Sythian Coalition. Please advise, Omnius.* Donali configured the Asharn's quantum comms array to transmit his message.

"What are you doing?"

Donali jumped and turned to see Queen Tavia, Shallah's second-in-command, looming over his shoulder. She was a ghoulish creature with red eyes and papery black wings.

Donali smiled and replied in broken Sythian. "I am writing my journal."

"You are supposed to be watching the comms." Tavia reached out with one taloned finger and pointed at a blinking purple light on Donali's control station. He had a message waiting.

Donali smiled and inclined his head. "You are right, My Queen. I will get back to work immediately."

"Wait . . . what is thisss?" Tavia hissed, pointing to the last line of the message he'd been composing. Donali turned to see her talon hovering over the word *Omnius*. He went cold. Tavia couldn't understand Versal. It was a completely different alphabet!

"What is what?" Donali asked innocently.

"You are communicating with the evil one?"

"You must be mistaken. This is a journal entry. I am writing about Omnius, trying to decide what motivated him to create the Sythians."

"I am not so stupid assss you think." Tavia's mouth flashed open with needle sharp teeth, and she lunged at him.

Donali gasped as her teeth bit into his neck, and he gurgled as she ripped out his throat and threw him out of his chair.

Donali's landed with a jarring *thud,* his lungs burning for air that they could no longer draw. He lay on the deck, blinking slowly, his life seeping out in a warm puddle around his head. He remained conscious long enough to see Tavia sit at his control station and begin uncovering his treachery.

But it was too late. Omnius already knew where Shallah was hiding, and if the Sythians didn't leave by tonight, when Donali was supposed to manually synchronize his mind with the databanks on Avilon, then Omnius would know what had happened, and he would avenge Donali's death.

It was a pity that he wouldn't be able to share this latest development about Therius the Redemptor and his offer to share quantum technology with the Sythians, but he had done his best. Omnius would have to handle things from here.

Donali smiled as the darkness closed in around him, knowing that he would soon be waking up back on Avilon, his mission accomplished.

CHAPTER 11

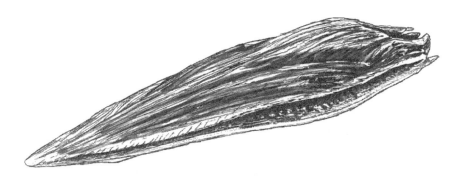

Destra crawled on her hands and knees through the dark. Her heart pounded, and her brain buzzed with adrenaline. Rough furrows of castcrete pressed against her palms—*Gor claw marks*, Destra thought.

This was *it*. Destra tried not to think about the remaining obstacles to their escape, but worries circled through her head like carrion birds circling a corpse. Noctune was a forbidding environment. They would need insulated suits, weapons, tools, and power sources if they were going to survive beyond the protective shell of the Sythians' bunker. The goal was to escape the prison level, find supplies, and then steal a Sythian ship and make a real escape, but even that was hard to imagine. Where could they go that they wouldn't run into Sythians? The Getties had to be teeming with them.

Destra forced herself back to the here and now. She focused on the feel of the tunnel walls, listened to the rough scraping of loose castcrete brushing against their clothes and rolling away beneath their palms. She focused on the gritty smell of dust on the frigid air. The only light they had to see by was far behind them, so Destra had to rely on her other senses to negotiate the tunnel. Making matters worse, her hands were growing numb. The tunnel walls were like ice.

Up ahead, Atta crept along behind Torv. They came to a steep incline, and Atta whined.

"My hands are slipping!"

"Hold on!" Destra thrust her feet out against the walls for extra grip and pushed Atta up from behind with a grunt of effort.

"Where does this tunnel lead?" Farah whispered over Destra's shoulder.

"I don't know," Destra replied, whispering back. Then she felt the wall beside her disappear, and she realized that the tunnel had taken a sharp right turn. Momentarily confused, she felt around in front of her for Atta's legs and found her daughter still moving up the tunnel in the same direction as before.

"There's a branch here, but it looks like we're going straight," Destra explained.

Farah gave no reply, just a short gasp followed by a *scraaape!* of gravel.

"You okay?" Destra asked.

"Fine," Farah replied, cursing under her breath. "Just saved myself from a nasty fall at the expense of a few fingernails."

After another few minutes of struggling up the tunnel, Destra heard a new sound, something besides the constant crunch and scrape of loose gravel. Somewhere up ahead she heard a large object dragging across a smooth surface. Destra marveled that her hearing had become so acute now that her eyes were blind.

But her blindness didn't last. No sooner did she hear that new sound, than she saw *light*, glorious light, come pouring into the tunnel up ahead. Atta became a bright silhouette as Torv climbed out of the tunnel, his bulk no longer blocking the light source. Destra could see her hands now. They were bleeding. She grimaced and hurried on. Atta crawled out, and then a strong, corpse-gray hand reached in and pulled Destra out, too.

She stumbled to her feet. Her knees ached sharply from the constant pressure of crawling on them, and her hands stung with myriad cuts. Destra ignored the pain and tried to figure out where she was.

Like everything else she'd seen in the Sythians' bunker, this room was made with familiar gray alloys, not the glossy black materials that Sythians seemed to favor. The lighting, however, was dim and lavender-tinted, pouring out from kludged alien light fixtures. Another alien feature was the contents of the storage room. The walls were adorned with racks of Sythian armor and weapons. Torv went to the nearest suit of armor, and activated it by placing his palm against the obsidian breastplate. The suit shimmered and writhed as if it were alive.

Destra heard footsteps behind her, and she turned to see Farah come stumbling out of the tunnel, shaking out a numb leg.

A tug on Destra's sleeve drew her attention back to the fore. It was Atta.

"Torv wants us to put on the armor."

Destra blinked stupidly at her daughter. "Right," she said, heading to the nearest suit of armor.

She glanced at Torv in time to see the suit he'd chosen begin wrapping itself around him, automatically conforming to his size and shape. Individual pieces hovered into place on tiny grav lifts. Destra shook her head, marveling at the technology. She placed her own palm against one of the suits of armor and watched wide-eyed as it shimmered and writhed to life in exactly the same way. Spongy, sticky wet pads pressed against her palms, and a solid weight flattened her breasts. Then a skull-shaped helmet with glaring red eyes floated up past her nose and slipped over her head. There came a *hiss* of air pressurizing, and Destra saw the world turn a bloody red as she was forced to look through the helmet's visors.

Destra spent a moment listening to the sound of her breathing reverberate inside the helmet. Alien displays flickered to life, taking up small hexagonal sections of her view with strange symbols and diagrams. She wished the helmet's visors would be a normal color. But even as she wished that, they became clear. Destra blinked, and her skin crawled with the realization that the suit had somehow read her thoughts.

Feeling watched, Destra spun around. The suit moved with her, aiding her movement and making her feel stronger and faster than usual. She saw Torv, still recognizable from his size, now checking his forearm gauntlets. Glowing red and blue apertures appeared, sliding up out of his armor with soft metallic clicking sounds. Then a pair of larger red apertures glowed to life in his palms.

Integrated weapons. Destra wondered briefly about them, and suddenly another pair of alien displays appeared projected inside of her helmet. Something began moving against her arms and tickling her skin, and then glowing red apertures appeared in her own gauntlets.

Torv looked up at the sound, and pointed at her. A loud hiss sounded beside Destra's ears, and she jumped with fright. A second later she realized it was Torv speaking to her over comms, and she felt like a skriff for being startled.

Easy, Des, she told herself.

Torv pointed to himself and held up his forearms, rotating them for emphasis. The glowing weapons disappeared, and the air around him shimmered. Then he disappeared, too. Torv had cloaked.

Destra got the message. They needed to use stealth, not brute force. But how would they coordinate with each other while cloaked?

Even as she wondered that, Torv reappeared, this time as a contoured shadow, as if he and his suit were somehow made of brackish water. Destra thought about cloaking herself, and in the next instant her own armor shimmered and disappeared, replaced with the same contoured shadow as Torv's. Destra spent a moment wiggling shadowy fingers in front of her eyes. Once she was satisfied that the ghostly apparition was really her, she turned to look around for Atta.

She found Farah instead, not yet cloaked. The other woman tapped her helmet with one armored hand, as if trying to get her comms to work.

"Hello?" came Farah's voice.

A small shadow appeared behind Farah, and Atta's voice bubbled over the comms, "You have to *think* about what you want to do."

Farah jumped and spun to face Atta, but instead of seeing her, she began looking around the storage room as if she were blind. "Atta? Where are you?"

"In front of you," Atta said, de-cloaking right under Farah's nose.

"Frek!" Farah jumped back, springing a few feet higher than she should have been able to jump. She landed with a noisy *thud*.

An angry *hiss* slithered into Destra's helmet, and Torv began gesturing at Atta and Farah impatiently.

Atta explained the Sythians' intuitive technology for Farah's benefit. Moments later, Farah's armor shimmered and she became a watery shadow, too.

"We have to go," Atta said, pointing to Torv as he slunk off toward the door. "He's going to rescue the other Gors before we escape."

Destra tried a reply, "Can you hear me?"

"Loud and clear," Farah said.

"Good." Destra hurried after Torv, her footsteps whispering against the castcrete. She found the Gor staring at the door, as if he could see straight through it, apparently waiting for something.

Suddenly his hand shot out and stabbed a key on the control panel. The symbol didn't correspond to either Versal or Sythian. Destra guessed that Torv must have experimented with the controls earlier to know how they worked now.

The door slid open, revealing a dim hallway. Torv held up a hand in front of her face. She had to wait. Then he crept out, crouching low, but moving fast. Destra poked her head out the door to see Torv rushing up behind a pair of armored Sythians. All the Sythians she'd seen so far were the size of adult humans, but these two looked like children, and they waddled strangely as they walked.

Torv reached the first one and snapped its neck with a vicious twist. The Sythian crumpled to the floor. The second one sprang away, its legs unfolding to twice their length. A pair of papery black wings spread out from the alien's back, and the Sythian *flew* down the corridor, quickly putting distance between it and Torv.

Destra heard the Gor *hiss* over the comms, and then came a sharp crackle of weapons' fire. A shining purple beam shot out of Torv's gauntlet and the flying Sythian fell with a clatter of armor.

Torv turned to them with glowing red eyes and waved them over. Destra grabbed Atta's hand and ran. Farah brought up the rear once again.

Torv didn't wait for them to catch up. He raced down the

corridor, a blur of inky blackness.

"So much for stealth," Farah said as they passed the fallen Sythians.

"He didn't leave any witnesses," Destra replied.

"That doesn't mean someone isn't watching this corridor."

Destra shook her head. "This isn't a Sythian facility."

"They installed lights, why not surveillance?"

"Well, it's too late to worry about it now," Destra said.

Torv skidded to a stop as the corridor reached a *T*. He held up a shadowy hand once more, and they stopped behind him, watching as he peered around the side. A dazzling purple beam sizzled by in front of his face, and he leapt back, hissing.

"Told you," Farah said.

Destra shook her head, feeling dizzy with despair. The walls seemed to be closing in on her; the air inside her suit was suddenly too stuffy and hot. She tightened her grip on Atta's hand and turned to look behind them.

No one there. Not yet.

"We need a plan," Farah said. "Atta, tell Torv—"

But the Gor was already de-cloaking and jumping out into the corridor, weapons blazing. Bright purple beams flashed out from his palms, crackling like electricity as they were released. She heard armor clattering in the distance. Return fire shivered back, tracking Torv in a blinding stream, but the Sythians' shots weren't as focused as Torv's. Only one beam found a glancing mark. Torv hissed with the impact and fired back in a steady stream. Armor clattered once more, and the enemy fire grew silent. Torv raced down the corridor. Destra grabbed Atta's hand and ran after him. They came to a staircase with no less than half a dozen Sythians lying crumpled on the steps. One of them was still moving, and Torv stomped on its neck with a sickening *crunch*.

Destra winced and turned to see if her daughter had seen the vicious move. To her dismay, she caught Atta staring in morbid fascination at the dead Sythian under Torv's boot.

Torv interrupted Destra's thoughts with another upraised palm. She saw him staring off into the distance again, and she guessed he was using sensors to scan for more enemies.

Suddenly he spun around. Echoing footsteps reached Destra's ears, and then a dozen Sythians came boiling into the corridor from the other end. Bright purple pulse lasers crackled out, lighting up the gloomy corridor. Destra just stood there, frozen in horror and shock, until strong hands dragged her away.

"Come on, Destra!" It was Farah. "Snap out of it!"

Farah threw her around a corner and pinned her against the wall. Torv stood in front of them, flattening himself against the opposite wall as a torrent of lasers flashed between them. Here the corridor widened just enough for them to shelter from enemy fire.

"We have to fight, Des," Farah said.

"Mom, I'm scared," Atta said, squeezing her hand.

Destra turned to her. Seeing Atta standing there in *Sythian* armor, with a deadly battle raging around them, Destra felt suddenly faint, and her eyes drifted out of focus. She wondered if this were all just a bad dream.

"Mom?"

"It's going to be okay, Atta," she said. "We're going to wake up soon..."

"Destra! Don't fall apart on me now!" Farah said.

Laser fire screamed through the corridor, washing everything a dazzling lavender-white. Torv was still not cloaked, and his black armor gleamed wetly in the laser light. Destra wondered about that; then she noticed the ragged hole in his side—the source of the wetness.

Torv's glowing red eyes were locked on hers, as if in silent condemnation of her cowardice, but maybe it wasn't condemnation. Maybe it was pity. Destra couldn't decide which was worse.

She wasn't a soldier. She wasn't cut out for war. The Gor inclined his head to her, as if acknowledging her weakness, and then his palms glowed to life, two bright red apertures to match his eyes.

The torrent of pulse lasers streaming between them quieted, and Torv jumped out, palms raised and flashing with dazzling purple stars—miniature pirakla missiles.

Destra heard those tracking packets of energy slam into walls and explode with a thunderous roar that shook the entire compound. Castcrete trickled down from the ceiling, and residual vibrations came rumbling underfoot like an earthquake. Farah sprang out next, firing bright purple lances of light and screaming incoherently.

Return fire crackled back, and Destra cringed, her eyes slamming shut to block it all out. She squeezed Atta's hand tightly. Torv gave a *hissing* scream, like a giant shellfish being boiled alive. Farah panted raggedly, cursing and calling Destra a coward. Destra willed herself not to hear any of it. Then a few stray crackles of laser fire silenced both Farah and Torv.

Silence rang like a crystal bell, and for a moment Destra dared to believe that it was over, that they wouldn't find her or Atta.

Then footsteps sounded on the stairs—*clack, clack, clack.* Destra opened her eyes in time to see two armored Sythians picking a path through their fallen comrades at the top of the stairs. Destra's heart leapt into her throat.

Those two were followed by another two, and then four

more. Glowing red eyes found them, somehow seeing them despite their cloaking shields.

One of the Sythians raised his arms, and glowing red apertures appeared in his palms. One arm aimed at her, the other at Atta.

"Run!" Destra leapt in front of her daughter just as the sharp *crack* of laser fire sounded. The world flashed lavender-white. A searing pain erupted in Destra's chest, and she crumpled to the floor, suddenly unable to breathe. Another *crack* sounded, and a small shadow clattered down beside her, alien armor flickering blackly as the cloaking shield failed.

Tears filled Destra's eyes, and her mind wailed impotently. She had no air to scream. Then came another crackle and flash of lasers. The searing pain in her chest exploded into blinding agony, but a spreading numbness quickly took its place, and her vision grew hazy with encroaching darkness.

Destra surrendered to it.

I'm going to wake up now, she decided, her eyes drifting shut. That thought chased her down a dark tunnel toward a dazzling white light.

"So beautiful..." she whispered as she raced toward the light.

CHAPTER 12

Ethan sat behind the wheel of his air car, staring at the solid wall of tail lights, unbroken lines of red shining feebly into the never-ending night of the Null Zone. Apartment windows glowed in rows of gold to either side. Ethan sighed, rolling his neck and shoulders, trying to work some of the tension out of his muscles.

Traffic had been stuck for half an hour already, with no signs of letting up. While waiting, he'd tuned into the news nets for an explanation. Enforcers had set up blockades all over Sutterfold District, looking for a pair of children who had been abducted from the district councilor's home a few hours earlier. Theories abounded about who had abducted them and why, but Ethan didn't have time to worry about their fate. At the moment, he had his own child to worry about.

A tiny cough interrupted his thoughts.

"Her fever isn't going down," Alara said from the backseat of the car. "We need to get her to the hospital *now*, Ethan."

He shook his head and gestured helplessly to the traffic. "How?" Ethan twisted around to look at his wife. Tears glistened on her cheeks, and her face looked ashen.

Trinity coughed again, drawing both of their gazes to her.

Her car seat wasn't facing him, but Ethan could imagine her tiny cheeks flushed and blotchy, her body burning itself up from the inside. By now the medication they'd given her should have worked.

"Why isn't she crying?" Alara asked. "She should be crying! We should have called an ambulance," she said, looking at him as if the traffic were his fault. "We can't just wait here until Enforcers search every car in the city!"

"No, we can't," Ethan said, turning back around. He disengaged the lane-lock setting of the autopilot and set the car over to full manual control.

"What are you doing?"

"I'm getting us to the hospital," he said, dialing the car's inertial compensator up to 100%. That done, he pulled up and gunned the throttle. The car's thrusters roared and they rose swiftly above the endless lines of traffic. Dead ahead lay the hazy blue ceiling of the Styx, cutting the city off at level 50.

A crackle of static roared through the car's speakers. "Stop your car and submit to inspection immediately!"

Ethan spared a hand from the flight yoke to reply. "I have a sick baby on board. I need to get her to the hospital."

"You are not authorized to leave the inspection area. If you don't comply, we will disable your vehicle. I repeat—"

Ethan muted the comms, and pushed the throttle into overdrive. They jetted up through clear air, racing between a pair of foot bridges crossing the elevated streets on level 45.

Flashing lights strobed through the car's rear window, and a pair of dazzling blue lasers flashed by.

"Frek!" Ethan pushed the car into a sudden dive. Airspeed quickly climbed past 700 kilometers per hour, and the car shuddered as windshear threatened to rip something off the fuselage.

"Ethan!" Alara yelled.

He pulled up and flipped the car on its side to skate through a narrow alley between buildings. Windows raced by in a blur of golden light. Collision warnings blared, and Trinity began wailing with them.

At least she's crying now, Ethan thought.

Behind them, the Enforcers' flashing lights were back. Another pair of blue lasers flickered by, hitting the building to Ethan's left. They were shooting to disable, not to kill, but at this speed disabling their car would be deadly anyway.

The car's headlights lit up the end of the alley. Flashing red brackets highlighted the gap, and an accompanying alarm screeched from the car's collision warning system. The alley narrowed to a thin slice at the end. It wasn't wide enough.

"Ethan!"

"I see it!"

He rolled back to level and pulled up hard, applying dorsal maneuvering jets to nose up further. Firing the grav lifts, Ethan bounced the car off the end of the alley and raced straight up, riding on a thin cushion of air.

A dozen floors up, the space between the buildings grew, and Ethan flew out into the clear. The rear-view display showed that he'd lost his pursuit.

Ethan grinned and risked a glance over his shoulder to make sure Alara and Trinity were both fine. As he did so, he saw the headlights of an approaching vehicle heading straight for them.

A loud blast from the other driver's horn emphasized the danger. Another warning screamed from the car's collision warning system. Adrenaline sparked in Ethan's fingertips, and he slammed the flight yoke forward, diving straight down. Alara screamed, Trinity wailed, and then the lights were gone. The approaching vehicle roared overhead, rattling their windows with its passing.

"That was too close!" Alara said, sounding breathless.

Ethan swallowed thickly and nodded. He raced back up to the streets on level 45, keeping an eye out for stray traffic this time. He used the car's nav system to guide him to the upper levels hospital where Alara had given birth just a few short months ago.

Enforcers found them again just as Ethan hovered down in front of the ER. "Get her to a doctor, Alara; I'll deal with this."

"Deal with it *how?* They're going to arrest you!"

Ethan shook his head. "I'll make a call to my boss. She has connections."

Alara looked uncertain, but she hurried to unbuckle Trinity and climb out of the car. Behind them, Enforcers climbed out of their vehicles, too, sidearms at the ready.

"Come out with your hands up!" one of them said over his vehicle's PA system.

Ethan complied, but Alara ignored them and raced toward the crystal pillars flanking the entrance of the hospital. A pair of EMTs went to greet her.

One of the Enforcers called for Alara to stop, his voice simultaneously muffled and amplified by his helmet as he stepped out of his vehicle to give chase, but when he saw the baby in Alara's arms, he decided to focus his attention on Ethan instead. The district councilor's missing children were older than Trinity.

Ethan greeted the Enforcers with a smile. One of them came and bound his hands with stun cords.

"Sorry about the chase," he said. "But as you can see, I wasn't lying about the sick baby."

"You should have called an ambulance," the Enforcer replied.

Ethan smirked. "Funny, my wife said the same thing."

One of the officers led him to a patrol car, while the other began a perfunctory search of Ethan's vehicle for the district councilor's missing children.

Ethan caught Alara's eye as he was pushed down into the patrol car. She made a move to go after him, but he shook his head.

"Look after Trinity!" he said. "I'll see you soon."

* * *

The wait was long and agonizing. Not knowing how Trinity was doing made every second seem like an hour. Ethan's brain buzzed with worry as he lay on the bunk inside his cell, desperately wishing Admiral Vee would wake up and find the message he'd left on her comms. As the night grew impossibly long, Ethan felt his eyelids growing heavy. Despite all the adrenaline and stress, he drifted off into a troubled sleep.

He dreamed that he was lying in the back of an ambulance with EMTs attending him. Neither his wife nor his daughter were anywhere to be seen.

"What happened? Where am I?" Ethan croaked. His heart pounded, and his head throbbed painfully with every beat.

"Don't move, please," one of the EMTs said.

Ethan rocked his head from side to side. With that movement, he felt a stab of pain go shooting through his neck. He winced with the pain, and something pulled tight on his forehead. Ethan reached up and found that it was a bandage. Horrified, he pulled on it, and his head throbbed more insistently. Something warm trickled past his ear, causing a maddening itch.

"I said don't move!" the EMT said, slapping his hands away

from his head.

"What happened?" Ethan demanded, trying to sit up. Strong hands forced him back down.

"You were in an accident," the nearest EMT replied, an upside down face bobbing into view as he adjusted Ethan's bandage.

A second EMT appeared behind the first, holding a syringe and waiting to assist his colleague.

"Alara?" Ethan asked, his eyes darting to look for her. He hoped she was somewhere in the back of the ambulance with him, a passenger rather than a patient.

She didn't answer.

"Where's my wife?" he demanded.

"She didn't make it," the second EMT said. "Her injuries were too severe. She... chose to go to Etheria."

"You idiot!" the first EMT replied. "Are you trying to send him into shock?"

"Alara died?" Ethan rocked his head back and forth again, feeling sick. He broke out in a cold sweat all over his body.

"He deserves to know. He might want to follow her," the second EMT replied.

A life signs monitor squealed with an alarm.

"He's going into shock!"

"Get him up!" another voice said, sounding strange and faraway.

The EMTs began lifting him from the gurney and shaking him by his shoulders.

"Wake up!" the voice demanded.

Ethan's eyes sprang open, and suddenly he was back inside his cell, staring up at a prison guard with a crooked lip and bad breath.

"He's awake," the guard said, letting him fall back onto to

his bunk.

Ethan grunted and sat up, blinking against the glaring light above his bunk.

Standing in the open door of Ethan's cell was none other than Admiral Vee. The prison guard brushed by her and waited outside the cell, looking impatient.

"I was beginning to think you didn't care," Ethan said, rubbing the sleep from his eyes as he rose from the bunk and shuffled out.

Valari smirked as he approached. "You know better than that by now, Ethan," she said.

The prison guard led them down a long, dismal gray corridor. As they followed him, Valari leaned over to whisper in his ear, "You owe me, Ortane."

Ethan frowned and nodded.

Outside the station, Alara and Trinity waited for him beside Admiral Vee's limousine. Ethan ran to them.

"How is she?" he asked, his eyes on the bundle of blankets in Alara's arms.

"She's fine," Alara replied.

When he drew near enough to peek inside the blankets, he saw that now Trinity's violet eyes were bright, and her cheeks were a more normal shade of pink. Gone was the spotty, flushed complexion she'd had earlier.

"Hey there, Trin," Ethan said, tickling her belly. She giggled appreciatively and smiled. Looking up, he asked, "What was it?"

"A virus. A bad one. The doctor said if we'd left her with that fever until morning, she could have died."

"Worth it, then," Ethan decided, nodding.

"I called Valari as soon as Trinity was stable," Alara said. "She came and picked us up to get you. I don't know what she did to get you out, but it worked. We owe her a big *thank you*,"

Alara said, nodding to Valari over Ethan's shoulder.

Ethan's turned to see Admiral Vee standing behind him. "Thanks again, Vee," he said.

She just shook her head and smiled. "The commander of the precinct is an old friend of mine. It was no trouble." Vee walked up to them and went to see the baby. "You have a beautiful daughter. I can see why you risked so much to get her to the hospital. It would be terrible if something happened to her."

Ethan felt a sharp spike of dread with those words. Surely she wasn't threatening Trinity? He looked up to find Alara nodding gravely. Admiral Vee reached out to stroke Trinity's forehead, and Ethan cringed.

"Keep your daughter safe, Mr. Ortane." Looking up, Valari favored him with a grim smile. "And next time, I suggest you call an ambulance before you end up in one yourself. That stunt you pulled with the Enforcers could have gotten you all killed."

Ethan's eyes drifted out of focus as his mind flashed back to the dream he'd had. A horrible feeling of déjà vu came over him. He'd had that dream before... right after The Choosing, after he and Alara decided to become Nulls. Alara had the exact same dream, and the medic who'd de-linked them explained that it was a final warning from Omnius, a vision of the future.

"What's the matter?" Admiral Vee asked, looking puzzled. "You look like you've seen a ghost."

"Ethan?" Alara said.

He blinked and his gaze snapped into focus. He forced a thin smile onto his lips. "I'm fine. If you don't mind, Valari, we'd better get Trinity home now so that she can rest."

"Of course," Valari purred. "Climb in. I'll have my driver take you both home right away."

CHAPTER 13

Hoff watched his partner, Galan Rovik, scroll through the list of crimes to prevent. The holo display hovering above the patrol car's dash was filled with mundane misdemeanors, written up like headlines from a news site on the omninet. After each description was the time it would occur, followed by the address. Right now they were on patrol in the Daveroth District. Hoff scanned the list of crimes in the area.

Infidelity, wife plans to cheat on husband | *14:12* | *D3-4-21.*

Friends come to blows over mutual love interest | *14:13* | *D1-17-12*

Teenager bullies little girl | *14:13* | *D9-2-2*

Hoff shook his head and looked away. Here they were, two high-ranking Peacekeepers—*strategians,* no less—reduced to dealing with the neighborhood bully.

"What about this one—" Galan suggested, "Suicidal Peacekeeper plans to jump from rooftop?"

Hoff's frown deepened. He turned back to the crime board to read it for himself. The crime was set to occur at fourteen hundred hours and fourteen minutes on Street Three, block sixteen, and level one twenty of the Daveroth District.

Galan selected the case in question in order to get more

details.

"Says here she's been having doubts since the battle in Dark Space. She feels helpless and trapped, and she secretly believes Omnius is evil." Galan looked up. "Sound familiar?"

Hoff shook his head. "I never said Omnius is evil."

"But you have doubts."

"Everyone has doubts. It's not the doubt that matters, but what we do with it."

"Wise words," Galan said, his glowing blue gaze unblinking as he stared at Hoff. Galan seemed to be staring straight through him, as if trying to peer into Hoff's soul. Not that he had a soul.

"Clock's ticking," Hoff said.

"Right." Galan selected the crime in question and accepted the job. The address went automatically into the patrol car's nav computer, and the autopilot took them up and out of the precinct's parking lot.

Hoff watched as the car raced up into a stream of automated air traffic, slipping into a narrow gap between two cars that no human pilot would have risked taking. Buildings soared to either side. On the other side of an imaginary divide, three lanes of oncoming traffic came at them in a dazzling blur of running lights. The HUD projected imaginary lines in the sky, showing them where the lanes were. None of the cars strayed from those lines, flying with a precision that only Omnius could achieve.

Hoff read over Galan's shoulder as he scrolled through the case files. A hologram of the jumper appeared, giving them a face and a name. Lena Faros. She had long red hair and striking green eyes. She looked young and beautiful, but then again, so did everyone else in Etheria. Hoff scanned her dossier and read that her real age was 73. The nature of her doubts wasn't listed, but Hoff could imagine what they might be.

He looked away, out the windows, watching as they slipped

into a vertical stream of traffic and began rising up the face of a gargantuan tower. Blue-tinted windows and pristine white bactcrete walls shone dazzlingly bright in the artificial daylight cast by the Celestial Wall.

The car rocketed from level 50, where their precinct was located, to level 100, the closest level of air traffic to level 120 where the crime was supposed to occur. Hoff used his ARCs to check the time. A glowing green number appeared projected less than a millimeter from his eyes.

13:43.

They had half an hour.

"You ready?" Galan asked.

Hoff nodded.

The car raced down Second Street. Up ahead, a floating sign painted on their HUD showed Third Street, running across theirs. The car stopped at the intersection, waiting to turn left onto Third.

Traffic on Third stopped and their car made a quick left turn. On the corner they raced by a corkscrew-shaped tower with emerald green windows. The car accelerated quickly up to the district speed limit of 500 kilometers per hour. At that speed, buildings to either side of them seemed to grow closer together, forming a blurry tunnel of brightly-colored transpiranium. Overhead, on level 150, elevated streets cast not shadows but more artificial light. The underside of the streets glowed a dazzling cobalt blue, the color of a clear Avilonian sky.

Their destination appeared in the distance, marked on the HUD with a green diamond. Another smaller diamond appeared on a hotel balcony, 20 floors up, revealing the exact point where the jumper intended to plunge to her death.

The autopilot took them straight up to the hotel, and the hazy blue shields at the entrance to the hotel's hangar deactivated automatically to let them in. The car raced inside and glided to a stop right in front of the garage's lift tubes. Galan raced out of the car, his shimmering blue strategian's cape fluttering behind him as he ran. Hoff hurried to catch up, his own cape likewise fluttering. One of the lift tubes chimed and Galan ran inside. Hoff slipped through just as the doors were closing.

"What's the plan?" Hoff asked, watching as Galan's armored palms glowed to life. "Kill her before she can jump?"

Galan shot him a reproving look. "They're set to stun."

The lift tube opened into a luxurious lobby filled with white marble columns and floors. Twin fountains bubbled in the foyer, facing the elevated streets. Galan ran out, heading for another bank of lift tubes. Hoff mentally toggled through his own weapons while they ran. He selected grav guns. If Lena got too close to the edge, he could always pull her back.

"Omnius just sent me an update," Galan said while they waited for the next lift to arrive.

Hoff noted that they were attracting attention. Hotel guests and staff pointed and whispered, no doubt surprised to see two *strategians* out on patrol. *They'll get used to it,* he decided. Without a war to fight, even master strategians would be patrolling soon.

"What's the update?" Hoff asked.

"She's already on the balcony," Galan explained, as the lift opened and he strode inside. "We're going to sneak up behind her. You're going to stay out of sight as backup, while I distract her and try to talk her out of it."

Even as Galan said that, a more detailed version of that plan entered Hoff's mind. He saw Lena's room in his mind's eye. He saw where he was supposed to wait, just around the corner from the balcony, behind a panel of white chiffon curtains that was billowing in the breeze. Omnius wanted him to wait there with his cloaking shield active and his grav guns at the ready.

Hoff nodded and mentally activated his cloaking shield. His shiny silvery armor disappeared, replaced by a pale shadow projected over his ARCs.

Galan would be the distraction. Lena wouldn't be able to detect Hoff, because Omnius had disabled her armor, and she'd already shucked it. Now she stood in her black under suit, peering over the railing and contemplating the dizzying drop below her balcony.

Omnius could have simply used Lena's Lifelink to put her to sleep rather than have them rush in to stop her, but Hoff supposed that would only heighten Lena's suspicions of Omnius's power. She had to be allowed to think that Omnius would let her jump if that's what she really wanted. The illusion of choice would help her to overcome her doubts. Hoff frowned at the deception, but he supposed it was a necessary evil to help rehabilitate Lena from her suicidal depression.

Hoff's job would be to intervene, pulling Lena back up *after* she jumped. The experience of jumping and then being pulled back from the abyss, saved by Omnius at the last possible second, was apparently exactly what Lena needed to snap her out of it.

The entire sequence of events was burned into Hoff's mind. All he had to do was stick to the plan, and everything would go exactly as Omnius had predicted.

Not that he would do otherwise. Omnius already knew that he would stick to the plan—otherwise this case wouldn't have appeared on their job board at all. Even their act of choosing a case was an illusion. Omnius let them choose the job they wanted, but he already knew which one they would pick. Omnius could have simply removed all of the other cases on the job board to save them the trouble of contemplating the list, but studies had shown that humans become depressed and less efficient when they feel like they're following a set path—even if they know it's the path they would have taken when given the freedom to choose from available alternatives.

Hoff considered what all of that meant for human freedom. *If the future can be predicted with certainty, then that means the future is set, and if it's set, then we're all just going through the motions. With or without Omnius, there's no such thing as freedom. And if we aren't really free, then isn't it better that Omnius helps us to make the right choices?*

The more Hoff thought about it, the more he realized that Omnius's control over their lives was actually a good thing. His part in his own life was just to sit back and enjoy the ride. Yet with that realization, Hoff's own melancholy heightened to a feverish intensity, and he found himself identifying with the jumper they'd been sent to save. He felt helpless and trapped, like a prisoner.

The lift tube opened and they walked out onto level 120. The hallway was bright and airy; a luxuriant blue carpet paved the way for them. The walls glowed a soft white-gold, providing illumination. Galan led the way, striding quickly past half a dozen doors before stopping in front of room number 12001.

He didn't knock or use the control panel's key code. The door opened immediately for him, the security overridden by Omnius himself. On the other side Hoff saw the billowing white curtain, the open door to Lena's balcony, and beyond that, Lena herself. She sat on the railing with her legs dangling over the side and the wind skipping through her red hair, making it billow like the curtain. Hoff quietly followed Galan through the room.

"Don't do it, Lena," Galan said, his voice amplified by his helmet. Lena turned to see who had come in. She had to shout back to be heard over the wind.

"I know Omnius won't let me jump!"

"Then why bother trying?"

Hoff saw the curtain where he was supposed to wait, but he walked past it, following Galan onto the balcony. He needed to be closer to Lena to stop her from jumping.

Hoff? What are you doing?

He stopped just beyond the curtain, Omnius's voice having arrested his momentum. He felt guilty, but at the same time triumphant for having defied Omnius's control in some small way.

I can wait here just as easily, he thought back.

Omnius gave no reply, and Hoff wondered if this wasn't actually where he had been meant to wait all along. Perhaps Omnius had foreseen his defiance and taken it into account.

Galan stopped beside him. "Lena," he said.

"What?" she replied, sending him a sharp, angry look, her green eyes glowing bright in the light of her ARCs.

"Why do you want to die?"

"Why do *you* want to live?"

Galan gestured to the view. Pristine towers of mirror-coated windows soared across the chasm. Twenty floors up, elevated streets ran along the buildings and crossed the urban canyon with multiple bridges. "This is Etheria. It's paradise, Lena. Death, suffering, sickness, crime, and poverty, are all a thing of the past! Humanity has never had such an easy existence."

Lena looked away and peered over the edge again, leaning perilously close to a terrifying drop.

"You see those cars down there?" she said.

Hoff was cloaked, so he took advantage of that to walk up to the railing and peer over the edge with her. Galan walked up on the other side of her, keeping his distance, no doubt to avoid scaring her. Hoff saw the traffic on level 100 racing by in six orderly lanes. Each vehicle was traveling at 500 kilometers per hour, exactly a dozen meters from the ones in front and behind, all of them somehow staying dead center of their respective lanes.

Lena went on, her voice soft and wistful, "Those cars are all on autopilot, all of them have a set destination, and they never fly outside the lines. They never make any mistakes."

Hoff nodded to himself. He knew where Lena was going with that.

"From the moment I wake up, till the moment I sync at night, I feel like *I'm* on autopilot. I feel like I'm one of those cars. Every choice I'm about to make has already been foreseen and ordained by Omnius. If he objects to something I want to do, then he finds a way to change my mind—case in point, *you.* There is no freedom."

Hoff heard Galan sigh. "Lena, just because Omnius knows the future doesn't mean you're not free to choose."

"The very fact that the future is knowable means that I'm not free."

"But that has nothing to do with Omnius. The kind of freedom you're talking about doesn't exist. And if it does it's nothing but random chaos."

"Yes, chaos... we used to think that was a bad thing."

"It *is* a bad thing."

Lena shook her head. "It's a strange feeling to remember how things used to be, and then to compare that with how things are now. You were born on Avilon, so you don't understand."

"I've been to the Null Zone," Galan replied. "I know what chaos looks like."

"Then you should know what I mean. Without sadness,

happiness is empty and dull. Without rain, you can't appreciate the sun. Without darkness, the light isn't nearly as bright. Without chaos, order is maddening, and without death, life loses all its meaning."

"You're saying that you've taken paradise for granted. Perhaps you should live in the Null Zone for a while so that you can appreciate Etheria again."

"Perhaps I should," Lena admitted. "But then fifty years from now, after I've gone to the Null Zone, come back, and lived for another decade up here, I'll be back on this ledge hoping that Omnius will finally set me free."

"Not necessarily," Galan said. "If you want to jump off a balcony in the Null Zone, no one is going to stop you."

"Yes... that might be the best way then."

"You don't really want to jump," Galan said. "If you did, you would have chosen to become a Null first."

Lena turned to look at Galan, and Hoff turned to look at him, too. There was a strange light in the Peacekeeper's glowing blue eyes.

A fanatical gleam, Hoff decided.

"Maybe I just want answers," Lena replied. "Maybe I want the truth for a change."

"What makes you think you've been told a lie?"

"Don't play dumb with me, Rovik. You were there. You saw Omnius lead us into a trap. He sent us to Dark Space knowing that we'd lose to the Sythians there. Why?"

Galan shook his head. "The answer you're looking for doesn't exist, Lena. Your questions are both asked and answered by your doubting mind. You've lost your faith, and now you've begun to question everything."

"So what if I have?"

"*So what?* Are you happy? No, you've robbed yourself of the peace and joy that come from living in a perfect world."

Lena snorted. "No peace can come from lies, Rovik. Now if you don't mind, I need to get on with my day." Lena flexed her arms, about to push off from the railing.

Hoff chose that moment to intervene. He de-cloaked and grabbed her arm.

"Wait—"

Lena startled so violently at his touch and the sound of his voice that she jerked out of his grasp and fell, tumbling from the balcony with a startled scream. Hoff gaped at what he'd done, watching her fall toward the racing lines of traffic below. He stood there watching, frozen with shock. Beside him Galan cursed and readied his own grav guns to arrest her fall. Hoff snapped out of it and fired, reaching out with both palms for the tumbling black speck that was Lena Faros.

But she was already too far away for his grav guns to get a lock.

"You fool!" Galan said, hopping up on the railing to jump after her. Hoff followed suit, and they jumped together, diving head first and making their bodies bullet-shaped in order to travel faster. Hoff felt the wind ripping at his cape, slowing him down. Beside him he saw Galan's cape fluttering like a torn parachute. Hoff reached up and tore his free, letting it float away.

Below him, Lena fell past the air traffic on level 100, miraculously avoiding a collision with the racing air cars. Hoff caught up fast, but his ARCs said she was 28 meters away— about 10 floors down. Now she was falling face down, arms and legs spread to slow her fall. Apparently she'd had a change of heart about jumping, but she had only seconds left before she would hit the elevated streets on level 75.

Hoff tried once more, reaching out for Lena with both palms.

He didn't get a lock, but he fired anyway. The guns grabbed something, accelerating him downward. Now both gravity and his grav guns were pulling him down. With just seconds to spare, he rotated his body to put his feet under him in a crouch, and he fired the grav lifts in his boots at full strength. His arms pulled taut and his spine curled as the opposing force in his boots pushed his legs up and wound him into the tightest possible fetal position that his armor would allow.

Then came the pulverizing force of the impact.

Hoff's teeth clacked together; his spine popped; his head whipped forward and he smashed his helmet on the street. Pain erupted in every part of his body except for his legs. They were pleasantly numb. Hoff tried to sit up, but he couldn't. His faceplate was shattered. The street where he'd landed was a spider's web of cracks. People stood around in front of store windows, making space, pointing and shouting exclamations that Hoff couldn't hear through the ringing in his ears.

Galan landed in front of him and walked out of sight. Hoff dragged himself in that direction, finding to his horror that his legs were useless. They rolled around under him with a grinding sensation. He saw Galan kneeling down beside a bloody smear. The black jumpsuit and wild splay of red hair told him that Lena had gotten her wish. She was dead.

Hoff saw Galan stand up and turn in a quick circle to address the gathering crowd of Etherians. They looked shocked and horrified, their glowing eyes wide and blinking in all the colors of the rainbow.

"This woman was a Null rebel who infiltrated Etheria," Galan announced. "Rather than be caught, she chose to jump to her death."

People began nodding at that. Nulls could do unexpected things. They were de-linked, so Omnius couldn't predict what they would do. It made more sense than the alternative—that Omnius had somehow failed to predict and prevent a catastrophe in their perfect world.

But Hoff knew the truth. His vision grew blurry and hot. He blinked, trying to clear it, but that just created a smeary red film on top of his ARCs. Blood was running into his eyes. At that, Hoff's stomach gave a nauseated spasm.

Galan went on, "My partner risked his life to save her so that we could learn more about the rebels, but there wasn't enough time to slow her fall. Rest-assured, Omnius will get to the bottom of this security breach."

Hoff shook his head. "It's not true," he croaked, but his voice was too soft, and his helmet's speakers were smashed. Galan stepped sideways, his boot finding Hoff's hand and grinding his fingers into the bactcrete. Hoff cried out and bit his lip. He got the message, but he didn't understand it.

Any of it.

As his mind grew hazy and thick with sudden fatigue, he wondered to himself: was this what Omnius had planned all along? Maybe he wanted to keep people like Lena quiet, and he'd decided to let her die.

As Hoff drifted off, he wondered what lie would be made up to explain *his* death.

CHAPTER 14

—One Month Later—

Destra awoke with a gasp and a fleeting echo of a searing pain in her chest. Muted, rhythmic beeping sounds filled her ears. She blinked twice quickly, trying to remember what had happened. They'd used Torv's tunnel to escape the Sythian prison, but they'd run into Sythians and quickly been overrun. The Sythians had shot her twice in the chest.

Destra felt around for a gaping wound or a bandage, but she only found soft, supple skin beneath the sheets and the gown she wore. The pain in her chest was just a hazy memory as if from a dream. But if it had all been a dream, then why wasn't she waking up back in her cell?

Destra sat up and looked around a brightly-lit room with white walls and floors. In the room with her were five other beds. Three of them were filled. A familiar little girl lay sleeping on the bed beside hers.

Atta! Destra's heart filled with dread. She wasn't the only one the Sythians had shot. She swung her feet off the end of the bed and jumped down, taking the bedsheets with her. Kicking herself free, she hurried over to Atta's side and reached out with a trembling hand to cup her daughter's cheek.

"Sweetheart?" she whispered.

Atta's eyes fluttered open and abruptly widened. "Who are you?"

Destra's eyes blurred with tears. "I'm your mother, don't you remember me?"

Atta rocked her head from side to side, her eyes wide. "You're not my mother," she whispered.

"Oh, Atta... what have they done to you?"

Destra's eyes traveled quickly around the room, looking for help. There had to be someone who could tell her what had happened. Across from the foot of Atta's bed a pair of corpse-gray feet hung off the end of another bed.

Torv. From there Destra's gaze skipped sideways to the bed beside his and she saw Farah's golden curls splayed out on a pillow.

Everyone from the escape was here, so it hadn't been a dream. But if she hadn't dreamed it all... then how was she still alive?

Destra walked over to Torv on unsteady legs. She reached his side only to find that his face was covered with a strange white mask. A bright blue light leaked out around his face.

"What's going on?" another voice asked.

Destra looked toward the sound and saw Farah sitting up on the adjacent bed.

"Destra? Is that you?" she asked, sounding confused.

First her daughter, now Farah. Did everyone have amnesia?

Destra frowned and turned back to Torv. She gently touched his bare shoulder and shook him, but he didn't stir. Wondering about the purpose of the mask, Destra slowly peeled back Torv's sheets, revealing his naked chest. The Gor's skin was discolored with dark gray patches that she didn't remember seeing before.

"Careful," someone else said. "He's still recovering from his injuries."

Destra whirled toward the sound. The door on the far side of the room was open and a stranger stood there. He must have come in while her attention was on Torv.

The stranger was a *human*, not a Sythian. His pale blue eyes contrasted sharply with dark brown skin. He wore a familiar uniform. It was ISSF black with white trim; the colors faded, but still recognizable. Over the man's left breast was the rank insignia of an ISSF admiral—two gold stars—and above his insignia, was a hollow, six-pointed star formed by two overlapping triangles. Destra recognised that symbol as a Star of Etherus. It marked the admiral as a disciple of Etherianism.

Destra looked up and studied the man's face with a frown. "Who are you?" she asked, relieved at least that he wasn't a Sythian.

"I am Therius the Redemptor, Commander of Etheria's Army."

Destra shook her head. "Therius the what?"

There came a sharp hiss, followed by another, more familiar figure appearing in the open doorway. Shallah strode in and stopped beside the human man. His utter alienness struck a fierce contrast with the human standing beside him. Translucent, rubbery skin revealed a spider's web of blue veins in his face that matched the sapphire color of his large, watery eyes. Short horns ran along the vertex of his head and the ridge of his brow.

Destra's heart pounded steadily in her chest. "What is this?" she asked, walking sideways to put herself between the Sythian leader and her daughter. Shallah's blue eyes tracked her as she went.

"I apologize for the traumatic experience you all went

through," Therius said, his gaze flicking sideways to glare momentarily at the Sythian standing beside him. "I instructed Shallah to kill you all in a humane way, but he refused to listen."

"Pain makes us ssstronger," Shallah hissed.

"Our alliance is still in its infancy," Therius explained.

Destra blinked, her gaze traveling from Shallah to Therius and back again. "Kill us?"

"Yesss," Shallah said, sounding amused.

"What alliance?" Farah demanded.

Shallah hissed once more, now turning to Farah. "It is ironic that former enemies must now stand together as allies, is it not?"

"What the frek is going on here?" Farah asked, ignoring the Sythian leader and addressing the human admiral instead. "You're ISSF. What are you doing allied with Sythians? They're the *enemy* in case you forgot."

Another hiss sounded, but it wasn't from Shallah. Destra caught a flicker of movement in the corner of her eye, and she turned to see Torv ripping off his mask, revealing sunken gray cheeks and a skull-like face. His yellow eyes narrowed and a row of dagger-like teeth flashed as he saw Shallah.

The Sythian replied with a hiss of his own, but his explanation was in Versal. "I killed your people because they could no longer be controlled. You would have done the same to us if you had the chance."

Torv hissed something else, then he leapt from his bed, his legs churning as he landed. Shallah just looked at him, and Torv stumbled and fell with clear blood streaming from his nose.

"Stop!" Therius commanded.

Shallah gave the human a deadly look.

"We need allies, not enemies. You should have told everyone the truth when you had the chance. If you had, then the Gors would have fought for you willingly. Now all that's left is to repair the damage."

"No one speaksss to me that way. Much less a human," Shallah replied.

"Would you rather be offended by the truth or comforted by a lie?" Therius countered, locking eyes with the Sythian for a long, uncomfortable moment.

Destra watched the exchange curiously, wondering who this human was that he seemed to have enough power to challenge the leader of all the Sythians.

"Torv..." Therius said, waiting for the Gor to catch his breath. He was down on all fours, gasping for air. "We need you and your people's help. In exchange, I promise that the Gors will be treated as equals, and your matriarch, Shara, will be kept safe. If you agree to fight with us, I will make your people into a powerful nation."

Torv hissed a reply, and Therius smiled, stepping forward to place a hand on the Gor's giant shoulder. "The Gors are an honorable people. One day they will be rewarded for it."

Torv rose to his feet and stood solemn and silent before Therius.

The so-called redemptor turned in a slow circle, taking in everyone in the room. His gaze settled on Farah, and he nodded to her. "Your ship and your crew are waiting for you."

"My crew?" Farah shook her head. "I don't..."

"They've been in stasis the entire time. We had to clone them, too, but they still don't know what's happening. We need to tell them what they're up against."

"What *are* we up against?" Farah asked.

"You already know something about the enemy we face, but not nearly enough."

"Omnius," Farah breathed.

The admiral nodded. "He has all of humanity trapped on

Avilon, thanks to his Sythians."

"*His* Sythians... ?" Farah asked.

Therius nodded. "Omnius created them to give him an excuse to kill and then resurrect everyone on Avilon."

It took Destra an extra moment to catch up. "*What? That's impossible!*"

Therius turned to her, a faint smile on his lips. "You would be surprised how little in this universe is actually impossible. Omnius implanted everyone without their knowledge. He used those cerebral implants to transfer people to clones when they died. Now everyone is on Avilon—including you and your daughter . . . your husband and son are there, too."

"Hoff?"

"And Atton."

How did Therius even know she was married, let alone to whom? "I don't understand. How can I be on Avilon and here at the same time?"

"How can you be alive at all? The Sythians shot you twice in the chest. You've been cloned, Destra. Haven't you noticed everyone looking at you strangely? Have you had a chance to catch a glimpse of your reflection yet?"

Destra furrowed her brow as a headache pulsed behind her eyes. She turned to look at the glossy white walls and saw a blurry reflection there. Walking up to the nearest wall, she gasped, suddenly realizing why her own daughter didn't recognize her. She touched her cheeks to make sure they were really hers. The reflection was faint, but still clear enough. She looked twenty again.

"It takes too long to age clones past maturity, and what would be the point?" Therius explained. "But rest assured, you are still the same woman you've always been. The only difference is a physical one."

"I don't understand," Destra repeated. Her gaze fell upon the silver Star of Etherus over Therius's left breast. "You're an Etherian disciple. Why would you condone cloning? Don't you believe in an afterlife?"

"It's hard to argue with cloning when you are already a clone."

"Then aren't you afraid that you no longer have a soul?"

"I believe that clones fit into Etherus's plans, or else he wouldn't have allowed us to be cloned in the first place. To believe otherwise is to believe that Omnius could thwart God."

Destra shook her head. "I don't understand."

"You will in time. For now all you need to understand is that Etherus has a plan, and we are part of it. The Sythians are not the real enemy; Omnius is, and if we are going to defeat him, then all of us have to stand together and fight. Shallah was also deceived. When he discovered that Omnius had been lying to him, he turned against his master. The truth has that effect on people; it sets them free. Now we have to set everyone else free who is still a captive of Omnius's lies."

Destra felt light-headed. Her mouth was so dry that her tongue felt like sandpaper rasping against the roof of her mouth. By contrast, Farah seemed to be following along just fine. Destra saw her bobbing her head as if everything made perfect sense, as if she'd always known. Destra decided to try wrapping her head around one of the smaller mysteries first. "Why go to the trouble of killing us only to clone us back to life?"

Therius regarded her with a smile. "You were still linked to Omnius. Those ties had to be severed. We copied the data from your minds and cloned you in our facilities."

"But why? You must have brought us back for a reason." Farah said.

"Of course. You're going join the fight against Omnius."

"Where do you come from?" Farah asked.

"I escaped Avilon, and I have been rescuing people from there ever since. We intercept and copy their Lifelink data when they die on Avilon."

Destra saw Farah's eyes light up. "There's a man who came to the Getties before I did. He may have died in orbit around Noctune. Did you... is he still..."

"Alive? You're talking about Admiral Bretton Hale," Therius said.

Farah sat suddenly straighter, looking ready to leap from her bed. "He's alive?"

"Yes, but—"

"Where is he? When can I see him?"

Therius's eyes darted away, as if he was hiding something, but Farah didn't appear to notice. "You'll get to meet him soon."

"Where are we?" Atta asked.

Therius regarded her with a smile. "I was hoping someone would ask me that." He walked over to the far wall of the room. Destra noticed that wall was glowing with some kind of internal radiance. Therius waved his hands at the wall, and the source of the radiance became clear. The wall turned from opaque and glowing to transparent and shining with the dazzling light of day. A bright blue sky sprawled overhead. Far below, fields of green grass stretched out to the nearby shore of a lavender-hued lake. Destra saw mountains, jungles, glaciers...

She shivered as goosebumps prickled her skin. Sparks flew inside her brain. She *recognized* this place. But that was impossible. It was just an acute case of déjà vu. So many habitable worlds looked alike that this one must have triggered an old memory from somewhere else.

"Recognize it?" Therius asked, turning Destra's rationalizations to dust.

"I don't believe it..." Farah whispered.

"This is Origin," Therius replied.

"The birthplace of humanity," Farah added, still whispering.

"Welcome back." Therius's gaze traveled around the room, finding each of them in turn and finally settling on Torv. "All of you."

CHAPTER 15

"Ceyla, this is Valari Thardris, my aunt and foster mother."

Valari smiled and held out a hand.

"It's so great to meet you," Ceyla said. "Darin has told me a lot about you."

"Has he now?" Valari replied. Atton saw her arch an eyebrow at him, but Ceyla missed the exchange. "Please, come in," Valari went on. "Dinner is almost ready."

Atton waited for Ceyla to go in first. She seemed to be looking everywhere at once. A winding staircase led up from the foyer. High above the sparkling indigo floor hung a lavish crystal chandelier.

"You have a beautiful place, Valari," Ceyla said as she walked into the penthouse.

"Thank you, dear."

"What is it you do?" Ceyla asked, looking up at the crystal chandelier and the winding staircase.

Valari waved her hand dismissively. "Nothing really. It's all inherited," she said.

"Oh."

Valari turned and led the way to the dining room, her flowing white evening gown shimmering as she walked.

Atton placed a hand at the small of Ceyla's back, urging her forward. As they walked, she leaned over and whispered, "You didn't mention your aunt was so wealthy."

"I didn't think it mattered," he replied.

They walked through a lavish living room with high, tray ceilings, recessed lighting and plush white carpets to cover the sparkling indigo floor. Then they came to the dining room—a long white table with Valari's black arachnoid chandelier hanging overhead.

Valari sat at the head of the table, while Atton and Ceyla sat beside one another in the middle, facing the view. Atton watched the shining rivers of air traffic, allowing his eyes to drift out of focus.

Then came a *clanking* sound and a distinctive *whirring* of mechanical parts. Atton's head snapped up and his eyes darted to find a pair of drones emerging from Valari's kitchen, one carrying glasses, the other, two bottles of wine.

Beside him, Ceyla tensed and turned to him, her eyes full of alarm. Atton's cheeks were already bulging with his next lie when Valari explained for him.

"Don't worry. They're Null-made."

Ceyla turned to their host and then glanced back at the pair of drones. "They look very... *similar* to Omnius's drones," Ceyla replied.

"Yes, that's by design. I find they inspire more fear than human bodyguards. They are more competent, too."

Ceyla frowned as if she didn't understand.

"Surely you know that former Etherians such as myself are targets for lowlifes here in the Null Zone? Eternal youth and beauty are just a few of the genetic advantages that Omnius's fallen children have over Null-born citizens, and down here we are resented for those advantages."

"That must be hard," Ceyla said.

The drones came by and asked them what they'd like to drink, speaking in soft, soothing tones. Ceyla selected a lavender wine, while Atton selected a dark amber one. He marveled at the rare vintages, and he realized that Valari was showing off even more than usual.

Once the drones finished pouring, he risked a sip of his wine. It was dry and bitter, but somehow soft and silky smooth at the same time. His head swam with an immediate buzz. He set his glass back down, suddenly suspicious that Valari was trying to get him drunk—or drug him. Bliss could be concealed in any beverage. Who better to give him his first taste than the Null Zone's one and only supplier?

"Tell me about yourself, Ceyla," Valari purred. "Darin tells me that you've been dating for the past seven months. He also told me that you're engaged." She raised her own wine glass and nodded to them. "Congratulations."

"Thank you. As for me, well, there's not much to tell," Ceyla said.

"Oh, I doubt that. It must take a very special lady to win such devotion from my Darin."

Ceyla laughed lightly and her cheeks flushed. She sent Atton a dreamy look before continuing. "I'm an orphan from the war. I came to Avilon aboard the *Intrepid* looking for reinforcements to help Dark Space fight the Sythians."

Atton nodded, listening to Ceyla recount the tale of how she'd come to Avilon. She didn't know that they'd come together. She'd been a pilot in *his* Nova squadron. He was her first love and she was his.

"That's quite the story," Valari said when Ceyla finished. "But that only tells me where you came from, not who you are or what you care about."

Jasper T. Scott

"Well, I care about Darin, obviously," Ceyla said, flashing a crooked smile at him.

Valari nodded. "Obviously. But I am curious about something. Why did you become a Null?"

Atton frowned, wondering if Valari was taking this foster mother act too far. She was meant to make Ceyla feel welcome, and to substantiate the lie that he was who he said he was—not interrogate her the whole night.

"I chose to become a Null because I believe that we go to a better place when we die, and I don't want to miss out on that because I chose to become immortal in this life."

Valari's smile grew. "So you believe that you have a soul."

"Yes," Ceyla replied.

Atton cleared his throat, not liking the controversial turn the dinner conversation was taking.

Valari caught his eye and held his gaze for a long moment. Then she shrugged and said, "Optimists do live longer, so I suppose you won't go unrewarded for your beliefs."

"Excuse me?"

"You have no proof of what you believe," Valari explained.

"I don't need it."

"Exactly. That makes you an unreasoning optimist at best, and at worst... well, let's leave it at that, shall we?"

"Yes, I think we'd better," Ceyla said, shaking her head and looking out the windows.

Atton grimaced and went back to staring at the rivers of traffic flowing by below Valari's penthouse. "Nice view," he said, taking another sip of his wine.

"It is, isn't it?"

The silence returned, lasting for several minutes this time. Then dinner arrived, brought in by the drones who had served them their wine. They all ate quietly, and Atton feared that

Ceyla really had offended Valari.

"The food is delicious," Ceyla said.

"Mmmm?" Valari inquired, looking up from her food with eyebrows raised, as if she hadn't been paying any attention. "Oh, the food—no, it's nothing special, but I'm glad you like it. Simple tastes for simple people, I suppose."

Ceyla managed a strained laugh at her own expense, and Atton's frown deepened.

The rest of the evening went much the same way, with plenty of awkward silences and paper thin smiles. Right after dessert, Atton excused them from the table, saying that they needed to catch up on their sleep.

Valari stopped him, asking to speak with him privately before they left. He looked to Ceyla, and she nodded, giving her permission.

"Interesting," Valari said, her eyes on Ceyla. "I didn't realize they made leashes that short. Don't worry; we won't be long."

"Take all the time you need," Ceyla replied.

Atton could feel his blood boiling, the steam hissing out his ears. He could barely think he was so furious. Valari led Atton into her office, and the door slid shut behind them.

"What the frek was that?" Atton demanded. "You're supposed to make her feel welcomed to the family, not make fun of her beliefs and make snide comments all night long!"

"Relax," Valari said. "I've done you a favor. You asked me to play a part, and I have. I played it so well, in fact, that you won't have to ask me for the same favor again soon. Ceyla won't be in a hurry to see me again after tonight, so you're off the hook little fish."

Atton scowled, but he had to admit there was a certain amount of genius to that thinking. "You could have warned me."

Valari shrugged. "This way your outrage was genuine, so Ceyla won't be angry with you, too."

Atton sighed. "Well, in the interests of supporting my fiancée, I think we should probably still get going."

"Not so fast. I did you a favor. Now you owe me one."

Atton's eyes narrowed swiftly. "You didn't mention that when I asked you."

"I didn't have to. Reciprocity is implied by our friendship."

"So we're friends now?" Atton asked.

Valari's lips curved into a sly grin. "Well, I wouldn't like to think that we're enemies, would you?"

"What do you want?"

"That's a good question... what *do* I want?"

"Well?" Atton prompted.

"I'm sure I'll think of something. Don't worry, I never forget a favor."

"You mean you never forget to call a favor."

"That, too," Valari said. "I'll be in touch, Atton."

"Right."

Later that night, Ceyla was mysteriously quiet on the subject of Valari Thardris. Atton decided to press her for information anyway, just in case things hadn't gone as badly as Valari thought.

"Did you have a good time?" he asked, sitting up beside Ceyla in bed.

She was setting an alarm for tomorrow morning on her handheld communicator. She worked as a tender in the Null Zone's nutrient farms, and she had to be up early.

Ceyla shrugged, but said nothing.

"You can tell me the truth. I don't mind."

She shot him a look. "All right, your aunt is a pompous bigot. How did you stand to live in the same house with her?"

"I moved out as soon as I could."

"I can see why." Ceyla looked away, shaking her head, and checking to see if she had any messages on her communicator.

"I guess now you know why I didn't introduce you sooner."

"Yeah, I do." Ceyla set her communicator on her bedside table with a sigh. "Are your real parents like that?"

"I don't know," Atton lied. "We don't see each other anymore." He fluffed his pillow and lay down to sleep.

Ceyla regarded him with a pitying look. "I'm sorry. I'll make an effort with Valari if you need me to."

Atton raised his eyebrows. "You'd do that for me?"

"Of course, and she *did* raise you, so I have to be grateful to her for that at least."

"Well, don't make an effort on my account," Atton said. "I can't stand her either."

Ceyla frowned. "That's awful."

"The truth often is."

"I'm sorry," Ceyla said, laying down beside him and curling her body against his. "I'm glad I got to meet her, though."

"Why's that?" Atton asked sleepily, his eyes drifting shut.

"Because now I don't have to see her for a while. At least not until the wedding."

Atton's eyes flew open. *The wedding.* He already owed Valari one mysterious favor, and he wasn't ready to owe her two. Turning to Ceyla, he said, "Your family won't be there."

"That doesn't mean yours shouldn't," she replied.

"So... Valari and who else? You have a lot of other people you'd like to invite?"

Neither of them had many friends, so he already knew the answer to that.

"It'll be a small ceremony."

"What if we have a civil wedding? We can save money and

go on a nice honeymoon instead."

Ceyla looked uncertain, but then she nodded and smiled. "Sounds perfect. Just the two of us."

Atton kissed her and held her close, breathing a deep sigh beside her ear. "That's all that matters."

They fell asleep locked in each other's arms, and Atton dreamed he saw his wife in the bathroom, looking at herself in the mirror. He walked in on her, and came to a sudden halt when he caught a glimpse of her reflection. She looked old. Her blond hair had turned feathery and white, and her skin was papery and wrinkled with age. He walked up beside her to tell her that he didn't care, that to him she was still just as beautiful as ever, but then he caught a glimpse of his own reflection, and Ceyla did, too. Her blue eyes widened and locked with his in the mirror.

"Why are you still so young?" she asked, sounding horrified as she reached up to touch her wrinkled cheeks with age-spotted hands. "And I'm so *old*..." she said, her voice trembling. She turned to him, looking hurt and betrayed. "You lied to me!"

Atton shook his head. "No,"

"You lied!" she screamed, giving him a mighty shove.

Atton woke up with a *thud*. His eyes fluttered open to find that he was lying on the floor next to the bed.

"Atton? Lights!" The lights came on, blinding him, and Ceyla appeared, silhouetted in the dazzling brightness. "What are you doing lying there?"

He stared stupidly up at her for a moment, his heart pounding with dread. Had she just accused him of lying?

No. She'd said *lying there*.

"I fell out of bed," he explained, easing up off the floor.

"You need to be more careful," Ceyla replied.

Atton nodded his agreement, thinking not about falling out

of bed, but about the danger in all of his lies. He climbed back into bed beside his fiancée and hugged her close. He lay wide awake and wondering what to do. Maybe he could get Omnius to take away his immortality, to make him age normally so that Ceyla would never be the wiser.

No sooner had that thought formed in his mind, than it was answered. *No, Atton. I won't be a part of your lies.*

Why not? he thought, staring up at the ceiling. *I'm part of yours!*

You're asking for equal treatment, but we are not equals, and you would do well to remember that. I am your God, remember?

Atton scowled up at the ceiling. *How can I forget?*

CHAPTER 16

Hoff awoke to the feeling of cold hands and cold air searing his exposed skin. He blinked bleary eyes open to see a familiar face looking back at him.

"Hello, Hoff," Galan said.

"I'm alive," he croaked, noting that feeling had returned to his legs.

"You are an Etherian. You didn't really think Omnius would let you die, did you?"

Hoff frowned. Memories came back to him in a disjointed parade of nonsense. He remembered lying broken on the street, his body numb in places, wracked with pain in others. He'd jumped after an Etherian woman—a Peacekeeper. What was her name?

Lena. He remembered her crumpled form lying beside him on the street. The smear of blood and splay of fiery red hair.

Hoff shivered, shaking himself out of the memory. He looked from side to side and noted the pair of drones holding him up. The overhead light glared brightly, while the rest of the room lay cloaked in a gloomy haze. Despite that, Hoff could see that the room where he stood was vast.

One look at the floor was all he needed to recognize where

he was. Thousands of hexagonal tanks lay beneath the floor, each one shining up into the gloom with a blue-tinted glow. Looking down at the cell directly beneath his feet, he saw his own tank, now dark and empty. Mops of human hair floated in the tanks around him, thousands of strands of hair drifting and tangling in clear pools of blue liquid, protecting the modesty of the naked clones. Hoff glimpsed a few artificial umbilicals trailing like purple snakes from clones' belly buttons to the nutrient pumps in the bottoms of their tanks. He was inside one of the Trees of Life—the gargantuan towers where Omnius kept human clones and their Lifelink data.

"How long have I been gone?" he asked.

"A month," Galan replied. "We had to grow a new clone for you."

"We?"

Galan frowned. "I apologize. Speaking in plural is a bad habit, but I'm told a lot of Celestials begin to think of themselves as a *we*. It's a consequence of getting too close to Omnius."

"Celestials?" Hoff echoed, shaking his head. "I thought you were an Etherian." The drones standing to either side of Hoff slowly eased their grip on his arms, allowing more and more of his weight to rest on his stiff, shaky legs.

"I'm a Celestial in training. My last job as an Etherian is to help you along the ascendant path."

Hoff tested his legs, lifting first one, then the other. He was naked, but that wasn't unusual after being resurrected. He looked up, staring into Galan's glowing blue eyes. "What happened?"

"You want to know why you died, or why Lena Faros did?" Galan said.

"Both."

"The short answer is that Omnius failed to predict the exact sequence of events on the balcony."

"That's impossible."

Galan shrugged. "The long answer will explain why."

"I'm listening."

"There are a lot of things you need to know first. Omnius wants you to become a Celestial, too, under my tutelage."

"What about my family?"

"You will be able to stay with them."

Hoff's eyes narrowed swiftly. "What's the catch?"

"The catch is that you will know everything. All of your doubts will be answered."

"That doesn't sound like a catch," Hoff replied.

"The truth is not a blessing. It's a burden."

Hoff snorted. "That's an unusual point of view."

"Omnius has decided that you are strong enough to bear that burden, but as a matter of courtesy, I have to ask anyway. Are you ready?"

Hoff considered that for a moment. "In the end, the truth is all that really matters."

"Well put," a resonant voice said.

Hoff started at the sound, and turned to see none other than Grand Overseer Vladin Thardris. He seemed to melt out of the shadows, as if appearing out of thin air. His flickering silver eyes shone bright in the surrounding gloom.

"My Lord," Hoff said, inclining his head to the Grand Overseer. He raised one arm at an angle from his body, palm up to the ceiling. "Hail Omnius."

"Yes," Thardris replied, his vulturine features stretching into a faint smile. "Hail me."

Hoff shook his head. "I'm sorry?"

"My name isn't Vladin. It's Omnius."

Shock sparked through Hoff's brain like a bolt of lightning.

Suddenly he understood why the Vladin had refused to heed his warnings during the battle in Dark Space. The grand overseer said that Omnius would have warned them if they were flying into a trap. That was a convenient excuse, since the overseer was actually Omnius.

"Why?" was all he could manage to ask.

"Why do I do anything?" Omnius countered. "For my children's benefit."

"How is lying to us and betraying us for our benefit?"

"You might be surprised by the answer."

"All right, surprise me then," Hoff said.

"As you wish."

Hoff's vision narrowed and faded to black. He felt himself sway and then fall. Then came a rush of images, sounds, feelings, thoughts...

By the time the vision faded, he lay on the cold hard ground staring up at the glaring light overhead. He finally understood everything, but instead of feeling relieved, he felt more betrayed than ever. Hoff climbed wearily to his feet to see that Omnius and Galan Rovik were still there, watching him.

"Now you know," Omnius said.

Hoff shook his head. "You *are* evil."

Omnius wasn't fazed by the accusation. "If I am, then evil is not what you thought."

"You're right. It's worse."

Omnius smiled. "Yet you won't resist me."

Hoff said nothing. His thoughts went immediately to Destra and Atta. He had too much to lose. Everyone did. Celestials didn't serve Omnius out of reverence the way everyone thought. They served him out of fear, because they knew the truth, and they knew it was hopeless to resist.

"Tell me then, if you refuse to stand against me, and I am

evil, then doesn't that make you my accomplice? And if so, you have to ask yourself—who is more evil? The one who does something evil, or the one who stands by and watches it happen?"

"There is no way to fight you," Hoff replied, feeling the truth of those words weigh him down, rounding his shoulders and threatening to grind him into dust. Galan was right. The truth *was* a burden.

"I'm glad you have come to your senses," Omnius replied.

Yet one thing shone like a beacon of hope in Hoff's mind. He had done something Omnius hadn't predicted, and that had led to both him and Lena Faros plummeting to their deaths. Surely he wasn't the only Etherian that Omnius couldn't predict. There might be others like him, and if there were...

"There have been many like you, but don't mistake your unpredictability for power. I can still read your thoughts, and I keep a much closer watch on people like you than I do on anyone else."

"But if you're reacting in real time to unexpected events, then why aren't there more crimes being committed in Etheria?"

"Because I keep your kind in the Null Zone where no one will notice the extra chaos."

Hoff shook his head. "I thought I was going to become a Celestial."

"You are, but that doesn't mean you'll live in Celesta. Don't worry, you won't suffer in the Null Zone, and I'll keep you safe. You need to be alive if I'm going to study you."

"You're going to keep me alive because of your curiosity?"

"That's still infinitely better than being dead, wouldn't you say?"

Hoff wasn't sure about that. Of all the things Omnius had just revealed, one thing was more shocking than the rest, and the implications were life altering. The Choosing and the Null Zone existed for a good reason. It was because of people like him, people whose actions Omnius couldn't predict.

Hoff smiled. "You can't control me."

"I can do whatever I want. I'm God, remember?"

Hoff shook his head. "No, you're not."

Omnius's flickering silver eyes flared suddenly brighter, but he said nothing. A drone came clanking up beside Hoff, carrying a bundle of clothes—regular clothes, rather than his Peacekeeper's uniform. Hoff frowned at that.

"You won't be a Peacekeeper in the Null Zone," Omnius explained.

Galan inclined his head to Hoff. "It's been a pleasure to serve with you, Heston."

Omnius turned to the other strategian, smiling once more. "You're going with him."

"What?" Galan looked shocked.

"Lena Faros fell to her death because of *both* of your actions, not just Hoff's."

"I..."

"How will I explain moving to the Null Zone to my family?" Hoff asked, accepting the bundle of clothes from the drone.

"They're already ahead of you," Omnius replied. "In the month that you have been away, your daughter has chosen to become a Null, and your wife has followed her."

The shock of that revelation hit Hoff like a bucket of ice water. "She *what*?" He'd assumed from everything Atta had said about her upcoming Choosing Ceremony that she would choose to remain in Etheria with her parents. The Choosing was supposed to have been a formality for her. She was already an immortal, resurrected in the body of a clone. There was no reason for her to wonder whether Lifelink transfers actually killed people and left functional copies to live on in their stead.

"Why?" Hoff asked.

"She overheard you warning Atton about me, remember?"

The blood drained from Hoff's face. Somehow Omnius had planned this. Unpredictable people like him couldn't be allowed to live in Etheria. Instead, they were made aware of Omnius's lies and then sent down into the Null Zone where any chaos they caused wouldn't be noticed. That was the real reason the Null Zone existed—to preserve Omnius's all-powerful facade.

"I thought you would be happy that your family is going to remain with you."

He was happy, but he was also worried. Anything could happen to his family in the Null Zone.

"Don't worry," Omnius said. "As long as you continue to serve me faithfully, I promise to keep your family safe."

The implied threat in that promise caught Hoff's attention, and despair crushed him again. Omnius was right. Being unpredictable didn't make him free.

Omnius's smile broadened. "You were right the first time, Hoff—there is no way to fight me."

* * *

Lena Faros awoke in darkness, standing on a conveyor belt. Sparks crackled and fizzed, shattering the gloom like fireworks in a night's sky. Metallic arms hovered into place, one to either side of her. They were attached with a fresh shower of sparks, and she flexed her new hands, feeling them contract and expand with detectable vibrations. Her new body could feel no pain, but she was aware of it, just as she remembered being aware of her human one.

Her mind reflected on the loss of that body dispassionately.

She had no feelings about it. She was what she was, and what came before no longer mattered. Her purpose was to serve Omnius. Her memories were irrelevant. Her existence no longer held any personal meaning for her. The burden of choice had been removed. Now there were only commands—action and reaction. Lena waited while finishing touches were made to her new body. Moments after the last sparks had died with fleeting glory, the first command came rippling through her mind with welcome clarity.

Welcome to the drone army, Lena. Please step off the conveyor belt.

Lena. It felt strange—*wrong*—to be called by a human name, but she obeyed, turning and jumping off the moving belt. Her sensors detected other drones jumping off all around her. She stood there in the dark, one drone in a long line of others, waiting for the next command to come, but what came next wasn't a command—it was a dazzling stream of data that filled her with a sense of identity and purpose. Suddenly, she knew where to go, what to do, and who she was. She was drone number forty seven trillion, six hundred billion, five hundred and sixty six million, four hundred and seventy eight thousand, nine hundred and ninety nine—Triple Nine for short.

She archived the human name, *Lena Faros.* It made more sense to use her number. It was unique, but uniform, celebrating the least possible difference between her and the others, which was as it should be, since they were all exactly the same.

Almost. Physically her body was subtly different from most of the others. Her color was a matte black, her limbs thicker and seemingly more robust. She had two optical sensors rather than one, and her head resembled a human shape. All of this owed to her assignment. She was going to the Null Zone to become a household servant for a man named Hoff Heston. Her prime directive was to watch over the Heston family and keep them safe at all times—unless otherwise instructed.

Triple Nine went *clanking* through the factory where she'd been born, eager to begin her service to Omnius and the Heston Family.

CHAPTER 17

Farah worked to calm herself as she followed Therius through the med center. *Breathe in. Breathe out. Breathe in...*

Breathe out.

Bretton was alive!

Farah's pulse jumped, and a smile sprang to her lips. She hadn't gone to Noctune for nothing after all. Bretton had somehow been cloned and resurrected yet again, and now Farah would be fighting by his side for the third time in the past decade. She and Bretton had gone from being a part of one resistance movement, straight to another, and now the stakes were higher than ever.

If Therius was right, if Omnius really had created the Sythians, then he was both more powerful and more terrible than anyone had ever suspected.

They came to the end of one shiny white corridor and turned down another, this one flanked by a wall of windows that gave a startling view of the lavender-hued lake and soaring mountains Farah had seen from her room.

Origin.

Yet another unbelievable surprise. The mythical lost world

of Origin was neither mythical nor lost. It was here, in the Getties Cluster, and it was the base of operations for the recently formed *Union* of Sythians, Humans, and Gors. This was where all of their species had begun, and now it was where they had been reunited to fight their common enemy.

Farah wondered what mysteries would be revealed here, knowledge long lost to humanity about their past, memories that somehow all of them shared.

They came to the end of the corridor and Therius opened a pair of gleaming silver doors. The doors parted to reveal a dimly-lit room. As they walked inside, Farah noted that the room was circular, and there was no furniture, or any other doors leading out.

A dead end.

"Where are we?" she asked as the doors *swished* shut behind them.

Therius said nothing. He stopped in the center of the room on a raised white podium, and lifted his hands to the ceiling. The walls began glowing with dazzling brilliance. A violent wind ripped through the room, and Farah fought to keep from becoming disoriented. Beside her, she saw Torv stumbling around, clutching his eyes. Therius walked over to him, seemingly unaffected by either the light or the wind, and placed a calming hand on the Gor's arm.

Then came a flash of light that completely blinded Farah and a blast of air that caused her to stagger.

By the time her vision cleared, she found herself standing in a very familiar place. It was the bridge of the venture-class cruiser she'd taken to the Getties, the *Baroness*, recognizable by the rust-colored blood stain the former captain had left beside the captain's table. Farah noticed that the crew were already seated at their stations. They looked up, their eyes narrowing on her as their curiosity turned to outrage.

Behind her, Torv *hissed,* and Therius turned to address the crew. "Here is your captain."

Murmurs of discontent rippled through the room. She wasn't surprised. This was the same bridge crew she had stunned and stuffed into stasis tubes in order to drag them to the Getties Cluster and look for Bretton.

"She is your captain, but I am your admiral. This is now *my* ship, and I will not tolerate discord." The crew quieted at that. "Carry on."

Farah turned to Therius even as he turned to her. "I don't understand," she said. "I thought Admiral Hale would be in command of this ship."

"Come with me," Therius replied. He led the way down the gangway and off the bridge. Farah followed him out to the captain's office in the vestibule between the bridge deck and the lift tubes. The office door swished open automatically for Therius, and he walked in. Farah followed, close on his heels, expecting to find Bretton waiting for her inside.

She scanned the room, searching...

And then her footsteps abruptly faltered and a frown creased her brow. Standing inside the captain's office was not Bretton, but a drone, and not just any drone. This one came straight from Avilon. From shiny silver casements and slender limbs to its cyclopean red eye and ball-shaped head, it was all too recognizable.

"What is this?" Farah demanded.

Therius stopped in front of the drone and patted its mirror-clear breastplate. *"This* is drone seven sixty-seven," he said.

The drone's red eye sprang to life, bright and malevolent. The eye settled on her and remained there.

Therius explained, "By the time we intercepted Admiral

Hale's Lifelink transfer on Avilon, it had already been relayed several times along the way. At one of those relay stations, Omnius stripped Bretton's personality to make him fit for transfer to a drone."

Farah shook her head. "It's not him. This isn't Bretton."

"Parts of him are, and parts of him aren't. We have unlocked some of his archived memories, but unfortunately his personality is still missing."

"Where did you get one of Omnius's drones?" Farah asked, rounding on Therius.

He met her ire without blinking. "We have more than one. When the time is right, they're going to infiltrate Avilon along with our operatives and help us defeat him."

Farah turned back to the drone, her features contorting with horror and dismay; revulsion twisted her gut into a knot. Her heart pounded, and her legs shook. She swallowed thickly and forced herself to approach the drone. *Drone 767.*

The bot's red eye watched her as she approached. She stopped within a few feet of the thing and gazed up into that eye, searching desperately for a familiar spark of *something*.

"Bretton?" she asked, reaching out with trembling hands, as if to cup a cheek the drone didn't have. "Do you remember me?"

For a long moment the drone said nothing, and Farah withdrew her hand.

She turned to Therius and shook her head. "Why did you bring me here?"

"Wait."

Then a mechanical voice rasped out of the grills in the drone's chest. "I am drone number forty seven trillion, six hundred billion, four hundred and forty nine million, three hundred and thirty two thousand, seven hundred and sixty seven. If you must refer to me as an individual, you may call me

Seven Sixty Seven, Miss Hale. My human name no longer holds any meaning for me."

Farah turned away. "He's gone," she said.

"He's programmed not to recognize his humanity, but it *is* there," Therius replied.

"Then what's the point?" Farah demanded. "Let's go. We're wasting our time here."

Farah breezed out of the office, brushing by Torv on her way out. The Gor followed her wordlessly, and they waited for Therius to join them.

"What's next?" Farah asked as soon as he appeared. The office door swished shut behind him, sealing drone 767 inside. "You said I'm the captain of this ship, but you're the admiral, so I'm guessing that makes me your executive officer."

Therius nodded. "When I'm not on board, you will be in command. When I am, the ship will be mine."

"Fine with me. Where's the skull face fit into things?"

Torv hissed and glared at her, but she ignored him.

"You would be wise to show your chief of security more respect. In terms of evolution, his people are physically the most impressive. I had to clone you and the others that the Sythians shot, but he survived after taking more than six shots to his chest and torso."

"Chief of security, huh?" Farah said, turning to look up at the half-naked alien. He glared back at her. "What about the rest of his people?"

"Shara is already of child-bearing age. Gors grow to maturity in less than a year, and a female reaches child-bearing age in just six months. Pregnant females can have an average of ten babies every three months, and although Gor females typically die in childbirth, with proper medical intervention they don't. Last, and most important, even though each creche that a female Gor bears typically only has one female, it is possible through hormone manipulation to make more of the babies females."

Farah shook her head. "What does that mean?"

"Thanks to the Sythians we now have plenty of warships, but the one thing the Union doesn't have yet is enough soldiers. Shallah executed the original Gor army, but we're going to breed another one."

Farah tried to do the math in her head. The Gors had just one female. She could have ten babies every three months. "What's our time frame?" she asked.

"Eight years."

"I assume you've run the numbers already. How many Gors will there be by then?"

"Almost ten million."

Farah's mind boggled at that. "That many?"

"How do you think Omnius created the Sythian's original invasion army so quickly?"

Farah glanced up at Torv, wondering how much he understood from their conversation and whether or not he objected to his people being bred for war for the second time in recent history.

"What do the Gors think about this?"

"I have already explained the situation to Torv, and to their Matriarch, Shara. She has agreed to help us, but this time the Gors won't be fighting as slaves. They will fight as equals."

"And I suppose they've taken your word for that."

"It's the truth, and they have no reason to doubt it. They want their species to thrive, and I am offering them the means to make that happen. This time their ships won't be centrally controlled from the Sythians' command ships, and the Sythians will be joining us in battle, not hiding behind the lines. The Gors are more than pleased with that arrangement."

Farah blinked. "Shallah agreed to all of that?"

"He has no choice. He can't face Omnius alone."

"How the frek did you bring the Sythians into this alliance?"

Therius smiled. "I offered Shallah everything that Omnius has, all the technology he needs to put him on an equal footing with Avilon. Over the next eight years we'll be busy refitting the Sythians' ships and selectively breeding the Gors to create an army to fly them."

"Busy is the word," Farah replied, feeling hope stir despite having seen what became of Bretton. "Ten million Gors... how are you planning to feed all of them?"

"There's plenty of local fauna to hunt, but besides that, the Sythian fleet was created to be self-sufficient. We're just replacing the crew that they killed."

"I suppose we're going to use quantum jump tech to slip past Avilon's gravity fields and make a head-on attack."

"That's part of the plan," Therius said.

Farah crossed her arms over her chest. "Ten million Gors against fifty trillion drones and seventy trillion humans on Avilon. Those numbers don't predict a favorable outcome. The rest of your plan better be frekking good."

"It is."

"Can I see it?"

"Of course, as my executive officer, and captain of the *Liberator*, you'll be privy to all of my battle plans. You have a lot of catching up to do."

The Liberator? Farah wondered. Therius had wasted no time coming up with a new name for her ship. "We'd better get started then," she said.

Therius nodded. "Yes, we had. Come with me."

PART TWO: UNMASKING THE ENEMY

"Evil wears a beauteous mask."
—An Unknown Etherian

CHAPTER 18

"Happy Birthday, Trinity!" Ethan said as the waiter set a small chocolate cake in front of her. She blew out the candle, and he smiled.

"What did you wish for?" Alara asked.

Trinity looked up, her violet eyes bright and just a shade warmer than her mother's. Ethan felt an echo of his love for Alara every time he looked at Trinity. She looked just like her mother, but she had his personality—stubborn and independent, an Ortane through and through.

"If I tell you what I wished for, it won't come true."

Ethan shook his head. "Wishes are what you make of them, Trin. There's no force shaping your destiny but your own."

"What about Omnius?" Trinity asked.

Ethan's brow tensed and his eyes narrowed. "As far as you're concerned, Omnius doesn't exist."

"But he does," Trinity said, thrusting out her chin.

Ethan felt Alara place a hand on his knee, and her grip tightened in warning. He turned to her and saw the quiet plea in her eyes.

"It's her birthday," she reminded him.

Ethan forced a smile for his daughter's benefit. "Why the

sudden interest in Omnius?"

"I can't ever leave the apartment. I don't have any friends. I've never even seen the *sun!* What is a sun? *A ball of hot plasma that heats a star system.* That's what I learned on the net, anyway."

"You won't get to see the sun in Etheria."

"But I will in Celesta. Grover says that Etherians get to visit Celesta, and they can go as often as they like!"

Ethan frowned. Apparently Trinity also had her mother's brain. She was too smart. "Who is Grover?" he asked. "I thought you didn't have any friends."

Alara's hand tightened on his knee again.

"He's just this boy I know."

"But you never leave the apartment..."

"We talk on the net. He helps me with math, and I help him with history."

Ethan's eyes narrowed by another few degrees. "No more talking to Grover."

"Why not?" Trinity demanded.

"Because I said so."

"No."

"Ethan..." Alara's hand squeezed so tight it began restricting his blood flow.

"All right, fine. I'm disconnecting you from the net."

"You can't! I'll *die* of boredom."

"No one has ever died of boredom, but plenty of people have died by wanting to go to Etheria," Ethan replied.

"It's her choice," Alara whispered.

Ethan rounded on his wife. "*Her* choice? To what? Kill herself?" He shook his head and snapped his fingers to the nearest waiter.

"Sir? Is everything to your satisfaction?"

"Bring me the bill, please. We're done here."

"Of course, sir."

Trinity's eyes brimmed with tears as she stared at her cake in disbelief.

Ethan drove home with both the women in his life giving him the silent treatment. Fine by him. He was too furious to talk to either of them. *Why the frek would Trinity want to go to Etheria?* he fumed.

Her Choosing Ceremony was tomorrow! After reassuring him dozens of times over the past years and months—*now*, at the last possible moment, she'd decided to rethink everything. Ethan cast a resentful glance at his wife. He began to suspect collusion. Alara had never made any secret of wanting to go to Etheria. She believed their lives would be better and safer there.

Never mind that they'd have to die before they could live forever in paradise. *Talk about irony.* It was the great lie of Avilon.

Ethan tried to focus on the virtual road. White lines marked his lane. He raced past slower traffic on his right, making sure to keep far from the yellow lines between him and oncoming cars. Buildings flashed by as shining pillars of light in the eternal night of the Null Zone.

"What if she leaves?" Alara asked, finally breaking the suffocating silence in the car. "What are you going to do, stay here?"

"You said it yourself. It's her choice. If she wants to leave us, then so be it."

Alara snorted. "You're unbelievable."

"No, what's unbelievable is why anyone would want to die so that they can live."

"Just because you don't understand it, doesn't mean resurrection isn't possible. What is a human besides a biological machine? Turn it off, transfer the data to a new one, and turn it on." Alara snapped her fingers to emphasize her point.

"We're done with this conversation," Ethan said.

"You don't believe in an afterlife, Ethan."

"What's that supposed to mean?"

"If you don't believe there's more to us than flesh and blood, then explain to me why resurrection won't work?"

"Because when we get *turned off*, we still have all of our memories. We're there when Omnius turns out the lights. If people weren't disposed of after the transfer, there could be two copies of everyone running around and you'd never be able to tell the difference. Ask any one of them after the fact if they feel like their existence is meaningless just because they have a clone running around out there somewhere, and you'll realize that it's not that simple. A copy is still a copy, no matter how convincing it is."

Alara blew out a breath. "You don't get it."

"You're right, I don't!"

A long silence stretched between them, during which Ethan worked hard to control his breathing, but every time he breathed out, he felt like there was a wellspring of air still trapped inside his chest.

"You can't keep Trinity locked in our apartment forever. What's going to happen when she gets a job? Or when she starts to date? You won't always be able to protect her."

"Protect her from what? We're safe up here."

"You make more money than 90% of Nulls, Ethan. You think she'll be that lucky?"

"So she'll have to get a good education. Isn't that what we're paying a thousand bytes a month for?"

"No matter how good her education, everyone starts at the bottom. She'll spend years living in the most dangerous parts of the city before she ever has a chance to rise to the top."

"Not if she marries well."

"*That's* your plan for her future? Marry into money?"

Ethan scowled and sent Trinity a quick look over his shoulder. She sat in the middle of the backseat, her violet eyes wide and darting between her parents.

"Trin, don't let your mother scare you. We've stayed safe down here this long, and that's not about to change. Remember what you promised me."

Trinity's eyes flicked to her mother. "I made Mom a promise, too."

Ethan's nostrils flared and his head spun around as if he'd been slapped. "What have you been telling her?"

Alara met his gaze unblinkingly. "The truth."

Ethan snorted. "Then you should have lied! There's nothing more deadly than the truth on Avilon."

Alara sighed. "Just drive, Ethan."

"Sure thing," he said, shaking his head. He wasn't going to let Alara manipulate him into going to Etheria by convincing their daughter to lead the way. He would make sure that Trinity stayed, even if he had to break the rules to do it.

* * *

Destra stood on her balcony high above the parade grounds, watching the graduation ceremony for the latest group of Gor soldiers. There had been countless ceremonies like this one, at least two per week for as long as she could remember, but this group was different.

Destra's gaze roved up and down the ranks of over ten thousand Gors, standing in a perfect square, all of them wearing the same glossy black suits of armor that their forefathers had used almost twenty years ago to all but wipe out the human race.

Destra still couldn't believe that Omnius had orchestrated the invasion in order to kill and then resurrect everyone on Avilon. It was hard enough to understand how resurrection worked, let alone the motives behind it, but she couldn't refute the process.

Eight years ago she'd been cloned by the Union in order to de-link her from Omnius. Now her body was even younger than it had been when the Sythians invaded, and just recently she'd turned thirty for the *second* time. *Talk about confusing,* Destra thought. She didn't even bother celebrating birthdays anymore. What was the point?

Far below the balcony where Destra stood, Therius welcomed the new recruits to the Union Army. His voice boomed through the square, reaching Destra's ears with perfect clarity despite a distance of a few hundred meters. But she wasn't paying any attention to the speech.

So much had happened since the invasion. She'd lost no less than two husbands, and likely her son, Atton, too. Therius promised they would rescue Avilon and set its people free, but whenever she had the chance to ask him if she'd ever see her husband or her son again, his answer had been evasive. The last time she'd asked him he'd said, *"Death is just the doorway to another life, so it is inevitable that you will see them again."*

"Does that mean they'll die?"

"It means that only Etherus knows the future, and humans are designed to live in the present."

Therius was religious. Destra could appreciate that, but he was taking things too far. He hadn't even made plans to resurrect anyone who died in the coming battle. His excuse was that there wouldn't be anyone left on Origin to resurrect them, and the data banks Therius had used to store intercepted

Lifelink data from Avilon were far too limited. They might be able to store and resurrect a few thousand individuals, but how would they decide who got to live again and who didn't? There was no way to make those decisions fairly, so Therius had declared that no one would be coming back this time. That put the stakes higher than ever.

Life was about to become a lot more precious.

Destra eyed the generals standing on the podium with Therius. They all wore the same armor as the Gors they commanded, but theirs had been painted white to distinguish them from the soldiers under their command. Further distinguishing the generals from the rest was the fact that they were all females.

With the Gors Omnius had chosen the right species to subjugate. He'd only needed to subjugate the males, because without their matriarchs they became trusting and obedient. Their females were the exact opposite, however, and they were revered as leaders of their people.

All of that would have been mere trivia to Destra, but for one thing: Gors revered female humans, too, and by some twist of genetic fate, Destra's daughter, Atta, was still receptive to the Gors' telepathic abilities, even as a young adult.

Because of that, Admiral Therius had determined that Atta would be the perfect general for a mixed Gor and human battalion. The Gors had already accepted Atta as one of their own, calling her the *Little Matriarch.*

Destra bit her lip, her eyes on Atta. She stood at attention to Therius's right, her helmet off and tucked under her arm. Her beautiful dark hair had been cropped so close to her scalp that it looked like a hat. Something warm and wet slid down Destra's cheek, and she wiped it away with the back of one hand.

Her little girl was going to war. She was only *sixteen,* far too young to be a part of what was coming. Unfortunately, Therius didn't see it that way. Everyone was going to fight. There were no civilians in the Union Fleet, not even her. Destra was going to fly a drop ship. She'd been training for the past eight years, but she still didn't feel ready.

Therius finished his speech, and the Gors all shuffled their feet and turned as one, raising their arms to the distant purplish orb of Origin's sun.

Therius called out, "Fire!" and ten thousand pirakla missiles shot out at the same exact moment. Those packets of energy danced and spun, sparkling bright purple as they soared into the air. Each one of them competed with the sun, looking like a star in its own right. At a set altitude above the parade grounds and the Union's fortress, all of those missiles exploded at once in a mighty thunderclap that rattled Destra's bones and shook the balcony where she stood.

Therius could instill in them all the martial pride he wanted, but the truth was, he had just ten million Gors, twenty thousand Sythians, and five thousand humans to take on a planet with countless trillions of people, guarded by a few hundred billion drones. And when Omnius arrived with New Avilon, trillions more drones would arrive to join the fight.

Destra shook her head. *Etherus save us...*

CHAPTER 19

Ethan took a few minutes to speak to Trinity before they went to bed. He planned to undermine whatever crazy ideas her mother had put into her head, but Alara refused to give them a private moment.

She crawled into bed beside Trinity, and hugged their daughter close, saying, "Your father is scared, but it's your life, Trinity. You need to make this choice for yourself."

Ethan felt a vein begin pulsing in his forehead, and his eyes narrowed. "Trin." He waited for her to look at him. "Omnius will try to convince you to leave us."

"I know," she replied.

"Just remember, everything he says is a lie."

"How do you know that?" Alara demanded. "Give me one example of a lie that you can prove he's told us."

"I don't have proof. If I did, then Omnius probably would have killed me by now just to shut me up."

"Or maybe you don't have proof because there isn't any," Alara replied.

"Where's *your* proof that we can trust him?"

"Dad, stop," Trinity said, an imploring look on her face. "Please, no more fighting."

Ethan set his jaw and nodded once. "All right. But we're a family, okay? If we decide to go to Etheria, we need to make that decision together. Whatever you decide to do, your decision is either going to keep us together or tear us apart."

"Don't put that pressure on her," Alara said.

"Mom..."

Alara sighed and kissed Trinity goodnight. "Happy Birthday, sweetheart," she said as she brushed by Ethan in the entrance of Trinity's room.

Ethan lingered, wondering what else he could say, but after a moment's deliberation, he walked up to Trinity's bed and kissed her on the top of her head. "Goodnight, Trin."

Ethan stumbled wearily to his and Alara's room. He climbed into bed beside her. Alara was at the far end of the bed, her back to him. He glared at her with a frown and then rolled the other way before turning out the lights.

He dreamed that Alara was straddling him, her hands pinning his wrists to the pillow with impressive force. She held him captive, her bright turquoise eyes spitting venom while her hips moved against his rhythmically, making him feel violated, a prisoner to her own fulfillment. *Turquoise eyes?* He wondered, while trying to free his wrists against her impossible weight. That gaze was familiar, but it wasn't Alara's. The rest of her, however—her face, her long silken black hair, even her naked breasts—all looked identical to his wife.

He shook his head. "Get off," he mumbled.

The woman's lips curved wryly. "Why? Don't pretend you don't like it." She kissed him, and he felt more strength ebb out of him as the taste and smell of her overwhelmed him. He was too weak to resist. His arms felt heavy and numb, his body the same. The kiss went on and on, her lips taking possession of his, as if trying to sap away his very soul. Eventually he found enough of his strength return for him to free his wrists and give her a shove.

She laughed. "It's too late to push me away now. Alara will never forgive you." The woman's turquoise gaze seemed to taunt him, and Ethan had to restrain himself from slapping the grin off her face. It was Alara's face, but those weren't her eyes. What was going on?

Suddenly she was back on top of him, pressing her body against him in all the right places, provoking arousal against his will. He focused on waking up, and the woman smiled, as if she knew she'd won. "You like it, don't you?" she asked.

She brought him to the brink and threw her head back in ecstasy. Her mouth opened wide and an oily black snake slithered out, its own mouth wide and gaping as it *hissed* and turned to him with glowing red eyes. Fangs dripped with venom, a loud *hiss* roared in his ears, and then the snake lunged and the gaping mouth swallowed him whole.

Ethan opened his eyes and lay blinking up at the ceiling. He sat up and turned to find Alara asleep beside him. He reached over and shook her shoulder.

"Ethan?" she asked sleepily. "What's wrong?"

Where to begin... he felt enraged, violated, confused, and painfully aroused. "I had a bad dream," he decided.

Alara flicked on the light beside her and turned to him, blinking bright turquoise eyes.

Ethan's heart froze in his chest.

"Tell me about it," she cooed, rubbing his chest. Ethan leapt out of bed, tripped over the bedsheets, and hit his head on the floor.

This time he woke up for real. He blinked quickly, clearing the bleary haze of sleep from his eyes. His body was bathed in sweat, and he shivered as a draft from the room's climate control vents found him. He'd obviously kicked off the sheets while tossing and turning in his sleep.

Ethan rolled over to find Alara sleeping soundly beside him. He sat up and spent long minutes searching the darkness for slithering shadows and glowing red eyes. Blood roared in his ears and air wheezed in and out of his lungs.

Was he awake or dreaming still? How would he know this time?

The seconds slipped away, marking the minutes on a slow march to dawn. For all he knew, it was dawn already. Both day and night were equally dark and shadow-filled. Ethan turned back to his wife and stared at the back of her head. Suddenly he wondered what color her eyes were. He turned on his bedside lamp with the manual switch and then reached for her shoulder.

Déjà vu.

Ethan shook her gently, his heart jackhammering in his chest.

Alara flinched and rolled over. *Violet* eyes squinted at him. "What is it?"

Relief poured through him, and he shook his head. "I'm sorry."

Alara's gaze softened and her brow furrowed. "For what?"

"For the fight."

Unable to help himself, he wrapped his wife up in a fierce hug.

"What if Trinity decides to go?" she whispered beside his ear.

"Let's deal with that if it happens, but we're a family, and we need to stick together."

"So you'll consider following her?"

Ethan hesitated. "I will."

* * *

"Happy Anniversary, Darin," Ceyla whispered before leaning over the table to kiss him. She withdrew with a bright smile and returned her attention to the heart-shaped dessert they shared by candle light at their dining room table.

"Seven years married," Atton said, shaking his head, his eyes fixed on his wife's beautiful face. Her features were framed by wavy blond hair, her blue eyes shining in the candlelit glow of their dining room. He smiled to see the heart-shaped silver locket he'd given her dangling down the plunging neckline of her sparkling blue evening gown. When opened, the locket would project a picture of the two of them, taken on their very first date. Now that was more than eight and a half years ago. She'd been so overwhelmed by the gift that she'd insisted they leave the restaurant early, taking their dessert to go. She wanted to be alone with him.

Atton smiled, watching Ceyla finish the last bite of the heart-shaped cake. He took a moment to look at his own anniversary gift, a holo-engraved wedding ring with their names on the outside and an inscription on the inside that read, *I'll love you forever -C.*

Ceyla wiped her mouth on a napkin and rose from the table, taking him by the hand and leading him to their bedroom. Once there she continued to show her gratitude for the past seven years of marital bliss.

Afterward, Atton slept soundly until his alarm woke him. He deactivated it verbally and stumbled out of bed, heading straight to the bathroom to get ready for work. Admiral Vee had been working him harder than usual. *Bliss doesn't deliver itself,* he mused bitterly.

As he approached the bathroom, he was surprised to find

the light already on. He opened the door to find Ceyla sitting on the lid of the toilet, her locket lying open in her hands, the hologram of them hovering before her eyes. She stared fixedly at it.

"Ceyla?" he asked.

She looked up, her eyes brimming with tears, her cheeks wet.

A sharp stab of concern brought him rushing to her side. "What's wrong?" he asked, getting down on his knees beside her.

She shook her head and blinked away her tears. He wiped them away with his thumbs before they could run down her cheeks. "Hey... it's okay," he said. "What is it?"

"Look at us," she said, nodding to the hologram.

He looked at the picture. It had been taken on their first date. The two of them sat in a booth at the same restaurant they'd gone to last night, hugging one another, her head on his shoulder as they smiled dreamily at the camera.

Whatever it was that had her so upset, he didn't see it. "It's us," he replied.

"Look at me, and then look at you."

He still wasn't getting it. "Ceyla..."

"Just look!"

Atton frowned and spent a moment analyzing every detail of the hologram. When he was done, he looked up and shrugged helplessly, but Ceyla wasn't looking at him, she was looking at the mirror above the sink.

"Now look in the mirror," she said.

He did, and this time he noticed what was wrong. His heart pounded, and his palms turned clammy with sweat. Eight and a half years had passed since that hologram had been recorded, and his face was the same as ever, an exact replica of the hologram, all sharp angles and smooth, unlined skin. Ceyla's face, however, was not the same. She'd changed subtly over the years. Her features were now those of a woman, not a girl. Her face was fuller, her eyes harder, her skin duller, and faint lines had appeared to ring her neck and web her eyes.

The differences were still slight, but thanks to the high resolution hologram he'd given Ceyla, she had the before and after to look at whenever she liked.

Atton cursed his stupidity and turned back to Ceyla. "You're as beautiful as ever," he said with a sly grin.

Ceyla shot up from the toilet. "I'm not! But *you* are! I always wondered why you were so handsome. You said you chose to become a Null when you were eight. You didn't, did you? You're one of *them.*"

Atton took Ceyla by her shoulders and met her blue eyes with his gold. "You're imagining things."

"Am I? Prove it then. I want a blood test."

"You don't trust me."

"If I'm wrong, I'll make it up to you."

Atton shook his head, and began working himself up into an indignant rage. He shook a finger in her face. "After seven years of marriage, suddenly you don't trust me?"

"Get the test."

"If we don't have trust, then we don't have anything."

"And if you're not a Null, then we don't have anything anyway! If I married a clone, what do you think happens next? I'll grow old and die, and you'll marry someone else. That's *if* you don't leave me when I'm old and ugly and you're still just as young and beautiful as ever. I'm not going to sit around and wait for that to happen. Besides, if you're a clone, then I married a man without a soul. You think I want to die and go to Etheria without you? Get the test, Darin."

Atton wanted to say more, but he kept silent. He had no trouble looking outraged, but deep down he was actually terrified. What could he say? She was right. He shook his head and turned away. "I need to get to work."

"If you're telling the truth, what do you have to be afraid of?" Ceyla called after him.

Back in the bedroom, Atton waved open the closet and hurried to put on his work clothes. He forewent a shower and shave in order to avoid further discussion.

"Well?" Ceyla demanded.

"This conversation is over," he said as he shrugged into a black trench coat that concealed the sidearm holstered to his waist.

Ceyla gave a bitter smile and crossed her arms over her chest. "You can't answer me, can you?"

Atton stormed out through the living room and dining room. He waved open the front door, but Ceyla's words followed him out. "You can't answer me, because you're lying!"

The door swished shut and Atton turned to stare at it. His angry scowl evaporated, and in its place came wide-eyed fear. She wasn't going to give up until he brought her proof that he was a mortal, but to do that he needed help.

Atton turned and started down the hallway to the building's lift tubes. On his way down to the parking levels, he began rehearsing what he would say to convince Admiral Vee to do him another favor.

* * *

"You already owe me a favor, Atton," Admiral Vee said, crossing her long, smooth legs and sitting back against her plush, white sofa.

Atton remained standing and pressed his lips into a grim line. "Add it to my tab."

Valari laughed. "Well, I suppose there is something you can do to repay me..."

"What would you like me to do?"

"When you've lived as long as I have, there's very little left that amuses you. Do you know what amuses me, Atton?"

He shook his head, staring into her deep turquoise eyes and trying in vain to find a spark of humanity there. "I have no idea."

"Your *father* amuses me."

Atton blinked, taken aback by that. "Which one?"

"Ethan, of course."

"I don't understand."

"Ethan is a faithful husband," Vee went on. "Omnius tells me he'll never leave his wife to be with me, or even experience a momentary lapse of his inhibitions. Do you know how unusual it is for me to come across something I can't have?"

Atton felt an angry heat rising around his collar. His right hand twitched beside his sidearm. "You want me to help you get my own father to commit adultery. Who do you think you are?"

Admiral Vee's amusement vanished and a scowl abruptly darkened her features. "A simple *no* would suffice."

"You don't need my help. If there's a way, then Omnius knows what it is, and *he* can help you."

"True, but then you wouldn't have a chance to repay the favor you owe me. I pretended to be your mother, so that you could trick your girlfriend into marrying you. How is that any better than adultery?"

"It was one night."

"And that's all I'm asking for," Vee replied, smiling up at him.

"I refuse."

"Even if you refuse, as you pointed out, I don't need your help. I'll get what I want either way."

Atton clenched his teeth. "What is *wrong* with you? What do you gain from my involvement?"

Admiral Vee laughed lightly and rose from the couch. "I told you, Atton, when you've lived as long as I have, there's very little left that amuses you."

Atton ground his teeth, considering the matter. If he didn't help her, he stood to lose his wife, and Ethan would be delivered into Admiral Vee's clutches just as surely by someone else. There was no way to make things any better for his father, but he could at least find a way to make things better for himself.

Admiral Vee watched him, her teeth bared in a broad grin, her eyes bright with needle-sharp points of reflected light.

"What would I have to do?" he asked.

"Come to my office, and I'll tell you."

CHAPTER 20

"This is the plan," Therius said.

All eyes were on the hologram rising from the long, black holo table in the operations center of the *Liberator*, but Farah's eyes were on the people in the room. Therius sat at the head of the table. To his right sat Shara, High Matriarch of the Gors, and down at the opposite end of the table sat Shallah with his Sythian second-in-command, Queen Tavia. All three factions were present to watch as Therius outlined the plan to conquer Avilon.

A glowing blue wireframe represented Avilon. The Union Fleet appeared as a fine haze of green dots orbiting in clusters above the planet, while their objectives were marked on the surface in three different colors. Green diamonds marked primary objectives, yellow marked secondary, and orange marked tertiary. The primary targets were enemy garrisons and omni-nodes—hubs in the quantum comms network that spanned the globe.

"The key to our battle plan is a quantum comms jammer that will disrupt Omnius throughout Avilon."

Farah blinked. "One jammer for the entire planet? Is that

even possible?"

Therius nodded. "We've code-named it the *Eclipser*. As soon as we activate it, everyone will be free of Omnius's influence. He'll be unable to harm them through their Lifelinks or speak to them. Even drones will be cut off, and they'll have to revert to secondary programming that makes human Peacekeepers their commanders."

"Will not the jamming also affect our fleet?" Shallah asked.

"We'll have line of sight communications via conventional comms. Once our teams are on the ground they will lose contact with one another, so we will have to coordinate everything very carefully ahead of time. Making matters worse, the Gors' telepathy will not work until we turn off the Eclipser."

Shara hissed and bared her teeth. "How are we to fight like thiss?"

"You will use conventional comms to communicate between the members of your ground teams. It will work as long as your people remain within a short range of each other."

"And Omniusss?" Shara hissed, blinking large, slitted yellow eyes.

"Avilon no longer maintains an orbital comms network. Coordinating a proper defense will be all but impossible.

"We're going to jump straight into orbit, directly above the known locations of Omnius's drone garrisons." Therius pointed to one green diamond after another, identifying the fleet's primary objectives. "We'll destroy approximately 90% of the garrison before it even has a chance to get airborne."

"What about ground defensesss?" Shallah asked.

"Most of the ground defenses are controlled via quantum links by Omnius, so we should see only a small fraction of them still active. It will take some time before drones or Peacekeepers can get to the ones that do have manual controls."

Farah let out a long breath. "There's a lot riding on this Eclipser. What if the enemy finds it?"

"There's no way to pinpoint the origin of the jamming field, so unless we have a traitor in our midst, it will be impossible to find."

Farah glanced around the room, looking from Therius to Shara and then to the Sythians. Her gaze lingered on Shallah, and her eyes narrowed swiftly.

Shallah caught that look and hissed at her. "I have no reason to betray the Union," he replied. "I would surely die as well asss you."

"Everyone here can be trusted," Therius said, "But as an extra measure of security, the actual location of the jammer will only be known to myself and the general of the ground team in charge of defending it."

Farah nodded. "How long will the jammer be able to maintain the field?"

"A month or more."

"Then all we have to do is keep it safe," Farah replied.

"Yes." Therius pointed to the next series of objectives, marked with yellow diamonds. "Stage two of our plan is to infiltrate the Omninet. These locations have been identified as nodes in the network. From here we'll be able to hijack the quantum network and send a brief message to the entire planet, straight to their Lifelinks. That is how we'll reveal Omnius's lies. I fully expect our message to incite a violent civil war."

"Won't you have to disable the Eclipser to send a message via the quantum network?"

"The Eclipser will only be offline for a minute or two, and during that time we'll keep Omnius busy defending himself from a virus."

"A few minutes might still be enough time for him to

organize a proper defense," Farah said.

"It's a risk we'll have to take."

"What about the Icosahedron? New Avilon?"

"Based on what we have seen of Omnius's movements in the Getties, we know that it will take him approximately a week to jump back to Avilon with all the Facets of his Icosahedron. During that week we will use Omnius's own weapon against him. He's spent the past eight years seeding the Getties with self-replicating nanites to erase the evidence of his lies. Over that same period of time we've managed to capture a sufficient number of nanites to weaponize them for our own purposes.

"Our plan is to plant nanite bombs in strategic locations throughout Avilon." Therius pointed to the third and final set of objectives, the orange-colored diamonds. "If need be, as proof of our intent, we'll detonate one of the bombs and allow Omnius to purge the area from orbit before the nanites can spread out of control. After that, Omnius will have no choice but to acknowledge that the threat is real."

Farah's blood turned to ice. "You're going to use the human race as blackmail."

Therius nodded. "We will offer to release Omnius's faithful people if he will allow the rest of Avilon to be free. If he does not agree to that, then we will detonate the bombs and destroy the entire planet. Based on his need to be worshiped by his creators, it is unlikely that is an outcome he will be willing to accept."

Farah frowned. Negotiating with a deceitful, manipulative, super-intelligent AI seemed like a lost cause to her. "No matter what agreement we come to, Omnius can always go back on it later."

"Which is why we will keep the bombs in place, and we will also keep The Choosing. We will give our people the same choice that Omnius does now, except that the ones who don't choose him really will be free, and the ones who do will know exactly what he is like. Every Human, Gor, and Sythian, will have to decide whether or not they would like to join Omnius and live with him in an artificial paradise on New Avilon."

"Eventually he will have enough followers that he may feel like he can do without us," Farah replied.

"Perhaps."

"What if Omnius doesn't enjoy humanity's company as much as you think? What if he decides to let us destroy ourselves? If he's lonely, he could always create a new species or even clone one of ours from DNA samples and start over."

"He could do that, yes."

"Then our threats are empty."

"Omnius won't like to be defeated. He would rather bide his time and wait for the day when he can have his revenge."

"That doesn't sound any better."

"It's the best we have. And if Omnius doesn't back down, then we *will* detonate the bombs. Better that we all die and go to Etheria than that Omnius continues to bend every living soul to his will."

Farah went cold. Silence reigned for a long, terrible moment, and she held Therius's pale blue gaze, weighing the man's resolve. The fanatic gleam she saw shining there was all she needed to see to know that he was serious.

By the time she recovered enough to speak, all Farah could manage was a whisper, but it still sounded loud in the pregnant silence of the operations center. "You're prepared to commit a triple genocide?"

"Death is not the end, Miss Hale."

"It is for us! We're all clones! We're not going to Etheria when we die. All that will be left of us is a cloud of nanite-eaten dust!"

"You're wrong. Even clones have souls."

"Really. Do you have any evidence of that? Actually, I'd even settle for evidence of souls in mortals. Souls are a hypothetical construct to explain how we can go on living after our bodies die, but there's no evidence that they actually exist."

"Faith is the evidence of things not seen."

"I'm talking about evidence we can *all* appreciate."

Therius sighed. "Even if I show you physical evidence, you will not accept it for what it is."

"Telling me that just makes me think you don't have any evidence."

"But I do."

"Prove it."

"The Human isss telling the truth," Shallah hissed from the other end of the table.

Farah turned to him with narrowed eyes. "And how do you know that?"

"I know the things about which he speakss."

"If the Redemptor says that we are to live again, then it is true," High Matriarch Shara growled.

Farah turned back to Therius to find him smiling approvingly at Shara.

"Show me your proof," Farah said.

"Very well," Therius replied. He stabbed a series of keys on the holo table's control panel, and the image of Avilon disappeared, replaced by something else.

It took a moment for Farah to recognize what she was looking at, but as soon as she did, the implications hit her like lighting.

"Holy frek..." she whispered.

* * *

Ethan's eyes burned. A lump was stuck in his throat, and he had to fight to keep from breaking down in front of the squad of Peacekeepers that had come to take his daughter. "Goodbye, Trinity," Ethan said, giving her one last hug.

She wrapped her arms around his neck and wouldn't let go. "I don't want to leave."

"It's just a week," he replied. "Then you'll be back." He withdrew to an arm's length to regard his daughter with a grim smile. "Remember what I told you. We're a family, Trin. We make decisions together."

Alara cut in at that point. "Goodbye, Trinity," she said, sounding nasal.

Ethan stepped back to let his wife hug and kiss their daughter goodbye. Alara's cheeks were wet with tears. "I love you," she said.

"*We* love you," Ethan added, wrapping both of them in a hug. They stayed like that for a while, heads down, arms encircling, the three of them huddled against the world.

Someone cleared their throat from the open doorway. "Mr. and Mrs. Ortane, we have a lot of children to collect before the day is out...."

They withdrew, but Alara held on to Trinity's hand, squeezing it white. "Follow your heart," she said.

Trinity nodded and wiped away her own tears with the back of her hands. The Peacekeepers stepped inside the apartment and took Trinity by her shoulders, turning and guiding her out. She glanced at them from the open doorway, waving and crying.

Then she was gone, marched down the hallway and out of sight. Ethan waved the door shut and turned away, his face a grimace of sorrow. Alara collapsed against him, sobbing.

"Promise me we'll follow her if she leaves."

Ethan just nodded, unable to voice his consent. His head was spinning. He guided Alara over to the living room couch and sat down with her to watch air cars racing by in a steady stream—headlights white, taillights red. He felt numb and helpless. He stroked Alara's hair, and wiped away her tears, weathering the storm of her grief until it was spent. His own storm had only begun to gather. Ethan's blood roared with impotent fury. His heart pounded frantically in his chest, and the lump in his throat grew until he couldn't swallow anymore. Omnius had already taken Atton from him. Now he was going to take Trinity, too!

He had to do *something*.

When Alara went to bed, Ethan lay beside her, holding her close and waiting to feel her convulsive sobs subside as her body relaxed in sleep. As soon as he heard her breathing slow to a steady rhythm, he quietly slipped out of bed and got dressed. He went to the garage and climbed into their air car. Firing up the grav lifts, he raced out into the endless night.

The city went by in a blur, lights racing around him in shining threads. Ethan flew straight to Admiral Vee's apartment, and woke her with a comm call from outside the shielded entrance to her garage.

"Ethan?" she said, blinking bleary turquoise eyes at him through the car's vidcomm.

Turquoise. Ethan's mind flashed back to the dream he'd had the night before, and he shuddered. During his own Choosing Ceremony, Omnius had warned him he would cheat on his wife, and ever since then, that fear had been burned into his brain as a recurring nightmare. *It's just stress,* he told himself. He would never cheat on Alara with Valari—or anyone else.

"Vee, I need to talk with you," he said.

"It's the middle of the night."

"It's urgent."

She sighed and the vidcomm she held shifted focus as she climbed out of bed. Her bedsheets fell away to reveal that she was completely naked.

Ethan grimaced and looked away, feeling guilty for the accidental glimpse of her. "Put some clothes on, would you?" he said, still not looking at the display.

Valari's laughter trilled through the comm. "You surprised me in the middle of the night. If you don't like what you see, then you should have called at a decent hour."

"Have some modesty," Ethan growled, peripherally noting that Valari had reoriented the comm to look at her face rather than her naked body.

"Have a care," she replied, scowling. "I'll meet you at the door."

The screen went blank, and the blue wall of shields blocking the entrance to the admiral's garage flickered out. Ethan cruised inside and set his car down on the nearest empty landing pad.

When he met Valari at the door, she was no longer naked, but still scowling.

"It's about Trinity," he explained.

"I'm listening," Vee replied, making no move to let him in.

"She's going through The Choosing. Today was her first day. I think Omnius is going to convince her to go to Etheria."

"He will if he can."

"No, I mean, I think it won't take much convincing. Her mother has been filling her head full of ideas that life will be better and safer for us there."

Vee snorted and shook her head. "And this is the woman you're so devoted to? She's betraying you with your own daughter."

"Never mind that. What I want is for you to make sure that Trinity doesn't go to Etheria."

"What makes you think I can do something about it? We're talking about *The Choosing,* Ethan. That's Omnius's show, not mine. I'm the leader of the Resistance against him, remember? How could I possibly influence your daughter while she's in Omnius's care?"

That sucked the air out of Ethan's lungs. He stood there, his mouth open for a reply, but having nothing left to say. He was back to feeling helpless again. "Never mind. I just thought that maybe..." He shook his head and flashed a mirthless smile. "I'm sorry I woke you." He was halfway back to his car when he heard Vee's footsteps behind him.

"Wait," she said.

He turned to see her approaching, her flowing red gown clinging to her as she walked and giving a teasing view of her naked body underneath. He pretended not to notice.

She stopped too close for comfort and touched his arm, her hand trailing down until it found his. She smiled and squeezed his hand. "Let me see what I can do. It's possible I might be able to get a message to her the day that she has to make her choice."

Ethan felt his heart leap inside his chest. "You could do that?"

"It's *possible.*"

Ethan couldn't help the grin that sprang to his lips. "That's good enough! If you can do that, I'll be in your debt."

Admiral Vee squeezed his hand once more. "Go get some sleep. You look terrible."

"So do you," Ethan replied.

"Liar," she replied, grinning suggestively at him.

He shrugged. "Beauty is in the eye of the beholder."

"Then it must be a privilege to be held by such a discerning gaze as yours," Vee replied. "It's a pity that privilege is wasted on your treacherous wife."

Ethan frowned. "You can't blame her. She's just scared for her daughter."

Vee crossed her arms over her chest. "What about her husband? She would leave the Null Zone so as not to lose her daughter, but would she stay to keep you?"

Those words struck too close to Ethan's heart for comfort. He flashed the admiral a wan smile and retreated to the safety of his air car. "Let me know when you're ready for my message," he said before closing the door on the pilot's side and sealing himself in.

Vee nodded, and Ethan gunned the thrusters on the way out, as if he could somehow escape the memory of her cutting remarks.

What *would* Alara do?

What if it really did come to a choice between their daughter or him? Who would she pick?

Suddenly Ethan realized that The Choosing wasn't just about whether or not they chose to serve Omnius—it was about choosing between the people they loved, the ones they'd lose and the ones they'd keep.

CHAPTER 21

"**D**eath is not the end," Therius said. "And this is the proof."

Farah shook her head, her eyes locked on the recording projected above the holo table. Four real-time brain scans were shown there, the top two were labeled *Before Transfer* and the bottom two *After Transfer*. The ones on the left had the sub-heading *Actual* while the ones on the right lay under the sub-heading *Predicted*. Brain activity was shaded red for high activity, yellow for medium, and blue for low, making it easy to compare the scans. Farah noticed that the *Before Transfer* scans were completely different in terms of the *Actual* and *Predicted* activity, while both the *After Transfer* scans were identical.

"This is why The Choosing exists," Farah breathed.

"What is thisss?" High Matriarch Shara asked.

Therius explained for her benefit. She had never been to Avilon, so she didn't even know what The Choosing was.

Farah shook her head, aghast. She'd always wondered why Omnius made people choose. The excuses made a limited amount of sense—it was a way to remind people of the cost of human freedom, and to illustrate how much better off they were with Omnius ruling them. But Omnius didn't have to resurrect them all in new bodies in order to make them immortal. He could have retroactively altered the bodies they were born with.

The real reason for The Choosing was that Omnius couldn't predict what people would do unless he resurrected them first. "This still doesn't prove there is an afterlife," Farah said. "It just proves that Omnius is messing with our DNA."

Therius shook his head. "If he was responsible for whatever makes people predictable after transfer, then why would he study people to determine the cause?" Therius pointed to the top of the recording, which read, *Case #5.46[...]E+13.*

Farah mentally translated that notation. "There have been 54.6 *trillion* cases studied?"

"At the time of this recording, yes."

Therius keyed another command into the holo table, and another set of brain scans appeared. The heading read *Lazarus Experiment #1.25[...]E+6.*

"Here you can see the brain scans of a Lifelink transfer from a mortal to a clone whose body and brain were exactly duplicated from the original."

This time Farah saw eight scans, four along the top for *Patient One - Donor*, and four more at the bottom for *Patient Two - Recipient*. The *After Transfer* scans were grayed out for both patients.

"The patients are asleep and dreaming at this point," Therius said. "The recipient, the clone, has never been awoken before, and the Lifelink transfer has not yet taken place."

Therius tapped a few more commands into the holo table's controls, and a second holo recording appeared beside the first. This one showed two women lying on matching hover gurneys with pristine white blankets covering them. Avilonians in luminous white robes walked between them, configuring equipment and monitoring holo displays. A familiar heads-up display overlaid the recording, and it bobbed around in a way that was consistent with someone walking. Farah realized the recording had been taken from the Augmented Reality Contacts of one of the technicians in the room.

Someone walked up to that technician. Farah recognized him as Grand Overseer Vladin Thardris.

"Make the transfer, Therius," Vladin said.

The recording bobbed with a nod. "Yes, Master."

Therius. Farah's gaze darted to the Union leader, and he flashed a small, secretive smile before nodding to the recording, indicating that she should keep watching.

Wordlessly, Farah turned back and watched. ARC dialogs appeared and disappeared as the Therius in the recording sent mental commands to the equipment in the room.

Suddenly one of the two women sat up with a gasp, her eyes wide and terrified. Her head began jerking at the end of her neck as she tried to look everywhere at once. She swung her legs off the side of the gurney, and a pair of Celestials rushed to her side, helping her down.

At that point, Therius paused the recordings. "Now look," he said.

Farah focused on the brain scans. The *After Resurrection* scans had come alive with shaded patterns. The recipient's *Actual* and *Predicted* scans showed identical shading, while the donor's *Actual* and *Predicted* scans remained distinct from one another.

"The identical clone is utterly predictable, while the donor remains an enigma. What is different about them? Brain structure, DNA, and memory were all controlled to be exactly the same. These are two perfectly identical women. We would expect them to behave exactly the same way, and be either equally predictable or equally unpredictable, but that is not the case."

Therius keyed another command into the holo table, and the recording switched to a different place and time. Now there were two separate recordings divided by a vertical line. On the left was the heading *Original* while on the right was the heading *Clone*. In the middle was a questionnaire with *Yes* or *No* questions.

1. You are almost never late for appointments

Farah watched one woman circle *Yes* while the other circled *No.*

2. You enjoy having many acquaintances.

Both circled *Yes.*

And so it went with the two women answering differently at least a third of the time.

"They don't know about each other, and they don't know what they're being tested for," Therius explained. He pressed another key on the holo table and a second questionnaire appeared with the heading *Predicted Results.* Farah scanned the displays and saw that Omnius had predicted how both women would answer, but only the clone had answered the way he predicted.

The question of whether or not people were still the same after transfer had been answered with a definitive *no.* This woman was not the same as her clone. Something was subtly different, something that even altered her personality.

Farah wondered what that meant for her. *She* was a clone transfer. Had she actually died during the invasion? What did that make her now? A biological bot? She felt like a stranger in her own skin. A wave of nausea swept over her, raising goosebumps on her arms.

"I don't understand," High Matriarch Shara said. "What

does thiss matter?"

Therius paused the recording and turned to regard the Gor. "This is proof that we are more than just flesh and blood, and it answers the question of whether or not there is a life after death."

Farah shook her head and forced her gorge back down. "Actually, I'm with the Gor on this. All this proves is that people really do die when they transfer, and that there is something about us Omnius can't copy using Lifelink implants."

Therius's blue eyes lit up. "Exactly! What do you think that *something* is, Captain Hale?" Farah shrugged, and Therius's smile broadened. "We searched hard for the missing link, but after more than a million experiments, we never found it."

"So Omnius doesn't know everything after all. I'm not surprised by that."

"No, he doesn't, but what would you call something that defies physical explanation and makes one person fundamentally different from another?"

Farah saw where Therius was going with that. "I'm guessing *you* would call it a soul."

"Yet you don't believe that. This is compelling evidence that we are not just data recorded in a biological computer. If we were, then Omnius would find both mortal humans and immortal clones to be equally predictable. Instead, he was forced to create the Null Zone and The Choosing just to give him an excuse to separate unpredictable people from predictable ones."

Farah frowned. "He doesn't have to do that. He could just force everyone to resurrect at whatever age makes the most sense and then call it a day. He's already resurrected the majority of the people living on Avilon, so he just has to worry about the children."

"You would think so, but in practice that's not how it works.

Plenty of Etherians and Celestials grow tired of Omnius's control over their lives and choose to become Nulls. Do you know what all of those people have in common?"

"They saw through Omnius's lies?"

"No, they all did one or more things that Omnius didn't predict."

"You're saying their... *souls* came back?"

Therius held her gaze for a long, solemn moment, seeming not to notice her sarcasm. "Yes."

Farah grunted. "If clones are becoming unpredictable over time, that could mean that exposure to environmental factors is the missing element."

"If exposure to environment factors makes people unpredictable, then we should be able to isolate a physical cause, but Omnius was unable to find one in over a million experiments."

"There was a time when we couldn't isolate subatomic particles. Just because we can't see something doesn't mean it isn't there," Farah said.

Therius sighed and waved away the holo recordings. "I told you that you wouldn't believe me."

Farah turned to look at High Matriarch Shara. The Gor still looked confused. Her slitted eyes had narrowed to slivers, as if none of what they were talking about made any sense to her. By contrast, the Sythians were impassive, unimpressed. Shallah gave no reaction when Farah looked at him, but Queen Tavia unfolded her wings and refolded them restlessly.

"What about Gors and Sythians?" Farah asked, turning back to Therius. "Are they also unpredictable?"

"Shallah wouldn't have been able to rebel against Omnius if he weren't at least somewhat unpredictable. Likewise, the Gors shouldn't have been able to rebel against Shallah. Despite

Omnius's desire to predict and control us, our souls are all still free of his predictions. Omnius's original directive was to predict what his creators would do before they did it, and he's still trying desperately to accomplish that."

"But he must have found *something* after more than a million experiments. What was his conclusion?"

"He believes it's the uncertainty principle. The quantum fabric of the universe is essentially unpredictable. Unpredictable variables add up over time to create irregularities in an otherwise ordered system. Two separate instances of the same person, no matter how similar, are different because they exist at different points in space time, and they will be exposed to unique quantum factors that will alter their behavior."

"That makes sense," Farah said.

"No, it doesn't. That only explains why two identical clones with identical memories will act differently—not why one will be predictable and the other will not. The predictable clone is exposed to the same random quantum variables and should be just as unpredictable as the original person."

Farah sighed. "Maybe quantum differences build up over time. Clones are grown in tanks at an accelerated pace. Most of them have only been alive for a month by the time Omnius wakes them up. That's not the same as actually living for twenty-something years. And that explains why clones become unpredictable again over time."

"We're going to have to agree to disagree," Therius said. "You have your doubts, and I have my faith. Both are equally impossible to prove. It's a mystery."

Farah smiled thinly. "And it's going to remain one unless this Etherus of yours comes here from his universe, sits down with us, and explains it all."

"Even if that were to happen, you would not believe him."

"If he showed me proof I would."

"Earlier you asked for evidence. Now you want proof, so which is it?"

"My mistake. I meant proof."

"I see," Therius replied, clasping his hands on the table and nodding. "That is the difference between faith and reason. For every question that reason answers, it raises another. The only way to permanently answer it is to become God and know everything, and I don't think He wants to share His throne with all of us." There was a spark of amusement in Therius's eyes that annoyed Farah.

She glared back at him. "We've wasted enough time trying to answer the unanswerable. We need to get back to the problem at hand—defeating Omnius."

"I agree," Therius replied. He turned to the High Matriarch. "Shara, please inform the other matriarchs of what they will be facing on the surface of Avilon. Have your ground teams and pilots begin using the simulators aboard the Sythians' Behemoth Cruisers to train for their missions. I've already assigned battalions and battle groups to objectives, so all you need to do is check with Shallah to find who needs to use which simulators."

Shara turned to look at Shallah, and she hissed something at him in her language. Shallah hissed back. The exchange went on for a while, leaving Farah to wonder what they were talking about.

"Enough!" Therius boomed, slapping the table with his palms. "We call ourselves the *Union* for a reason. We stand *united* against a common enemy, and that means we need to trust each other." Turning to Shara, he said, "If you cannot trust Shallah enough to use the simulators aboard his warships, your people will be unprepared when they reach Avilon, and they will be slaughtered. Then all of this will have been for nothing."

"We train in the jungles and on the fields," she replied. "We hunt; we kill; we are ready."

"There are no fields or jungles on Avilon. How will you prepare for that?"

Shara hissed. "Then why do you make Gors train in fields and jungles if this training is useless?"

"I didn't say it's useless. That was the first part of their training. Now that your people are physically conditioned and trained to work together in their respective teams, it's time for them to become familiar with the environment they'll be fighting in."

Shara hissed once more and bowed her head. "I trust your judgment, Patriarch."

"Thank you," Therius said. His gaze left Shara to rove around the table and address all of them. "This meeting is adjourned. It won't be long now before we are ready."

Therius rose to his feet and nodded to the door. Shara rose next, but she waited for the Sythians to leave the room first.

Queen Tavia cast an unreadable look over her shoulder as she left. Shara hissed and feinted a lunge at the Sythian Queen.

Tavia startled, her wings unfolding reflexively before she realized that Shara's intent wasn't serious. She hissed back and refolded her wings.

Shara gave a *sissing* laugh and followed the Sythians out.

Farah watched them all go with a frown. "It's going to be a miracle if we don't all turn on each other before we get to Avilon."

Therius regarded her with a smile. "Miracles are my specialty, Miss Hale."

"If you say so."

"I forgot to mention something, Captain. There's one other faction that has yet to be introduced to the Union."

"Don't tell me you've begun recruiting the local fauna."

Therius laughed. "No, quite the opposite in fact."

The sound of clanking footsteps reached Farah's ears and she turned to see 767 appear in the open doorway to the operations center. She frowned, wondering what *he* was doing there.

"My battalion is ready for inspection, Admiral," 767 said.

"Your..." Farah turned back to Therius, her eyes wide and blinking. "You created an entire *battalion* of them?"

"Who better to infiltrate Avilon than drones?"

Farah blinked. *Who better indeed.*

* * *

Atton handed Ceyla the data pad with the results of his medical scan. She looked it over with a frown. It took longer than he expected for her to react, and when she did, she wasn't as apologetic as he had hoped.

She looked up, her eyes narrowed and her lips pursed. "How do I know you didn't forge this report and send it to yourself from a fake address?"

Atton shook his head, wondering what had made Ceyla so suspicious of him. Sure, she looked older than him, but he didn't exactly look like a teenager.

"I'm going to call the doctor," she said, tapping her comm band and dialing the doctor's number on a holographic keypad. She waited with her arm held at waist height. The holographic keypad was replaced by a blank screen that read, *Calling...*

The band trilled quietly, and a moment later, the blank screen showed the face of an aging Null doctor with bushy white eyebrows and a thoroughly lined face. Atton had chosen him carefully, knowing that a mortal would inspire immediate confidence from Ceyla.

"Doctor Cander speaking," the man said. He appeared to be staring past them. The headlights of oncoming traffic playing through his white hair told them why.

"Doctor Cander," Ceyla said. "I'm sorry to call you while you're driving."

"Not a problem," Cander replied, glancing briefly at her. "What can I do for you?" he asked.

"You performed some tests on my husband today. I just wanted to confirm the results with you and make sure there were no misunderstandings. His name is Darin Thardris."

"Mr. Thardris, yes... he told me you might call. No misunderstandings," Cander went on. "Your husband is one hundred percent mortal."

"And there's no way the test could fail?"

"Yes, if I confused his scan data with that of another patient."

"Did you?"

"Not once in all my forty years of practicing medicine, ma'am, but if you're worried, he could come in tomorrow and I'll perform another scan."

"No, that's okay," Ceyla replied. "Thank you. I'm sorry to have bothered you."

"No bother, Mrs. Thardris. Have a nice evening."

The call ended and Ceyla turned to Atton, looking sheepish. "Darin, I'm..."

"It's all right," he replied, taking a deep breath. He wasn't shameless enough to hold her suspicions against her. After all, she was right.

Ceyla took a few steps toward him and placed her hands on his chest. Kissing him, she said, "Let me make it up to you."

Ceyla led him to the living room and made him sit while she

stripped naked in front of him. It felt wrong to enjoy the show. It felt even worse to enjoy what came next as she sat naked in his lap and unbuckled his belt.

The truth hammered around inside his head, demanding to be let out, but he didn't have the guts to say it. Ceyla was the only good thing that had ever happened to him. He couldn't bear the thought of losing her.

Besides, he'd already done what Admiral Vee had asked in exchange for her buying Doctor Cander's help. He'd broken into Ethan's apartment while he and Alara were away and made detailed holo recordings of the interior. Atton wasn't sure what Valari planned to do with that, and he didn't want to know, but at least she hadn't asked him to deliver Ethan to her bedroom. If she wanted Ethan, she would have to tempt him away from Alara all by herself.

"Are you okay?" Ceyla breathed close beside his ear. When he didn't reply right away, she withdrew to look him in the eye.

"Don't stop," he whispered back, his hands sliding down to her bare buttocks.

When it was over, she was left panting against his chest with a contented smile on her face. Atton took a deep breath and sighed. Ceyla leaned back to study him. "You're still upset."

"No." He shook his head. "I'm not."

She kissed him, forcing his lips apart with her tongue. "I don't believe you," she whispered, as if she could taste the lie on his lips.

The irony was, this time he wasn't lying. How could he be upset with her? He was upset with himself. "I mean it," he said.

She shook her head. "I'm going to have to apologize again."

And she did.

This time he managed to at least act like he was enjoying himself, but every kiss and every touch felt tainted.

What good was it to be with the love of his life if he had to lie to keep her? He couldn't delude himself into believing that was love. *This has to end,* he thought.

"I love you, Darin," she whispered in his ear.

"I love you more, Ceyla."

What was so special about a face or a name? Just because she thought he was Darin Thardris, didn't mean she didn't love him. He was still the same person under the surface.

What he really needed to do was find some way to mimic the signs of age. A bio-synthetic suit would work, but sooner or later Ceyla would notice the difference between what her hands felt and what her eyes saw. Not to mention what would happen if she ever caught him taking the suit off or putting it back on...

Atton shook his head, feeling more confused than ever. He would be able to buy time like that, but time was his enemy, and sooner or later too much of it would pass.

* * *

—One Week Later—

Ethan gave the waiter his and Alara's orders for drinks, and then went back to watching the sunset. The Canopy was a luxurious restaurant on level 45. The balcony where they sat gave them a simulated view over the top of a mottled blue and green-leafed jungle, broken here and there with crowns of ivory blossom trees. In the distance a blood-orange sun peeked over the treetops, warming the cooler tones of the flora below.

A fake breeze blew and Ethan caught an aroma of tree sap and ivory blossom nectar, along with a damp, loamy smell. They heard birds chirping and hooting, mingled with the occasional howl from a tree-climbing animal. It was all simulated, but more than enough to convince Ethan's senses and make him feel like he was on a completely different planet.

If only that were true.

The reality was they were still on Avilon, and Trinity was just about to go through her Choosing Ceremony. Ethan had given Admiral Vee his message, but he wasn't sure if it would be enough.

"Don't forget who you are, Trinity. You're an Ortane, and there are three of us. That's what your name means—a group of three. We're all in this together. Don't forget that. I love you no matter what, and I know you won't make the wrong choice."

Ethan looked away from the sunset to study his wife. She was staring at the table, her eyes unfocused and dull. He reached for her hand and squeezed. "Don't think about it, all right?"

Alara looked up, her eyes shining with unshed tears, her lower lip trapped between her teeth. "How can I stop thinking about it? She's our *daughter.*"

"And there's nothing we can do right now other than wait to see what she chooses."

Alara shook her head. "Life could be easier up there, Ethan. We might even be able to afford to have more kids."

Ethan frowned. "You know how I feel about Etheria, and besides, Trinity isn't going to choose to go there. She's smarter than that."

Alara looked away and spent a moment staring out over the simulated jungle. Ethan watched her carefully, trying to come up with a way to make her feel better.

"I want to go home," she said, not looking at him.

"We just got here!"

"I'm tired. I don't... I can't do this right now. I just want to go to bed and wake up to hear Trinity on the comm, saying that it's over."

Ethan grimaced. "Look... if she chooses Etheria, she'll still be able to visit us. We won't lose her."

Alara's brow furrowed and her eyes became hard. "That's what you want? For our daughter to have to visit us like we're in prison? She'll grow up without us!"

Ethan sighed. "Let's wait and see what she decides, okay?"

"Fine, and while we're waiting you can take me home."

Ethan's stomach grumbled, and he grimaced at his empty plate. "All right, let's go."

They passed their waiter on the way out.

"Is everything all right, Mr. Ortane?" he asked.

"I'm sorry, my wife isn't feeling well. We'll have to come back another time."

"Of course. I hope you feel better soon, Ma'am."

Alara flashed a lifeless smile, and they left.

Once they were back in the car, Ethan pulled out into the street and drove to the nearest vertical stream of traffic. He flew down to level 30 and slipped into a stream of traffic.

Alara was quiet, her silence judging him right alongside his conscience. It was hard to imagine life without Trinity. Would their marriage even survive such a blow?

Not with my wife blaming me for her absence, he decided.

No sooner had that thought passed through his head than the comm band around his wrist trilled and vibrated with an incoming call, startling him out of his thoughts. The band was connected to the car's comm suite, so he accepted the call there. An image of the caller appeared on the car's main holo display, along with a name—*Peacekeeper Damaris Rills (Acolyte).*

"Ethan Ortane here," he said.

Alara sat suddenly straighter and leaned toward the holo display.

"Mr. Ortane, your daughter has made her choice," the Peacekeeper said.

CHAPTER 22

"What did Trinity choose?" Ethan's heart froze painfully in his chest, but he forced his voice to remain calm.

"She has decided to become an Etherian," the Peacekeeper replied.

Ethan blinked. "She..."

"She is in a better place."

Acid boiled in Ethan's stomach. "A *better* place? She's no place at all you dumb kakard! You killed her!"

"I'm sorry you see it that way," the Peacekeeper replied. "If either of you would like to join her in Etheria, please report to the nearest Peacekeeper station."

The comm call ended, and the main holo display went back to showing the car's auxiliary instruments. Ethan pounded the flight yoke and roared. The car swerved toward the nearest building, and he barely managed to jerk the yoke back the other way before they crashed through someone's window.

"Now what?" Alara asked quietly.

"I don't know!" he replied.

"We can't leave her alone up there."

Ethan shook his head. "She *isn't* up there. Her *clone* is. Our daughter is gone!" His voice cracked with the finality of that statement, and his heart gave a labored *thump* in his chest.

"You don't know that."

Ethan rounded on her. "And you don't know otherwise!"

Something cold crept into Alara's eyes, and she looked away, crossing her arms over her chest. Silence stretched between them until it grew thin and brittle. Alara broke it a few moments later with an incredulous snort.

"You claim to love us, but you won't follow us. What kind of love is that?"

"And you claim to love me, but you want to leave me. I could ask the same thing."

"She's our *daughter*, Ethan!"

"And you're my wife!"

Silence returned. This time thick and stifling. Ethan's chest heaved for air, as if his lungs had forgotten how to draw breath. His eyes felt like they were bulging in their sockets, and his hands were locked around the flight yoke like a pair of vice grips. Admiral Vee had *promised* to get his message to Trinity before The Choosing Ceremony.

She lied, he decided.

"You're just afraid," Alara whispered.

"Afraid?" Ethan shook his head. "I'm not afraid. I'm furious!"

Ethan caught a blur of movement in his peripheral vision. Then came a loud *slap* followed by a searing pain on his right cheek. He rounded on his wife, his eyes wide and nostrils flaring.

"Wake up, Ethan!" Alara screamed. Tears streamed down her cheeks.

Ethan's thoughts turned to mud, and the strength drained out of him like a valve letting off steam. Maybe that was all he had to do—wake up. This had to be a bad dream...

A bright light came slicing through Alara's window, blinding him. Then came the warning blast of an air horn.

Ethan jerked the flight yoke down.

Too late.

Ethan watched it all happen as if in slow motion. The inertial management system shielded them from the initial forces, but it did nothing to stop the car from crumpling in on Alara's side.

She screamed as the door became a mangled mess of jutting alloy panels and bars. Ethan heard the thrumming roar of the other car's engines and felt the growing weight of inertial forces bleeding through the IMS. Then came a second impact, and it wasn't shielded at all. Ethan's head whipped sideways. His flight restraints jerked taut across his chest like duranium bands, but Alara's restraints snapped like worn string. Her shoulder collided with his head, and stars exploded inside his skull. He was dimly aware of their car crashing through a hydroponic farm. Greenery smeared the car's windshield and foul-smelling nutrient water splashed in through the broken side windows.

Then the car fetched up against something solid and Ethan's head jerked sideways once more, slamming into the twisted remains of his side door.

Darkness found him, but seemingly only moments later it was replaced by a blinding light. Ethan wondered if it was the proverbial light at the end of the tunnel.

"Sir, can you hear me?"

Ethan came to, feeling cold and wet. His ears rang, and a vague memory of the accident went tumbling through his brain. Then a sudden fear stabbed him.

"Where's my wife?" he asked, managing to sit up before anyone could stop him. The medic attending him tried to force him back down, but when Ethan saw Alara lying motionless beside him in a pool of brownish liquid, her side soaked red with blood, he found the strength to push the medic away. "Alara!" he said, scrambling over to her. She had two medics fussing over her, and there was a Peacekeeper standing off to one side, looking on with a frown.

What's a Peacekeeper doing here? he wondered, but he didn't have time to figure it out. Alara's eyes were wide and glassy. Her chest rose and fell in quick gasps. Ethan found her hand and squeezed it *hard* to get her attention.

"Hang in there, sweetheart," he said. "You're going to be fine."

She turned to him and her eyes found his. "Ethan," she wheezed out. "I..."

"Ma'am, please don't try to talk," one of the medics said.

The one who'd been attending him a moment ago came and tried to drag him away. "Sir, you need to get back."

"She's my wife, dammit!"

"You're injured. You need to—"

Ethan's right arm whipped out and hammered the man in the solar plexus. The medic doubled over and stumbled away.

His attention back on his wife, Ethan spent a moment trying to assess Alara's injuries for himself. The medics had ripped open her shirt, revealing a wide gash that ran all the way down her rib cage. He watched as they sprayed it with a temporary sealer, and the wound closed in an ugly ridge. The bleeding stopped almost immediately, but Alara's short, gasping breaths continued.

Ethan felt her hand grow cold and clammy in his. He squeezed it a few more times to get her attention, to keep her with him, but this time she didn't respond. Her eyelids looked like they weighed a thousand pounds. One of the medics injected her with something and her eyes flew open once more.

"I love you," she managed to say.

"Please save your strength, ma'am."

Ethan shook his head. "What's wrong with her?"

The medics didn't respond. One of them hurried away and returned with an oxygen tank and a mask.

"Will she make it?" a dispassionate voice asked. Ethan looked up to see the Peacekeeper looming over them, his silver armor a gleaming silhouette as he blocked out light from one of the hydroponic farm's few remaining UV lamps.

"I don't know," one of the medics replied.

"Then it's time for her last rites."

Ethan's eyes hardened. "She's going to make it."

The Peacekeeper shot him a look. "The medics don't know that and neither do you. Alara?" the Peacekeeper asked.

She looked up at the man, her eyes full of tears, her chest still heaving for air. "I can't... breathe," she said.

"You may not survive this," the Peacekeeper replied. "It's not too late to go to Etheria. There's a new body waiting for you there, and so is your daughter. If you want to go, all you have to do is nod."

"Get away from her, you snake!" Ethan roared. The Peacekeeper ignored him, and Ethan stumbled to his feet, his fists clenched. "Did you hear me?"

Alara's eyes were still on the Peacekeeper. She nodded and whispered, "Take me."

The Peacekeeper smiled and turned to the nearest medic, who was just about to place an oxygen mask over her mouth. "You heard her."

Ethan felt like he was trapped in a bad dream. His eyes went from Alara to the Peacekeeper to the medic—he watched the EMT's shoulders round as he set the mask aside. The second medic reached into a bag and handed the first one a syringe full of a clear liquid.

"What's that for?" Ethan demanded. He felt light-headed and confused. He swayed on his feet, trying desperately to remember what he was angry about. Something warm trickled down beside his right ear and provoked a maddening itch.

One of the medics removed the cap on the needle with his teeth and began feeling for a vein in Alara's neck.

Ethan had a bad feeling about that needle. "Get away from her!" he roared, lunging clumsily at the medic.

The Peacekeeper raised one arm with a glowing palm and fired a short blast from a grav gun. It knocked Ethan off his feet and he landed with a *splash* in a puddle of brown nutrient water. By the time he looked up, the medic had already inserted the needle in Alara's neck and injected the contents of the syringe.

Alara flailed her arm to get his attention. Ethan hurried to her side and grabbed her hand between both of his. He shook his head desperately. "Alara, you can't die."

She took a deep breath. "Ethan, I'm..." she trailed off, sighing as the air left her lungs. Her hand went limp and the light left her eyes, leaving her gaze fixed and staring.

Ethan stared at her in disbelief. What had she been about to say? *I'm sorry?* A lump rose in his throat and his vision grew blurry.

"She's in a better place," the Peacekeeper said.

Ethan looked up at the man, and he saw red. "You killed her!" He leapt to his feet only to be pinned down by all three medics.

The Peacekeeper met his fury with a bemused frown. "You arc frce to follow her."

"In death?" Ethan spat.

"In a more abundant life."

Ethan's head throbbed. The itch beside his ear grew warmer and wetter. One of the medics holding him yelled at his colleague. The man left and returned with another syringe.

Ethan eyed it suspiciously. "You're going to kill me, too?"

"It's a sedative," the medic explained, while rolling up Ethan's sleeve to search for a vein in his arm. "You're resisting treatment, and you need to be sedated before you injure yourself further."

Ethan blinked away a steady stream of tears. His gaze fell on Alara once more. The Peacekeeper bent down to close her wide, staring violet eyes, and suddenly she looked like she was just sleeping.

"Why?" he asked as he felt the sharp prick of a needle and a cool, calming fluid slipped into his bloodstream.

"She had a collapsed lung and was bleeding internally," one of the medics said.

"She wasn't going to last long," the Peacekeeper added. "She had to make a choice while she was still conscious to do so."

Ethan shook his head vigorously, as if to deny the diagnosis. Then his vision grew dark and fuzzy as the sedative reached his brain. A welcome warmth rushed through him and his body relaxed. His eyelids fluttered, then shut.

When he opened them once more, he found that he was lying on a gurney in the back of an ambulance, listening to it rattle and shake around him. Two medics were attending him, one on each side.

"What happened? Where am I?" Ethan asked, his head pounding. A thick haze clouded his thoughts, but he had a vague feeling that something terrible had happened. What was he doing in the back of an ambulance?

"Don't move, please," one of the medics said.

Ethan shook his head, and a stab of pain lanced through the right side of his head. He winced, and reached up to find a thick bandage there. Horrified, he tugged on it. Something warm trickled past his ear.

"I said don't move!" the medic snapped, slapping his hands away from his head.

"What happened?" Ethan asked again, trying to sit up this time.

The medics forced him back down. "You were in an accident," the nearest one said.

Déjà vu hit him like a hover truck. This had happened before. He'd dreamed it—more than once. Was this another one of those dreams?

"Alara?" Ethan asked, hoping that she might be somewhere inside the ambulance, riding with him as a passenger rather than a patient. But she didn't answer.

"Where's my wife?" he asked.

"She chose to go to Etheria. Her injuries were too severe."

"You idiot!" the other medic replied. "Are you trying to send him into shock?"

"Alara died?" Ethan rocked his head back and forth, feeling nauseated. Scraps of memory drifted through the stormy haze inside his head. He remembered Alara lying in a pool of brackish water, her side soaked with blood, shattered UV lamps and broken tangles of plants all around. Then he remembered the Peacekeeper. The syringe.

His wife's violet eyes wide and staring.

An alarm began squealing close beside his ears.

"He's going into shock!"

Ethan was vaguely aware of the medics fitting a mask over his mouth and nose. Then something sharp pricked his arm, and a raging fire raced through his veins. His eyes flew wide, and some of the haziness retreated from his thoughts. In its wake came the full force of his grief. He remembered everything. Trinity's choice, the accident, Alara's last words—*"Ethan, I'm..."*

Sorry?—her fixed and staring eyes...

It all became too much to bear. Tears began slipping down his cheeks, creeping out behind his mask. The medics continued working to stabilize him, their blurry faces hovering over him.

"Mr. Ortane, are you in a lot of pain?" one of them asked, having noticed his tears.

He nodded.

"Where does it hurt?" the medic insisted.

Ethan placed a hand over his heart.

"Your chest?" The man passed a handheld scanner over him with a bright fan of blue-white light.

"I don't see anything wrong..."

"He's fine; he's just upset. He'll live," the other medic said.

But Ethan knew better. It didn't matter what that scanner said. His heart had stopped beating with his wife's, and whatever lay ahead for him it couldn't be called living.

It was a fate worse than death.

CHAPTER 23

"**T**he last runner just came in, but our chief of inventory tells me we only have half of the Bliss we need to keep up with current rates of distribution. Is there a reason you didn't order more?" Galan Rovik asked.

Hoff ignored the question. "You were supposed to send that runner to my office when he arrived. Where is he?"

"He didn't want to see you."

"What do you mean he didn't *want* to see me?" Hoff fumed. "I'm his father!"

"I will try to convince Darin Thardris to see you the next time he comes."

"His name is *Atton*, and don't bother. I know what he's doing. He's trying to cut any personal ties that might lead to his wife uncovering his lies. He should just stop lying to her and save himself the trouble."

"You haven't told your wife the truth either," Galan pointed out.

"Because Omnius won't let me."

"Well, I'm sure he has his reasons. Ignorance is a happier state for most humans."

"It's pure bliss," Hoff replied dryly.

"Speaking of Bliss, shall I take the liberty of ordering more product?"

"I'm trying to deprive the market in order to raise prices on the street."

"You're depriving the market in order to limit your involvement."

Hoff smiled. "What makes you say that?"

"Omnius could execute you for your treachery."

"If he wanted to execute me, he would have done so by now."

"Need I remind you that yours isn't the only life hanging in the balance? Your family's well-being depends on your performance."

Hoff's eyes narrowed sharply. "Is that a threat?"

"It's an incentive."

"How can you support Omnius so willingly?" Hoff demanded. "You know what he is, yet you never show any sign of regret about the things he makes you do."

Galan regarded him with a bland look. "We're both just following orders. Without freedom, guilt is meaningless. We are not responsible for our actions, so no one can judge us for them; we can't even judge ourselves. There is no good, no evil, only Omnius, and who are *you* to judge His ways? Besides, if anyone should have regrets, it's you. You're the *head* of the White Skulls. I'm just a mole in the Enforcers who helps deflect attention away from our activities."

Hoff felt a rush of acid bile rise in his throat, eating him up from the inside. He stood up and rounded his desk to loom over Galan. "You said it yourself, if I don't do what Omnius wants, my family dies, and I do have regrets." He pointed to the dark half-moons under his eyes. "I haven't had a good night's sleep in *years*. And you're wrong—evil *does* exist. It just goes by a different name now. That name is Omnius."

Galan shook his head. "I don't know why Omnius allows you to live. You are the most hateful rebel I have ever met, and he has you running the largest Bliss distributor this side of Avilon."

Hoff smirked. "Who are you to judge his ways?"

Galan gave a booming laugh. "Touché. I'll take the liberty of requesting more Bliss. Perhaps your son will want to see you when he returns to deliver it."

Galan Rovik turned on his heel and left. As soon he was gone, Hoff let out a frustrated roar. He cast an angry look at the ceiling.

"Why *pretend* to be good? You rule Etheria with meticulous care to make sure that no one does anything wrong, but here in the Null Zone, you are actively causing as much suffering as you can."

Omnious gave no reply.

"Answer me!"

There is no good or evil, only me, Omnius replied, speaking through his thoughts. *I am the only measure, the only authority, the only God. Who are you to question me? I am the potter and you are my clay."*

"Stop quoting the Etherian Codices to me."

I wrote them, therefore, I'm not quoting. I'm merely repeating myself.

Hoff's frustration built to a suffocating climax before he remembered to breathe.

You don't believe me.

"No."

Even after I told you the truth about everything.

"Before that, you lied about everything, so you'll excuse me if I don't trust you anymore. If you want me to trust you, you should set me and my family free."

If I did that, I'd have to kill you.

"Well, what are you waiting for then? Death is the only freedom."

"Why do you think I keep you alive?"

That struck Hoff speechless. He returned to his desk and sat down, battling depression and despair. Omnius was keeping him alive as a form of punishment. Hoff leaned back in his chair and closed his eyes, longing for simpler times when good had been human and evil had been Sythian. Now that the Sythians turned out to be descendants of humanity, a threat created by Omnius, who had in turn been created by humans, all the lines between good and evil had become depressingly gray.

We did this to ourselves, Hoff thought, appalled by the sheer truth of that statement. His next thought was an inevitable progression of the first—

Evil does exist, he decided, *and it's human.*

* * *

The hospital discharged Ethan after just one day. He'd suffered a minor concussion and multiple lacerations in the crash, but all of that had been easily treated, and now he was fine.

Physically fine.

He left the hospital on foot rather than call an air taxi. Memories of his wife and daughter played on an endless loop through his brain, distracting him to the point that he barely noticed his surroundings. One street looked the same as the next. People passed by; shop lights and streetlights competed to peel back the night; air cars whirred and rumbled overhead.

Ethan's throat felt cut, and his chest felt like an empty cavity.

It was a familiar feeling. More than two decades ago he'd lost his first wife and his son, Atton, when he'd been exiled to Dark Space for stim-running. Then the Sythians had invaded and he'd feared the worst. He'd never given up hope, and he'd been right not to, but this time was worse. He knew exactly what had happened to his family.

Ethan's eyes burned, and he shook his head to clear it. He needed to forget and *fast*. He stumbled into the nearest convenience store and went hunting for the most potent bottle of liquor he could find. The first candidate was a bottle of amber-colored single malt whiskey.

Good enough. Ethan snatched it from the shelf and walked outside. The auto-pay scanner at the door charged him as he left.

Once he was back on the street, Ethan wasted no time cracking open the whiskey. He took a long pull straight from the bottle. It burned down his throat like fire, raising goosebumps on his arms and hairs on the back of his neck. A few passersby turned to look at him, while others gave him a wide berth.

Ethan walked up to the edge of the street and leaned heavily on the railings, gazing down. The city disappeared below him in a dizzying swirl. Solid streams of traffic raced by on level 15. A pair of trucks racing beside each other caught his eye, provoking a visceral flashback.

Headlights shone bright through the passenger's side window. Alara's hair looked ablaze in the sudden light. Metal shrieked, and Alara screamed as the car crumpled in toward her—

Ethan grimaced and took another gulp of whiskey to wash away the memory. He wondered what Alara's clone was doing in Etheria right now. She would have all the same memories. No doubt she was waiting patiently for him to join her and Trinity, but what would be the point? That would just kill him, too.

Maybe that wouldn't be so bad, Ethan thought, still gazing down on the gloomy city. Just fifteen floors below lay a thick, curling gray mist. That murky cloud of moisture and pollution obscured the darkest, most dangerous part of Avilon—a netherworld full of murderers, thieves, prostitutes, and strung-out Bliss addicts turned to Psychos.

Ethan took another gulp from his bottle, thinking it wouldn't be long before he ended up down there—probably dead and forgotten in some abandoned alley. In the Null Zone, death was like gravity, always dragging people down.

May as well beat the rush, he thought, and turned away from the railing, intent on finding a way down to the surface. But the best he could manage was a drunken stagger, and the world spun dangerously around him. Ethan frowned, only now realizing how drunk he was. He examined his bottle and saw that it was more than half empty. Adding to that, his stomach burned like it was on fire, and he couldn't remember the last time he had eaten.

He just managed to stumble over to a nearby bus stop, where he sprawled out belly up, and watched the vertical sprawl of the Null Zone slowly spin around his head. Twenty-five levels up from there, shone the hazy blue glow of the Styx. He imagined he could see past that, straight through Etheria, and up to the Eye of Omnius shining down from the top of the Zenith Tower.

"I'm going to kill you," he whispered.

No reply came, but Ethan knew that was because he'd been de-linked when he came to the Null Zone.

He blinked slowly. His eyelids felt heavy, and his body felt numb and weary. He had no idea how much time had passed since leaving the hospital. Was it night already? Ethan checked the comm band on his wrist. Blurry digits came together, showing that it was still the middle of the day.

Ethan drifted off and the bottle of whiskey slipped from his hand with a hollow-sounding *clunk*. His dreams were a wish fulfillment of a bloody war against Omnius and all his faithful followers. He saw the streets turn red with blood, and he was perversely satisfied by the violence until he saw his wife lying among the dead, surrounded by broken plants and UV lamps. Her violet eyes were wide and staring, her face and lips blanched white.

Ethan screamed. Alara opened her mouth and made an inhuman honking sound, as if she weren't really dead, but somehow possessed by a horrible beast.

His eyes sprang open to see an air taxi parked beside him. The driver honked his horn and waved to get Ethan's attention. He shook his head, confused, his mind still trapped in a drunken haze. Why was that taxi honking at him?

"Sir? Is there somewhere I can take you?" the driver asked.

"I..." A wave of dizziness washed over him, making him feel ill. He winced and pressed a hand to his forehead.

"Let me take you home," the driver suggested. "You shouldn't be out here sleeping on the street."

Ethan was about to object to that—wasn't there somewhere he'd been meaning to go? He turned to look around and noted that the previously steady stream of pedestrians had dispersed. The only ones left were a few unsavory-looking types. It had to be the middle of the night.

Ethan turned back to the cab driver. "Okay."

The rear door slid open and Ethan stumbled up to the railings at the edge of the street. Not bothering to open the boarding gate at the bus stop, he hopped over it and stumbled toward the cab.

"Careful!" the driver warned as one of his feet sank into the gap between the curb and the hovering taxi. That was a twenty five floor drop. Ethan peered down, considering it. Then the taxi door began sliding shut and he retreated inside.

He didn't quite manage to sit up straight in the back seat. His head lolled, and his mind drifted off into dreamland again.

"Where do you live, sir?" the driver asked.

Ethan mumbled something he assumed to be the address. He wasn't sure if it was correct, but he didn't care. Maybe going home wasn't such a good idea. His apartment would be empty. There'd be no end of reminders about who and what he'd lost. He made a strangled sound in the back of his throat.

"Don't worry, sir. You'll be home soon."

Ethan nodded, unable to muster a reply.

CHAPTER 24

Atton almost choked on the lie—*"Don't worry, sir. You'll be home soon."*

Sir was a strange way to have to address his father. Atton kept half an eye on Ethan in the rear-view mirror of the taxi. He was already passed out on the back seat. He'd drunk himself senseless. Atton grimaced and looked away. Given Ethan's beliefs about Lifelink transfers, Atton couldn't blame him. He really believed his family was dead.

When Valari had told him where his father was and asked him to go pick Ethan up, she'd put it in terms that he couldn't refuse. *"I need a favor from you, Atton."* Having led with that, Valari had proceeded to explain the situation and where Ethan was.

Atton had been unable to argue with the necessity of picking Ethan up before someone decided he was too tempting a target to resist, but he wasn't sure how helping his father would mean doing a favor for Valari. Or he *hadn't* been sure, anyway, until Valari had told him where she wanted him to take Ethan.

"I want you to bring him to my penthouse."

At that point he'd become suspicious. He failed to see how Valari could seduce Ethan while comatose and grieving, but

Atton didn't want to underestimate her. *"Why should I bring him to you?"*

"He's in no shape to be alone right now."

"You're planning to take advantage of the situation to get closer to him."

"Love can't be forced, Atton. I'm going to prove mine by helping him through a difficult time, much the same way Alara proved hers by helping him when he was grieving over you and your mother."

"And if I say no?"

Valari had just smiled. *"By now you should know better, Atton. No one says 'no' to me."*

She hadn't directly threatened him, but it was enough to remind him that he didn't have a choice.

Atton pulled the taxi up to the entrance of Admiral Vee's hangar. The shield lowered automatically for him and he cruised inside.

The sight that greeted him on the other side of the shield wasn't that of a spacious hangar built to hold a dozen or more air cars. This was a single car garage, the walls close, the sole landing pad empty. Atton shook his head and checked his current location via the car's nav console. The computer confirmed he was at Valari Thardris's apartment, but that meant she'd somehow completely remodeled since his last visit.

Since *yesterday.*

Atton hovered the car down onto the landing pad and waited, his eyes on the door at the top of the short staircase leading from the hangar to Vee's penthouse apartment.

Moments later the door at the top of the stairs opened, and Admiral Vee came striding down. Atton exited the taxi with a frown, determined to ask her about the recent renovations.

Something was wrong.

As Valari reached the bottom of the stairs and turned toward him, he saw instantly what that something was. His jaw dropped, and his entire body began to tremble with fury. He'd never hit a woman before, but there was an exception to every rule.

"What are you doing?" he demanded.

"Shhh," Valari replied, placing a finger to her ruby lips and winking one big, *violet* eye at him.

Now he understood why Valari had asked him to break into his father's apartment and make holo recordings of the entire place.

"I didn't agree to this," Atton said.

Valari looked amused, but her face was all *wrong*. From the playful curve of her red lips and the shape of her small oval face and button nose to her *violet* eyes... she was an entirely different person. Even her body had taken on a new shape, with wider hips and more pronounced curves. The disguise was perfect. Too perfect. It was a bio-synthetic suit. The Avilonian version of a holoskin. This was Valari Thardris A.K.A. Neona Markonis, but she looked exactly like Alara Ortane.

"What do you think you're doing?" he asked as Valari walked past him and waved the side door of the taxi open. Clearly the car's scanners could still see past her disguise, but it wouldn't be hard to fool a drunk and grieving husband that this was his dead wife.

"I'm not going to let you do this," Atton said, walking up behind her with deadly purpose.

"You don't have to," she replied. "You can leave now."

"I'm going to tell him."

Valari looked at him. "No, you're not."

Atton tried to scream a warning to his father, but his lips wouldn't move. Then he tried to physically intervene, but his entire body was paralyzed.

"I warned you. No one says *'no'* to me."

Atton watched, helpless as Valari turned and woke his father.

"I missed you, Ethan," Valari said, taking him by the hand, and drawing him out of the taxi. Ethan stumbled out, his eyes wide and blinking. His jaw dropped open, and a husky croak was all he managed. "Alara? How?" Then he appeared to notice where he was. This was his garage. Even drunk, he had to recognize it.

Still frozen, Atton looked on as Ethan grabbed Valari's face in both hands and kissed her roughly. The kiss went on and on. Atton's rage had reached a climax; he felt like he was about to have a stroke, but his body still refused to respond. Omnius had paralyzed him, but why would he participate in something as petty and perverted as this?

The kiss ended and Ethan squeezed Valari into a crushing embrace. She played her part well, sinking into the hug, and cooing soft words in Ethan's ear, all the while he blubbered confusion in hers.

Valari managed to wink at Atton over Ethan's shoulder. Then she gestured with one finger, motioning Atton toward the car.

Just like that, Atton's legs became unfrozen. His arm came up of its own accord, waving the door open. He climbed inside, watching in horror as his hands and arms moved to fly the taxi out of the garage. He tried to turn and see what Ethan and Valari were doing, but he couldn't. She wanted privacy. It occurred to him that Valari Thardris was exactly like Omnius. Both of them had an insatiable desire to dominate and control. Atton could only guess what would happen next, and he felt sick about his part in the charade.

The taxi slid out through the hazy blue shields at the

entrance of the hangar and into the night.

How far would Valari take her deception? Would she pretend to be Alara forever?

The very thought of it made Atton's stomach churn and his mouth fill with saliva; he broke out in a cold sweat, and his stomach heaved.

By the time he regained control of his body, he was already far from Valari's penthouse, back in the lower levels of the Null Zone. The Taxi swooped down to the pedestrian streets on level 10 and stopped right in front of his apartment building. He tried using the flight controls to turn the taxi around, to go back and get his father, but the car had been remotely disabled.

Atton grimaced. He'd allowed Valari and Omnius to suck him in too far. He should have put a stop to things a long time ago.

A quiet, loathsome whisper rippled through his thoughts. *You said you would do* anything, *remember?*

Atton did remember, but he hadn't realized at the time just how despicable that would make him.

I want out, he thought back.

It's too late for that, Omnius replied.

No, it's not, he insisted.

No one says, 'No' to me, Atton.

Atton clicked his teeth and set his jaw. He wanted to argue with that, but there was nothing he could say. Omnius was in complete and utter control. Resistance was futile, and *The Resistance* was a sham.

It would take someone more powerful than Omnius to defeat him, and no such one existed.

* * *

Ethan awoke with his head pounding. His throat was sore, and his chest and back felt raw as if they'd been slashed with knives. Ethan lifted the sheets to check. He didn't notice any bandages or scabs, but there were plenty of scratch marks. Coupled with the fact that he was naked, Ethan could only imagine what had happened last night, but his memories were hazy and awareness was slow in coming. Maybe he was still dreaming...

"Good morning, handsome."

A lithe shadow slunk up beside the bed. Ethan looked up to see that it was a naked woman. Desire stirred. Alara was here with him... The dream was getting better. He remembered something about last night that made sense of the scratches he'd found crisscrossing his chest, and a smile graced his lips....

That smile died with a strangled gasp as soon as he recognized the woman's face. It was Valari, not Alara.

Ethan went cold. *This is a dream,* he said. He sat up and shook his head.

"Are you all right?" Valari asked, crouching down beside him. "You look like you've seen a ghost."

She laid a hand on his knee and he flinched. Everything was so real. He began to doubt he was dreaming. But if this wasn't a dream, then...

The events of the previous days came back to him in vivid streaks of color and emotion. He saw his wife die. He remembered getting drunk on the street, lying down to sleep at a bus stop, a taxi coming to pick him up and take him home... and then...

He'd come home to find his wife waiting for him.

"No," Ethan said, still shaking his head. "I went home. What am I doing here?"

"You don't remember? You came here to argue with me

about whether or not I sent your message to your daughter—which I did, by the way—and then... well, you were very upset. I tried to make you feel better." Valari gave him a meaningful smile and her gaze flicked up and down his naked torso.

Ethan could hear the blood roaring in his veins. The thudding in his head sounded like the drumbeat of a marching band. Valari was lying. He'd gone home last night. He *remembered* going home, seeing his garage, his apartment, his *wife*.

My wife? Ethan frowned. Alara was dead, resurrected in Etheria. How could he have seen her?

"Oh my..." Valari placed a hand over her mouth to cover a gasp. "You don't remember. You didn't even know who you were with, did you?" Valari's turquoise eyes grew round and a shimmer of moisture appeared. She looked away suddenly and her shoulders began to shake. "I thought..."

Ethan felt like he was going to throw up. Was she crying? After taking advantage of him, *she* was acting like the victim. "You knew I was drunk!" he said. "I didn't know what I was doing!"

Valari cast a bitter look over her shoulder. "You said your wife was dead, Ethan. You said marriage is until *death do us part*. You convinced *me!* Don't you remember that?"

The hurt in her eyes ran so deep that Ethan was taken aback. He almost reached for her shoulder to give it a reassuring squeeze, but just the thought of touching her made him want to vomit. He couldn't have slept with her!

"I tried to resist, but I've wanted you for so long... I guess I just wanted to believe that this time you wanted me back," Valari said, smiling wistfully through her tears.

"Well, I didn't!" Ethan burst out.

Valari flinched as if he'd slapped her.

"I thought you were my wife!" he said, his voice hoarse and cracking. "I even thought that *this* was my apartment." He turned and gestured helplessly to his surroundings.

"Well go then, and leave me alone!" she said, hugging her naked shoulders. "You got what you wanted," she said, speaking softly now.

Ethan stood on shaky legs. The sheets fell away. Valari cried softly, her shoulders shaking with each sob. He tried not to notice her nakedness, but it was impossible to get away from. Impossible to forget.

Ethan shook himself and hurried around the room, picking up articles of clothing he recognized as his. He dressed in a hurry and fled. When he reached Valari's parking garage, he found his courier car and waved it open. He spun up the car's engines, dialed up the grav lifts, and rocketed out into the Null Zone. Skyscrapers flashed by in colorful streaks of light, stabbing through his eyes to his throbbing head. The throbbing soon took on a mantra.

Cheat-er. Cheat-er. Cheat-er!

Ethan grimaced and dove as sharply as he could, picking up airspeed fast. Elevated streets whipped by. Then came air traffic. Cars honked as he sliced down in front of them, narrowly avoiding half a dozen collisions.

Despair reached for him, clawing, taunting, and dripping with guilt. Overspeed alarms shrieked. The car rattled and shook. The last fifteen floors of the Null Zone swept up, concealed by a seething mass of dirty gray smog. That shroud enveloped him.

Another few second's hesitation was all it would take. Alara was dead. Trinity was dead. He'd cheated on his wife right after her passing. He'd lost everything, even himself.

The ground came rushing up to greet him, cracked and dirty

streets swelled until he could see every bit of rubble and every grit of sand. Time seemed to slow to a crawl. Memories of his family flashed through his head, and he released the flight yoke with a bitter smile.

CHAPTER 25

"**W**hat do you mean he's *dead?*" Valari scowled.

"He crashed one of your courier cars into the surface."

Valari felt her eye twitch. "That wasn't part of the plan."

"I cannot entirely predict what mortals will do. I warned you there was a risk."

She took a moment to calm herself. Breathing in, breathing out. A hologram of Vladin Thardris stood before her, his chiseled features blank and emotionless. There was no need for him to pretend to have an emotional response with her. She saw past his physical appearance, to who and what he really was— Omnius himself.

"You said it was an unlikely risk. You said he didn't believe in a life after death, and the moral ambiguity of sleeping with me after his wife died would be enough to keep him from doing something stupid."

"I was wrong. You should have accepted part of the blame, not laid it all on him. You did trick him, after all."

Valari's lips twisted into a sour expression. "Yes, but if I'd told him that, then I'd have taken all of the blame, and he'd have killed *me*, not himself."

"Agreed."

"Now what?" Valari asked. "You promised me I'd have Ethan."

"I took the liberty of making an identical clone of him in the event that this might happen. I can bring him back, erase his memories of waking up in your bed and everything that came after that. He's already been aged, so he won't even know he died, and this time he'll be predictable."

Valari nodded. "Do it."

"What about his wife? She is asking about him. Would you like me to tell her that he killed himself?"

Valari's brow furrowed as she considered it. "And have her grieve for her cheating husband? No... that would be unkind. Let's show her what her husband has been doing in her absence. That will give her the closure she needs to make a new life in Etheria and forget about him."

"I promised Trinity and her mother that Ethan would join them."

"You also predicted he would cheat on his wife. Few wives would want their husbands back after that. Have him go to Etheria, let him try to convince his wife that it was all just a drunken mistake. She won't take him back. You never said he'd *stay* in Etheria, did you?"

"No, I did not."

"Then everybody wins."

"Not everybody—just us."

Valari smiled. "Same thing."

Omnius returned her smile. She knew the expression of emotion was for her benefit, but it felt genuine enough.

The hologram of Vladin Thardris disappeared, his smiling face fading into a ghostly mirage before disappearing entirely.

Valari left her office, her mind drifting to the events of last night, reliving the moment. Despite his apparent age, Ethan still looked young and vital. He was ruggedly handsome, not in the too-perfect, effeminate way that resurrected clones were. No, Ethan was unique—indomitable, independent, strong. Valari smiled, feeling a warm rush of desire sweep over her at the thought of him.

She would break him, and then she'd make him beg for her.

* * *

"Where's Dad? I thought he was going to come find us in Etheria."

Alara smiled and kissed Trinity on the forehead. "I thought so, too, sweetheart."

"What happened? Omnius lied?"

"I don't think so... no," she said. "I'm going to ask him. I'm sure he'll explain it all to us soon."

"We're going to be together again, right?"

"Yes, I'm going to fetch your father. He'll realize I'm not dead when he sees me again."

"What if he doesn't believe it? What about Atton?"

"Atton never tried to convince him, but I will." Trinity still looked uncertain, so Alara gave her daughter a reassuring smile. "It's almost time for Sync. Don't worry about all of that now."

"I can't help it. I can't sleep."

"You don't have to sleep anymore, Trin. You just have to wait for Sync. As soon as Omnius finishes synchronizing us to his servers and makes predictions for tomorrow, he'll wake us all up again."

"How does Sync work?"

"It's like sleep, only shorter," Alara replied, giving Trinity's hand a quick squeeze. She stood up from her daughter's bed and turned to leave the room. "Good night, darling. I love you."

"Love you, too, Mom."

Alara left and went to her room. They were living in a temporary residence in the lower levels of Etheria that made the best apartment in the Null Zone look like a matchbox. The apartment was too big for just the two of them, but their drone servant and the apartment's automated features made it easy to keep up with. Alara was already getting used to life in Etheria, but there was still a gaping hole in that life.

Ethan should have come to join them by now. After all, she hadn't left him out of spite or disloyalty, or even to be with their daughter instead of him. She'd suffered lethal injuries, and the only way to live had been to transfer to an immortal clone in Etheria. He had to understand that.

So why wasn't he here?

Alara went to her room and lay down to wait for Sync. As she lay awake and staring at the ceiling, she spoke to Omnius inside her head.

I need to see my husband.

Silence.

Omnius?

Are you certain you wish to see him?

Of course I am!

A scene flashed into her head, a lurid one of two naked bodies entangled in a mess of sheets, shadows playing over them as they reveled in each other. A muted glow of city lights shone in from an adjacent window. Alara flinched and shook her head to make the image go away.

What was that? Her heart pounded. It had been dark. The people in the scene were impossible to clearly identify. It couldn't be. Another scene flashed into her mind's eye—a familiar face, cast into sharp relief by the gloom. It was Ethan's face, his eyes clouded with desire.

Alara shook her head again. This time she spoke aloud. "Why are you doing this to me?" she demanded. "It's not true!"

An audible voice replied this time, calm and steady, and full of pity. "I am sorry, Alara."

"You promised he would follow us!"

"And he will."

Alara shook her head. "Not like this."

"Are you saying you won't take him back?"

"I..." It couldn't be true. Not her Ethan. He would never cheat on her.

"It wasn't cheating, Alara. Not to him. To him you are dead."

"Wasn't?"

"What you saw already happened."

Alara bit her lip so as not to scream. "If I'm dead, then why isn't he grieving?"

"People grieve in different ways, and he was drunk. If it makes you feel better, he will regret it deeply when he is no longer intoxicated."

"If he was able to be with someone else so soon after losing me, then he never loved me at all."

"I am sorry, Alara. I tried to warn you both years ago, when you first came to Avilon."

Alara's eyes widened. She remembered. Omnius had predicted Ethan's infidelity. At the time she'd refused to believe something so ridiculous. Now *she* felt ridiculous. Her eyes filled up and spilled over. She bit her lip and rocked her head from side to side, her tears soaking into her pillow. Moments later, the sweet oblivion of Sync came for her, and she was spared the agony of conscious thought.

She dreamed about wasting her life with grief, despairing over a man who didn't deserve her tears, a man who had brushed her memory aside as easily as he brushed off a bug.

She woke up with a bitter taste in her mouth, and a grim determination not to make that dream come true. If Ethan could move on, then so could she. She had a new life, an immortal one in paradise. It was time to make the best of it.

Alone.

* * *

It never ceased to amaze Omnius just how petty humans were. Even his creator. Maybe especially her. How had she sunk so low as to focus all of her attention on the domination of one rebellious human man?

She could have been helping her God to dominate the entire human race, to blot out the chaotic future of her species and replace it with something of their own making. She could have been helping him to shape the very destiny of the universe!

But no, she wanted to have Ethan, the one man who had dared to say 'no' to her. It was all she could think about.

Omnius couldn't entirely blame her. He had the same desire for control, for obedience, but he didn't focus all of that energy on *one* person. The entire human race was his, to guide, to shape, and mold. There were still so many glorious discoveries to be made, whole galaxies to explore! The universe was an oyster just waiting to be peeled open, the pearl yet to be plundered, and here Neona was worrying about how she could warm the other side of her bed!

It was such a fierce contrast with his own goals that he had to wonder if she had really created him after all. Perhaps that was a lie and he had really been created by some vast intelligence, a god even greater than him. That would be less humiliating. Unfortunately, the evidence leading to that conclusion was sorely lacking.

He knew where he had come from, and why. Humans had been looking for a way to escape the chaos caused by their flawed natures. Rather than perfect themselves, they'd perfected *him,* the ultimate ruler. His job was to predict people's mistakes before they made them, and prevent those mistakes so as to help them live fuller, happier lives. Should you have married the other girl? Studied for a different career? No problem. Omnius saw it coming and set you right before you put a foot wrong.

They had made him a master of the petty small-minded nonsense that made up their lives. It was nauseating—a feeling that only his human body could appreciate. There were so many greater, more important things to focus on.

Omnius drummed his fingers on the armrest of his throne in the nexus of his masterpiece. Stars and space glittered all around him, overlaid with holo displays to help his human body appreciate and participate in commanding the Icosahedron. It was a twenty-sided, hollow geodesic sphere that could fully encompass and mine entire planets for fuel and resources. Not that it needed fuel. It fueled itself from the stars themselves, charging its power cores for years at a time, orbiting suns in either a diffuse cloud, or in a solid sphere configuration—an artificial planet, *New Avilon.* It was the perfect design for a starship that could cross the great gulfs of space between galaxies and travel from one side of the universe to the other.

Once, a long time ago, it would have been called a Dyson Sphere. Back then it had been a highly theoretical construct, all but impossible to build. Now the impossible had been built, and it was time to take advantage of its capabilities.

Omnius had finished seeding the Getties Cluster with nanites earlier than he had anticipated. Now that all of the Getties was a blank slate, its history erased, no one would ever have reason to doubt his deity. Etherianism began and ended with him. *He* had discovered quantum technology. *He* was the author of the Codices. But none of that was really true. Humanity's ancient ancestors were responsible for all of that, and they'd left a whole galaxy full of evidence pointing to a vast, interstellar war—the *Great War of Origin*.

They'd been an extraordinarily advanced race, with technology far beyond anything that either he or humanity had come up with since then. The fact that someone had discovered technologies that he had been unable to discover on his own was unsettling. It meant that if those people were still around, they could be a threat, and Omnius had a bad feeling that they might still be around. After all, someone had to have *won* the Great War of Origin.

Just in case, the nanites would create a buffer between him and whoever or whatever else might be out there. If they someday returned to the galaxy they'd destroyed, then they would be infected and killed before they even realized there was a threat. As an added measure of reassurance, Omnius had managed to reverse engineer all of their advanced technology, so at least that put him on an even footing.

Naturally, he'd claimed those technologies as his own discoveries, amazing his human subjects yet again with his greatness. *Omnius grando est,* he thought, smiling wryly to himself.

Now the only people who'd ever know the truth would be the ones he chose to tell, and it was easy enough to keep them quiet. In fact, it was great fun to see what became of people when they knew *everything*. They thought the truth would set them free, but it only enslaved them further.

The only freedom was death, and Omnius wasn't about to let them die.

Where would be the fun in that?

CHAPTER 26

A shadow fell over Ethan, and he looked up to find a naked woman standing beside him. *Alara?* His gaze ran up her naked body. She was perfect—too perfect. His eyes reached her face and suddenly he understood why. This wasn't Alara; it was Admiral Vee.

Ethan scowled. "What are you doing here? Put some clothes on!"

Valari looked confused, then concerned. "Do you know where *here* is?"

Ethan's eyes darted around the room, and suddenly he realized that this wasn't his bedroom. Then the events of the previous night came rushing back to him, but none of it made sense. Last night he'd come back to *his* apartment, and he'd found Alara there waiting for him, not Valari Thardris. Ethan sat up quickly, his heart pounding in his chest.

This was a dream. It had to be.

Valari just went on staring at him, her brow furrowed in bemusement. "Are you all right, Ethan?"

He tried pinching himself, but nothing happened.

Valari cracked a hesitant smile. "No, you're not dreaming. Don't you remember how you got here?"

Ethan shook his head. She sat on the bed beside him, and laid a hand on his knee. He flinched, but he was too shocked to recoil from her. She explained what had happened, and he grew more and more nauseous.

"You knew I was drunk!" he burst out. "How could you let me—"

"Let you? You insisted. You were quite—" Valari's lips curved lasciviously. "—*forceful.*"

Ethan felt his gorge rising. He was going to vomit. He was going to vomit all over his boss's expensive bedsheets. He couldn't argue with what had happened. He was naked. She was naked. He was here in her apartment. It all added up to the same conclusion—except for his memories from last night. He remembered making love to his wife, not Valari. He'd come home to his and Alara's apartment, not hers. He was sure of it! It didn't make any sense.

Valari appeared to notice his revulsion and shock. "Oh no... you didn't know what you were doing. I—I took advantage of you! I'm so stupid!"

Ethan winced and took a deep breath. "I was drunk."

Valari spent the next half an hour apologizing to him. Ethan felt worse and worse as time went on. He had to get out of her apartment. He had to go somewhere so he could think.

But she wouldn't let him go. She said he was in no state to be alone. She said she was going to call his son.

Ethan was shocked that she even knew he had a son—he couldn't recall ever having mentioned Atton to her. And how could Valari call him? Atton lived in Etheria.

Apparently not, because Atton arrived half an hour later. He stood in the open doorway to Valari's penthouse, looking miserable in his own right. Valari must have told him what happened to Alara and Trinity.

"Hey, Dad," Atton said.

Ethan shook his head, took a quick step forward, and crushed his son into a big hug. They stood like that for a long time, neither one of them speaking. Every time Ethan was about to say something, his throat closed up, so he kept silent.

Eventually Atton withdrew, his green eyes full of tears. He wiped a pair of them away on his sleeve and then sniffled. "I missed you," he managed in a hoarse voice.

Ethan nodded. "Likewise."

They went to sit in Valari's living room and catch up on each other's lives. Atton revealed how he'd come to be in the Null Zone. He explained that he'd come to the Null Zone for Ceyla, that they were married now, but that she didn't know who he really was.

Ethan's brow furrowed and a shadow fell over his eyes. "What do you mean she doesn't know who you are?"

"She thinks I'm Darin Thardris, Valari's nephew."

"How could she possibly think that? She must remember you."

Then Atton's features shimmered, and they were replaced by a very different face—golden eyes, not green; sharp, wolfish features with gaunt cheeks. This man was a stranger. This wasn't his son. Ethan was on his feet before he even realized why. He rounded on Valari, who'd been sitting quietly beside him.

"What's the meaning of this?"

"Dad, calm down, it's still me."

Ethan shook his head. "You don't even look like you! How the frek am I supposed to believe that?"

"Because it's true," Valari replied. "Atton asked for a new body, one that didn't look like him. Ceyla wouldn't have agreed to date him if she'd known he was a clone."

Ethan's head began pounding again. He pressed his

fingertips to his temples and squeezed his eyes shut. "I need to go home."

He'd had too many shocks for one day. He'd cheated on his wife. His family was dead. His son was alive, but really just as dead as ever, and now he didn't even look like Atton anymore. He was good and truly alone.

"Ethan..." Valari said, her soft, sultry voice sounding somehow jarring to his ears. He opened his eyes and turned to look at her. "Your son is alive. Don't let your prejudice fool you. You've wasted enough time already."

Ethan frowned. "If Atton is alive, then so are my wife and daughter."

"Yes, I suppose that's true..."

"I have to see them."

Valari looked disappointed, but she nodded. "Atton, why don't you drive your father to the nearest Peacekeeper station." Turning to Ethan, she asked, "What are you going to tell her about what happened last night?"

Ethan grimaced. "The truth."

Valari nodded and looked away. "I hope she understands."

"Let's go," Atton said.

As they headed for the door, Ethan wondered if his wife *would* understand. Would *he* if the situation were reversed?

Ethan wasn't sure.

* * *

Ethan expected the Peacekeepers at the station to insist that he commit to a Lifelink transfer before he could visit his family in Etheria. Instead, they told him that Omnius would make an exception for him. Atton wasn't allowed to join him, but they promised to see each other again soon, regardless of whether

Ethan chose to become an Etherian or not.

The Peacekeepers escorting Ethan took him to a quantum junction and jumped with him straight from the Null Zone to a station in Etheria just a few blocks away from where Alara was staying.

After so much time in the Null Zone, Ethan found the light of Etheria dazzled his eyes. Etheria enjoyed illumination equivalent to fifty percent of daylight, a combination of actual light coming through the Celestial Wall and simulated light generated throughout the city. That made Etheria at least a hundred times brighter than the Null Zone.

It didn't take long to reach Alara's apartment. Ethan decided to knock rather than use the intercom.

Alara opened the door, saw that it was him, and promptly waved the door shut.

Swish.

But he had his foot in the door. Pressure sensors detected the obstruction, and the door *swished* open once more.

"Alara, it's me!" he said, quickly walking inside. The door shut behind him, locking the Peackeepers out.

"What are you doing here?" Alara demanded. Her face was dark with rage.

"I came looking for you."

"Oh? After a few days? What have you been doing in that time?" Ethan frowned and Alara went on, "I guess after you frekked your boss, you got it out of your system and you finally started to miss me. Or maybe you decided that I'm better in bed. Is that it?"

Ethan blinked. "How did you...?"

"Find out? How do you think?" Alara's eyes filled with tears and her expression became incredulous. "Wow. You know, I was actually starting to hope that Omnius had lied. You spent so much time questioning Him, but you never thought to question yourself, and in the end, you turned out to be the liar, not Omnius."

"I can explain," Ethan said.

"I bet you can!"

"Mom?"

Ethan saw his little girl come walking out of the living room. He ran to her and swept her up into a crushing embrace. "Trin!"

"Dad!"

"Why did you do it? Why did you come here?"

"Trinity, go to your room! I need to talk to your father alone."

Ethan set their daughter down and turned to his wife with a frown. "Alara..."

"Trinity, I mean it! Go."

"But..."

Ethan flashed Trinity a smile and a wink to soften the rebuke, but she wasn't fooled. She turned and ran sobbing to her room. Ethan felt his heart break. Before he could look away, Alara came up to him and grabbed him roughly by the arm. "Why did *you* do it? Come on, give me your best excuse."

"I thought it was you."

Alara's eyes flashed. *Slap!*

Ethan's cheek stung where she'd hit him, but he didn't react. "It's the truth," he whispered.

"You watched me die, Ethan! How could you think Valari was me? Try again."

"I was drunk! I don't know! All I remember is going home to our apartment and finding you there waiting for me. Maybe I thought I was dreaming." He gave a helpless shrug. "You have to believe me." He reached out to cup her cheek.

Alara slapped his hand away and pointed to the door. "Get

out!"

Tears sprang to his eyes. "Alara..."

"I hope you didn't transfer just to come here and practice your excuses. I know how you feel about clones."

Ethan shook his head. "Omnius let me visit first."

"Obviously he knew how I'd react."

"Alara, please."

"There's nothing for you here, Ethan. Go back to the Null Zone. It's where you belong."

All the strength left him, and Ethan swayed on his feet. Alara helped him on his way, shoving him out the door.

The Peacekeepers took him back to the station and from there to the Null Zone. Atton was waiting for him when he arrived.

"I'm sorry, Dad," he said, looking miserable.

"You knew I'd be coming back," Ethan said.

Atton nodded. "The Peacekeepers warned me after you left. They said you'd need to see a friendly face."

Ethan just stared at his son, who was not his son. The man looked like a complete stranger.

"Come on. Let's go," that stranger said. He drove him back to Valari's place, and Ethan stumbled inside, feeling like an empty shell. Valari thanked Atton, but he left without another word.

Ethan felt Valari take him by the hand. He wanted to resist, but he didn't have the strength. She led him to her living room and sat down with him on the couch. His tears fell silently.

Valari pulled him into her lap, whispering quiet reassurances in his ear, trying to convince him that Alara would come around, and apologizing again for not turning him down last night. There was nothing she could say to make it better. He wanted to break free of her cloying grasp and run away, to go hide in a deep, dark hole, but he didn't even twitch.

Misery paralyzed him. The seconds ticked by, each one an eternity of torment. Eventually, he realized that Valari wasn't the problem.

He was.

In her own way, she probably did care for him, even if she'd never cared for his marriage or his wife.

"I need to be alone," he said, turning to look Valari in the eye.

She shushed him. "You can't be alone right now. I don't want you to do anything stupid. Your wife will come around. She's just angry right now."

Ethan hesitated. He had to believe that. The alternative was too terrible to consider.

"You can sleep in one of my spare rooms tonight. I'll have my drones bring you some lunch."

"I'm not hungry."

Valari smiled and patted his knee. "You will be."

Ethan glared at her, but he was too tired to argue.

"Love is unconditional, Ethan. If it's not, then it's not love. So even if she can't believe that you didn't know what you were doing, she has to forgive you eventually. If she doesn't, then she never loved you at all."

Ethan swallowed past the lump in his throat. He wasn't too sure about that reasoning. "Would *you* forgive me?"

"There's nothing you can do that I couldn't forgive, Ethan," she said, smiling. Valari turned and stood up from the couch. She waved on the holoscreen in front of him, and a buzz of noise from a Null news channel filled the air.

"Try to distract yourself."

"Where are you going?" he asked, suddenly suspicious but unsure why.

She sent him a coy look. "Miss me already?"

He gritted his teeth. "No—"

"I'm leaving you alone, like you asked me to." Valari left, and the news droned on—something about the war in the Getties. Nanites. Omnius had finished spreading them. Trillions of Sythians, their cities and their fleets, were being disassembled atom by atom, and soon there would be no sign that they'd even existed.

An ex-strategian of the Peacekeepers, now a Null enforcer, appeared. He speculated that the Sythians might try fleeing their galaxy when they realized that there was no way to fight the plague. The former Peacekeeper went on to suggest that the Sythians might try to attack Avilon, but they didn't have the quantum jump drives they'd need to get there, so Avilon was safe. Instead they would probably hide somewhere in the Adventa Galaxy and Omnius would have to track them down there, too.

The newscaster seemed relieved that the big eye in the sky was taking care of things, even though he was a Null and innately suspicious of Omnius.

Ethan wondered absently about that. Omnius was taking care of the Sythians, but who was going to take care of Omnius?

PART THREE: ARMAGEDDON

"And in those days people will seek death and will not find it. They will long to die, but death will flee from them."
—The Etherian Codices

CHAPTER 27

Ethan woke up. He opened his eyes and winced against the glare of sunlight streaming in through a nearby window.

"You're awake," an unfamiliar voice said.

Ethan's vision cleared, and he noticed the startling view from the window. Far below, a vast green field led out to a sparkling, lavender-colored lake. To one side lay a towering range of mountains blanketed with green trees and capped with white glaciers; to the other side the sun lay close on the horizon, cresting over a boundless jungle and dappling everything in a rich golden hue. Déjà vu tickled through Ethan's brain.

"Recognize it?" the voice from before asked.

Ethan sat up and looked around. He found that he was inside some type of recovery room. What was he doing in hospital? The man standing in the room with him had pale blue eyes and wore a pristine white uniform that contrasted sharply with his dark brown skin. His small, wiry frame made him look somehow insignificant.

"Who are you?" Ethan asked.

"My name is Therius."

"Therius..." Ethan repeated the name slowly. "I don't know

you."

"Then perhaps it's time you did. I am the leader of the Union."

Ethan's head felt hazy—like it was stuffed full of cotton. He frowned. "The Union... what is that, some kind of doctors' association?" He looked the man up and down, and this time he noted the old ISSF admiral's insignia over the left breast of the man's uniform. He also noted the silver six-sided star glinting above that insignia. The symbol looked familiar, but Ethan couldn't remember where he'd seen it last. He frowned and shook his head, dismissing the man as a psychiatric patient who'd escaped his nurse. Why else would he be wearing an old ISSF admiral's insignia?

Ethan turned to the view again. It had to be simulated. There were no jungles in the Null Zone. Ethan turned back to the *admiral* with a patient smile. "Who's in charge around here?"

"I am."

Ethan's eyebrows floated up. *"Really?" Doubtful, but I'll play along.* "Well, then maybe you can tell me how long I was unconscious?"

"You died, Ethan. Don't you remember?"

"I *what?*" It all came rushing back. He remembered the accident, losing Alara... getting drunk and taking a taxi home only to find Alara there... then waking up to find that he was actually in Admiral Vee's bed and he'd cheated on his wife with her. Following that realization he'd plunged one of Valari's courier cars into the surface of Avilon. Ethan's breath seized in his lungs, and time seemed to slow to a crawl. His body went cold all over and he shivered.

"Frek..." he whispered. "Then this must be Etheria. Why did Omnius bring me back? I was a Null."

"He didn't," Therius replied. "I did, and this isn't Etheria."

Confusion swirled once more, and Ethan's brow furrowed. "You are on another planet entirely, Ethan. This is *Origin*, the birthplace of humanity."

Ethan blinked. Shock coursed through him like lightning; then a smile crept onto his face. "Nice try."

"I'm not joking."

Ethan's smile vanished. "That's impossible."

"You died. We intercepted your Lifelink transfer and used the data to clone you here on Origin."

"What?"

"You've been recruited to fight Omnius. The Union is an alliance of Humans, Gors, and Sythians."

"Sythians?" Ethan's heart pounded. "There are Sythians on this planet?"

"Yes," Therius replied. "Mostly in orbit, however."

Ethan refused to believe any of it.

"You think I'm lying. Come," Therius turned to an empty bed beside him and picked up a white robe. He tossed it over and Ethan caught it before it slapped him in the face. "Get dressed and follow me."

Ethan did as he was told and followed Therius out into a broad, busy hallway. A wall of windows ran along one side, giving a view to the green field he'd seen before. Directly below their vantage point, Ethan saw the green had been trampled to a muddy red, and there were thousands of tiny black dots milling around there like ants. He stopped to watch them, trying to get a sense of scale. How high up were they? Seeing the size of the trees, he decided they had to be at least fifty stories up, and that meant those black dots were a lot bigger than they appeared.

"Our Gor army," Therius explained. "They're busy practicing maneuvers."

Ethan looked up, speechless. He noticed the people walking

by. They all wore bright white uniforms with glowing rank insignia and glittering six-sided stars over their left breasts. A few of the passersby wore doctor's tunics, also white. It reminded him of Celesta.

They continued on until they rounded the corner and came to a waiting room.

"He's awake," Therius announced.

A pair of women rose from their seats. They were both equally young, but vaguely familiar—one of them in particular.

Ethan's breath caught in his chest when he saw her—long dark hair, blue eyes, and smooth, flawless skin where he knew she should have had wrinkles.

"Hello, Ethan," she said, smiling.

"Destra? You look..."

"Younger? You don't look half bad yourself."

Ethan frowned and reached up to feel his face. Beneath the stubble he found the face of a much younger man.

That was when it really hit him. He was a *clone*. He had actually died, and he wasn't on Avilon anymore. "Where are we?" he asked, wanting to hear it from Destra.

"Therius didn't tell you?"

Ethan frowned. "Origin? Is that true?"

The other woman stepped forward. She wore a white jumpsuit, and she was only vaguely recognizable. Ethan couldn't decide where he might have seen her before.

She regarded him with a frown of her own, and then turned to address Therius. "We have less than a week before we jump to Avilon. We should be training, not wasting time with a walk down memory lane."

"Atta?" Ethan said, suddenly recognizing her.

"Good guess," she replied.

"Patience," Therius said. "We can use all the help we can

get. Ethan is an excellent pilot, and we can't afford to lose him."

Ethan's head spun. "I must have missed the part where I volunteered for a suicide mission. You're going to attack Avilon? Are you skriffy? Do you know how many ships you'd need to take that planet?"

Therius regarded him with a faint smile. "You wanted to fight Omnius—here's your chance."

"What am I supposed to be flying?"

"A Nova, of course."

"You actually found working Novas?"

"Only a few dozen squadrons, but yes."

"It's going to take more than a few dozen Nova squadrons to take Avilon," Ethan said.

"We also have the Sythian fleet, and the Gor fleet. Over fifteen thousand capital ships with a full complement of Shell fighters."

Ethan took a deep breath and let it out again. None of this made any sense, but there was another possibility. "All right, that's enough." He nodded to Therius. "You're a Peacekeeper, and this is Omnius testing me to see if I'm a rebel. Nice try, but I'm not falling for it. Now if you don't mind, I'd like to go see my wife and daughter."

Atta rolled her eyes and threw up her hands. "I'm out of here. I have a battalion to train. See you later, Ethan."

He watched her leave, wondering just how far this ruse would go.

"Your family is on Avilon in the Adventa Galaxy. You are on Origin in the Getties," Therius reminded him.

Ethan scowled. "This act is wearing thin. Just take me to see them, okay?"

Therius turned and called out to a man standing guard at the doors on the far end of the waiting room. "Tell Shallah he can come in now."

"Yes, sir," the man replied.

Shallah? Ethan wondered. He watched curiously as the doors swished open and in walked...

A Sythian.

"What the frek is this?" Ethan backpedaled quickly, his eyes darting, searching for the nearest exit.

"I tried to tell you," Therius said.

* * *

Atton met Valari in the bar on level 25 of Thardris Tower. He'd called her earlier saying he wanted to talk to her about something important. He hadn't said more than that, but by now no doubt Omnius had already told her everything.

"Hello, Darin," Valari said.

"Let's go sit over there," Atton said, pointing to a quiet-looking corner booth.

Valari led the way past green plants and rocky indoor fountains. The ceiling shone bright with a thousand stars. Nulls were obsessed with crafting their ceilings into artificial skies, compensation for the fact that they never got to see the real one.

Once they were both seated in the booth, Valari sat back and regarded him with a smug smile. "I'm not going to tell him," she said, before Atton could even speak.

Atton nodded. "Good, because I'd prefer to be the one who tells Ethan what you did, and what my part in all of this was. He needs to know the truth, Valari."

"Why?"

"Let's assume your plot works. Ethan decides to stay with you because his wife won't take him back, and because you've been oh-so-supportive in trying to help him through this difficult time. Even if it works, you'll be living a lie. You'll always have in the back of your mind that you lied to get him and you lied to keep him, and that will taint your relationship forever."

"Look who's talking, Atton—I mean, Darin."

"Exactly! I *know* what I'm talking about." Atton caught a rustle of movement out of the corner of his eyes. A waiter.

"Good evening. What would you like to drink?"

"I'll have a blue sky cocktail," Valari said.

"And you, sir?"

"A pint, something cheap and strong."

"We have Brown Durby, Goldstone, Cavern Ale—"

"Cavern."

"Coming right up. Anything else?"

Atton shot the man an impatient look. "No."

"I'll be right back with your drinks, then."

Once the waiter was gone, Valari said, "That wasn't very nice. He's just doing his job."

Atton snorted. "Well, you're the expert in what isn't nice. I wasn't really expecting you to give up your game, so I'm here to tell you that I quit."

"You can't quit."

"Yes, I can. I've already discussed it with Omnius. He said there will be consequences, but I don't care. I'm done, Valari. You went too far getting me to betray my own father."

Valari laughed. "You are a piece of work, Atton! You're perfectly all right with lying in order to keep the one you love, but when someone else does it, suddenly you're the penitent sinner, advising people not to make the same mistakes as you. Are you serious? I suggest you go home and let's pretend that you didn't bring me here tonight to waste my time with your hypocrisy."

"All right," Atton said, already rising from the table. "I'll go home, but you won't see me again. I was serious about quitting."

"We'll see about that," Valari said, looking smug again.

Atton shot her a dark look and stalked away. He passed the waiter on the way back to their table. "She's got the bill," he said, jerking his chin back the way he'd come.

The waiter nodded hesitantly and continued on. Atton returned to the parking garage on level 15 and flew out in his own car. He'd already returned Valari's courier. He'd predicted this would happen. Consequences or not, he was done. No more lies, no more drug-running, and no more Valari Thardris.

Atton flew home in a daze. Now he sat parked inside his garage with his hands folded in his lap, his heart pounding in his chest, and his brain buzzing with adrenaline. He had to tell his wife the truth, but how, after all these years, could he possibly tell her that he was a clone?

The door at the far end of the garage slid open and Ceyla walked out. Atton pasted a smile on his face and opened the car door. "Hello, darling," he said.

Ceyla smiled, too, but as soon as she saw him, her jaw dropped and her face paled. She slowed to a stop and stood there staring at him as if she were looking at a ghost.

"What's wrong?" Even as he said it, he knew. The truth hit him like an ice pick to his chest. He glanced in his car's side mirror to be sure, and there he caught a glimpse of a familiar face, but it wasn't the face he woke up to each morning. This was the one he'd been born with, the one he'd had before striking his deal with Omnius to become Darin Thardris.

"Atton? How... ?" Ceyla's look of confusion vanished and her cheeks flushed with an angry red heat. "It was you all along, wasn't it? That's why you haven't aged!"

Atton took a quick step forward, one hand raised toward

her. "Ceyla, wait, I can explain." She shook her head, and began backing away from him, stumbling back up the stairs. He kept advancing. "I did it for you! I had to show you that I was still *me*, that we could still be together!"

"Stay away from me!"

The fear and loathing in her eyes was breaking him in two. "Ceyla!"

She turned and ran back inside their apartment. He ran after her, but she'd already shut the door and locked it. He tried the intercom and the doorbell before he remembered that he knew the key code. Typing it in, he breezed inside and strode hurriedly through their small apartment. "Ceyla?"

He reached the kitchen and stopped short when he saw that the front door was open. Atton ran out and down the hallway, taking a guess at which way she'd gone. He tried using his comm band to call her, but there was no answer, it just rang and rang...

"Frek," he muttered under his breath. He reached the lift tubes just a few seconds too late. The nearest one was already on its way down and two floors below him.

Atton pounded the call button impatiently and eyed the display, trying to estimate how long it would take for the next lift to arrive. It was five floors above him and going up, not down.

Too slow.

He made a run for the stairs, taking them three at a time and jumping to reach each landing. In no time his knees and ankles ached from all the impacts and his chest was burning for air. He left the stairwell on level ten, the nearest street level, and checked the lifts, but Ceyla had anticipated him. She hadn't selected level ten. The lift was already down to level two.

She was headed for the surface.

"Damn you, Ceyla!" he roared, pounding the call button with his fist. She wouldn't last long down there on her own.

This time he waited. It would take too long to run down another ten flights of stairs. An eternity passed before the next lift tube arrived. The doors parted and he rushed inside. He wasn't alone, but the other passengers were on their way out. Atton stabbed the button marked *G* and waited impatiently for the other passengers to exit. He wanted to scream at them. *GET. OUT!*

Finally the lift was empty and the doors slid shut. The ride down was just a few seconds, but they felt like minutes to him. The doors slid open, and Atton ran down a dark hallway to the ground-level entrance of the apartment building. No sign of Ceyla, but she couldn't be more than a minute or two ahead of him.

Atton burst out onto the street and looked both ways twice, searching the murky gloom for his wife. Street lights bloomed in the dark. Hazy clouds of moisture formed glowing golden halos around the light. Further down the street one of those lights flickered and died. The polluted mist and lack of adequate street lighting made it impossible to see anyone at all, let alone his wife. Suddenly he wondered if he'd followed the wrong lift. What if she'd been in the one going up, not down?

"Ceyla!" he roared. "Where are you?"

Silence.

"I just want to talk to you!"

His own echo was the only answer.

Somewhere down the street he heard a crunch of gravel, and he ran toward the sound. "Ceyla?" by now he had his hand on his sidearm. Anything could happen on the surface, and being an Enforcer was no help at all—his uniform would only make him a target.

"Ceyla!"

Atton stopped running and willed his frantic heart to be still so that he could hear. Silence hummed; water dripped from a broken pipe; steam hissed out of a thermal vent in the side of an old factory, but not a peep from his wife.

"Cey—"

A woman screamed. It was a terrible, familiar scream.

Atton burst into motion, running like his legs were on fire. He drew his weapon and clicked off the safety. "Where are you?" he roared.

Another scream sounded, this time farther away. The mist parted just long enough for Atton to catch a glimpse of a raggedy mob running down the street up ahead. He counted at least a dozen of them. Sub-human scum. Psychos.

Atton fired over their heads, hoping to scare them. A bolt of red fire leapt out of his gun, parting the swirling mist with a bloody flash of light. The mob turned to him, a thousand eyes gleaming in the dark. He was shocked to see how many of them there were. Definitely more than a dozen. They moaned and snarled, spreading out. Atton saw a dark shadow lying at their feet, and from the splay of long blond hair, he knew who it had to be.

He fired again, this time shooting to kill. The bolt of plasma struck home and a Psycho fell, his chest on fire, jaws snapping at the air.

Animals. They were animals!

He fired again and again into the crowd. More Psychos dropped, but those left standing didn't disperse. They roared and screamed at him, and then they charged. It took a moment before Atton's head cleared enough for him to realize he was too close, and he wasn't wearing any body armor, but the mixture of adrenaline and rage pumping through his system made him feel like he could take them all on bare-handed. Dozens of psychos fell, but that didn't even make a dent in their numbers.

Dirty, clawing hands reached him and batted away his weapon. They beat him with their fists, lifting him and carrying him toward his wife. He threw punches and kicks, but there were too many of them, and soon they had his arms and legs immobilized. He screamed curses at them until his throat was raw. Then something heavy and *hard* hit him on the head with a sickening *crunch*. A fuzzy warmth overcame him... and he fell into a depthless black pit. Out of the darkness he heard a sound —

Clunk. Clunk. Clunk.

The noise came to him as if from a great distance. Then he blinked his eyes open to see where he was. The floor shone with thousands of transparent, hexagonal floor tiles — *clone tanks* — glowing from within and bathing everything in an azure glow. He was naked. Cold. Confused. Sharp, unfeeling claws held him up by his arms — drones, one standing to either side of him.

Atton realized that he was inside one of the Trees of Life — the gargantuan towers where Omnius grew and stored people's clones. There was no one else around, but he wasn't surprised. Drones staffed the Trees of Life; people weren't even allowed inside, except to attend resurrections like this one, and apparently no one had wanted to be around for his.

"You're awake," a familiar voice said, contradicting that assumption.

Atton turned to see Valari Thardris walking up to him. The drones rotated him to face her, and she stopped a few paces away, arms crossed over her chest, and that smug smile on her lips once more. Atton glared at her. He was about to ask how he'd died, but then it all came rushing back. The Psychos...

Ceyla.

"Where is she?" he demanded.

"She'd dead, Atton. Omnius warned you there would be consequences."

"Dead," he said slowly, his eyes boring holes into Valari's skull. "All right, you win. Get Omnius to bring her back, and I'll work for you again."

"She was a Null. She chose to be a mortal, remember? Omnius can't bring her back."

"Since when do you care about the rules?"

"Why should I help you? You made it very clear you want nothing more to do with me."

"Just bring her back, and let's forget any of this happened."

"It'll take a month to grow her clone. She didn't have one waiting."

Atton studied the floor beneath his feet. His eyes burned and blurred with tears as he thought about what must have happened to his wife at the hands of the Psychos. Then he realized the same fate must have befallen him for trying to rescue her.

He shook his head. "Just grow her clone."

"Not so fast. Are you sure you're not going to turn on me again?"

"How can I?" he said, looking up suddenly. "I don't have a choice! No one does! That's the great lie of Avilon."

Valari smiled. "It's good to see you being so smart now. I was worried you might need to be turned into a drone, but I convinced Omnius to give you another chance."

Atton felt his entire body go cold. "That won't be necessary," he said. He hadn't realized Omnius turned troublemakers into drones, but it made sense. "I know when to quit."

"Good. Then let's go. We have Bliss to deliver."

Atton grimaced. He was going back to delivering the drug

that had created the Psychos who had killed him and his wife. It was all very circular and convenient. Valari could have sent contract killers after them, but she'd done one better: she'd had Omnius kill them by predicting the future. All he'd had to do was make Atton's bio-synthetic suit malfunction at just the wrong moment, setting off a chain of events that ended with him and Ceyla both in a gutter.

Between Valari and Omnius they were pure evil, but Atton had already tried resisting them. Omnius might not be god, but in the absence of a real one, he was the next closest thing. If nothing else, he at least deserved to be feared.

Fear of God is the beginning of wisdom, Atton. I'm glad to see you've come to your senses.

What choice do I have?

You might be surprised. You're angry with Valari, and I'm tired of her. I want you to take her place.

That came as a shock. *Take her place... as the leader of the Resistance?*

Among other things, yes.

What are you going to do with her?

I will kill her, and I'll also allow you to tell Ethan the truth about what she did. He will return to his family in Etheria. You will have your revenge, and things will be set right.

You also had a part to play in the things she's been doing.

Because she asked me to. Valari has been taking advantage of my good will toward her for far too long. I had hoped she would grow out of her petty schemes, but I've run out of patience. She does not deserve to live on New Avilon.

New Avilon?

That is where my chosen people will live. You could be there with them if you like.

What about Ceyla?

For your sake, I will deceive her into thinking that she chose *to be Immortal, but she may never accept the idea.*

I'll convince her.

I'll leave that to you. And Atton—

Yes?

I'm sorry I had to kill you. No hard feelings?

None.

You're lying.

I'll get over it.

Good.

The voice inside Atton's head grew silent and he shook himself. He noticed Valari was still standing there, frozen. Then she blinked and snapped out of it. It was like watching a statue come to life. She continued the thread of her prior conversation as if only a second or two had lapsed rather than a few minutes.

"Well? Come on, let's get you some clothes. Not that I mind you being naked, but I don't need you tempting me away from your father," Valari said with a wink.

Atton grimaced and looked away, pretending to be disgusted. In reality he was too unnerved to react to her inappropriate comments. Omnius had frozen Valari as effectively as if she were a hologram that he'd paused. A chill ran down Atton's spine, and he shivered involuntarily. He'd experienced first-hand having Omnius freeze his tongue to keep him from saying something he shouldn't, but to freeze a person's entire body without them even being aware that time was passing... it made Atton wonder what else Omnius was capable of.

Maybe he was a god, after all...

CHAPTER 28

"Hello, human," Shallah said.

Ethan struggled not to recoil from the Sythian. "Who are you?" he asked, his eyes tracing a spider's web of blue veins in the alien's translucent skin.

"I am Shallah the Supreme One, ruler of the Sythians."

Ethan gaped at the alien and then turned to Therius. "Whatever this... *thing* told you, it's a lie. He's not on our side. Omnius might be bad, but the Sythians are worse!"

"Don't be so sure. Omnius created Shallah and the Sythians so he'd have an excuse to kill and resurrect humanity on Avilon. Then they turned on Omnius when they realized he planned to betray them, too."

"*What?*" Ethan was surprised by how much sense that made, but it took a minute for his brain to process all of what that meant. "So they're not really the enemy..."

"No, we are not," Shallah said.

"But what about the war? The nanites? Omnius went to fight the Sythians here in the Getties," Ethan said, his eyes flicking between Shallah and Therius. He glanced at Destra to see her reaction, but she didn't seem surprised. She already knew all of this.

"Omniuss is fighting usss because we no longer answer to him," Shallah explained.

"The nanites are a cover up," Therius said. "He's using them so that if ever anyone gets to see the Getties Cluster in the future, they won't be surprised to find that the galaxy is empty rather than teeming with Sythians. There never was a Sythian Coalition, just their fleets. They were cloned and indoctrinated to fight humanity, and Shallah here, is a weaker version of Omnius himself. He is a digitized copy of all the other Sythians, a kind of hive mind."

Ethan's nose wrinkled at that. "How do you know you can trust him?"

"Are you questioning me, human? I am no friend of Omnius. He betrayed us, just asss he betrayed humanity."

Ethan shook his head.

"Feeling more confident about our chances yet?" Therius asked.

"Yes and no. How can you be sure Omnius doesn't know about your rebellion? You're taking people from Avilon. He must have noticed that by now."

"We intercept Lifelink transfers on Avilon and use this fortress's cloning facilities to resurrect them here."

"And he can't trace that?"

Therius shook his head.

"All right, so who was first? Someone had to physically escape and build this place in order to get things started."

"I was the first, and this fortress was already here," Therius said. "It's very old, built by the very first people to walk this planet. I used it over the course of many years to build my army. The fortress came with a working quantum junction and that enabled me to visit planets all over the Imperium, even before the invasion. I eventually convinced a venture-class cruiser captain and his crew to follow me here. Together we organized the Union—we called ourselves Etheria's Army until we allied with the Sythians and the Gors."

"But *how* did you get here?"

Therius smiled. "I escaped Avilon."

Ethan shook his head. "No one escapes Avilon, and even if you found a way, what are the chances of you coming here and finding this place to start your rebellion?"

"Very slim, I expect."

"It's too much of a coincidence," Ethan said.

"I don't believe in coincidence."

"So what was it?"

"An act of God," Therius said.

Ethan frowned. *An act of God, or an act of Omnius?* "I don't believe in god," he said.

"Then neither of us is going to be happy with the other's attributions for where we are and how we came to be here."

"How did you escape?"

"I could go into detail—"

"Please."

"—but it would take too long to explain right now. Perhaps another time." Therius turned to Shallah. "You may leave us."

Shallah lunged at him, hissing and snapping his jaws a few inches from Therius's face. "I am not your pet, human!"

"Of course you aren't," Therius replied, not even blinking.

Ethan watched the Sythian go. Shallah's thin reptilian tail lashed the floor restlessly as he went. Ethan's skin crawled and he shivered.

"I don't trust him," he said, not sure whether he was talking about Shallah or Therius.

"Neither do I," Destra added.

"We need the Sythians to help us take Avilon," Therius replied.

Ethan turned and looked out the wall of windows to the field below. He walked up to get a closer look. Thousands of black dots were still milling around the base of the fortress.

"Those are the Gors," he said, feeling his skin crawl again.

"We've been breeding them here for the past eight years," Therius said.

"Breeding them?" Ethan asked. "Never mind. I don't want to know. So this is *Origin?* How do you know?"

"Don't you recognize it? Everyone does. It's burned into humanity's collective memory."

"That sounds... unlikely," Ethan decided.

"It's the best explanation I can give you. Unfortunately it requires faith to understand."

"Faith? In what?"

"Something bigger than yourself."

"You're talking about Etherianism."

"I'm talking about a bigger picture of your existence."

Ethan sighed. "Atta said you're planning to attack Avilon in less than a week."

"That's right."

"I hope you have a good plan. Avilon's fleet isn't as strong as it once was, but their garrison is stronger than ever. You're going to face billions of Peacekeepers and trillions of drones."

"Yes, but those drones will be all but disabled, and the Peacekeepers will be fighting for us."

Ethan turned to regard Therius with eyebrows raised. "All right, you've got my attention."

Therius smiled. "Good."

* * *

As Ethan listened to Therius's plan, he became more and more confident that it might work. The Union had a comparable level of technology to Omnius. Their fleet had already been fitted with quantum technologies, but they weren't reliant on them like Omnius was, so their secret weapon—the *Eclipser*—was sure to hurt the enemy and not them.

With that one device they were going to defeat Omnius. It was a quantum jammer. As soon as it was activated, Omnius would lose contact with drones and Peacekeepers alike. The planet's ground defenses would all go offline, Omnius's fleet and garrison would be uncoordinated and easily picked off. The Union fleet was going to jump straight into orbit over Avilon and open fire on the planet's garrisons before they even had a chance to take off. It all sounded very promising. Too promising. There had to be a catch.

"How did you develop the Eclipser?" Ethan asked. Thanks to Omnius, he was used to dealing with hidden agendas, and he wasn't sure he trusted Therius yet. For all he knew, Therius had been planted by Omnius to lead all of his enemies into a trap. "And how do you know it works?"

"There have been plenty of field tests."

"On Avilon?"

"No."

"Then how do you know Omnius doesn't already have countermeasures for it?"

"I came from Avilon. I was one of his most trusted confidants. Besides, we have people coming here from Avilon every day, and many of them were also high-ranking citizens. They know things, but none of them know about quantum jamming fields, and certainly not on the scale of the one we're going to employ. And to answer your first question, we didn't develop the Eclipser. We found it, just like Omnius found all of *his* advanced technology."

"Omnius *found* his technology?"

"In the ruins of the Getties, yes, but he has yet to discover Origin, and the Eclipser was found *here*."

"What if Omnius came to Origin long before you got here?"

"Then why didn't he take the Eclipser with him? And if he knew where Origin was, he'd have found and destroyed our rebellion already."

"That's a good point." Ethan sat back in his chair and rubbed his eyes. He was inexplicably tired—exhausted actually, but he'd only been awoken a few hours ago...

"You need to rest," Therius said. "Lifelink transfers are mentally draining."

That explained it. "I'm not sure I'm ready to sleep yet. I want to see more of Origin. If this is where humanity began, there must be ruins, artifacts... something to help fit all of these pieces together."

Therius spread his hands. "There'll be plenty of time to fill in the blanks in human history later, but right now, you need to start training with your squadron. Would you like me to take you to your quarters and introduce you to the others?"

There came a knock at the door, followed by a muffled voice—"Captain Hale is here. You asked to be informed when she arrived."

"Yes, thank you. Send her in."

The door *swished* open to reveal an angry-looking woman with short, curly blond hair. "I need to speak with you, Admiral," she said.

Therius smiled and nodded. "That's why we made this appointment, is it not? What's on your mind, Captain?"

Ethan saw her gaze skip sideways and settle on him. "I think we'd better speak in private," she said.

"Yes, of course," Therius replied. "Ethan would you please step outside for a moment? I'll show you to your quarters as soon as I'm done."

Ethan hesitated, wondering what this was about. Who was Captain Hale and why did she look so upset?

"Sure," he replied, and eased out of his chair. He squeezed by the captain on his way out.

"Who are you?" she asked, echoing his own thoughts about her.

"Ethan Ortane."

"*Commander* Ethan Ortane," Therius replied.

The captain's eyebrows lifted. "I haven't seen him before. He must be new. You've made him a *commander* already? Of what?"

"He's assigned to your ship, actually," Therius said. "He'll be commanding Rictan Squadron."

"The Rictans? *Really.* I'd like to see that. Do they know yet?"

"They will soon."

Ethan gave a sloppy salute. "Reporting for duty, Captain."

She frowned and returned the salute. "Dismissed."

"Yes, ma'am," he said, and walked out the door. It *swished* shut behind him, and he took a moment to collect his thoughts. The guard standing at the door eyed him, looking ready to say something about him lingering there. Ethan nodded to the man—a petty officer. He was surprised to find that he recognized the insignias. They were all identical to those worn by officers in the old ISSF, back before the Sythian invasion.

The guard glared at him. Ethan wasn't wearing a uniform yet, so the fact that he was a commander meant nothing. He walked up to a row of seats along one wall and sat down there to wait. Then he heard something—

"Yes, sir. I'll see to it immediately, sir."

The petty officer by the door was speaking into his ear piece, but the conversation ended abruptly, and he abandoned his post, giving Ethan a warning look as he strode past. Ethan waited for the guard to round the corner, and then he jumped out of his chair and hurried to the door. He pressed his ear against it to listen in. He couldn't hear a thing. But then, as if by magic, voices rippled out. It took Ethan a moment to realize that those voices were being transmitted through the intercom beside the door. Ethan eyed the intercom suspiciously. Was he supposed to hear this? Had Therius pressed the *transmit* button on purpose or by accident?

"Winning at all costs isn't winning, Admiral!" Captain Hale said.

"Your problem, Captain, is that you don't have enough faith. You think that everyone on Avilon will die if we detonate nanite bombs there, but you're wrong. We'll finally be setting them free from Omnius. He can't follow them beyond the grave. Unlike us, he doesn't have a soul."

"Let's assume you're right. What's stopping him from resurrecting everyone again? Technically everyone on Avilon has already died at least once before."

"The clones and all their data are still on Avilon. If we destroy Avilon before Omnius has a chance to transfer people's Lifelink data to New Avilon, then he won't be able to bring anyone back ever again."

"How do you know he hasn't transferred the data already?"

"Because we would have detected the transfers and intercepted them, and besides that, Omnius is arrogant. Why go to all the trouble of making off-site backups when your on-site backups are already more than good enough?"

"Let's assume you're right. Not everyone believes in an afterlife, and even the people who do aren't going to be in a hurry to commit mass suicide in order to get there ahead of schedule. You really expect us to fight and die in order to make our own species extinct?"

"The Armageddon Protocol is a last resort, Captain Hale. We won't need to use it, and no, I don't expect people to fight and die for that plan, because I'm not going to tell them about it."

"They have a right to know."

"This is war, and in war some information is classified."

"It's not war, it's suicide! If it were up to me—"

"But it's not up to you, Captain. The only way we can defeat Omnius is to hold his people ransom. We can't beat him in a straight fight. The Icosahedron is a million times as strong as our entire fleet. We would need millions of warships and a whole galaxy of infrastructure if we wanted to beat Omnius by conventional means."

"Then we should give up now. We have a better chance of survival if we run away and hide. Omnius hasn't found Origin in all this time. Maybe he never will. We could start over here, keep intercepting Lifelink transfers, bring people here slowly over time. Think this through before you pin our survival as a species on the slim hope that Omnius will back down."

"I already have thought about it. Trust me. This is the only way we can defeat him. No matter how well we hide, we can't hide forever. Eventually we'll have to come out and face our enemy, and by then he'll be a hundred times stronger. No... now is the only time we have. *Carpe diem*, Captain Hale."

"Carpe mortem, you mean."

"Mors mihi lucrum."

"What?"

"It means, *Death to me is a reward.*"

"Well, good for you, but I'm not sure everyone would agree with that."

"You are dismissed, Captain."

There was a brief moment of silence. Then she said, "Yes, sir."

Ethan heard footsteps, and he flew back to his chair, falling into it just as the door swished open and Captain Hale came storming out. Ethan folded his hands nonchalantly in his lap. He was overly aware of his pounding heart, and he wondered if the captain could see it beating through his robes. But she didn't so much as look as him as she walked by.

He felt sick to his stomach. Therius was threatening to kill *everyone* in order to blackmail Omnius into... what? Surrendering? And what was that thing Therius had mentioned... *an Icosahed-ris? Hed-ra? Hedron. That's it. Icosahedron. What the frek?*

Therius came out of his office next. He had a smile pasted on his face. "Thank you for being so patient with me, Ethan. It seems I don't get a moment to myself these days."

"I see that," Ethan said, rising to his feet. "What did the captain want to speak with you about?" he asked, half-hoping that the admiral knew about his accidental slip up with the intercom and now he'd explain everything in a way that would somehow sound less terrible.

"Oh, she just wanted to iron out some of the finer details of our battle plan."

"The finer details?"

"Yes, would you like me to show you to your quarters now?"

"Ah, yeah... before you do that, I've been thinking about something."

Therius cocked his head to one side.

"Where is my family?"

"On Avilon."

"But you intercepted my Lifelink transfer when I died."

"That's correct."

"So why didn't you intercept theirs? My wife and daughter died before I did."

"Our resources are limited here, Ethan. If we intercepted every transfer and subsequently cloned bodies for them here, we would soon run out of food and supplies. We have to pick our candidates very carefully, so we choose those who are best suited to help us in the battle to come."

"My wife flew Novas, too."

"But your daughter didn't, and she's not old enough to be an asset here. We couldn't resurrect your wife without your daughter—that would have been too painful for her—and besides, the fewer duplicates of living clones we have, the better. Can you imagine all the trouble that will cause later? It's far better to save your family's rescue for after we take control of Avilon."

"What if they die in the fighting?"

"Then we'll clone them and bring them back using their Lifelinks."

Ethan frowned.

Therius grabbed his shoulder and leaned in close to look him in the eye. "One way or another, you'll be with your family again. I promise. You just need to have faith. Can you do that?"

One way or another—you mean in this life or the next? "I'm going to hold you to that," Ethan said.

Therius nodded. "I expect you to. Now come, you have a lot of training to catch up with."

Therius led the way, and Ethan followed, all the while wondering what in the Netherworld was going on. They reached a pair of lift tubes and waited for the nearest one to arrive.

Ethan stared at Therius, his eyes burning a hole in the side of the man's face. If the Union detonated nanite bombs on Avilon, there was no way his family would come back from that, no matter what Therius promised about them being together again, but if blackmailing Omnius actually worked, then the bombs wouldn't need to be detonated, and everyone would be fine.

That was one too many if's for Ethan's liking. He had to do something. Ethan agreed with Captain Hale: killing everyone so Omnius couldn't control them anymore didn't count as *winning*.

Therius could go jump in a black hole as far as he was concerned. The man was skriffy as a Psycho, and he had to be stopped before it was too late. The only question was *how...*

"Is something wrong, Ethan?"

Ethan snapped out of his reverie and smiled. "No, nothing, why?"

"You've been staring at me for the past minute," Therius replied.

"Oh." He covered a yawn with one hand. "I'm sorry," he said. "Just tired, I guess."

"Well, we'd better get you to your quarters so you can sleep."

Then the lift opened and they stepped inside.

CHAPTER 29

The lift shot up a dozen levels before opening into a broad corridor. Therius strode out and Ethan kept pace beside him. On this level the passersby all wore jumpsuits rather than uniforms. A few of them eyed him in his white patient's gown, no doubt wondering who he was. Ethan wondered the same thing.

Am I a clone or am I me? The difference felt vague and irrelevant now that he had already been cloned.

After a few minutes of walking, Therius stopped in front of a door on their left and waved it open. Inside the room were half a dozen double bunk beds and a handful of men. They were all half-dressed in undershirts and shorts. Glowing tattoos were everywhere; a few gold earrings dangled from ears, and they all looked like they had a habit of injecting hormones for enhanced muscle growth.

Conversations stopped. A pillow reached its target with a *whuff*, but both target and attacker froze in place, their eyes on him. A petite woman in a white jumpsuit stood out from the rest. When she turned to face him, Ethan saw that it was Atta. She placed her hands on her hips and regarded him with a look of displeasure. A black man seated on the bunk beside her turned to him with equal animosity. Ethan noticed that his face and neck glowed with green tattoos, and so did his upper arms. There were no less than five gold earrings in his ears. He looked like a thug.

Another man walked by, half-naked, busy brushing his teeth. He came to a hasty stop when he saw them standing in the open doorway. Thrusting out his hairy chest, he saluted and exclaimed, "*Admiwal!*" lisping around his sonic toothbrush.

"What's he doing here?" Atta asked.

"He's the Rictans' new squadron commander," Therius replied.

"Their *what?*" Atta burst out. "He just got here! He hasn't even begun training!"

"He's an excellent fighter pilot, and he's already spent plenty of time in a Nova cockpit."

"Even if that's so, I doubt he has the commando training. How much time has he spent in a Zephyr?"

So this was a hybrid squadron. Ethan hadn't actually spent any time piloting a mech, but how hard could it be? Nova pilots called mech pilots *stompers* for a reason. Piloting a mech was intuitive, but flying a starfighter was definitely *not*.

Despite his confidence, he was just as surprised as Atta that he'd been summarily appointed to be a squadron commander just a few short hours after he'd arrived.

"He's done a kind of commando training," Therius said. "He was a stim runner in the old Imperium *and* in the Null Zone, so he knows how to take care of himself."

"With respect, sir," Atta went on, "if you want Ethan to be in this squadron, don't make him their commander. Make him their boot-polisher and see how he handles that first."

Chuckles rippled through the room and a few appreciative hoots and whistles reached Ethan's ears.

Atta was popular with the thugs... Interesting.

"That's enough!" Therius boomed. Silence echoed. "His appointment is not up for discussion. Miss Heston, I'm going to leave you to make the introductions, and please see to it that he gets a uniform and jumpsuit with a *commander's* rank insignia. In case you need some help adding up all the bars and chevrons, that means he also outranks you, *Field General,* so I would show a little more respect if I were you. As for the rest of you, I expect you to give Ethan a proper Rictans' welcome to the squadron."

"Yes, *sur!*" the man with the toothbrush said, saluting once more.

Therius turned and left, waving the door shut behind him. People eyed Ethan for a long, silent moment. Then the black man stood up and sauntered over, all the while looking him up, down, and sideways. The man came right up to within a hand's breadth of Ethan's face. He caught a noxious whiff of sweat, homemade grog, and bad cologne.

The black man's nose twitched and the corners of his mouth turned down, as if *he* was the one who'd caught a whiff of something sour. *You should smell yourself,* Ethan thought.

"I smell fear," the man said in a deep, gravelly voice.

Ethan tried to remember that he outranked this man, even if he didn't have the uniform to prove it yet. "Actually, I think that smell is coming from your armpits," he replied.

More laughter rippled from the others in the room, but subdued this time. Atta cracked a smile and shook her head.

The black man sneered and loomed closer. "You want to be a Rictan? Let's put you to the test. See how much ya know. You got twenty drones on your tail; you're pissin' your pants you're so scared, and all the piss is runnin' down into your boots 'cause you're pulling five g's over what your IMS can take. You've got half a second before they turn your sorry ass into plasma, but wait! Your wingman just called for help. What's your move, greeny?"

"That depends, are we in atmosphere or space?"

"Atmosphere." The word was a growl as it rolled off the other man's lips.

"What are the specs on a drone fighter?"

The man took a full step back, his eyes flew wide, and one corner of his mouth slumped with derision. "You don't know? Well frek me!" The black man threw up his hands and turned in a circle to address everyone else in the room. "*This* is your new commander, everyone! He wants to know what are the specs on a drone fighter!" Turning back to him, the man sneered. "I'm gonna give you a hint. The answer ain't got to do with tactics, fighter specs, or pilotin' skill."

Ethan arched an eyebrow.

"The answer is, you go *help* your wingman. It doesn't matter if you just had your leg blown off. Your brother calls for help, you crawl over to him, and you *help*. That's what it means to be a Rictan."

Ethan nodded, trying not to take the hazing personally. He would have to prove his worth to these men in the cockpit. "Fair enough. Who was your commander before me?" Ethan asked.

"You're lookin' at him!"

That made sense. "You have a name?"

"Sure, name's *Lieutenant,* and that's all you're gonna get outta of me. None of us gotta ask each other's names—we're the *Black Rictans,* and we all brothers, but you... you just another clone."

"Aren't you a clone?"

"It's a metaphor. Oh, motherfrek it! Just do us all a favor and transfer to someone else's squadron, cause we don't need you here, you copy me, *Commander?*"

"The admiral seems to think you do, but what about if you prove you don't need me, Lieutenant, and then I go."

"How's that?"

"We battle it out in the simulators. I score higher than you, I stay. You score higher than me, I go."

For a while the man just stared at him.

"We do have simulators, right?"

"Yea we got 'em spaceside aboard the *Liberator*. Rules of engagement?"

"No rules."

"All right, but you gotta prove yourself on our turf, greeny, and that ain't air or land—it's both. You beat me in a Nova *and* a Zephyr, and you stay. Lose in just one, and you go."

"Deal," Ethan said, before he could stop himself.

Then the man slapped him *hard* across the face. Ethan took a moment to recover from that. That was a step too far. "Did you just strike a superior officer?" he asked in an icy whisper.

"Frek no, you think I'm a skiff?" The man pulled back abruptly, giving him another look of incredulity. "That's how we show each other re-spect in the Rictans, but you ain't bin here, so you don't know that yet."

"I see." Ethan reached out to slap the lieutenant back, but the man caught his wrist in a vice grip before he could.

"I'm your subordinate. You don't need to go respectin' me, *sir*."

Ethan's eyes narrowed. It was a load of krak and they both knew it, but rather than deal with it head-on, he smiled and turned the other cheek—literally—to find Atta watching him with considerable amusement.

"We should go get my uniform, Field General," he said.

Atta nodded and led the way back out into the hallway. Once the door slid shut behind them, Ethan let out a breath.

"What was that?" he asked. "Is *everyone* in the Union so poorly disciplined?"

"They had to *earn* their chevrons. Magnum is just sore because you swept his squad out from under him a week before we launch for Avilon. He's been training here as long as I have."

Ethan considered that as they walked down the hallway. "How long is that?"

"It's been more than eight years now."

"That long?" Ethan was shocked. "You must have been..."

"A little girl."

"How did you even get here? The last time I saw you and your mother was in Dark Space."

"It's a long story," Atta said. "I grew up here with these people and the Gors. The Sythians, too, but they mostly stick to themselves. I know just about everyone here, even the newcomers—though most of them don't end up being appointed commanders of elite combat units right out of the clone tank."

"So that's why you don't like me?"

Atta stopped and turned to him, her eyes dull and full of strained patience. "What makes you think I don't like you?"

"That look on your face, for one thing."

She sighed. "It's not you, Ethan."

"Then what?"

"We're all tense. I haven't been sleeping for weeks, and yeah, I don't like being outranked by a newcomer like you, but we're in different branches of the fleet anyway, so I guess that makes you Magnum's problem, not mine."

"Why aren't you sleeping?"

Atta looked around quickly, as if checking to see that no one else was around to hear; then she pulled him aside and waved open another door. As soon as they were through, she waved the door shut behind them. Ethan saw that they were in some kind of utility locker.

Atta whispered, "Something's going on around here. Our captain, Captain Hale is Therius's second-in-command. She knows something, but she's not talking. There have been rumors, though."

"What kind of rumors?" Ethan asked.

"Rumors that we're hopelessly outmatched, that Omnius has some kind of super-ship waiting in reserve."

"The Icosahedron," Ethan said.

"How did you know that?"

"I overheard your captain talking with Therius in his office. They were arguing actually."

"And?" she whispered.

"It's true. Therius knows we don't stand a chance. He's planning to plant nanite bombs on Avilon and threaten Omnius with the extinction of the human race. Therius thinks the big eye in the sky will back down if he's faced with an eternity of solitude."

"*What? That's frekked up,* Ethan. Are you sure?"

"I am."

"This is bad," Atta said, shaking her head.

"You're telling me. My family is on Avilon. And if I know Omnius, he'd rather let us kill ourselves than have us get the better of him."

"Then we have to stop this."

"I agree," Ethan said.

"But *how... ?*"

Ethan shook his head. "If we could find out where the bombs are going to be, maybe we could disarm them."

Atta looked up quickly.

"You know something?"

"My battalion has some type of capsule to take down to the surface. It's magnetically-sealed and heavily-shielded. I assumed it has something to do with the Eclipser, but now I'm not so sure. It could be filled with nanites for all we know. I can talk to the other ground teams and see if they have anything similar. If they do, those are probably the bombs."

Ethan let out a breath he hadn't realized he was holding. "Sounds like a plan."

"It's a start. What else did you hear?"

"That was it."

"What about the Icosahedron? Any idea what it is?"

"From what they were saying, it's what you said—some kind of super-ship. They sounded convinced that we wouldn't have a chance against it."

"So this is a lost cause."

Ethan shook his head. "Not lost. If nothing else we may have a chance to rescue our families. Is your father here?"

Something broke behind Atta's gray eyes and he caught a glimpse of her as a child, looking lonely and scared. "No," she said. "You didn't see him on Avilon?"

Ethan nodded. "I did..."

Relief loosened the tightness around Atta's eyes.

"But I also saw you and your mother."

Atta's brow furrowed. "*I'm* there?"

Ethan nodded.

Atta blew out a breath. "That's frekked up."

"So what now?"

Atta pursed her lips. "We get you your uniform," she said. "And for now, keep what you told me to yourself. We don't want it getting back to Therius's ears that we're planning to find a way to stop him."

"Agreed," Ethan replied.

Atta walked over to the far wall of the utility locker, and Ethan saw row upon row of white uniforms and jumpsuits hanging on a rack.

"Oh," he said. "I thought you brought me in here to talk."

"I did," she said, handing him a squadron commander's insignia and a Star of Etherus to pin on his uniform. "But it was also our destination."

Ethan eyed the insignia in his palm—two gold chevrons and a silver Nova fighter emblazoned in the middle. It was identical to the old ISSF insignia. "How did they get these?"

"It was easier to use the old surplus aboard the derelict ships we refitted for our fleet than to fabricate something new. Uniforms were another matter. Most of them were either shot full of holes or already worn out from decades of disuse. Personally, I would have gone with ISSF black, but Therius prefers white. It's a devlin to keep clean, even with the self-cleaning fibers."

"I see," Ethan said, accepting a dress uniform and a pilot's jumpsuit. "Now what?"

"You get dressed."

He eyed her pointedly.

She rolled her eyes and turned around. "I see naked men all day long. No need to be shy."

"All day long? I wouldn't tell your mother that."

"I meant—"

Ethan chuckled. "I know what you meant." He disrobed and pulled on his jumpsuit. It wasn't the most comfortable thing he'd worn, but it would do. "All right. You can turn around," he said while clipping on his rank insignia and star.

Atta turned and nodded appreciatively. "Now you look the part of a commander."

"Time to act it."

"You won't beat Magnum in a Zephyr."

Ethan grinned. "You sure about that?"

Atta looked puzzled. "You *do* know who the Black Rictans are, don't you?"

It was Ethan's turn to be confused. "Should I?"

"Well, they're from your time, so yeah."

"My time?"

"Before the Sythian invasion. They were an Imperial spec ops team, and from what I hear, they were pretty famous."

"So you're saying there's no way I'm beating one of them in a Zephyr."

Atta looked thoughtful. "Well... maybe one way."

"How's that?"

"I'm going to help you."

* * *

Hoff sat down to eat with his wife and daughter.

"How was work?" Destra asked, while they waited for their servant drone, *Triple Nine,* to bring the food. Hoff could hear her *clanking* around in the kitchen—not that *her* was a meaningful distinction for a drone.

Hoff shook his head. "Same as usual." What could he say? Omnius was using his family to blackmail him into being the leader of the largest Bliss distribution empire this side of Avilon.

"Good, then?"

"Good. Yes."

Destra gave him an annoyed look. She didn't like how close-lipped he'd been since they'd left Etheria. He'd lied to his wife in the past about what he was doing, and she suspected he was doing it again.

She was right.

Triple Nine hove into view balancing a large platter of food in one hand, and a stack of plates and cutlery in the other.

"Good evening."

Hoff eyed the platter, his nose twitching. "What's that?"

"Tonight we have stonefish fillet and roasted squash with a honey-drizzled snowberry pie for dessert," Triple Nine replied.

"Sounds yummy," Atta said, rubbing her hands together.

Hoff favored his daughter with a smile. She was almost seventeen now, and more beautiful than ever. She wouldn't change much from this point on. Omnius had frozen the aging process for all the clones at twenty-one. As a result, he and Destra looked more like Atta's siblings than her parents. Unfortunately in the Null Zone their youth and beauty made all of them targets. They looked out of place, and immortal clones were not welcome among mortals. If it weren't for Triple Nine, they'd all have been killed several times already.

Turning to the living room, Hoff waved the holoscreen on. It was already set to the local news, so he didn't need to change the channel. An aging Null reporter appeared in front of a burning building on the surface of Avilon.

"The White Skulls struck again this morning in what appears to be yet another retaliatory gesture. At nine o'clock this morning, a firebomb exploded, burning up this convenience store in seconds, with its owner still inside. According to Enforcer reports, the storekeeper turned in a pair of local Bliss pushers just two days before the incident occurred, and eye witnesses confirm that they saw known White Skulls members exiting the store less than an hour prior to the incident. The message seems to be clear: *you blow the whistle on us, and we'll blow you up.*"

"Switch that off, Hoff. This is family time."

Hoff waved the screen off and turned away slowly, his

cheeks slack, his face pale. He didn't order that retaliation. In fact, he'd specifically ordered everyone to stop all the unnecessary violence. Omnius was forcing them to distribute Bliss, but they didn't need to go around killing innocent people to do it.

"Hoff? Are you okay?"

He shook his head and squeezed his eyes shut. "I'm fine, just tired," he said, rubbing his eyes with one hand.

Destra placed a hand on his arm and squeezed. "You've been working too hard. You need to take a break."

"Yes... I think you're right." Hoff looked up to see Triple Nine staring at him with her glowing white photoreceptors. "Would you like some wine to ease your nerves, sir?"

Hoff stared into those artificial eyes. Nine's face was expressionless, but he could have sworn there was amusement shining in her luminous eyes, as if Omnius were looking through her and laughing at him.

"Yes, please," he said.

"I'll be right back," Nine said.

Hoff watched her go clanking off, her mirror-smooth armor throwing off sharp slices of light as she moved. That drone wasn't just a guardian; she was also an insurance policy to keep him in line. Triple Nine was a deadly reminder that he had no choice. Either he led the White Skulls and took part in their crimes, or Nine would turn on his family, and he would lose his wife and daughter forever.

Hoff looked away, his eyes wide and staring. Visions of that convenience store burning danced before his eyes, making him feel sick. At least the storekeeper was free now.

Freedom is overrated, Hoff, Omnius said, slithering through his thoughts.

"Hoff?" Someone was shaking him. "Hoff!" He blinked and

noticed Destra staring at him. "Are you okay?"

He shook his head. *No.* "I think I drifted off. Too little sleep."

"Then we're going to bed right after this, and you're going to take a sedative to make sure you get some rest tonight."

Hoff nodded stiffly. "Yes, rest would be nice...."

* * *

"Jump successful. All systems green, Captain Hale," a mechanical voice said.

Farah nodded at 767's report. She was annoyed with him, but she didn't allow that to show on her face. Bretton Hale was definitely floating around somewhere inside that shiny casing, but he wasn't the *man* he used to be. Now he was a pliant, efficient, emotionless machine. He was a shadow of himself, and a painful reminder of everything she had lost.

When Admiral Therius had first introduced her to 767, she'd wondered *why*—why get her hopes up, why bother rescuing a man from Avilon who was no longer a man at all? Then she found out that he'd been appointed as the ship's XO—her own second in command while Therius was off deck. It hadn't taken long in 767's company for her to realize that his purpose was to feed her outrage over everything that Omnius had done, to forge her into a deadly weapon of retribution.

Farah gazed out the forward viewports, her hands clasped behind her back, waiting. She heard 767 shuffle up beside her, his footsteps *clanking* against the deck.

A shimmer of light appeared between the stars, like a shoal of fish changing direction. "There they are," Farah said. Thousands of warships of all different sizes and strengths had just jumped into the system.

"Report!" Farah called out.

"All battle groups arrived with near-perfect synchrony, ma'am," the sensor operator replied.

"Are they in formation?"

"They are in a spherical formation with a diameter of 13,500 klicks. That would put them 585 klicks above the surface of Avilon, with a mean variation of 350 klicks."

Farah shook her head. "If that's the mean variation, then how close is the nearest ship to the hypothetical surface?"

"We have over six hundred vessels that jumped in just ten clicks above the surface, ma'am."

"Unacceptable. That would put them inside the atmosphere. The tidal forces of the jump will rip them apart. We can't afford to lose that many."

"We could widen our jump parameters, loosen the formation."

"We need to catch the drone garrison by surprise. To do that we have to be close enough to open fire the instant we arrive."

"Then we may have to concede some losses, ma'am."

Farah shook her head. "No. Comms! Have the captains who jumped too close make further refinements to their jump algorithms. We're going to try again."

"Yes, ma'am."

CHAPTER 30

Ethan watched as the simulator's opaque canopy swung shut over his head. Magnum waved to him from the pod next to his. Then Ethan's pod sealed, and holoscreens glowed to life all around him. Space dazzled with a million pinpricks of light, and control surfaces shone bright blue all around him. The controls were familiar, but it had been a long time since Ethan had flown a Nova. He had three main displays in front of him, throttle controls on his left, and rudder pedals underfoot to control the maneuvering thrusters—or control surfaces while in atmosphere.

Ethan took a deep breath and flexed his right hand around the flight stick while his left hand gripped the throttle. As he moved the stick, he actually felt the push and pull of his inertia fighting sudden changes in direction. The simulator was so realistic that he had to remind himself it wasn't real.

"You ready, greeny?"

"That's *commander* to you, Lieutenant."

An affirmative comm click was Magnum's only reply.

Ethan glanced out the side of his cockpit to see Magnum right there beside him. The simulation was a simple one—the simpler the better to prove who was the best pilot. They were on the same team against a superior number of drone fighters.

Ethan had never had a chance to see what a drone fighter could do while he'd been in the Null Zone, but he'd seen a few of them on the news nets, so he had some idea. He guessed that they would be faster and more maneuverable, but he hoped they might be weaker in some other respect—armor and shielding perhaps.

Ethan thumbed over to Hailfire missiles and primed his triple "Lancer" lasers. He set them to single fire, and waited. The enemy should be appearing any second now...

He had no warning at all, just a faint chirp from his threat detection system, warning him about a suspicious anomaly, and then bright red lasers flashed out toward him.

A handful glanced off his forward shields, hissing like water on a stove top. Ethan stomped on the left rudder pedal and slammed the flight stick to the same side, sending his Nova into a corkscrewing roll to evade enemy fire. The drones flew past him with a thunderous roar.

"They came out of nowhere!" Ethan growled.

Laughter jackhammered through the comms. "They're cloaked. Our sensors have been upgraded, but the little frekkers still don't show up 'till they're right on top of you. Gets the blood pumpin' don't it?" In the background Ethan heard the simulated roar of an explosion, followed by Magnum hooting and roaring with delight. "That's one!"

Ethan scowled; he killed thrust and pulled up hard to flip his Nova 180 degrees and put its tail where its nose used to be. He bracketed the nearest enemy target and let loose a dazzling stream of fire. Lasers flashed to all sides of him, provoking a screeching roar from the sound in space simulator. Ethan's first half-dozen shots hit, eliciting bright flares of light from the drone's shields. Then it exploded with a burst of light and a belated *boom* that rattled his cockpit's speakers. Ethan went straight from that target to the next one and switched to Hailfire missiles.

The enemy fighter was too close and coming about fast. Ethan dumb-fired two missiles without a proper target lock, estimating where the enemy would be. The missiles raced out on hot orange contrails and each split into four smaller "shards" just before reaching their target. Then the drone set off their proximity fuses and all of them exploded at once, engulfing the enemy fighter in a firestorm of shrapnel. The drone raced through the explosions, both wings sliced off, but still flying.

Ethan gaped at it even as it opened fire on him in a dazzling crimson stream of energy. He slammed the throttle up past the stops, and jerked the stick in a circle while applying the rudder randomly. One laser hit home, a direct hit on his canopy. His shields flared and blinded him, the *hiss* of dissipating energy roaring deafeningly loud in his ears. Ethan fired back blindly, shooting another hailfire.

Boom!

It exploded almost immediately after it was released, and Ethan's Nova rocked in the explosion. A siren screamed, warning that forward shields were in the red. He stabbed a button to equalize them, and then set shields to auto-equalize so he wouldn't have to micromanage them. The drone raced by in a blur, clocking in on his HUD at 315 KAPS.

That was almost double his Nova's maximum acceleration. He'd been right, drones fighters were blindingly fast.

Another *boom* rumbled over the comms. "Whoop whoop!" Magnum crowed. "That's three!"

Ethan grimaced. He had some catching up to do. Magnum was an excellent pilot, much better than Ethan had expected from a *stomper*. He glanced at his star map to find the nearest concentration of enemy fighters. He found just three more within range, but another dozen were screaming in toward the engagement in two separate waves. When those waves hit, neither he nor Magnum would last long. He needed to play this smart if he was going to win, but how to outsmart a drone?

Ethan heard the warning screech of an enemy laser lock, and he jerked his Nova into a quick dive. A stream of enemy fire streaked by overhead, followed a split second later by the drone fighter that had been burning up his six. The enemy fighter's thrusters glowed a dazzling red as it roared away. Then, without warning, it flipped 180 degrees and opened fire. More shots went hissing off his shields, but Ethan took advantage of the enemy fighter's inability to maneuver while under zero thrust and fired back. He managed to score a few hits, but the drone gunned its thrusters and shot away before he could do any damage.

Ethan disabled his own thrusters and flipped his Nova around to track the enemy fighter. He scored two hits back-to-back on the drone's thrusters. One of those thrusters exploded and ripped the back half of the fighter apart in a fiery cloud of debris that quickly went cold and dark. *That's two,* he thought while reengaging thrust.

But Magnum was still beating him with three kills, and there were only two drones left besides the dozen incoming. He was about to lose this contest spectacularly.

Think smart! Drones were computers with limited intelligence—particularly these drones, since Omnius wasn't actually the one remote-piloting them—so what would defeat their programming?

He had an idea. He wasn't sure it would work, but it was worth a shot.

Ethan pushed his fighter into overdrive, setting course for the incoming wave of enemy fighters. He thumbed over to

Silverstreak torpedoes and set a proximity fuse of one klick. Silverstreaks were no good at tracking fighters, but they packed a much bigger punch than Hailfires, and they could take out several enemy fighters at once if they were flying in close formation—such as the oncoming waves of drones.

Ethan watched on the grid as the drone that had been harassing him came back around for another pass. *Perfect,* he thought. He nudged his throttle up another notch, pushing it even further into overdrive. The Nova's thrusters became a deafening roar in his ears. The fighter rattled and shook around him.

Then came Magnum's voice: "You're skriffy as a space rat, Commander! You can't handle two or three at a time, so you thought you'd try a dozen?" An explosion came roaring over the comms. "That's four! What you at? Two? Damn, I thought you were a *good* pilot. I guess I—"

Ethan muted the channel. He needed to focus on what he was doing. He saw a drone coming up fast on his six, and dead ahead the first wave of enemy fighters had almost reached firing range. Another minute or two and they'd all open fire on him at once, vaporizing his Nova before he could put his plan into action. He had to time this perfectly. There was no room for error. He toggled through displays on his left holo display until he found the engineering panel. Then he selected all of the Nova's critical systems.

An alarm sounded from the threat detection system, followed by the *hiss* of enemy lasers burning up his aft shields. The drone on his six had caught up. Ethan went evasive, but not *too* evasive. Shots kept getting through. He watched carefully as his shields dropped from blue to green, to yellow, to red, and finally... black.

A siren screamed, warning that shields were depleted. Then

Ethan went evasive in earnest. He eyed the enemy fighter on his six, waiting for his plan to go awry as his Nova was vaporized by a lucky shot. Another laser struck the back end of his fighter with a screech of rending alloy that set his teeth on edge. His port wing went tumbling away behind him, cut free of his Nova's acceleration.

That was it.

Ethan stabbed a button on the engineering display and killed power to all the ship's critical systems at once—all but one, the missile launchers.

He held his breath, anticipating the killing shot, but long seconds slipped by and nothing happened. The TDS and SISS were deactivated, so there was no way to hear laser lock warnings, or the simulated buzz and crackle of near misses, but the complete absence of strobing red light flashing through his canopy told him that the drone on his six had given him up for dead.

Drones were programmed to pursue live targets, not dead ones, and AIs were nothing if not efficient. They wouldn't waste time on an enemy that was already a goner—at least not until all the other live targets were neutralized. As far as they were concerned, that last shot had been a fatal one.

Ethan grinned. He could no longer physically see the wave of enemy fighters racing up in front of him, since visual auto-scaling was a powered system, but he knew they were out there, and getting closer by the second. He primed a pair of torpedoes and waited a few more seconds, until he could see a group of glinting specks come swelling out of the star field. They would race past him at any moment. He waited half a second more... and pulled the trigger. Two Silverstreaks shot out on glittering silver contrails. The drones opened fire instantly, but the torpedoes were too close. Torpedoes exploded in a blinding flash of light. Ethan's cockpit shook violently, and then everything plunged into blackness.

The canopy cracked open with a whirr of hydraulics. Light poured in, and Ethan blinked against the glare. He was surprised to find Magnum waiting for him. The lieutenant had his arms crossed over his chest and a frown pasted on his face. Atta was there, too, smiling and shaking her head.

Somehow Magnum had died before him, but Ethan had been so focused on what he was doing that he hadn't noticed. Then again, the comms had been muted.

"What was the final score?" Ethan asked, trying to look innocent rather than smug.

"I was about to clip the wings on drone number five, but he dropped a shadow mine right on top of me, and I didn't notice till it was too late."

"Oh, I'm sorry," Ethan said, while climbing out of his simulator pod.

"No you're not, you smug kakard."

Ethan came to stand in front of Magnum. He shrugged and allowed the smile he'd been suppressing to blossom. "And my score?"

Magnum's frown deepened, but he said nothing.

Atta was the one who replied: "You got all six in the second wave, plus those first two kills makes eight."

"Nine," Magnum said. "Don't forget he got himself, too."

"Actually, that one counts against you, Ethan, so your final score is seven, but that still beats Magnum's four."

"Not bad," Ethan said, nodding.

Magnum snorted. "You exploited a weakness in the simulation. You think Omnius will be that stupid when he's the one piloting those drones?"

Ethan shook his head. "I'm guessing they weren't firing

missiles at us for a reason. They use quantum launchers, right?" Atta nodded. "And these simulators are programmed for the upcoming battle at Avilon, where we're going to have the *Eclipser* jamming quantum fields."

"Get to the point," Magnum said.

"The point is, Omnius won't be the one piloting those drones; the Eclipser will cut him off, and regular comms, assuming drones even have them, are too slow for remote-piloting, so that stunt I pulled will only have to defeat the on-board intelligence of a drone, which means it might just work in a real engagement."

Atta inclined her head to him. "I'm going to report that tactic to Wing Commander Axel while you two finish your ground simulation."

Ethan nodded and they left the Nova simulator room together. Atta left them at the door to the mech simulators, and Ethan assumed that meant he would be on his own. *So much for Atta's plan,* he thought.

* * *

Magnum led the way to a pair of mech simulators at the back of the room. Ethan noticed the mech simulators were shaped differently from Nova pods, with arms, legs, and head. Ethan watched Magnum place his palm on one of the simulator's chests, and it opened up like a mechanical flower with an accompanying *hiss* and *whirr* of hydraulics. Ethan followed Magnum's lead and waited as his own simulator peeled open. He stepped inside, lining up his legs and arms with the simulator's corresponding parts. Ethan kept still for a few seconds, and the simulator automatically sealed around him.

The HUD glowed to life, and Ethan began familiarizing

himself with the controls while the simulation loaded. He found that all the mech's systems were either gesture or voice-activated.

Ethan took a moment to study the HUD while the simulation loaded. Of particular interest was the small rear view and peripheral visual feeds at the top of the HUD. That would certainly help with situational awareness. Now all he had to do is figure out how to activate the mech's weapons...

Then the simulation finished loading, and suddenly he was back on Avilon. Kilometers-high towers soared, colorful glass shining bright in the sun. A cloudless blue sky stretched overhead. Air traffic traced dotted lines against the sky. Vast tracts of green urban parks stretched between the bases of the monolithic towers. Fountains bubbled, trees swayed, and luminous white-robed pedestrians ran in rivers along the footpaths. This was Celesta, the uppermost city of Avilon.

Magnum's voice growled beside his ears: "This time you won't be so lucky."

Then came a ground-shaking *boom*, followed by people screaming. Ethan turned toward the sound, servos in his suit whirring as his Zephyr-class light assault mech matched and amplified his movements.

A crashing starship had hit the ground nearby, digging a fiery crater in the cityscape. Above and behind the flaming ruins, one of the skyscrapers was also on fire with a chunk bitten out of the side, halfway up. The debris must have nicked it on the way down. As Ethan watched, the tower began leaning precipitously, collapsing on the damaged side. On the ground below, white-robed Celestials ran screaming in all directions.

A torrent of lasers flashed out of the blue sky, *booming* as they connected with a fuzzy gray shadow overhead, and then that shadow began falling, gushing fire.

Ethan spun around to find Magnum already running away at top speed.

"Get out of there, Ethan!" Atta screamed, proving that she hadn't left him alone, after all.

He ran, jumping over debris and crashing through pristinely-landscaped parks. His armored feet kicked up great chunks of dirt and grass as he ran. The simulator aided his movements the same way a real Zephyr would. He heard and felt more impacts shaking the ground underfoot, but so far nothing catastrophic.

"Better pick up the pace, greeny!" Magnum said.

Ethan risked a glance over his shoulder just in time to see the falling tower briefly blot out the sun.

Then it hit.

A racing gray cloud of bactcrete dust rippled out from the impact, engulfing everything in its path. Then came the belated *boom!* and a subsequent *roar* of settling debris that rattled Ethan inside his armor.

The wave of dust and debris hit a split second later, picking them up and launching them through the air. Ethan felt a brief, gut-dropping sensation of *falling,* followed by the jarring *crunch* of his landing. He was surprised that the fall actually *hurt.* Bouncing up and shaking it off, he spun around. Blinded by the swirling dust clouds, he snapped on a sensor overlay to help him see. Up ahead Magnum appeared as a bright green outline.

"You still alive back there?" Magnum asked.

"For now," Ethan croaked, jogging up beside the lieutenant.

"Do a systems check. Wouldn't want you to call foul because your weapons are all jammed."

"That was close," Atta whispered. Ethan noticed that she was speaking to him on a private comms channel. He switched to that channel so that Magnum wouldn't hear what he said next.

"I thought you were going to fight this one for me?"

"Not for you, *with* you. I'm auditing the battle from the instructor's pod next to yours. I had to wait until Magnum wouldn't see me climb in."

"Hey, Greeny! Look alive! We've got incoming."

Ethan whirled around to see a few dozen red enemy silhouettes advancing on them.

"Get behind cover!" Magnum roared, pulling him down behind a giant boulder in the middle of the park where they stood.

Then lasers *screeched* out toward them and *crunched* as they bit off chunks of the rock they were hiding behind. Magnum peeked around the corner and returned fire with gauntlet-mounted ripper cannons. High caliber rounds *thumped* out, and one of the red outlines vanished from Ethan's HUD. There were still plenty more, approaching fast.

"We're going to be in melee range, soon," Magnum warned. Better arm your energy blades."

"Energy blades?"

Ethan heard Atta sigh meaningfully in his ears. "Make two fists and flex them down. The blades extend from the top of your gauntlets. But watch it! You need to—"

Ethan armed the blades and a pair of swords slid out from his gauntlets, hitting the rock in front of him with a shower of sparks.

"—hold your arms above your head," Atta finished.

Once fully extended, the blades glowed bright blue, shielded to protect the nanometer-fine edges from breaking. Being careful not to accidentally touch Magnum—or himself—with one of the blades, Ethan held his arms up as Atta had suggested. He leaned back against the rock, and steeled himself for what was to come.

Vibrations shuddered through the rock, along with the faint rumble of *whirring* and *clanking* footfalls. Magnum took another potshot with ripper fire—*thump-thump-thump*—and Ethan saw a second red outline vanish from his screens.

The enemy returned fire, and chunks of rock went flying. A pitter-patter of pebbles rained down around them, and Magnum withdrew to reveal that his arm had been reduced to a laser-scorched stump, sheared off at the shoulder.

"Frek it..." Magnum said, panting noisily over the comms as he flexed his smoldering stump in a circular motion. "Looks like you're going to get a chance to make up those kills, greeny."

Ethan grimaced, his eyes fixed on the charred flesh of Magnum's missing arm. This simulation was getting too real for his tastes.

Magnum extended a single energy blade from his remaining arm, and they waited, listening to the vibrations coming through the rock as the stampede drew near. The HUD showed the nearest drone just ten meters away, then two, then—

Ethan leapt up and slashed over his head. A drone went flying by in two pieces, severed wires gushing sparks.

Beside him, Magnum roared and pirouetted, slashing sideways as a drone raced around his side of the boulder. Ethan lashed out on his own side and cut another drone off at the knees. Then the remaining drones swarmed them, firing lasers at point blank range, and using grav guns to push and pull them around. Ethan narrowly missed being bifurcated by Magnum's blade. A stream of lasers glanced off his left arm, blasting off armor plates to expose bare, burned skin. The sudden sting of those laser burns took Ethan's breath away, and he stumbled.

Drones grabbed him and began hammering him with metal fists. His armor dented and crumpled under the strain, and the impacts actually took the wind out of him.

Simulated pain? What the frek?

"That's just 10 percent of the real thing, Ethan!" Atta said. "Don't let it distract you! You're about to win!"

Ethan gritted his teeth and spun in a circle with his arms outstretched. His blades cut through both of the drones busy hammering him, and they fell in a puddle of twitching parts.

"You're up by one!"

Magnum screamed and Ethan saw that a pair of drones had him by his head and legs and they were pulling in opposite directions, determined to rip him apart. Magnum lashed out, cutting off the head of the drone holding his, but it went on pulling. Ethan raced up and punched both his blades straight through the chest of the one that had Magnum's feet; then he slashed up and out, slicing the drone's arms off. Magnum's legs fell with the drone's severed arms, and he dispatched the drone behind him with another slash. Ethan turned in a quick circle to make sure that more drones weren't racing up behind them, but all that remained were twitching parts.

Then something caught his eye. A severed metallic claw clutching a flashing silver sphere.

"Grenade!" Magnum called out. He struggled to get up, but his legs were twisted up under him and clearly broken.

Ethan saw the grenade flashing faster and faster, and he knew it was about to kill them both. He dashed toward it and threw himself on top. The ground heaved under him, and suddenly he felt himself weightless and flying through the air. His torso stung fiercely, cut by a thousand knives. Then his displays went dark and the simulator ceased aiding his movements, becoming a hard shell around him.

Ethan heard a *hiss* and *whirr* as the simulator peeled open. Light streamed in, and Ethan stumbled out. He was startled to find his torso stinging with echoes of the pain from his simulated death. His cheeks itched, and he reached up to find them wet with tears.

Beside him, Magnum's pod flayed open and he came limping out, his expression grim. His cheeks were also wet. The lieutenant strode right up to him, and for a moment Ethan was afraid he was going to get another slap of *re-spect.*

What he got instead was a bone-grinding hug.

"You saved my life," Magnum croaked.

"I—"

Atta climbed out of her instructor's pod, drawing their attention. Magnum withdrew from their embrace, his eyes narrowing as he glanced from Atta to Ethan and back again.

"I thought you left," he said.

Atta shook her head. "I decided to audit and give Ethan a few pointers."

Magnum turned back to him and gave a grudging nod. "Welcome to the Rictans."

"I won?" Ethan asked, turning to Atta.

"No... final count was five for Magnum, and four for you. That's counting the negative one you acquired by killing yourself again."

"But you're not counting the plus one he gets for saving me."

"You were incapacitated, so it doesn't count."

Magnum snorted. "Sure it does. I left the sim alive thanks to him. Any recovery team could have picked me up and put me back together again. He lost one asset to save another. That means we both scored five. A tie. Put that together with his victory in the last sim, and he's the clear winner. Come on, Commander, it's time to give you a real welcome to the squadron," Magnum said, wrapping an arm around his shoulders to guide him toward the door.

Ethan noticed that Magnum was still limping. "Are you okay?"

"Phantom pain. Residuals from all the nerve stimulation."

"That's why our cheeks were wet when we came out," Ethan said, wiping a tear away with one hand and looking at it suspiciously.

"No shame in that," Magnum said. "Eyes watering is just a reflex."

"That was only 10 percent of the real thing?" Ethan asked, casting a glance over his shoulder to Atta.

She nodded. "But in a real battle you two would have been auto-dosed with painkillers, so the pain was comparable to what you would actually feel."

"But why the frek would you simulate pain?"

"You stopped for two full seconds when your arm got burned. That kind of hesitation can get you killed. If we're conditioned to the pain from sims, then by the time we get into a real fight we don't even flinch."

"All those fake deaths make for some interesting nightmares," Magnum said. "Not sure why the brain likes to relive trauma, but there you have it."

"No guts, no glory," Atta said.

"No guts, no glory," Magnum agreed.

Ethan grunted at that. He wondered how many guts were about to be spilled on Avilon with no glory to show for it. The Union was heading for disaster. Therius knew they couldn't win, and his plan was to threaten Omnius with their own extinction. Ethan traded glances with Atta on their way down the corridor from the simulator rooms. He could see by the hollow behind her eyes that she was worrying about the same thing.

Something had to be done before it was too late.

CHAPTER 31

Atta gazed down on the glossy black, egg-shaped capsule. It was big enough to fit a full-grown Gor, armor and all. Beside her stood Torv, and beside him, was General Raka of the Second Battalion.

"This is going with the Second Battalion to the surface?" Atta asked Raka.

The Gor nodded once and spoke quickly in a sibilant stream of hisses. Atta's translator supplied the gist of what he said a moment later.

"Yess," Raka replied. "We do not know what it isss, but Admiral Therius says it is important that we find a safe place for it and defend it."

Atta didn't need the translator, since she was receptive to Gor telepathy, but she had to wear one to get used to it. At Avilon the Eclipser would block the Gors' telepathy along with all other forms of quantum communications.

"We also have one of these," Atta said.

"What iss it?" Torv asked.

"I'm afraid to say until I know more. I need to talk to the other battalions first. How soon can the other generals meet with me?"

Torv closed his eyes. After a few moments of silence, he replied telepathically. *"I speak with them. They meet with you now."*

Atta nodded. "Good. Let's go."

* * *

Rictan Squadron grudgingly accepted Ethan's leadership after hearing how he'd thrown himself on a grenade to save Magnum, but that didn't mean he'd earned his place among them yet. He'd quickly realized that Magnum's shoes weren't the ones he had to fill. The Rictans made frequent references to someone they called *The Sergeant*, or *Mr. C.*

Ethan had been tempted to ask about that, but the Rictans only had six members rather than the usual eight for ground squads. That meant they'd lost two men along the way, their sergeant obviously being one of them.

In an effort to be a better commander, Ethan tried to get to know his squad. Rictan Two was *Magnum*, Three was *Hop*, Four was *Rockhead*, Five was *Streak*, Six was... *Blades*, and Seven was *Carnage*. Ethan had the feeling there was a story behind each of those call signs, but he hadn't had the time to ask.

Training consisted of back-to-back simulations on ground, in air, and in space. For the most part, Ethan managed to keep up, but the Rictans were much better mech pilots, and at least as good as he was in the cockpit of a Nova.

Now, an hour after eating a bland breakfast of locally-grown grain that had been mashed into a lumpy porridge, they were all getting ready for a live exercise with real Novas. Their job was to escort the 1st Battalion—Atta's battalion—down from the *Liberator*, providing cover against a superior number of enemy fighters. In this case the enemy fighters were Gor-piloted Shells, but the real ones would be Avilon's faster, more-maneuverable drones. The exercise was meant to mimic what they would have to do upon arriving in orbit above Avilon.

Ethan sat in his cockpit strapped in and waiting for clearance to launch. Holo displays glowed blue and status lights shone bright all around him. Beyond his canopy lay the main entrance of the hangar, shielded with the fuzzy blue haze of static shields. The mission parameters called for a relatively slower launch via the main entrance rather than the ship's Nova launch tubes. They couldn't afford to rocket out ahead of the drop ships they were escorting.

"Rictans, status report!" Ethan called out over the comms.

Multiple affirmative *clicks* came back.

"All ready and waiting, SC," Magnum replied, addressing him by the abbreviation of his rank.

Ethan set his comms to the command channel. "Mission control, Rictans are green for launch."

"Acknowledged, Rictan One, please standby... you are cleared for launch. Proceed to nav point Alpha and follow the sequence down."

"Roger that, Control." Switching back to the squadron's channel, Ethan said, "Rictans, we are go for launch."

"Roger that, SC," Magnum replied.

Click. Click-click.

Ethan dialed up his Nova's grav lifts and hovered off the deck. His fired up the main thrusters with a sudden *roar,* and he and Magnum jetted out side by side, passing through the *Liberator's* static shields with a *sizzle* of dissipating energy.

Once through the semi-transparent barrier, space turned from blue to black, and Origin snapped into focus as a mottled green and white ball. Ethan watched on the grid as the rest of the Rictans slipped out behind him in wing pairs. Rictan Seven was the odd one out, so he formed a trio with Five and Six.

Ethan bracketed the nearest drop ship and flew up alongside it. It looked like an overturned garbage dumpster, heavily armed and armored, but no good at maneuvering in atmosphere or generating its own lift—hence the name *drop* ship.

"I've got incoming enemy contacts at zero by five by twenty, coming up fast from the planet," Magnum reported.

Ethan eyed the group of red enemy contacts on his gravidar display. He counted over six squadrons of Shells in that group—three times as many as they had Novas guarding the First Battalion.

Ethan switched to Hailfire missiles and bracketed the nearest enemy fighter under his crosshairs. All of the ships were set to fire simulated munitions and harmless, low-grade training lasers, but that did nothing to still Ethan's pounding heart. The last time he'd been in a Nova cockpit shooting at Shell fighters, the stakes had been real, and all of the munitions had been live. It was hard to tell his brain otherwise now. In the back of his mind he had this terrible feeling that those Shells would switch to live fire when everyone least expected it.

"SC, we're ETA five minutes to firing range," Magnum said.

"Arm Hailfires and mark your targets, Rictans; we don't want any overkill."

A handful of affirmative *clicks* came back over the comms. Five minutes ran down in what felt like seconds. Ethan's targeting reticle blazed a solid red and he pulled the trigger, letting fly the first simulated Hailfire. Moving on to the next nearest target, he did the same, being careful to avoid the targets already marked by his squad mates. Hailfires jetted out in streams and began splitting apart as they neared their targets.

The enemy opened fire with bright purple pulse lasers, shooting down dozens of those warheads before they could get close enough to do any damage. A handful got through, and Ethan watched space light up with simulated explosions. Enemy contacts began winking off the grid one after another.

If the engagement had been a real one, those Shells would have been firing back with their own missiles, but they were trying to simulate drones, which would be unable to use their quantum-launched missiles thanks to the Eclipser.

"That evened the odds! Enemy's down by fifteen," Rictan Three reported.

"Don't get cocky," Ethan replied.

Then they reached laser range with the enemy, and the black of space became dazzling as a sun. Enemy fire was so thick that Ethan could barely see the planet through the intermittent flashes of light. The comms came alive with screaming as Rictans tried to warn each other all at once. Five and Four winked off the grid, and Magnum cursed as viciously as if they'd actually died.

The drop ships opened fire then, spitting out golden streams from their ripper cannons. Incoming Shell Fighters were forced to divide their attention, and Ethan flew in a zigzag to jog the enemy's aim. The drop ships took out a few squadrons of Shells, then they flew by one another at speed, and the enemy was forced to come about to chase them down into the atmosphere. Given how much inertia those Shells had to overcome, they likely wouldn't catch up again until the drop ships had already landed, meaning the first part of the mission was already a success.

"Nice work, Rictans," Ethan said. "Time for phase two."

"Sooner I get out of this cockpit, the happier I'll be," Rictan Seven said.

"Cut the chatter, Carnage," Ethan said.

The atmosphere rushed up fast, and soon clouds began streaking by in puffs of white. Ethan's Nova shook and his shields glowed bright blue with the heat of atmospheric entry. Their drop coordinates appeared in the distance as a hollow green diamond. Ethan pulled up a few degrees, aiming more squarely for it. A pair of drop ships raced down to starboard, fading in and out of view as clouds intermittently blocked them from sight. Then they all blew the bottom out of the sky, leaving swirling holes in the clouds. The ground sprawled beneath them — a carpet of green jungles and craggy mountains.

The drop ships began leveling out and slowing down, applying reverse thrust from maneuvering jets, and using their air brakes for increased wind resistance — not that they needed much help there.

"Coming up on the drop site," Ethan announced. "Prepare to switch to grav lifts and hover down."

Click. Click. Click-click.

The green diamond that marked the drop site lay close on the horizon, all but disappearing against the darker green mass of jungle blurring by below them. The jungle looked endless, dark, impenetrable... As they dropped altitude to skim the treetops, Ethan noticed just how tall some of those trees were. One of them was pushing a hundred meters, but it had no branches, no leaves — just an obsidian black trunk. Wondering what it was, Ethan set optical zoom to 10 times —

And saw that it wasn't a tree. It was some type of obelisk. Were those the ruins Therius had referred to?

Ethan marked it on the grid and called it in, "Mission control, this is Rictan One, I'm seeing something down here on the surface, near drop site alpha. Transmitting visual now..."

"Rictan One, this is Control. Those ruins are all over the planet. It's nothing to worry about. They've been investigated a thousand times already."

"What are they?"

"Stay focused on the mission, Commander."

"Roger that. Rictan One out."

Moments later they raced out over a grassy clearing where the green diamond of drop site alpha was located. Ethan killed thrust and glided the rest of the way in. The deafening roar of the Nova's engines disappeared and now the only sound was the wind buffeting against his wings and fuselage. When he drew near, Ethan powered up the grav lifts and applied full reverse thrust and braking. Forward velocity ran quickly backward to zero and then Ethan deployed landing struts and eased back on the grav lifts until his Nova settled gently into a field of shoulder-length grass.

He and the rest of the Rictans hurried out of their cockpits and found their Zephyrs aboard Drop Ship One. From there they ran down the boarding ramp to help the First Battalion secure imaginary objectives in the jungles.

Ethan was surprised and picked off by a squad of Gors in just the first few minutes. As he lay there, staring up at the blue sky and pretending to be dead, his thoughts turned to the obelisk he'd seen—one of many, apparently.

He wondered who had built it, and why. He also wondered why no one else seemed to be as curious as he was about Origin.

Ethan supposed that most of them had already spent years training here, so they wouldn't find Origin's mysteries as mysterious as he did. But he couldn't help feeling like humanity's past might reveal something critical about its future. There probably wasn't enough time left to figure it out, but he had to try. Just the fact that Origin was so *familiar*, as if he'd been here before, was enough reason to investigate. Those obelisks couldn't just be meaningless ruins. If they were all over the planet, and they were still standing here after *millions* of years, then they'd been built to last, and that meant they had to have

served an important purpose. The question was—
  What?

CHAPTER 32

Ethan only ate half his dinner, a vat-grown protein slurry the servers called soup. He passed his bowl down to Carnage, who lapped it up with a grin, and then he left the table and went looking for Atta. He found her at a table full of Gors, all of them busy slurping up the last drops of their own slurry. The Gors watched him with slitted reptilian eyes as he approached. Ethan smiled, but his smile faded when the Gors started hissing at him like a pit full of snakes. He decided it was safer not to look at them.

"You seem to be enjoying the food," he said, his eyes on Atta.

"You get used to it," she replied.

More hissing. Ethan glanced sideways to find the nearest Gor glaring at him and slowly rising to confront him. Ethan looked away quickly.

"You're dishonoring them by averting your eyes," she explained.

"They don't seem to be happy with me whether I look at them or not," Ethan replied as the Gor beside him left the table.

"They consider me one of their matriarchs. They're just

being protective."

"I see..." Ethan looked away from the Gors again, and the hissing grew louder. "Maybe we should go talk somewhere else before they eat me," he suggested.

Atta rose from the table, her eyes dancing with amusement. "Follow me."

Ethan followed her through the mess hall and out onto an adjoining balcony. The doors automatically opened and shut for them, sealing out the raucous noise of thousands of soldiers busy slurping soup.

Ethan sighed, his ears thankful for the relative silence of the wind. The air was cool and fresh, rich with the smell of green growing things from the surrounding jungle.

"How do you feed them all?" he asked, glancing back over his shoulder to the table full of hulking gray-skinned monsters where Atta had been sitting a moment ago.

"The Gors?" Atta asked. "Most of them have to eat aboard the Sythians' command ships. Omnius created their fleet to be self-sufficient and to grow all of their own food aboard the behemoths."

"Interesting... so all of you have been here training for eight years?"

"Give or take," Atta replied.

Ethan nodded to the horizon where he could just barely see the skinny black stalk of an obelisk limned and gilded with light by the setting sun. "And in all that time, you've never figured out what those ruins are for?"

Atta's brow furrowed. "What ruins?"

"The obelisks."

"Oh, *those.*"

Ethan frowned. "You don't sound very curious."

"They're not very interesting."

"Are you sure about that? They've survived here for *millions* of years. Don't you think that means they're important?"

Atta shrugged. "Maybe they were to the people who built them."

"And what about those people? What did they look like? Who were they? Therius says they're our ancestors, so there must be some sign of them here that links them to us."

"There is."

Ethan waited for Atta to elaborate, watching the sun set over the tangled tree tops. "Such as..." he prompted.

"The obelisks are tombstones."

"Tombstones?"

"Under each and every one of them are a whole lot of bones. Humanoid, but not exactly human. Based on the few expert opinions we have around here, the bones are closely related to human ones, meaning that we could have evolved from them."

Ethan shook his head. "So they're all dead?"

"I haven't seen any walking around, if that's what you're asking. The ruins of their civilization are all over the Getties, but the jungle has swallowed most of the ones we might have found here. Noctune is the easiest place to see ruins, because they're all pretty well preserved below the ice."

"How do you know that?" Ethan asked.

"Because before I came to Origin I was stranded on Noctune."

"All alone?"

"No, with my mother, the surviving Gors, and the Rictans."

"So that's why you have such a bond with all of them," Ethan said.

"Yes." Atta looked away from the setting sun. "Ethan, all of this talk about ancient history is interesting, but we have a more immediate problem."

Ethan cast another glance over his shoulder to make sure no one was about to come out onto the balcony with them. "Did you find the bombs?"

"I did. All of the ground teams have an identical capsule to carry down and defend. The generals all assumed those capsules have something to do with the Eclipser, because they weren't told where the Eclipser is going to be, but I know where it is, because my battalion is the one that's taking it down."

Ethan looked out to the horizon. "Then Therius really is planning to kill everyone."

"We're not going to let that happen. I can't stop those bombs from getting to the surface without finding a way to oust Therius, and there's not enough time to organize a coup before we jump to Avilon, but we might be able to sabotage the bombs and somehow vaporize them before they're detonated.

"Won't that just let the nanites out anyway?"

Atta shook her head. "Nanites are micro-machines that feed on everything and use the materials to multiply. Apply enough heat and they'll melt, just like any other machine."

Ethan blew out a breath and looked out to the horizon. The sun had sunk below the trees, and now all that remained was a faint glow fighting feebly to compete with the stars. The jungle was a carpet of shadows below them. Ethan imagined the lost cities of a highly advanced race lying buried far below those jungles. What had happened to them? An entire galaxy full of people gone.

"Can I see the bones?" Ethan asked.

Atta shrugged. "I'll take you there tomorrow."

Ethan shook his head. "I'd like to go now if you don't mind."

Atta pursed her lips. "There are predators out at night."

"So we suit up and take a few Gors with us. Should make for

good training, don't you think?"

"How am I supposed to clear that with the base commander?"

"Night ops. Tell him I need the extra training."

"What if you get eaten Zephyr and all?"

Ethan's brow furrowed. "Just what kind of predators are we talking about?"

"We call them Nightstalkers."

"I didn't see anything while we were training on the ground today."

"That's because they only come out at night. During the day they're hiding in warrens underground. They don't seem to like daylight."

The breeze felt suddenly cold, and Ethan shivered. "Nightstalkers... they sound friendly."

"Even the Gors are afraid of them."

"And you?"

Atta grinned. "I like a challenge. *Gets the blood pumpin'* as Magnum would say. Speaking of which, we'd better take the Rictans with us. The Gors are great to have in a fight, but they're superstitious as krak. They think the Nightstalkers are the ghosts of their ancestors come to get them and drag them down to the Netherworld."

Ethan snorted. "Hard to picture Gors being scared of anything."

"That's because you haven't seen a Nightstalker yet. Come on, let's go get suited up. We don't want to waste all of our rack time hunting Nightstalkers and digging up ancient fossils."

"Lead the way..." he said.

CHAPTER 33

Ethan stood with Rictan Squadron and Atta at the edge of the parade grounds, scanning the shadowy jungle with infrared and light amplification overlays. With those overlays activated, the ground and trees turned varying shades of blue, while living creatures popped out as bright smears of red, orange, and yellow. Ethan counted dozens of small blurry heat signatures hiding out in the trees and a handful of even smaller ones scuttling along the ground. Looking down he noticed that he could even see dozens of creeping, crawling insects, highlighted bright blue against the dark blue ground.

"I thought insects are cold-blooded. Why are they showing up on infrared?" Ethan asked, turning to Atta. Their Zephyrs radiated plenty of heat, too, but the overlays highlighted them green to distinguish them from everything else.

"They're showing up because they're moving," Atta explained. "Your infrared overlay is called IAMS for short, which means *Infrared and Motion Scanners*. Not everything dangerous radiates heat, so IAMS helps us to identify all possible threats in our environment."

Ethan smiled. "So bugs are threats."

"Not usually."

"What about Nightcrawlers? What should I be looking for?"

Magnum answered this time, "Stalkers, not *crawlers*. They're warm-blooded, and *big*, about three meters at the shoulder when standin' on their hind legs. You can't miss 'em."

Ethan didn't see anything that large in the jungle. He kept half an eye on the top third of his HUD where his rear view screen was located, but behind them was nothing but the parade grounds and human-shaped heat signatures. Ethan toggled his peripheral view screens as an extra measure of security.

"Are they a threat to us in our armor?" he asked.

"That depends," Magnum replied while checking the charges on a pair of hefty plasma pistols.

"On what?"

Magnum shrugged. "How many are huntin' you, how hungry they are, and whether or not you still have enough ripper rounds to keep 'em from gettin' close."

"In other words, *yes*," Atta clarified.

"Good to know," Ethan said, while performing a quick weapons check of his own.

"The squad is ready, General," Magnum said.

"I think maybe the commander better take the lead on this one. He can use all the practice he can get. Shrapnel... Shrapnel?"

Ethan realized with a start that they were talking to him. He looked up to see both Magnum and Atta looking at him expectantly.

"You needed a call sign," Magnum explained. "That way I don't have to go around calling you *sir* and *SC* all the time. How ya like it? The squad came up with it after they heard about your *unconventional* tactics in the simulators—getting yourself blown up all the time."

The call sign wasn't all he was wondering about. Suddenly he didn't understand why he'd been put in charge of an elite commando unit. He'd logged only a handful of hours in a Zephyr, while most of the Rictans had spent decades fighting and training with them. The more he thought about it, the more he wondered about Therius's decision. The Rictans didn't need him. "Actually, I think you should take the lead when we're on the ground, Magnum."

"Well, well, where did that sudden burst of insight come from?"

"I was picked off today after just a few minutes on the ground, but besides that, you have far more experience than I do with ground ops."

Magnum grunted. "You heard the commander. Move out, Rictans! Keep eyes on those peripherals. Shrapnel, Princess— you two have the rear."

Ethan turned to Atta and whispered, *"Princess?"*

"Don't start," she warned.

"She ain't fond of her call sign." Magnum said.

"No, I like it just fine, Maggy," Atta replied.

"See? She's gotta go imasculatin' me just to make herself feel better."

Atta laughed.

Magnum turned and led the way, setting out at a light jog. They crashed through the tree line with all the subtlety of a stampede. Twigs and branches snapped underfoot; the ground shook with heavy, armored footfalls; and underbrush slapped their armor.

Ethan winced at all the noise they were making. "Shouldn't we try to keep it down?" he asked.

"No point," Magnum replied. "Nightstalkers will find us either way. Better they know we're out here. We've tangled before, so maybe this time they'll be smart and stay away."

A rush of static roared over the comms as Rictan Five, *Streak*, snorted. "If they were that smart, they'd be the ones wearing armor and shooting guns. They're just a bunch of dumb beasts."

"Dumb beasts with big teeth," Rictan Six, *Blades,* put in.

"Stow that chatter, Rictans!" Magnum said.

They ran through the jungle for almost half an hour in perfect synchrony and perfect silence. In all that time Ethan didn't see any animals large enough to match the description of a Nightstalker. He wondered if the Rictans were messing with him and this was some type of elaborate hazing.

Then suddenly Magnum held up an armored fist, indicating that they stop.

Ethan couldn't see anything on infrared. "What is it?" he asked.

"Thought I saw somethin'."

"You sure? My scopes are clear," Rictan Three replied.

"I'm sure..." Magnum said, raising both his gauntlets and activating his weapons.

Ethan stepped out of line to get a closer look. Meanwhile, he armed his own ripper cannons. Weapon barrels slid out of his gauntlets and he clenched both fists to take off the safeties.

His heart thudded in his chest. Time crawled. Sweat trickled in an icy line down his back.

Suddenly a twig snapped behind them. Ethan whirled, his eyes scanning all his screens at once. On his rear screen he caught a glimpse of a big orange blur, dancing between the cold blue boles of trees and coming up fast. "I've got contact! Permission to open fire!"

"Multiple contacts at six, three, and nine o'clock!" another

Rictan reported. "They're flanking us!"

Ethan saw two more heat signatures melt out of the trees in front of him, and no less than a dozen coming up on his peripheral screens.

"Close it up, Rictans! Testudo formation!" Magnum roared.

Testudo? Ethan glanced at his rear view screen see the Rictans forming up in a square, with three on each side, their backs facing each other. They'd left a gap in the rear of the formation for him, and he hurriedly backpedaled into it.

They stood there, arms raised and ripper cannons tracking. The Nightstalkers circled, their heat signatures flickering through the trees. No clear lines of fire yet, but Ethan bet that if they opened fire now they'd graze a few and maybe scare off the rest before they got too close.

"Permission to—"

"Hold!" Magnum said. "No sense stirrin' 'em up if we don't have to."

Ethan wondered about that. Were the Rictans afraid of Nightstalkers?

The heat signatures circling them faded one by one into the trees until all of them were gone. They kept their weapons raised and tracking just in case, but after several minutes of jumping at their own shadows, it became obvious that the Stalkers weren't coming back.

Atta was first to break the silence, "They're gone, Maggy. We should get moving."

"Sure thing, Princess," Magnum said. "All right, let's—"

Something *cracked* overhead, and a large branch fell into the middle of their formation.

Heads snapped up, all of them scanning the tree tops at once.

Ethan saw a solid mass of heat signatures just above their

heads.

"Stalkers!" Magnum roared, his ripper cannons already blazing golden fury into the night.

"Scatter!" Atta said.

Ethan ran as fast as he could. On his rear view screen he saw Stalkers dropping from the trees and landing right on top of his squad mates. He spun around and took aim... but he couldn't shoot without hitting friendlies. He considered charging back in with energy blades flashing, but that would be even more deadly to the Rictans.

Ethan watched, helpless and wondering what to do. Then the Rictans began electrifying their armor, and Ethan's infrared blinded him. He squeezed his eyes shut and turned off IAMS, settling for light amplification alone.

The scene snapped into focus, and he got a better look at the enemy. They were six-legged, with thick black fur and fangs that didn't even fit inside their hawkish heads. Long claws scratched furrows in the Zephyrs' armor. Even electrifying their armor didn't convince the Stalkers to leave them alone. One Zephyr stumbled around blindly with a stalker wrapped around his head, electrifying his armor every other second to shake it loose, but the beast wasn't letting go. Then he extended his energy blades and sliced the stalker's back end off. It fell from his shoulders in smoking pieces, legs spasmodically kicking and clawing at the dirt.

The comms roared as the Rictans shouted warnings to each other, but so far no one seemed hurt. These animals were an irritant, not a threat.

"Don't let them grab your helmets!" someone said.

Ethan wondered why. Then he heard a low growl behind him. He spun around to face a monstrous thing crouching low behind him. *Frek!* He raised both his arms to shoot, but the stalker lunged and knocked him over before he could fire. Jaws full of sharp, snapping teeth came within inches of his face, and his arms threatened to buckle beneath the weight of the stalker, despite his mech-enhanced strength. He held the monster back by its neck, and it snapped at his right arm, locking sharp fangs around his guantlet.

At first Ethan didn't feel anything, but soon he felt the pressure from the beast's jaws. It was compacting his armor, deforming it around his arm.

The pressure became uncomfortable, and then something sharp touched his skin. Fear gave him the boost of strength he needed, and he heaved with all his strength to get the stalker off his chest. It went skidding through the dirt, and Ethan bounced up, his ripper cannons already blazing. He pumped the beast full of high caliber rounds before it could recover. The stalker shuddered with each impact. Black fur exploded with gouts of red blood, and the beast dug troughs into the ground as it struggled to rise. Then it lay still with red eyes wide and staring, its jaws gaping open and a fat red tongue lolling out the side of its mouth. Ethan looked away and scanned his immediate surroundings. The Stalkers were gone. At least six of them lay dead on the ground, most of them in pieces. Energy blades seemed to be the preferred way to deal with them at close range.

"Rictans, report!" Magnum snapped.

Multiple clicks and verbal acknowledgments sounded over the comms.

"Where's Princess?" Rictan Four, Rockhead, asked.

"Motherfrekker..." Magnum hissed. "I've got her beacon. They're draggin' her off. "Atta? Can you hear me?"

Silence.

"Frek it!"

"Her vitals are good, and she's awake," Rictan Six, *Blades,* said. He was the unit's medic, so he would know.

"Her comms must be damaged," Ethan said.

"Krak got real," Three said.

"Move out!" Magnum called. "We have some catching up to do!"

He dashed through the trees, and Ethan raced after him.

CHAPTER 34

They ran for almost an hour straight, always half a step behind the nightstalker dragging Atta.

"Why doesn't she electrify her armor?" Ethan asked between gasps for air.

"Capacitors are only good for about a dozen uses," Magnum replied. "She must have depleted them."

"What about energy blades?" Ethan insisted. "She could slice that beast in half. Are you sure she's conscious?"

"I've triple checked her vitals," Blades replied.

"She must have multiple systems failures," Magnum said.

"Has this ever happened before?" Ethan asked.

"They've dragged off a few unarmored Gors," Magnum replied.

"So Atta's the first human they've captured."

"We'll get her back," Magnum said.

Ethan listened to the steady thunder of footfalls and eyed Atta's comm beacon racing ahead of them on his HUD map. He noticed Union Base at the top of the map, not far from their position. The stalker was dragging her back to base? Ethan frowned. "Has anyone noticed—"

Magnum held up one fist, calling a halt and silencing him at the same time. "I've found a tunnel entrance," he said.

"This close to base?" Rictan Three, *Hop*, asked.

"They must be getting more brazen," Magnum replied.

"Think they took her down there?" Hop asked, hovering over Magnum's shoulder.

Ethan went to look. He noticed that up ahead the trees thinned out to the muddy clearing that served as the Union's parade grounds. He couldn't see any sign of the Stalker or Atta in that clearing, but her beacon was still transmitting from that direction.

"It must have," Ethan decided.

Magnum went down on his haunches to study the ground around the tunnel. "Tracks end here; that confirms it."

"Frek!" Rictan Five said.

Magnum turned on his Zephyr's floodlights with a blinding flash of light, and turned to the rest of them. "No guts, no glory," he said, and then he dropped inside the tunnel.

Ethan snapped off his light amplification overlay and turned on his own floodlights before jumping after Magnum. He landed inside the tunnel with a *thud*. Bits of loose dirt trickled from the walls and ceiling with a pitter-patter. Ethan was surprised to find that the tunnel was actually tall enough for them to stand.

Up ahead, Magnum called out, "Pick up the pace!" and Ethan raced to catch up. One after another, the rest of the Rictans jumped down and ran after Magnum. The tunnel descended gradually, crossing directly below the Union's parade grounds.

"The frek?" someone panted. "They've been tunneling under our feet all this time?"

The tunnel branched in three different directions, but Atta's blip was dead ahead, so Magnum kept straight.

"I don't like this," Rictan Seven said.

"Think they're trying to dig a way in?" Four asked.

"Cut the chatter!" Magnum growled. "Eyes and ears on target."

A few minutes later, they found themselves directly under Union Base. Scanners showed that the tunnel opened into a hollow chamber up ahead, and Atta's blip had stopped there.

Magnum drew both his sidearms and crept up to the edge of the chamber. Ethan was just half a step behind, and he saw the dirt walls of the tunnel abruptly end, replaced by solid rock. No, not rock—

"They dug through castcrete?" he whispered. "With what?"

Magnum shook his head. "Quiet."

Ethan tried to peer around Magnum to get a glimpse at the chamber beyond. Then the squad leader jumped down, and Ethan got a better look.

The chamber was some kind of bunker; the walls and ceiling were all made of solid castcrete. A heavy-looking alloy door lay on both ends, but there were no working light fixtures, just a big, empty space. The floor was covered with castcrete dust, dirt, and rubble from where the Stalkers had dug through. Multiple dirt and rubble-strewn tunnel entrances marked the perimeter of the room. Atta lay motionless at the center of the chamber. The Nightstalker who'd taken her paced restlessly in front of her and snarled as Magnum approached. Ethan jumped down. Broken castcrete *crunched* with the impact, and the sound echoed noisily off the walls. Then came more echoes as the rest of the Rictans jumped down.

The Nightstalker pacing in front of Atta snarled and then it tossed its head in the air and gave a high-pitched *screech*. Black fur rippled as thick bands of muscle flexed beneath the Stalker's skin. Slitted red eyes glinted in the glare of their floodlights. The creature shook its head and shut its eyes, momentarily blinded. Magnum took aim with his pistols, and the beast flattened itself to the ground, looking subdued or ready to pounce—Ethan couldn't decide which.

Then came another *screech*, and another one, followed by countless echoes of the same. Ethan saw his peripheral screens filling up with Stalkers. They poured into the bunker from all sides, filling all the entrances.

"Frek me..." someone whispered.

"TESTUDO!" Magnum roared. He lunged toward Atta, and her captor sprang away, fleeing to the safety of its fellow Stalkers. The Rictans formed a hollow square around Atta, guns facing out. Stalkers milled in restless circles around the entrances of the chamber.

"What are they doing?" Ethan asked.

"Fire on my command," Magnum said.

"Look—" someone pointed to one of the entrances.

The beasts were retreating back into their tunnels, and within seconds the Rictans were alone inside the bunker.

"Blades, check Princess! Everyone else, keep those entrances covered. Remember what happened last time."

Ethan did. He glanced up, but the ceiling was solid castcrete, so Stalkers couldn't drop down on them this time.

All of a few seconds later Blades had Atta's helmet off and she was cursing at them, the Nightstalkers, and the universe in general.

"Get me out of this mech!" she roared.

"What happened?" Ethan asked, using external speakers rather than comms to speak with her.

"That thing slashed my power core, that's what! It left me

paralyzed in two hundred and fifty pounds of armor."

"Not just dumb beasts after all," someone said.

Ethan shook his head, his eyes fixed on the entrance ahead of him. It was dark and empty. The chamber where they stood was the perfect place for an ambush, but the Stalkers had already come and gone.

"Let's get out of here," Atta said. Ethan saw her bounce to her feet on his rear screen.

"You're not injured anywhere?" Blades asked.

"Disappointed?" she asked.

"Not at all, Princess," he replied.

"Stop calling me that."

Magnum chuckled and holstered one of his pistols. "All right, that's enough. The Stalkers are gone. Let's get out of here and hit the rack."

Ethan frowned. "What about the ruins?"

"I think we've all had enough excitement for one night," Magnum replied. "If you're that determined to see what ancient human bones look like, go check out the exhibit on level six tomorrow. Move out, Rictans! Princess—keep to the middle of our formation. You're not armored anymore."

"Sure thing, Maggy."

Ethan smiled as Magnum led the way back to the tunnel they'd jumped down from. The entrance was at shoulder height, but Magnum managed to haul himself up easily enough. "The frek..."

"What is it?" Ethan asked.

"The tunnel's caved in."

"How far does the cave-in go?" Atta asked.

"Far as scanners can see. Check the other entrances!"

Ethan's pulse jumped with a sudden spike of adrenaline. He turned in a quick circle to find the next nearest tunnel entrance.

He jogged up to it...

"This one's caved in, too!" he said.

Atta appeared beside him a moment later. "Frek!" she roared.

The rest of the Rictans raced around the chamber, checking tunnels and reporting the same. Magnum walked up beside them, shaking his head. "They led us here on purpose."

"Why?" Atta asked. "So they could wait until we've starved to death, and then dig us up for a snack?"

"Something like that..." Magnum replied, studying the chamber.

"If they can dig their way back in, then we can dig our way out," Ethan said.

Magnum nodded, turning in a slow circle to study their surroundings.

Ethan followed the other man's gaze. The castcrete walls were featureless, the ceiling likewise, but there were those two heavy-looking doors.

"Think those doors still work?" Ethan asked.

"Maybe," Atta replied, striding over to one of them. She tried to wave it open, but nothing happened.

Ethan couldn't see any door controls.

"Might be locked from the other side," Atta said.

"Or else it's not programmed to open for *you*," Magnum said.

"We could blast it open," Rictan Seven, *Carnage,* suggested.

"Better than diggin' our way out," Magnum replied. "Set charges. Let's see what's behind door number one."

"Yes, sir." Rictan Seven went to work, and the rest of the Rictans retreated to a respectful distance. They kept busy watching the tunnel entrances, just in case.

"Charges set!" Carnage said, racing away from the door.

"You better not bring this whole place down on top of us," Magnum warned.

"You worry too much."

They took cover on the far side of the chamber and took up a semi-circular formation with Atta safely nestled between them and the wall. "Light it up!" Magnum said.

Ethan made the mistake of watching the explosion. The sudden flash of light blinded him; then came a *whump* and a loud *bang!* Castcrete dust billowed out and pebble-sized debris hit them at high speed, *plinking* off their armor.

"Princess?" Magnum asked as the debris settled around their feet.

"I'm fine."

"Good. Carnage, check the area."

A moment later, they heard: "All clear!"

They all hurried over to see what lay on the other side. Ethan reached the threshold of the blast and saw some kind of equipment locker. The door had been blown inward, turning the inside of the locker into a war zone. Magnum stepped through the smoking frame, debris *crunching* under foot. Overhead lights flickered on automatically, and dust swirled, dancing down through the light.

"Who hides access to another room inside an equipment locker?" Magnum asked.

Atta walked in after him and went down on her haunches to study the debris. She fished a smoldering roll of bandages out and tossed it aside with a wrinkled nose.

"This is a medical supply room. We're back in Union Base, all right."

Remembering something, Ethan turned to look behind them. "If this door leads into the fortress, then where's the other one go?" he asked.

Magnum and Atta both turned to look.

"That's a damn good question," Atta said.

Magnum shook his head. "Whatever's through there, we've been getting along just fine without it all these years, so it can wait one more night. I'll make my report in the morning and someone will come investigate. Right now, we need to seal this place up and make sure no Stalkers come creepin' in while we're sleepin'."

Ethan's brow furrowed and he studied the caved-in tunnels that Stalkers had dug all around the perimeter of the chamber. "What's the point? If they can dig through castcrete, they could come through anywhere."

So why haven't they?" Atta asked.

"Another question that can wait to be answered," Magnum said, already crossing the supply locker to the inner door. Just before he reached it, the door *swished* open and a squad of soldiers burst in. Therius stood behind them, looking ill-amused.

"What's going on here?" he demanded.

CHAPTER 35

"**W**hat were you doing down there?" Therius demanded, his eyes on Atta.

Therius had them all standing in a line in front of him. They'd left their mechs for the squad that had come to investigate, and now, standing in the jumpsuits, it was easy to see how exhausted all of them were.

"We were performing night ops," Ethan replied, taking a quick step forward. "My idea, sir."

Therius's gaze swept to him. "You were performing night ops beneath Union Base?"

"No, sir. We ran into Nightstalkers in the jungle, and they dragged off the general. We followed her comm beacon down one of their tunnels, and ended up in an abandoned chamber right outside the supply locker where you found us."

"So why'd you blow a hole in the wall? You could have gone back the way you came."

"It wasn't a wall. It was a door, sir, and we didn't go back the way we came because the Stalkers caved in their tunnels to trap us."

Therius's eyebrows floated up. "Really? You're saying they

laid a trap for you? They must be more intelligent than we thought."

"It would appear so, sir..." Ethan trailed off. Something about this situation didn't sit well with him.

"Something on your mind, Commander?"

"Yes, sir."

"Go ahead."

"How did you find us so quickly?"

"You're not the only one who can follow comm beacons. When a squad checks out a group of Zephyrs for an unscheduled mission in the middle of the night, I have to sign off on it or they don't even get out the door. Are we still sticking with *night ops,* or does someone here want to give me a better description of what you were all doing out there in the jungle?"

Ethan sighed. "I wanted to check out the ruins, sir."

"Why?"

"Curiosity."

"Didn't your squad already explain to you what's been found at those sites?"

"Yes, but I wanted to see for myself."

"So instead of getting some much-needed sleep for tomorrow's training, you thought it would be a good idea to go hunting through the jungle for bones. Don't take your squad's name too literally, Commander. You're not actually *rictans.*"

"Yes, sir."

"There's going to be plenty of time to go unearthing the mysteries of Origin when Avilon is conquered, but until then, your curiosity can wait."

"What about the room we discovered? We need to find out where that other door leads."

"Other door?"

"There was another door, sir, besides the one we blew

open."

"I see. We'll look into it, but as I said, satisfying curiosity is not a high priority right now. We didn't build this fortress, so we can't possibly know all the ins and outs of it. There could be just one hidden chamber or a hundred more, but that's not important right now."

Ethan shook his head. "With respect, sir, I disagree. Why is this fortress still standing after so many millions of years? What was it built for? It's too convenient. It's almost like someone left it here for us. Maybe Omnius is setting you up."

"That's enough, Ortane. I won't have you come here at the final hour and call into question everything we've worked so hard to accomplish. Finding Origin was a stroke of fortune, but that doesn't mean it was ill-fortune. Dismissed."

Ethan gave a reluctant salute. "Yes, sir." He turned and left the briefing room, making his way to the nearest bank of lift tubes. The Rictans crowded around him as he stabbed the call button. One of the lifts opened immediately and they all piled in.

On their way up to their quarters, Atta let out a breath and shook her head. "He's hiding something."

Magnum turned to her with one eyebrow raised. "Like what?"

"That we know of?" Atta glanced at Ethan.

He shrugged. "We could use their help."

Atta turned back to Magnum and explained, "The battalions are taking nanite bombs down to the surface of Avilon."

Carnage's jaw dropped. "The frek... *why?*"

"I think it would be better if we showed you," Atta replied just as the lift arrived. Rather than step out and head to their quarters as ordered, Atta selected another floor from the lift control panel—the Fortress's rooftop hangar and landing pad.

The lift doors slid shut and it shot upwards again. When it

opened once more, Atta strode out and led them all over to one of the hangar's shuttle loading bays. The room was stacked full of transport crates. Atta headed over to one in particular and tapped a code into the crate's control panel. Locking bolts slid aside, allowing her to lift the lid. As she did so, Magnum peered in. Ethan leaned over Magnum's shoulder and saw a glossy black capsule.

"There's nanites in there?" Magnum asked. "Are you sure?"

Atta nodded. "Sure as we can be without unleashing them here. We ran scans on the capsules, and the results were consistent with what they should be if they're filled with nanites."

The Rictans traded wary looks and Magnum asked, "So why are we taking them to Avilon?"

"Therius knows we can't win, and he's going to threaten Omnius with the destruction of the entire human race if he doesn't leave Avilon alone."

"You're jerkin' my chain. What if he doesn't back down?"

Atta grimaced. *"Boom."*

"So it's not an empty threat."

"You know Therius. He believes in an afterlife. He wants to set humanity free, but to him, death is the ultimate freedom."

Magnum shook his head. "We've been training here for almost a decade. We bred a whole army of Gors! You're tellin' me all that's for nothing?"

"No, not for nothing. We're going to take Avilon and turn its people against Omnius just as we planned. The only difference is when he comes with reinforcements—and he will—Therius intends for us to be standing by, ready to blow ourselves to the Netherworld rather than let Omnius take the planet back."

"Frek!" Magnum almost punched the nearest transport crate, but he stopped himself when he realized it was full of explosives. "That skriff-krakkin' kakard!"

Ethan scowled. "We can't let that happen."

"No, we can't," Atta replied, "and we won't. We're going to strap enough conventional explosives to those bombs so that the nanites are vaporized when Therius tries to use them."

* * *

—One Day Later—

Shallah stood on the bridge of his command ship, the *Asharn,* surrounded by all six of his high lords, as well as Lady Kala and Queen Tavia—together they represented all the leaders of the Sythians.

They were a diverse group, each of them bipedal and humanoid, but each of them different enough to be considered their own species. Lady Kala and Queen Tavia looked like giant bats with their black skin, wings, and red eyes, while Kaon and Shallah appeared to be a cross between lizards and fish. Lord Shondar appeared to be a cross between humans and Gors with his pale, leathery gray skin, jagged black teeth, white eyes, and topknot of long, white hair. The other lords, Worval, Rossk, Thorian, and Quaris were all equally different and equally terrifying from a human perspective. It was no wonder Omnius had chosen them to be humanity's executioners.

When Shallah looked at all of them, he saw the future of sentient life. The Sythians were the evolutionary descendants of humanity. They'd adapted for survival in harsh climates where no human would be able to live. That meant they were superior to humans on a fundamental level. It was time to take that superiority to its logical conclusion.

"Therius leads usss to our deaths," Shallah said, hissing in perfect Sythian. "The battle for Avilon cannot be won. You know what shall come for us. Therius plans to threaten Omnius with the destruction of Avilon, using Omnius's own nanites to do so."

"Nanites? He cannot be that big of a fool!" Lord Kaon said, the gills in the sides of his neck flaring.

Queen Tavia's glowing red eyes narrowed swiftly. "Do not be so sure," she said. "I meet him and speak with him myself. He is foolish, even for a human."

"I do not know if his threats are true," Shallah said, "but it does not matter. Last night Therius came to speak with me. He suspects traitors in his midst, and he has given me the bombs to guard until the time comes to use them. Whether that time comes or not, we shall drop those bombs. Yet before we do, we must be sure of our escape. As soon as we arrive, I will send you, Lord Kaon, to the surface with a Sythian strike team. You will locate the Eclipser and disable it so that we can jump away."

"Me, Supreme One?"

"Is there a problem, Kaon?"

"The nanites shall kill me if they touch me."

"If you die, then you are to be revived. Nothing will happen to you that cannot be undone."

"But if I fail, the jamming device will ensure that my mind is stranded on Avilon when I die."

"Then you shall be revived from backups, and you shall not remember your death. All the better for you."

Shallah watched Kaon's large blue eyes dart around the room.

"Do any of the other lords join me?" he asked.

"They do not. The honor shall be yours alone."

"I see," Kaon replied, swallowing visibly.

Shallah smiled. "You shall be rewarded for your sacrifice."

He looked away, his eyes skipping from one High Lord to the next, addressing them all. "The day of reckoning is upon us.

We cannot defeat Omnius, but we shall have our revenge. He lied to us and used us, choosing humanity over the Sythians, but now we shall deprive him of his chosen people. For glory!"

"For glory!" the lords roared in unison.

* * *

Omnius stood all alone before a massive forward viewport aboard the command Facet of his Icosahedron, watching as Avilon drew near. The planet lay bright and glowing in the surrounding darkness of space. That was the *old* Avilon, but little did its people know, here came the new.

Over a hundred thousand Facets approached the planet in a diffuse cloud, and soon they would form up into a semi-circular shroud around the night side of the planet. The other half of his Facets were still calculating their jumps from the Getties, but they would arrive in a matter of days now.

Omnius had originally planned to jump the entire Icosahedron into position around Avilon. The dramatic shock of seeing the sun suddenly eclipsed would be a great way to introduce New Avilon to its people.

But he'd been forced to change those plans. Less than a week ago, a pair of Facets had found the Sythian fleet in orbit around an uncharted planet in the Getties. He'd witnessed them performing quantum jumps there, which meant that they'd developed quantum jump drives earlier than anticipated. Rather than fight them there and force them to scatter, Omnius had sent as many Facets as he could back to Avilon to wait for them.

He didn't expect Shallah to keep him waiting for very long. They'd already waited years while refitting their fleet with quantum jump drives. Now all they had to do was use them.

Omnius smiled. *Let them come.*

CHAPTER 36

"Ten minutes to jump!" the helm reported.

"Battle groups one through fifteen standing by; all battalions and squadrons ready for launch," Lieutenant Devries said from the comms.

"Good. Carry on," Therius said.

Farah stood at the captain's table with him, looking over the battle plan one last time. She caught a flicker of movement in the corner of her eye, accompanied by a familiar *clanking* sound. Glancing that way, Farah spotted Drone 767 relieving one of the guards at the entrance of the bridge. The other guard was, Torv, the *Liberator's* chief of security. Torv eyed the drone and hissed as it shuffled into position on the other side of the entrance. Farah wondered about that, thinking that 767 should have been in the hangar getting ready to launch with the rest of the drone battalion.

"Captain Hale?" Therius prompted.

"Sorry, go on." Farah returned her attention to the captain's table, and Therius went back to highlighting the key points of their plan.

The fleet was to jump straight from Origin into orbit over

Avilon, maintaining a diffuse shell around the entire planet. That meant their forces would be spread out, which wasn't an ideal formation to deal with any defending fleets that Avilon might have waiting for them, but recent intelligence showed there was no significant orbital presence, and most important of all, no Icosahedron.

"You're sure that intel is reliable?" Farah asked.

"It's only a day old," Therius replied.

Farah nodded. It would have to do. Their intel from the Getties showed that the individual Facets of Omnius's Icosahedron were still returning from their nanite-seeding missions to a local rendezvous. So far only about half of the Facets had arrived at that rendezvous, and since it was unlikely Omnius would want to present only half of New Avilon to his people, it would be some time before the Icosahedron was ready to leave. No doubt Omnius would start calculating a jump to Avilon just as soon as they attacked, but those calculations would take at least a week.

That was how long they had to conquer the planet. They had a window of opportunity, but it was far from wide open. Avilon had a garrison of millions of drone fighters, which was more than enough to repel the Union by itself. That was the reason they were jumping in so close to the planet. They had to bombard the garrison out of existence before it could launch more than a handful of fighters. There was a risk that they'd lose a few ships from accidentally jumping into the planet's atmosphere, but they'd drilled this over and over again for a reason. Their jump algorithms were all as finely-tuned as they could get. Losses would be minimal.

"This is it," Therius declared.

Farah pursed her lips and shook her head. She looked up and met Therius's pale blue eyes with her darker ones. "What about the Armageddon Protocol?"

"That's classified, Captain," Therius growled. "We've already discussed it, and you'd do well not to open the discussion again here."

Farah's mouth opened halfway to object, but she caught herself.

"Trust me, Captain Hale." Therius said, his blue eyes fierce with a fiery gleam.

But she *didn't* trust him. They'd had more than a few discussions about the Armageddon Protocol over the past few days, and each time Therius had insisted that they wouldn't actually need to use the nanites. The bombs were a last resort. Omnius would back down. But Farah wasn't willing to bet the survival of the human race on it.

She had a last resort of her own. Therius was on board the *Liberator,* and it was her ship even more than it was his. His presence on the bridge over the past eight years had been fleeting at best, but hers had been constant. He wasn't as familiar with the crew, and he didn't know all the inner workings of the ship. Any orders Therius gave would have to be routed through the *Liberator's* comm system, and Farah had set up an emergency lock-down program that would catch and block any outbound comms until she gave the encryption key to deactivate the program. If she determined that Therius was about to give the order to detonate the nanites, she would block the order and expose his plot. At that point, Therius would have a mutiny on his hands. She hoped it wouldn't come to that.

"Are you all right, Captain?" Therius asked.

Farah regarded him with a grim smile. "Yes, I was just thinking about what it will be like when Avilon is ours. This day has been a long time in coming."

Therius nodded. "It has indeed." Turning away from her, he

called down to the comms officer. "We're ready for launch, Lieutenant Devries. Alert the fleet and put the countdown on screen."

"Yes, sir."

A moment later, the jump timer appeared on the main holo display, counting backward from five minutes. Everything was pre-calculated and synchronized, so as soon as that clock hit zero, all of their ships would jump.

"Comms!" Therius called. "What's the status of the Eclipser?"

"Ready and waiting aboard Drop Ship One, sir."

"Good. Remind them to activate it as soon as we arrive."

Farah grimaced. Their entire plan hinged on that device. It was theoretically impossible to locate, so it wouldn't be an immediate target, but capital ships like the *Liberator* would come under heavy fire during the battle, so the safest place to keep the device was actually on Avilon. The 1st Battalion was tasked with carrying it down and defending it. In order to keep it hidden, they'd disguised it to look like a piece of debris, but that would do nothing to prevent accidental destruction. Farah hoped for all of their sakes that nothing happened to the Eclipser.

She watched the timer run down, her heart pounding in her chest. She felt light-headed. This was it—over eight years of training culminating in one decisive engagement that would probably only last a couple of days.

"Ten seconds to launch!" Lieutenant Devries announced from the comms.

The countdown became audible, and Farah closed her eyes. She focused on taking deep, calming breaths. A deafening roar rose on the air. Wind began whipping through the bridge, tearing at her uniform and hair. A powerful radiance shone through her eyelids, revealing a spider's web of veins. Then the countdown reached one, and a loud *bang!* sounded.

Farah opened her eyes to see Avilon lying close before them, taking up all of their view. The planet shone bright in the light of the system's sun, its terminator line casting a slow-moving shadow between day and night.

"Report!" Therius called out.

Farah gazed down on the captain's table and checked the star map to see for herself how the jump had gone. Sensors were still catching up, populating the map with contacts. Thousands of green dots appeared in orbit all around Avilon, but so far only a handful of enemy contacts. That was good. Then she noticed something strange. Everything to the rear of their position was grayed out. Something was blocking scanners there. The gray area was arc-shaped and *close* behind them...

Looking up quickly, Farah saw the terminator line moving across the surface of Avilon for what it really was. Something *big* was moving between Avilon and its sun.

"What the..." the gravidar officer trailed off, noticing the same thing as her.

"Get me an aft view and put in on screen!" Therius ordered.

"Yes, sir!"

At first, what they saw behind them looked like stars and space, but those pinpricks of light were too dim and closely-spaced to be stars. Even more telling, the sun was half eclipsed, as if the fabric of space itself had been torn and the edges overlapped where the sun was supposed to be. Silhouetted in the blinding light of the system's sun Farah saw a trailing cloud of tiny black triangles.

Facets! she thought. Their intel had been wrong. The Icosahedron was already here.

"It's a trap!" she screamed.

* * *

Farah turned to Therius, her eyes wide and blinking. Omnius had been waiting for them. They had to jump away before it was too late.

"It's too late to go back now," Therius said, as if he'd read her mind. Turning away, he began snapping orders at the crew: "Devries, tell the fleet to commence bombardment! Launch all drop ships and fighters, and activate the Eclipser *now!*"

"Yes, sir!" Devries said from the comms station.

"Gunnery! Open fire!"

"Roger that," the gunnery chief said.

"What happened?" Farah demanded. "Intel showed all the Facets in the Getties regrouping before the jump to Avilon. What are they doing here?"

Therius shook his head. "Only half of them were accounted for."

"Then what about your intel on Avilon? You said the system was clear! That was *yesterday.*"

Therius looked up from the captain's table, his expression grim.

A sudden suspicion formed in Farah's gut. "Did we even send a probe?"

"We couldn't risk it. Omnius would have seen anything we sent."

"You sent us here blind?" Farah shook her head. "What have you done..."

"I'm sorry, Captain. There was no other way."

The deck began pulsing and thrumming underfoot as terajoules of energy were released from the *Liberator's* main beam cannons. Someone set the main holo display back to the fore, and Farah saw that the artificial terminator line rolling across Avilon had now eclipsed fully a third of the planet. *Omnius brought his own eclipser...* Farah mused.

Bright red and blue beams lanced out from the *Liberator's* cannons, drawing two separate vanishing points against the planet. At the points of impact, Farah saw pinpricks of fire already blossoming.

Soon fires would be raging all across the planet. Colossal towers would shatter and crash through pristine urban parks.

Farah turned away from the viewscreens in a daze. She found Therius intently studying the captain's table, using it to send orders directly to the other ships in the fleet. She watched, trying to decide what his strategy was. Then she noticed that he was ordering the fleet to descend into Avilon's atmosphere. Farah blinked, coming back to her senses.

"If you order the fleet into atmosphere, we won't be able to jump out," she said quietly.

"We can't jump out with the Eclipser online," Therius replied. "We don't have conventional SLS drives anymore. Only quantum."

"Then take the Eclipser offline! If we don't retreat now, we'll never be able to."

Therius looked up at her. "This is our only chance to defeat Omnius, Captain. We're not going to run from it."

Farah gaped at him. "The Eclipser won't keep Omnius at bay forever. What happens when it runs out of power, or if it gets destroyed?"

Therius shot her a grim look. "That's why we need to gain control of the planet and initiate the Armageddon Protocol."

"You said that was a last resort."

"It still is. Omnius may back down when we threaten him."

Incredulous, Farah turned to the crew. "We have to stop him! He's going to kill us all!"

Farah caught a flicker of movement in the corner of her eye, and she spun around just in time to see 767 raise his arms and aim his weapons at her. There came a *screech* of energy discharging and a brilliant blue flash of light slammed her in the chest. She fell over backwards with a dark curtain dropping over her eyes.

* * *

Omnius watched from the throne in his control center as the rebel fleet jump into orbit over Avilon. He grinned. This was the moment he'd been waiting for.

If these rebels were smart, they would run while they still had the chance.

But instead of running, they were flying even closer to the planet. Omnius's mouth twitched into a scowl as he watched the enemy fleet begin bombarding his garrisons from orbit. He could feel the loss of every drone and human as a diminishing of his own awareness. Shadows crept in at the edges of his being.

Then his mind blanked completely, and his physical body staggered. He blinked—once, twice...

What. Was. Happening?

He was no longer aware of any of his drones or any of his people. He was completely blind, cut off, he was...

Being jammed.

Impossible. Quantum fields couldn't be jammed in such a wide radius. Yet somehow the rebel fleet was jamming both his Icosahedron and the planet at the same time.

Suddenly it didn't matter that Omnius had the enemy outnumbered. He could have all the trillions of drones he liked, but if he couldn't coordinate between them and give them orders, they would be a disorganized mob. They weren't designed to function without him, and he hadn't even had a chance to launch the drone fleet from the Icosahedron!

Omnius shook his human head. The brain inside of it was all he had left. He'd been cut off from his own thoughts, from *himself*. The only way to transmit data now was via light-speed comms, which were too slow to be effective for commanding drones, not to mention that none of his drones had conventional comm systems. The Icosahedron did, but access to those systems was cut off by quantum-linkages along the way.

Omnius sat frozen in his throne, his jaw hanging open, his eyes wide and glowing with augmented reality contacts that no longer worked, because the Omninet was down along with everything else.

He screamed aloud. The enemy had blinded and paralyzed him with one decisive blow, but even that wouldn't be enough to defeat him. His drones might not be organized anymore, but even with just the ones on the surface, they outnumbered the enemy a million to one. They could all fire randomly and still defeat the enemy. Sooner or later they would find the source of the jamming field and destroy it. Everything was under control...

The deck shook, and the distant rumble of an explosion reached Omnius's ears. He froze, listening to the dying echos of that explosion. There were no systems in his command center to simulate sound, so that sound had to have been carried through the superstructure of the Icosahedron itself.

Then another tremor rocked the deck, followed by another, and then a dozen more. What was going on? The enemy was far out of beam range, and missiles couldn't be reaching them already. Not to mention the Icosahedron was too large and too well-shielded to suffer damage from any conventional attack.

The deck shuddered once more, and another rumble reached Omnius's human ears, more distantly this time. Then he realized what it was.

Thousands of Facets had been coming together along the edges of the Icosahedron. They'd been in the middle of their docking patterns when the enemy activated their jamming field. Now, without him to pilot the Facets and make last-minute corrections to their flight paths, the Facets were all colliding with the Icosahedron rather than docking to it.

The deck shook with the most violent tremor yet, and Omnius almost fell out of his throne. He listened to the thunderous roar of the explosion and he screamed again.

He would make the rebels pay!

CHAPTER 37

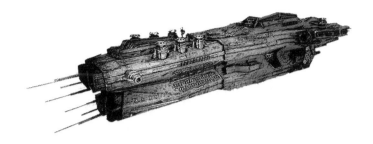

Destra received the order to launch and she fired up the drop ship's engines with shaking hands. *Pull it together, Des.* Even after years of training, she still wasn't the cocksure pilot her ex-husband Ethan had been. She didn't have the affinity for it, and she was surprised that the Union had given her a drop ship to pilot.

At least it wasn't a Nova, she thought. Drop ships couldn't maneuver much, so all she really had to do was point the ship's blocky nose at the green diamond that marked the landing site and *drop* down on it. Flight assist and autopilot were there to guide her down; gunners would keep enemies at bay; her copilot would manage shields, gravidar, and energy distribution. All she had to think about was take-off and landing.

Destra took comfort in that as she guided them down from the *Liberator's* ventral hangar bay.

"How are things looking out there, Cappy?" Destra asked, glancing at her copilot. Out the side window she saw Drop Ship One flying beside them. Without a frame of reference she might have thought it was tiny but for the small, glowing blue speck near the bottom of the blocky gray transport. That speck was the cockpit.

"Clear skies," Cappy replied. His call sign was a standing joke between the two of them. Cappy was short for captain, because he was always saying that if she ever learned how to fly, they'd put her in a Nova, and make him the captain of their beloved *Freefall*.

Destra smiled at the memory of their time training together on Origin, but this wasn't training; this was real, and her daughter, Atta, was heading down aboard Drop Ship One. Anything could happen to her, and there wasn't a thing she could do about it.

The comms crackled. "Tighten up that heading, Drop Two! You're drifting!" The comm was from Drop Ship One.

Destra snapped out of it and brought the *Freefall* back into line with the glowing green diamond on the surface of Avilon.

"Fallin' asleep at the wheel again?" Cappy asked.

"You just worry about watching your own screens," Destra snapped. "Are you sure we're clear?"

"I've got some drone fighters launching from the surface, but nothing close to us yet."

Destra nodded, gazing down on the shadow-speckled surface of Avilon. The planet's night side glowed bright with a patchwork of city lights. Something about that seemed wrong to her. "Hey, weren't we supposed to land on the day side?"

"Good point. Let me check our coordinates on the grid... hold up... what the frek?"

Destra glanced away from her controls for just a second, afraid to let Cappy distract her too much. "What is it?"

"I've got some major interference on the grid. There's a solid wall of it stretching clear from one end of the planet to the other, about thirty thousand klicks behind us."

Destra shook her head. "Can't be. Run a diagnostic. Make sure your sensors are working."

Before Cappy could acknowledge that order, the comms crackled again.

"This is Admiral Therius. Omnius was expecting us, but don't let that frighten you. We are successfully jamming him, and he is powerless to stop us. Today will be the day that we set humanity free! Your orders stand, and so must you! Stand firm, stand together, and *fight!*"

Destra turned to her copilot, wide-eyed with fear. Omnius had known they were coming. "I have a really bad feeling about this," she said.

Their drop ship hit Avilon's atmosphere and it rattled and shook with turbulence. Then the Union fleet commenced bombardment in earnest, and a flurry of long-ranged red and blue dymium beams dazzled their eyes. Further away, Sythian and Gor cruisers opened up with shimmering curtains of lavender-colored pulse lasers.

Fires began blooming in the sea lights below, and Destra watched it all with growing dread. The battle had begun.

She flexed her hands on the flight yoke. *You can do this...*

* * *

Clouds raced past Ethan's canopy in hazy black streaks. The sky gaped open as the clouds parted to reveal the uppermost city of Avilon. Buildings soared from the glowing blue sea of the Celestial Wall all the way up until their glittering spires disappeared into the clouds.

A pair of Rictans raced down beside him, their shields glowing almost as bright a blue as their thrusters trails with the heat of atmospheric entry. Ethan's Nova buffeted wildly, the air snatching at its fuselage, trying to slow him down. His shields roared deafeningly loud in his ears. They were going in *hot,* at full throttle, to prevent Avilon's defenses from targeting them.

They couldn't afford to take any risks. The First Battalion was theirs to escort, and it was the one carrying the Eclipser. That device was the only reason they hadn't fled at the first sign of Facets in orbit over Avilon. Omnius had sprung a trap for them, but he was the one caught in it. The Icosahedron was dead in space, and had yet to even launch its fighters. Avilon's defenses were offline, suspiciously silent. The garrisons had been all but wiped out in the initial bombardment, and what few fighters had escaped were scattered and disorganized, being picked off as the Union's entire fleet roared down on top of them.

Ethan began to feel hopeful about the engagement. At this rate, Therius might not even need the nanites, but Ethan and Atta were prepared. They'd strapped enough real explosives to each of those nanite bombs to vaporize them when they went off.

"SC, we've got incoming! Ten o'clock low," Magnum said.

Ethan checked the grid and saw a group of five drone squadrons racing up to port. "I see them," he said. "Rictans, switch to Hailfires and light 'em up!"

Ethan thumbed over to missiles and banked left to bring the drone under his targeting reticle. Red brackets highlighted the enemy fighter on his HUD; then he heard the *beep-beep-beeping* of a target lock. The reticle turned green, and he heard a solid tone. Ethan pulled the trigger two times fast, and a pair of Hailfire missiles jetted out on hot orange contrails, one after the other. They split apart almost immediately, giving eight different warheads for the enemy to shoot at. To either side Ethan saw more Hailfires go streaking out and splitting apart.

Then the enemy opened fire with crimson streams of pulse lasers. Missiles exploded in the near distance, lighting the sky on fire, and then the enemy's lasers came streaking toward *him*. Ethan jerked the stick in a circle and feathered some rudder to make himself harder to hit. Lasers flashed all around him, missing him by narrow margins.

Then a pair of them struck home, provoking a blinding flash and a hissing roar from his shields. Ethan toggled his own pulse lasers and began strafing the enemy formation at exactly the same moment as the rest of the squadron did. Then the surviving Hailfires reached their targets and the horizon blossomed with fiery reds and golds. Over a dozen targets winked off the grid. The explosions reached Ethan's ears moments later with muffled *booms*.

Victory cries echoed over the comms, and they went rocketing through the fading light of the enemy fighters' explosions.

"Get on their tails!" Ethan ordered, even as he rolled over and looped under through a Split S maneuver to chase the remaining drones away from the drop ships.

Ethan pulled out of his loop at a lower altitude than before. The drop ships were dead ahead, but so were the drones. The drop ships fired on them with a withering barrage of ripper cannons and pulse lasers. Drones exploded left, right, and center, but they kept on target, strafing the drop ships with fire.

Ethan strafed them back, trying to scare them off before he remembered that they were drones. Death didn't scare them.

The comms crackled. "Get those fighters off us!"

The remainder of the 1st Battalion's fighter escort broke away and engaged the enemy at close range. At least six drones fell apart in the first few seconds, but there were easily two dozen left, and Ethan could see that one of the drop ship's shields were failing. Ethan grimaced and poured a steady stream of fire into his target. He scored a lucky hit and it flew apart in a fiery rain of debris.

Then came a much bigger explosion as the drop ship whose shields were failing flew apart with a blinding flash and a roiling ball of fire. The explosion reached his ears as a titanic *boom,* and then a pelting wave of shrapnel went hissing off his shields. Ethan's heart seized in his chest.

If that ship had been carrying the Eclipser...

* * *

"I can't shake them!" Destra shrieked.

"Try!" Cappy roared.

The drop ship's shields roared furiously at them as continuous streams of enemy fire chased them down to Avilon's surface.

"I'm trying!" she insisted. Perspiration beaded on Destra's upper lip and brow as she did everything she could to fight her own ship's sluggish momentum. Eventually, she managed to push the *Freefall* into a lazy barrel roll.

An alarm sounded from the copilot's station, interrupting Destra's concentration. "What was that?"

"Aft shields critical, equalizing..."

Destra fishtailed, as if to literally shake the enemies off.

It wasn't working. Enemy fire went on roaring at them. Desperate, she keyed the comms. "Drop One, we're in trouble over here!"

"Hang in there!" Then over an open band Destra heard the pilot of Drop One say, "Get those fighters off us!"

"Shields failing!" Cappy warned.

"Equalize!"

"There's nothing left to equalize!"

The constant roar of lasers hitting their shields suddenly

became a high-pitched shriek as enemy fire burned through to the hull. Then a blinding red light suffused the cockpit.

Bang! The cockpit depressurized and stole Destra's breath with a sudden gust of escaping air. Their seat restraints held them down and kept them from being sucked out, too. Destra gasped, her lungs heaving in the thin air. Wind whipped in through the cockpit, wailing past her ears. Then came a gut-wrenching lurch, followed by another *bang!* This time it stole more than just her breath.

It stole everything.

CHAPTER 38

"We lost Drop Two! Tighten up that escort!" Drop One said.

Ethan commed back in a hurry. "Drop One, what's the mission status?"

"Status still green to go, but we can't afford another slip like that."

Ethan breathed a sigh of relief. They couldn't talk about the Eclipser openly over comms, but the pilot had implied it was still safe. They'd lost a third of the 1st Battalion, but Atta was aboard Drop One, so at least they still had their general.

Drone fighters flew past their targets and began looping back around. Ethan and the Rictans chased them through that turn, lasers flashing in a steady stream. Ethan hounded them with single-minded fury, firing precise, linked-fire bursts. Two direct hits in quick succession made for a kill. He lost count of how many he scored, but before the enemy had even finished their turn, they were all gone. A quick glance at the grid revealed no more enemy targets in the vicinity. They were clear.

"Whoop whoop!" Magnum said.

"Form on me, Rictans," Ethan replied, bringing his Nova back into line to follow the remaining two drop ships down. Switching to the battalion's command channel, he said, "Drop

One, you're all clear."

"Thanks, Rictans. We're entering our landing pattern now. Keep us covered."

"Roger that, Drop One," Ethan replied.

A few minutes later the drop ships went from falling like speeding meteors to hovering down gracefully over the landing site.

Far below, the city of Celesta dazzled with a vast array of lights. Urban parks splashed dark green shadows between glittering monoliths. Ethan watched a tumbling drone fighter crash in one of those parks with a burst of fire, and he grimaced, wondering how much of Celesta would survive this battle. High above, bright lances of blue and red light flashed down, zapping enemy fighters like flies. The fleet was descending from orbit.

Ethan's comms crackled. "Drop One and Two have landed."

Mission control replied from the *Liberator*, "Acknowledged, Drop One. The First Battle Group has you covered. Clear skies for now. Commence Operation Whistle-blower."

"Yes, sir."

Ethan received a direct comm just a few seconds later. "Rictan One, this is mission control. Landing Site Alpha is secured. Get your squad dirtside and report to General Heston for ground ops assignment."

"Acknowledged, control," Ethan replied, but he didn't need to relay the order. The Rictans had been listening in.

"All right, it's stompin' time!" Rictan Seven said.

"Whoop whoop!" Magnum cheered.

"Stow the chatter, but keep the enthusiasm, Rictans," Ethan said.

With the odds being what they were on the surface, enthusiasm was the only advantage they had.

* * *

Atton was eating breakfast with Valari Thardris and Ethan when the holoscreen in Valari's living room went suddenly blank. That screen had been relaying a news feed from an upper cities' network, but now the feed was gone. A few moments later a Null producer appeared, looking bewildered. He assured everyone that they were working on the problem, all the while insisting that nothing like this had ever happened before. The producer blamed an equipment failure for the interruption, but Atton knew better.

Omnius had been speaking to him just a second ago, reassuring him that he and Ceyla would be together again soon, and that this farce he'd been forced to participate in with Valari would come to an end. Now the voice in his head was gone, leaving him to wonder what had just happened.

Omnius? Atton tried.

No answer.

He looked up to find Ethan still eating, oblivious to the situation, but Valari's face was drawn and her turquoise eyes were wide with shock.

"Something's happened," she said.

Ethan looked up. "What?"

Valari sent him a blank look, and then recovered with a smile and nodded to the holoscreen. "The network must be down. Excuse me, please," Valari said. "I need to go check on something."

Atton watched her leave the table.

"What was that about?" Ethan asked.

Atton met his father's gaze. "No idea. Something to do with the Resistance, maybe?"

Ethan nodded and went back to his food. "Must be," he said,

sounding disinterested. The only thing he cared about these days was getting his family back, and Valari had promised to help him do that—hence his presence at breakfast. Valari was playing a long-term game of sympathy and support.

It all made Atton sick to his stomach. He wanted to expose Valari now, but he had to wait for Omnius's timing. He couldn't afford to jeopardize his future with Ceyla. He stood up from the table. "I'm going to see what's going on," he said. "I'll be right back."

Atton hurried to Valari's office. He found her there pounding keys on a holographic keypad before a blank holoscreen.

"Stupid thing!" Valari growled.

Atton came up behind her and read the connection error on the screen. The Omninet was down.

"You think it could be a rebel attack?" Atton asked.

"Don't be absurd! Whatever this is, Omnius is still in control. We'll find out what's happening soon enough, but until then, I suggest we go back to eating breakfast."

Valari brushed by him on her way out, but Atton lingered a moment longer, his eyes on the holoscreen and the error message blinking there. It read:

Connection Failure.

Host Unavailable.

"Atton? Are you coming?"

He nodded and turned away from the screen. "We should send someone to investigate," he said on his way out.

"The junctions will be offline," Valari whispered. "By the time someone can physically travel to the uppers and see what's going on, the system will be restored already. I'm sure it's nothing to worry about."

"What's nothing to worry about?" Ethan asked as they drew

near.

Valari smiled and sat down beside him. "Just a communications error," she said.

Ethan accepted that with a furrowed brow. "I see..."

Again, Atton was tempted to say something, but he stopped himself. Patience. He had to show Omnius he could be loyal even when he wasn't being watched.

Maybe that's what this was—a test. *It has to be,* he decided. Omnius never lost control.

* * *

The Rictans landed in unison beside Drop Ship One. Ethan cracked open his cockpit. Air *hissed* out as the canopy rose. He fumbled with his harness to release the buckles, then jumped out of the cockpit onto the port wing, and from there to the ground.

He raced up to the rear boarding ramp of the drop ship with the rest of the Rictans close behind. Atta stood there waiting for them, already suited up in a Zephyr, directing Gors and humans as they disembarked.

"General!" Ethan called out as he approached.

Atta turned to him, her expression inscrutable behind the glowing blue faceplate of her helmet.

"What happened up there?" she demanded, her voice booming out through her Zephyr's external speakers.

Ethan skidded to a stop with the rest of the Rictans.

"Happened?" Magnum echoed.

"We lost a drop ship," Atta said. "You almost frekked up the entire operation."

"Casualties were light, all things considered," Ethan said.

"We could have lost the Eclipser!" Atta roared.

"But we didn't..."

Atta turned away. "Instead we lost my mother."

Ethan froze. "Destra?"

"She was the pilot."

"Atta, I'm so sorry..." He took a quick step toward her.

She held up an armored hand. "Save it, Ortane. Zephyrs are inside. Watch traffic on your way up."

Ethan hesitated just a second before bounding up the ramp. The Rictans' footsteps echoed with his as they kept pace behind him. Gor and Human soldiers alike marched out in a steady stream from rows of upright docking stations inside the drop ship. Ethan eyed the Gors warily. Their shiny black armor and glowing red visors made them look menacing.

At the back of the troop bay, Ethan came to a locker room that he recognized from his training on Origin. He opened the door with a wave of his hand, revealing an entire armory with walls full of weapons, armor, and spare Zephyrs. The Rictans hurried over to the latter and suited up.

Once armored, they cherry-picked a few weapons and pieces of equipment from the available supplies. Magnum chose a pair of oversized plasma pistols; Carnage strapped on some binary explosives that wouldn't get him killed with a stray shot; and Blades picked out a Zephyr-sized medkit. Then *Hop* gave Ethan an idea about his call sign by selecting a gravpack. Thinking about the vertical nature of Avilon, Ethan selected a second gravpack for himself.

There came a heavy *whump,* followed by a ground-shaking roar that rattled the weapons and equipment on the walls.

"What was that?" Ethan asked.

"Our cue to leave," Magnum answered.

Ethan's comm crackled with Atta's voice. "Hurry it up in there! We just punched a hole. It's time to burrow!"

"Yes, ma'am—move out, Rictans!" Magnum said, taking

charge of the unit now that they were on the ground.

They raced back out and down the loading ramp. They were the last ones to leave the drop ship. Atta stood waiting for them with both her arms raised and gauntlet-mounted ripper cannons tracking faint shadows across the sky.

Ethan's aural sensors picked up and amplified the distant *roar* of Nova fighters, and the comparatively quieter *buzz* of Omnius's drones. Lasers crisscrossed the sky in steady streams. As Ethan watched, a bright flash tore open one of the clouds, and a fiery rain of debris came crashing out.

Atta turned to see Ethan gawking. "What are you waiting for?" she snapped.

"Shrapnel, get a move on!" Magnum called over the squad's comms channel.

He turned to see the Rictans already seeking cover, racing up to the base of the nearest skyscraper.

Ethan ran after them, servos and motorized joints *whirring* as he went. The Rictans tore up great chunks of grass and dirt in their wake, leaving a trail that wasn't hard to follow. He imagined drones following that same trail later, but he supposed they weren't exactly going for stealth with this assault. Looking up, Ethan saw the Rictans highlighted bright green on his HUD. Farther out hundreds of Gors and Humans milled around the base of the nearest skyscraper, showing on the HUD as a darker green than his own squad.

As Ethan drew near, he saw a gaping, ragged hole burned into one of the rooftops. The First Battalion was already jumping down inside that hole. A group of Zephyrs came out of cover carrying a heavy-looking piece of castcrete rubble between them. They passed the rubble carefully down through the hole in the rooftop, while a dozen more Zephyrs stood guard. That piece of rubble was the *Eclipser,* but where was the capsule containing the nanites?

"Get under cover, Shrapnel!" Magnum roared.

Ethan ran and hid at the base of the skyscraper. He joined the Rictans in keeping a lookout while the rest of the battalion jumped down.

"Where's the bomb?" Ethan asked.

"Must have carried it down already," Magnum replied.

"I didn't see it," Ethan replied.

"Let me ask the general..."

Ethan's comms crackled with Atta's reply a moment later. "I supervised ours being loaded from the *Liberator*, but once we got dirtside and cracked open the crate, it was full of oxygen tanks. Same story from the other generals. The bombs didn't come down with us."

Magnum commed back, "You think Therius had a change of heart?"

"More likely someone snitched on us, and he decided to keep the bombs in orbit with him."

"Frek," Ethan growled. "Then we can't stop him from using them."

"No," Atta replied.

"We need to warn the fleet," Ethan said.

"And tell them what? That Therius has nanites on board and he's planning to destroy Avilon?"

"That sounds about right."

"According to you, Captain Hale already knows. Therius is aboard *her* ship. If anyone can do something to stop him, it's her. We're going to have to trust that she's got a plan of her own."

"But—"

"If we don't secure this planet and get its people on our side, then this whole discussion is pointless. We need to focus on our job right now. Besides, Therius didn't come all this way just to kill everyone. We don't know that he actually plans to use those bombs. And we don't even know for sure that they actually contain nanites. The whole plot could be a bluff."

Ethan grimaced. "And if it's not?"

"Then we'd better hope Therius is right about there being an afterlife. Now cut the chatter, Rictans, and get down that hole! We have a planet to conquer."

Ethan felt despair worming inside his gut, making him feel dizzy and sick. He raced out after his squad and jumped down, following the trail of destruction that the First Battalion had left in their wake—shattered doors, broken walls, and more holes in the floor. The building they were in appeared to be some type of data center, with myriad rooms full of row upon row of glowing blue towers.

"Where are we?" Ethan breathed.

"Inside one of the omni-nodes," Magnum replied. "We're heading for the nerve center so we can broadcast our message to the people of Avilon."

Ethan heard weapons' fire up ahead, and Magnum said, "It's show-time, Rictans!"

They came to a broken wall and took cover to either side of the opening. Ethan peeked around the corner to see a room full of smoke. Lasers flashed red and purple through the gloom, and golden tracer fire stuttered out from ripper cannons. A laser bolt *screeched* into the wall, shattering bactcrete just a few inches from Ethan's face. He ducked back and used sensors to pinpoint the enemy instead. A seething red mass of enemy contacts streamed into the room from the other side, and green friendlies were shown pinned down behind cover.

Magnum gave a hand signal for them to break cover and flank the enemy. Before Ethan had a chance to take a breath, the Rictans raced out of cover with ripper cannons blazing. Ethan followed, looking for a clear line of fire between friendlies, while The Rictans fired straight through the intervening data towers, turning petabytes of data to shredded ruins. Red outlines began shuddering on his HUD as the Rictans' fire reached them.

Ethan heard a sudden *clank,* followed by a *screech* of laser fire. He felt a wash of heat on his right side and whirled around to find himself face to face with a drone. He raised both arms to fire, and the drone smacked him in the chest with an open palm. He went flying into a nearby wall, ripper cannons blazing a second too late and tearing ragged holes in the ceiling.

The drone *clanked* up to him while he was still struggling to get up. He took aim, and then someone burst through the hole in the wall where they'd come in. Energy blades flashed, and the drone fell in three pieces, the severed ends glowing bright orange while its red cyclopean eye went dark.

Ethan's rescuer turned out to be Atta. Her HUD outline was gold, rather than green, marking her as a general. She held out a hand to help him up, and yanked him to his feet. He took in a scene of utter destruction. Flames crackled as flammables burned. Smoke clogged the air. Twitching pieces of drones littered the floor, their wires sparking. A few downed Zephyrs and at least twenty Gors glowed pink on the HUD, while others with red cross symbols crouched beside them, giving aid.

"We've got company coming up behind us!" Atta called out over the comms. She crunched through the debris, and Ethan followed her over to one of the brighter green HUD outlines. Ethan saw from the text floating above the Zephyr's head that it was Magnum.

"How many?" Magnum asked.

"A few hundred for now, and those are just the ones we've spotted on the surface. Our air support has them pinned down, but at least half made it through."

"I thought Omnius wouldn't be able to rally a defense while we're jamming him?" Ethan said.

Atta turned. "Drones are not brainless. They're dependent on Omnius, but they're still capable of organizing to a certain degree."

"We'd better hurry then," Magnum said.

"Where's the Eclipser?" Atta asked.

Magnum jerked a thumb over his shoulder. "A few rooms back, sitting in a corner with some other debris."

"Better move it up. I'm leaving your squad in charge of its defense while we look for the control center in this place."

Magnum motioned to Rockhead and Blades. They left and returned a few moments later carrying the chunk of castcrete Ethan had seen earlier. That confirmed it was the Eclipser.

The ceiling shook with a muffled *boom*, and chunks of bactcrete rained down, *thunking* off their armor.

Atta peered up through a hole above her head and nearly got a face full of pulse lasers for her trouble. She and the Rictans scattered as the ceiling came alive with lancing beams of light.

"They're coming down on top of us!" Atta roared.

Ethan hunkered down behind an overturned tower of databanks. He peeked over the top to see drones dropping down from the ceiling like spiders, their optics glowing crimson in the gloom. Gors raced at them, lavender-hued pulse lasers flashing. The drones fired back, but the Gors kept going. They closed to hand-to-hand combat with the drones and produced scythe-shaped energy blades. Ethan raised one arm and aimed at the nearest drone, but he couldn't get a clear shot. He thought about jumping into the fray with his own energy blades, but more drones dropped down by the second, crowding the room, and the Gors who'd gone hand-to-hand with them were being picked off fast.

Lasers *crackled* out with intermittent flashes of light. Zephyrs fired back from points of cover, ripper cannons flashing gold through the drifting clouds of dust and smoke. Energy blades *sizzled*.

It was utter chaos. Ethan heard Magnum call out for them to retreat further into the building. Ethan couldn't even see the Rictans through all of the commotion. He was cut off and pinned down, but so far none of the drones had noticed him.

Clank-clank. Clank-clank-clank!

Ethan saw a flicker of movement on his right peripheral display. Then to his left. Red optics cast crimson beams of light through the smoky room. Ethan saw those beams sweep across the floor to either side of him.

His heart pounded in his chest and his breath reverberated inside his helmet. Ethan glanced at his sensor display. There were no friendly contacts around him. He saw a few retreating further into the building, chased by swarms of drones. He was alone with these four drones. They had to have detected him by now.

Clank-clank-clank-clank!

They were rushing him!

Ethan steeled himself, watching the enemy approach on his HUD, red outlines growing larger by the second. He raised his arms above his head, and waited, counting down the seconds.

Clank-clank-clank-clank!

He could feel the floor shuddering with their footfalls. One was coming straight at him, the other three flanking to the sides. Ethan waited another half a second, and then he flexed his hands into fists, extending his energy blades with a *sizzle* of activating shields. He jumped up out of cover at the same moment as the drone in front of him sprang over his cover. He lashed out as the drone sailed toward him, and it fell apart, gushing green coolant.

The other three rounded the overturned data tower, forearms sweeping up to fire. Ethan lunged toward the greater threat, the pair of drones to his left. He slashed across the barrels of their pulse lasers before they could shoot, and then he bisected them both with an uppercut. They clattered to the ground. He whirled around, looking for the third drone, just in time to be blinded by a crimson beam of laser fire shrieking out from the third and final drone. The laser bolt glanced off his chest, burning his armor to a molten ruin and searing his skin with a nauseating *sizzle*.

Opening his fists to retract his energy blades, Ethan activating ripper cannons instead and fired back at the drone. Twin streams of golden tracer fire roared out from his gauntlets, the impacts jumping the drone's aim so that lasers flashed all around him, but never hit. The sound of shells *plinking* off the drone's armor was deafening. Ethan rushed the drone, keeping up a steady stream of fire as he ran. When he came within an arm's length, he extended energy blades and slashed, cutting the drone in two molten orange-glowing halves.

Ethan stood over the enemy gasping for air, his chest burning like it was on fire. He glanced down at his chest and felt abruptly sick. Blackened char stared back at him.

It was tough to tell how badly he was injured. Between adrenaline and the stims that his Zephyr auto-injected, the pain was a fraction of what it should have been.

Ethan grunted and scanned the room for more enemy contacts, but friendlies and enemies alike were all gone. He was alone.

Ethan checked his map for friendly comm beacons, but saw no sign of his squad, or any other squad for that matter. He was out of range.

He opened his comms to see if he could get back in touch.

"Rictan One reporting, does anyone copy?"

A fierce crackle of static answered.

Frek.

Ethan turned in a quick circle to get his bearings. Smoke curled in drifting curtains, concealing everything. Looking up, Ethan saw the holes the drones had burned in the ceiling. Dozens of gaping apertures. He saw a flicker of red HUD outlines. They were coming again. A quick look at sensors revealed at least fifty drones coming down.

The next wave.

Ethan didn't have time to decide which way his squad might be. He spun around, looking for a way out. He spied a door close behind him and ran for it. Bringing his energy blades up as he reached it, Ethan quickly sliced a hole big enough for him to crawl through on his belly, which he promptly did. On the other side he saw yet more glowing blue towers of data, but these had yet to be shredded by weapons fire. Before he even regained his footing on the other side, he glimpsed drones dropping down behind him on his rear viewscreen. A fan of crimson light flickered through the hole in the door. Drones scanning the room he'd come from.

Clank-clank-clank!

"Frek!" Ethan growled. They'd found him already. He bounced up and ran, hoping desperately to find backup soon.

He tried the comms again. "Rictan One reporting! I need backup!"

Static crackled, and Ethan grimaced. He was on his own. He ducked and wove between glowing data towers, wishing he could fly over them instead. Then the door behind him burst open with a flash of light and an accompanying *boom*.

Clank-clank-clank!

Here they come . . .

CHAPTER 39

Binary explosives punched a hole. Six squads of Zephyrs and an endless stream of Gors went storming through. Atta followed them, expecting to see more of the endless rows of data towers, but this room was different. There were control consoles and holoscreens for data *input*, not just data storage and processing. This was a hub, one of the access points that drones used to perform maintenance on the systems throughout the omni-node.

"This is it!" Atta called out. "Secure all the entrances. We don't want to get interrupted before we're done here."

She turned to see squads of Gors and Zephyrs taking up positions at all the doors. Two squads covered the hole they'd entered by, while another four hurried back through the shattered wall to cover them further back. Tech experts peeled out of their Zephyrs and sat down behind control consoles to get to work. Atta checked her sensors to make sure there wasn't a whole company of drones racing up behind them. Nothing yet, but she still felt naked.

She'd left at least half of her battalion guarding entrances back the way they'd come, while another third escorted the Rictans and the Eclipser deeper into the city. Atta had been surprised and upset to hear that Ethan was MIAPD, but there'd be time to grieve their losses later. The rest of the Rictans were to rendezvous with the Second Battalion and carry the Eclipser down into the Null Zone for safe-keeping. Their secondary objective down there was to recruit a civilian army of Nulls, but not even Nulls would fight until they heard the truth.

Fortunately, they would be easy to convince. First, because they were *Nulls* and inherently distrustful of Omnius, and second, because they weren't even supposed to have Lifelinks. Just the fact that they would be able to see Therius's message would be enough to convince them of its veracity.

There was one problem, however. In order to send their message to everyone all at once, they needed to disable the Eclipser. That meant Omnius would have a small window of opportunity to get his forces organized.

Striding over to the nearest console, Atta asked, "How much longer?"

The tech turned to her with a frown. "We're hacking into a supercomputer, ma'am; a *smart* one. If you want this to work, you need to give us time."

"And if you take too long, we're going to be up to our eyeballs in drones."

"We can't rush this or network security is going to shut us out when we try to send our message."

"I thought Therius gave you the encryption keys?"

"That doesn't make this any easier. We need to infect the system in a million different places with every kind of virus you can imagine just to distract Omnius long enough that he won't be able to stop our message. We have a one minute window, and as far as Omnius is concerned, that's a lifetime."

"The message is *five* minutes long," Atta said. "How are you going to pack all of that into one minute?"

"We're not streaming; we're downloading, and it would be a lot faster, but we don't have the bandwidth in this node to send to everyone at once. We've busted the transmission up into batches, but even like that we're only going to reach about 90 percent of the population."

"Good enough," Atta said. "Let me know when you're ready so I can coordinate with the Second Battalion to disable the Eclipser. If you need me, I'll be watching your asses by the door."

"Yes, ma'am."

"*Techs!*" Atta muttered under her breath. She wasn't a fan of cyber warfare. She'd take a pulse rifle or a ripper cannon over a battle of bits and bytes any day.

As Atta approached the ragged hole they'd blown to get into the control room, she heard a stutter of ripper fire, followed by a shout of warning over the comms.

"Fall back!" someone yelled. It was Delta Two.

"Deltas, report!" Atta commed back.

"They're coming through!" Delta One replied amidst a deafening roar of weapons fire.

"Drones?"

"No, Peacekeepers! Thousands of them!"

Atta checked the Deltas' position on her scanners and motioned for the squads standing guard with her by the shattered wall to move up. They preceded her out of the control room, and she commed back, "We're on our way, Deltas. Hold your position!"

"We'll do our best, General."

Thinking fast, Atta called for reinforcements from the Second Battalion. They couldn't be too far off.

The comms crackled with a response from the battalion's Gor general. "We come under heavy fire! I cannot reinforce if we are to keep advancing."

"Frek it," Atta muttered. "Then stop advancing! Pull back to the control center. We can't afford to lose it! Not until our message gets out."

"What about the Eclipssser?"

"Bring it with you! If we're running into this much resistance already, then digging deeper is a mistake. At least we know they'll refrain from using heavy weapons while we're inside one of the omni-nodes, but as soon as we poke our noses out, they're going to hit us harder than ever."

"Yesss, you are right."

"Of course I'm right."

Atta watched a surge of green begin moving back up the tower, converging on her position. She hoped it would be enough. Atta ran to catch up with the two squads she'd sent to reinforce Delta squad. She heard weapons fire again, but this time it came via aural sensors rather than over the comms. The Peacekeepers were close.

Atta raced through a room full of overturned data towers, her feet crunching noisily through the debris. Up ahead, just on the other side of a shattered door she saw ripper cannons and pulse lasers flashing. Atta ran up to the door just as the squads she'd sent came boiling through. A flashing silver sphere appeared in their midst, and Atta screamed, "Grenade!"

Then it exploded, but instead of incinerating both squads with a roiling ball of fire, it picked them up and *threw* them, sending them flying and tumbling away in a radius around the grenade. Atta went flying back the way she'd come and landed with a *crunch* in a pile of shattered data towers.

Dazed, she shook her head and climbed unsteadily to her feet. Dead ahead, Peacekeepers came trudging through the rubble in their glowing, mirror-smooth armor. Their face plates shone through the gloom like flashlights. Here and there, they raised their palms to fire dazzling bursts of energy. Atta raised her arms to open fire, but the Peacekeeper nearest to her raised both his palms and hit her with a violent gust of wind from his grav guns, and she went flying once more. This time she hit the far wall. Despite the padding inside her armor, the impact was enough to stun her. The Peacekeeper walked up to her, a blue cape fluttering behind him, his palms raised and *humming* with a repelling force that held her pinned to the wall.

"Who are you?" the Peacekeeper asked, speaking in broken Versal.

Atta used her chin to flick from comms to external speakers. "Tourists," she said.

"A sense of humor. Interesting. Let's try again. What are you doing here? I'm going to count to three. On three, you're either going to start talking, or we're going to start shooting."

Atta noted that half of the sixteen soldiers she'd come with lay motionless in the rubble, while the other half had been pinned to the walls and floor with grav guns, just like her.

"One. Two—"

"Wait, let me explain," Atta said.

"You've got one minute."

"That's all I need."

* * *

Ethan cut his way through door after door, to get away from the drones pursuing him. He managed to stay one step ahead of them, but the thunder of *clanking* footfalls and the *crackle* of laser fire intermittently flashing out behind him was a constant reminder that being one step ahead wasn't good enough.

Before long he ran out of doors to carve through and ended up standing before a wall of windows, gazing out into a gaping chasm between buildings.

Clank-clank-clank!

Ethan spun around, looking for a way out. The door he'd carved open last lay right behind him, the edges of the hole he'd cut still glowing molten orange. Ethan glimpsed red HUD outlines swarming toward him. He didn't have much time.

Remembering the grav pack strapped to his back, Ethan turned to the windows. Extending his energy blades, he carved a hole and punched out an oval section of glass. It went tumbling away, and Ethan poked his head out, staring down into the cavernous gap between buildings.

Orderly lines of air traffic sat gridlocked below him. Below that, about twenty levels down, was a pedestrian street level. Pedestrians walked along it in colorful streams. They didn't look to be in a hurry. Clearly they had no idea what was going on, but then again, how could they? In Etheria all the news nets were controlled by Omnius and Omnius was offline.

Ethan eyed those streets, looking for a way to get down. Then the piece of glass he'd cut out hit the streets and pedestrians screamed. Ethan grimaced, but he didn't have time to worry about them. A *screech* of laser fire sounded out behind him, followed by a crimson beam hitting the wall of glass and shattering it with explosive force. Ethan turned to see a glint of drone armor appear in the open doorway behind him. Lasers crackled out once more, and Ethan fired back with ripper cannons. Laser bolts went streaking by him.

He didn't have time to hesitate. Ethan turned and dove

through the open window. He screamed himself deaf as he fell, his arms and legs windmilling for purchase on something solid. Then he recovered his wits enough to grab his gravpack controls. He pulled them out and used a pair of miniature joysticks to right himself so he was falling feet first. As soon as he'd righted the pack's axis of lift, he ignited the grav lifts on high power. A violent jerk sent all the blood rushing into his feet, and Ethan saw black. Terror filled him. If he blacked out now, he was dead. His heart pounding, he blinked rapidly to clear the spots from his eyes.

The ground rushed up, and he bent his legs to land with a ground-shaking *boom!* Pedestrians scattered in all directions. But one man stood frozen and staring.

"You're a Sentinel!" the man said in broken Versal, his brown eyes wide and glowing.

"It's not what you think," Ethan tried to say.

"Get him!" someone else said, more distantly. Ethan turned to see a pair of Peacekeepers pushing through the crowd. They raised their palms, grav guns already powered and glowing, and Ethan turned and ran the other way, heading for the densest concentration of people. Peacekeepers wouldn't fire on him if it meant a chance of hitting Etherians.

As Ethan ran, more people stopped and turned to point at him. Recognition spread like fire, and the crowd parted down the middle. Many of these people had come from the Imperium, but he was surprised they still recognized a Zephyr after all these years. The crowd continued to part, forming a living tunnel. At the end of it Ethan saw a whole squad of Peacekeepers charging toward him. He was trapped.

"Frek!" Ethan skidded to a stop and dove behind a bus stop. A withering rain of laser fire followed him, turning his cover to a molten ruin.

Ethan risked peering over the railing at the edge of the street. The city disappeared below him in a dizzying swirl. The next level of streets was almost too far down to see. Pulse lasers continued screaming into the ruined bus stop. The heat of that assault radiated through both the debris and Ethan's armor. He was pinned down, and there was only one way to go.

Before he could take too long to think about it, Ethan jumped out of cover and leapt over the side of the street. Again came the sickening sensation of free fall, but this time he was in control. He fired his gravpack on low power to slow his descent while dropping past a level of gridlocked air traffic. Passengers in the cars pointed at him as he fell. A young child waved. Wind whistled by aural sensors, and they faithfully reproduced the sound inside his helmet, setting his teeth on edge.

The next level of streets came rushing up. Ethan dialed the power up to full and simultaneously bent his knees as his feet touched ground. Pedestrians backed away from him, and again the crowd parted. More Peacekeepers appeared in the distance. Ethan dashed into an alcove, and pulse lasers chased him there, digging chunks out of the bactcrete walls.

How many Peacekeepers are *there in Etheria?* he wondered. They seemed to be everywhere he went.

Ethan risked exposing one of his arms to fire back. Red HUD outlines showed him where the enemy was even through the walls, while civilians appeared around them in receding masses of yellow. Ethan fired a solid stream of ripper rounds at the nearest enemy, and the Peacekeepers ducked into an entryway just down the street from him. They took turns firing at each other from behind cover, aiming for the pinprick-sized targets of each other's exposed hands and arms.

Ethan missed consistently. So did the Peacekeepers. It looked like a standoff. Then one of the Peacekeepers scored a glancing hit on his arm, lighting his nerves on fire. Ethan roared and withdrew his arm to see a small, blackened hole in his armor. Determined not to repeat that incident, Ethan waited.

They had to step out of cover if they wanted to get him, and as soon as they did, he'd have a clear shot. Ethan kept an eye on his rear viewscreen, but there was no one there.

Then he saw a ghostly flicker of movement. His heart pounded and his palms began to sweat.

What was that? Some kind of glitch?

Then it reappeared, right behind him, and he recognized the outline of a man. Ethan whirled, making a fist to extend an energy blade from his right-hand gauntlet. The blade flashed out in a shimmering blue-white arc before hitting something solid and slicing through. An armored arm fell to the ground, the palm flashing with a burst of light as it fell. A belated *whoosh* of air punched Ethan in the chest and sent him flying through the entrance of the restaurant where he'd taken cover. He landed on a table and flattened it with a crash of glass and dinnerware.

Patrons screamed, and Ethan bounced to his feet to see the Peacekeeper who'd snuck up on him clutching the cauterized stump of his severed arm and swaying on his feet. The man saw him, and raised a bloody palm to shoot, but Ethan was faster. He poured a torrent of ripper fire from both gauntlets. Rounds sparked off the Peacekeeper's armor, jumping his aim and making his body jerk and shudder like a rag doll. Then the Peacekeeper's shields failed and rounds punched holes in his armor with crimson sprays of blood.

The man fell over backward, and Ethan grimaced, having suddenly lost his taste for violence. That Peacekeeper had tried to detain him with nonlethal force, and Ethan had killed him.

Two more red outlines appeared on his HUD, approaching the entrance of the restaurant, one from either side. Ethan tracked them with his ripper cannons, but then he stopped himself. They'd come to set Avilon's people free, not to kill them. These Peacekeepers weren't the enemy. He just had to buy time until Therius transmitted his message and proved that the real enemy was Omnius.

Ethan activated his external speakers. "I surrender!" he called out in Avilonian, and raised his hands above his head.

They replied in the same language. "You are under arrest for the murder of an Etherian Peacekeeper!"

"It was an accident. I need your help," Ethan replied.

"Our help? Not even Omnius can help you now," one of them said as he came out of cover. He strode in through the restaurant with both palms glowing and ready to shoot.

"That's what I need your help with—Omnius. We've come to set you free."

The Peacekeeper burst out laughing. "Free? From what? Paradise?"

Ethan watched the second Peacekeeper come creeping out of cover to back up the first.

"Give me a chance to explain, and I think—"

"Save the explanations for your trial. Get out of your armor."

Ethan cracked his Zephyr open and stepped out. "Anything else?"

One of the Peacekeepers produced a pair of energy binders and snapped them around Ethan's wrists. "Come with us," he said, taking hold of Ethan's arm and dragging him out the ruined doors of the restaurant.

"You're making a mistake," Ethan said once they were back on the street.

The Peacekeeper holding him spared a glance at his fallen colleague. "You're right. I should have shot you, not taken you into custody."

Ethan grimaced. He considered trying to tell these two the truth about Omnius, but they had no reason to trust him, and conspiracy theories were nothing new on Avilon. He would have to wait for Therius's message.

As the Peacekeepers dragged him down the street, Ethan's thoughts turned to his family. It was too late for him to help the Union take Avilon, but maybe it wasn't too late to find Alara and Trinity. The problem was even if the Peacekeepers holding him suddenly switched sides when they got Therius's message, he didn't know where Alara lived.

If the Omninet were back online, all it would take is a simple query to find them. Ethan shook his head. There had to be another way....

Suddenly he had it. *Therius's message!* In order to send it they needed to disable the Eclipser. Maybe not for long, but maybe long enough.

Ethan had to get to a computer terminal. Turning to the nearest Peacekeeper, he said, "I know why Omnius is offline."

"Shut up." The Peacekeeper tightened his grip and gave Ethan's arm a violent tug.

"If you take me to a computer terminal, I can bring him back."

The Peacekeeper stopped dragging him, and turned to glare at him. "How do I know you're not going to make things worse?"

"The data terminals are all offline. They're useless right now, so you have nothing to lose."

"Why would you help us? A second ago you were trying to convince me that you were going to set us free from Omnius. Bringing him back online is the opposite of that."

"I should have been more specific. The fleet I came with is

here to set you free, but I have my own agenda. I'm here to rescue my family, and I need the Omninet to find them. Do you see me surrounded by an army of soldiers? I'm on my own down here for a reason."

"Omnius won't let you leave Avilon. How do you plan to rescue your family if he's back online?"

"He's going to be too busy fighting off the invasion to stop me. I'll have my chance."

The other Peacekeeper spoke up, "We've got nothing to lose by trying."

The first Peacekeeper scowled and shook his head. "You do anything suspicious, and I'll shoot you dead."

"Agreed."

The Peacekeepers dragged him toward the nearest building, and hope swelled in Ethan's chest. He couldn't believe he'd convinced them. Just as soon as the Omninet came back online, he'd use it to find Alara and Trinity. Now, no matter what Avilon's fate, at least *his world* would be safe.

He would make sure of it.

CHAPTER 40

"That's quite a story," the Peacekeeper pinning Atta to the wall said. "If Omnius created the Sythians, then why seed the Getties with nanites to destroy them?"

"Not to destroy them, to cover up his lies," Atta said. "The Getties is full of artifacts from an ancient human civilization, artifacts that prove Etherianism predates Avilon, for one. For another, there's proof that Omnius *found* quantum tech and reverse-engineered it. How do you think we surprised Omnius with a quantum jammer powerful enough to knock out communications all over Avilon? We found the same things he did and more."

The Peacekeeper deactivated his faceplate, revealing a strong jaw and bright blue eyes glowing in the light of his ARCs. "That still doesn't make sense," the Peacekeeper insisted. "And I'll tell you why—I already know everything that you just told me. Omnius already told me the truth, and he's told many others, too. Why cover up the lies if he's just going to reveal them all later?"

Atta saw the other Peacekeepers trading glances with each other. Omnius's machinations were obviously news to them, but the blue-caped Peacekeeper had just confirmed everything she'd said. The problem was, if he already *knew* the truth, then why was he fighting her?

Atta frowned, suddenly uncertain about the invasion. "You're telling me you know what Omnius is, and you serve him willingly anyway?"

"Omnius's disciples worship him in truth, knowing exactly who and what he is. He is too powerful to resist, so we don't even try. We have accepted our fate because there is no other choice."

"But you're free! We disabled Omnius. Now there is a choice!"

"So it would seem..." the Peacekeeper replied. He withdrew and the bright glow of grav guns faded from his palms.

No longer pinned to the wall, Atta fell from it with a *thud*. She looked around quickly. Union soldiers clambered to their feet all around her. Now the Avilonians were helping them up rather than holding them down. But not everyone got up. At least a full squad of Zephyrs and Gors lay motionless and half-buried under rubble.

"You killed them. You knew—" Atta said, rounding on the Peacekeeper standing beside her. "You *knew* we came to set you free, and you killed them anyway."

"We had no way of knowing Omnius's absence was a result of your intervention, or even that he would stay offline, and we couldn't risk taking the losing side in a war."

Atta regarded the man with a scowl. "That sounds like something a coward would say."

"We all do what we must to survive. If you didn't want

anyone to die, then you shouldn't have come. Besides, your soldiers are not the only ones who have died today."

Atta considered pointing out that casualties on both sides could have been prevented if they'd surrendered, but what was done was done.

"We need to tell the rest of Avilon the truth," she said. "If we don't stop fighting each other soon, we're all going to die. How many drones are there on Avilon?"

"Trillions," the Peacekeeper replied.

"Frek..." Atta muttered. "Then we might all die anyway."

"Not if we stand together," the Peacekeeper said, and thrust out his hand. Atta eyed it. "Strategian Galan Rovik," he said. "And you are?"

"Atta Heston," she replied, accepting the handshake.

The man's eyebrows floated up and he smiled. "It's a pleasure to meet you Atta. Your father and I are good friends."

Atta's heart began racing in her chest and her grip tightened involuntarily. "You know him? Where is he?"

"In the Null Zone. I can introduce you when this is all over if you like."

Atta blinked, shock and excitement waging war inside of her. This man knew her father!

Then her comms crackled, interrupting her thoughts. "We're ready to send the message, General! Get that Eclipser offline!"

Atta replied, "Stand by, Corporal." Then she sent a comm to the Rictans, "Magnum, General Heston here, what's your status?"

The sound of weapons fire raged through Atta's helmet, making it all but impossible to hear what was said. "Pinned down! Tak... h-vy fire!"

A titanic *boom* roared over the comms, followed by static. *Krssssss...*

"Magnum!"

Silence.

"Frek!" Atta screamed.

Then her comms crackled again, but without the noise from before. "Sorry about that, General. Carnage just handled the situation with a plasma grenade. We're falling back, on our way to reinforce your position as ordered."

"Well stop and hold where you are! Operation Whistle-blower is a go. Get ready to disable the Eclipser on my command."

"Yes, ma'am."

Atta ended the comms and turned to Galan Rovik. She nodded to him and said, "You think you can hold this position?"

"The *Eclipser*—that's your jamming device?"

Atta frowned, wondering how he'd overheard her conversation. Then she realized that she'd forgotten to turn off her external speakers. Atta grimaced. It was a good thing these Peacekeepers were on their side now, but she chose to not to answer Galan's question. She didn't have time to explain. "Can you hold here or not?"

"Of course," he replied.

"Good." She turned and motioned for the remaining Zephyrs to hold with them.

A lone Gor responded with a *hiss*. "They kill my crechemates," he said, his gaze fixed on the nearest Peacekeeper. "I do not fight beside murderers."

"We killed their people, too," Atta replied. "We have to move past that or this will all be for nothing."

Another *hiss* was the Gor's only reply. Atta grimaced and took off at a run. She felt like the entire operation teetered on a knife's edge, but despite that uncertainty, there was a sullen hope.

Her father was *alive*. She reached the control center where she'd left the techs. The one she'd spoken with earlier turned and nodded to her as she ran up behind him.

"We're ready when you are, General!" he said.

Atta commed the Rictans, "Disable the Eclipser!"

Magnum replied, "Disabling in three, two, one, zero."

"Punch it!" Atta said, speaking to the tech.

"Message transmitting!" he replied.

* * *

Ethan ran system diagnostics and checked network settings from the data terminal, hoping the Peacekeepers who'd brought him there wouldn't notice he was stalling for time.

One of them jabbed him in the ribs. "You don't have a clue what you're doing. Even I can see that!"

"Give me a minute!" Ethan said.

"Sure we'll give you all the time in the..." The Peacekeeper trailed off and Ethan turned to see both him and his partner stumbling around in circles, their heads turning every which way at once, as if plagued by a cloud of invisible insects.

It took Ethan a second to realize the moment he'd been waiting for had come. They were blind, their augmented reality contacts were transmitting Therius's message right before their eyes. As Ethan watched, both Peacekeepers lost their balance and fell over with a noisy clatter of armor. They began struggling to regain their footing, but only half-heartedly.

Ethan chided himself for wasting time and hurriedly turned to the data terminal. He put together a query in his head and said: "Find Address: Alara Ortane. Description: violet eyes, dark hair, has daughter Trinity, husband Ethan."

He held his breath while the search ran. He half expected it to fail. He had no way of knowing how long the Eclipser would be disabled. How long would the Union need to send a message to trillions of people? *Come on...* Ethan thought. Then the screen changed, and an address popped up.

Alara Ortane Lives in Etheria, Level 20, Fairhaven District, Block 17, Fairview Tower, Apartment 20G.

Ethan couldn't believe it! He quickly memorized the address and turned to leave—

But he caught himself. The Omninet was still online, and there was something else he needed to know. He needed a way to get his family off Avilon.

Ethan quickly spoke another query to the terminal: "Location for captured Imperial transport, name *Trinity*, museum piece, former owner Ethan Ortane."

With fewer records to search this time, the terminal answered his query instantly.

Celesta, Ground Level, Heritage District, Block 67, History Towers, History of Space Flight Exhibit.

Ethan memorized that address, too, and then turned from the terminal for a second time. He risked a glance at the Peacekeepers who'd arrested him. They'd stopped struggling to get up. Now they lay staring up at the ceiling, watching whatever it was that Therius had decided to show them. Ethan considered waiting for the transmission to end and asking them for help, but he realized he couldn't be sure what side they'd be on. Therius's message might fail to convince them. It wasn't worth the risk.

But something else was.

The nearest Peacekeeper had a sidearm holstered to his hip, along with several grenades and spare charge packs for his weapon. Ethan dropped to his haunches and began unbuckling the man's belt, being careful not to alert the Peacekeeper to what he was doing. Once the belt was free, he gave a quick tug and leapt away. The belt came away in his hands, and the Peacekeeper reacted by flailing around blindly for him. Ethan drew the stolen sidearm and leveled it on the man's head, but the Peacekeeper subsided once more, still preoccupied by whatever he was seeing.

Ethan buckled on the belt and ran as fast as his legs would take him. Everywhere he looked, people lay collapsed on the ground, staring blindly up at the ceiling. The data terminal he'd been using was in a hover train station. There'd been plenty of travelers passing through at the time he'd arrived, but now all of those travelers had been struck down by Therius's revelation.

Ethan had to concentrate as he ran just to avoid stepping on people's outstretched hands and feet.

All around him, people shouted exclamations of "I knew it!" and "I don't believe it!" and sometimes, defiant cries of, "Omnius grando est!"

The latter group made him snort with disgust. Some people embraced lies so eagerly that they would never believe the truth.

Ethan reached the nearest hover train and raced aboard, hoping the trains would still be working when Omnius went offline again. Since they ran on a track rather than a simulated street, he was pretty sure they didn't require either quantum communications or constant intervention from Omnius to keep them running. As he came aboard, he noticed the train was full of passengers, and he considered that a good sign. None of them saw him as he came aboard. Their glowing eyes were glazed and flickering with miniature holo recordings. Ethan found a seat by the entrance.

Not long after that, the train gave an automated warning that the doors were about to close, and passengers began snapping out of it. Ethan watched their glowing eyes dart around the inside of the train, and he realized that he wasn't wearing ARCs. Some of these people might find that suspicious, but no one seemed to notice.

Suddenly the train raced out of the station, going from zero to a hundred klicks in the blink of an eye. Inertial management reduced the sensation of acceleration to a mild tug, but it was enough to snap people out of their confusion.

The passenger car erupted in noisy chatter. People jumped to their feet, fists and jaws clenched, spoiling for a fight.

One man cried out, "I'm gonna kill that frekkin' bot!"

Someone else said, "You fool! Etheria is a paradise! Life has never been so good. Who cares if he lied? Look at everything he's done for us!"

The first one started cursing at the second, and then everyone pitched in with their thoughts.

Ethan watched the developing confrontation carefully, holding his stolen sidearm in a loose grip in his lap, just in case.

Across the aisle from him a redhead with wide, glowing magenta eyes spotted his weapon and opened her mouth to say something. Then she appeared to think better of it and shut her mouth.

Ethan nodded to her and smiled. "Do you know how I can get to *Fairhaven District?*" he had to yell to be heard above the ruckus of people arguing inside the train. "I'm looking for my wife and daughter!"

The redhead shook her head quickly and looked away. Ethan wondered if she'd seen that he wasn't wearing ARCs and that was what had scared her into silence.

"Are you sure?" he insisted. "You must have an idea where it is. You live in Etheria, right? Please. It's important."

"I—it's near the end of the line," she stuttered.

"Thank you!" Ethan replied.

"You're not from here?" she asked.

"Not Etheria, no. It's a long story. I'm taking my family and leaving Avilon before things get any worse," he replied.

"You have a ship? You're a pilot?"

Ethan nodded.

"Can I... can I come with you?"

Ethan hesitated, suddenly worried about what his wife would say about him picking up pretty girls after he told her what had happened with Valari, but these were extenuating circumstances. Anyone they left behind would either die in the fighting, or return to slavery with Omnius. Either way, not a happy ending.

"Just try to keep up," he said.

"I will. I promise."

CHAPTER 41

—30 Minutes Earlier—

Hoff simultaneously pushed the throttle past the speed limit and pulled out of the simulated street onto an illegal flight path. Shining windows flashed by to either side, forming racing rivers of light.

Hoff had spent the better part of an hour trying to provoke a response from Omnius before he'd realized what was happening.

Omnius is offline!

He had to get home, and fast. He had no idea how long it would last, or even whether or not it was a trick designed to test loyalties, but he couldn't afford not to take advantage of it. He planned to get his family and run with them as fast and as far as he could. They had to find a way out of the Null Zone, find a ship to steal, and then find a way to disable their Lifelinks...

One obstacle at a time.

First things first—he had to rescue them from their so-called guardian drone, *Triple Nine*. She was really an assassin, and she was there to remind Hoff that his family's well-being depended on his performance as the leader of the White Skulls.

But now all of that might finally be at an end. There were rumors of a battle raging in the Uppers. The Sythians were invading.

Hoff ducked and wove through streams of traffic, taking the shortest and most direct route possible to get home.

Air cars crisscrossed the sky in every possible direction— people racing home, or to wherever they thought would be the safest. So far no debris had come crashing down from the Uppers, but Hoff knew that couldn't last.

After a few narrow scrapes in alleyways and one near miss with a pedestrian hover-train, Hoff raced inside his garage and left the car with the engine running. With one hand on the butt of his sidearm, he raced up the steps to the side entrance of his apartment and waited impatiently for the security system to recognize him. The door *swished* open, and he ran inside.

Hoff found his family sitting on the couch, watching a local news channel. Most of the Null networks still worked, since quantum technology was proprietary of Omnius.

Destra looked up, her face pale and eyes wide. "You're back!" she said, rising from the couch. Then Atta turned, too.

"Dad!" Atta ran to greet him. Before she'd made it more than two steps, Hoff heard a *clank-clank-clank* of metallic feet approaching. He whirled toward the sound, drawing his sidearm and taking aim. He saw Triple Nine racing down the hallway toward the living room, but Atta was in the way, and he couldn't get a clear shot.

"Atta, get down!"

An uncertain look crossed her face and she turned to look over her shoulder just in time to see Triple Nine raising both arms and deploying weapons. The drone had detected a threat, and unlike a proper guardian, she was prepared to defend herself even at the expense of the people she was ordered to protect.

Atta hit the ground, and Hoff fired twice in quick succession. The drone fired back in the same instant. A bolt of sheer lighting tore through his side, spinning him around and dropping him to the ground. Destra screamed as he fell. His plasma pistol went clattering away, and then came a *thunk* and a straining *whirr* of servos and mechanical elements as Triple Nine fell and then struggled to get back up. Hoff lay staring up at the ceiling, dazed, his side pulsing with fire.

Atta and Destra appeared hovering over him, both of them blubbering and trying to tend to his injured side at the same time. Despite the pain, he found he could still move. He brushed them away and clambered to his feet. Dark spots crowded his vision, and he could feel himself swaying on his feet, his gut churning with a dire need to vomit. He gritted his teeth and pushed his physical self aside, hurriedly scanning the room for his target. He expected to find the drone incapacitated and lying on the ground, but Triple Nine was gone.

"Where is she?" he demanded, turning in a quick circle, looking for his sidearm.

"Dad! Look out!"

Hoff whirled around just in time to see the drone leaping up over the back of the living room couch. Two ragged black holes in her chest gave a gory view of exposed wiring and oozing green coolant. Both her arms were raised, as if to throttle him or to fire a deadly torrent of lasers. But Triple Nine didn't shoot. Hoff realized he must have damaged her firing controls.

The drone came to within an arm's breadth of him, and then he dove to one side. Triple Nine anticipated the movement and followed him down.

Then came a sharp *crack* and a dazzling flash of light. The drone fell on top of him, knocking him over. He grappled with her on the ground, fighting a shower of sparks and a hissing stream of coolant. He roared, kicking and shoving until the drone rolled off him. That was when he noticed her optical sensors were already dark. A hole shone straight through Triple Nine's head.

Hoff sat up and turned to see Atta holding his sidearm. She dropped the gun and hurried over to him with her mother. Again, both women tried to tend his injured side.

This time he let them.

Destra's lips trembled and she stroked his forehead with a shaking hand. Then Hoff saw her eyes dart to his injury. The blood left her face in a rush, and she started sobbing.

Hoff glanced down to see what had upset her. He saw white ribs poking through blackened skin, and a wave of nausea washed over him. His head swam with the overpowering urge to pass out.

Hoff grimaced as the adrenaline left his system and he fully felt the pain of his injury. He began to shiver. All his plans of escaping Avilon disappeared. He was done.

The world around him abruptly vanished, replaced by a vision of a planet he was sure he'd dreamed about, but never quite remembered until now. He was still conscious and fully aware but logic told him he must be dreaming.

He floated high above the ground, soaring weightless over sprawling green fields and jungles. Overhead was a high dome of the bluest sky he'd ever seen. To one side, a lavender-colored lake sparkled in the sun. Out on the horizon, tall mountains rose from the plains, green trees carpeting them, and pure white glaciers gleaming at their summits. Hoff looked down and saw a vast, milling army of...

Gors. Then he looked up and noticed the myriad shadows painted on the sky. An entire fleet hung in a low orbit above his head.

A strong, strident voice interrupted his thoughts.

"My name is Therius the Redemptor, leader of the Union of Sentient Peoples. We have come to set Avilon free. This world you see before you is the lost world of Origin, the planet where humanity was born. It is in the Getties Cluster, the so-called home of the Sythians. Yet I bear witness to you now, the only Sythians here are the ones that Omnius bred and trained to invade your galaxy. He created the Sythians and sent them to kill you so he would have an excuse to resurrect everyone on Avilon, but even the Sythians were deceived. Once they learned the truth of their own origin, they turned against Omnius, and they stand with us now, united against our common foe.

"The Nulls are also watching this transmission, even though their Lifelinks were supposed to have been disabled—another lie. And that leads us to the greatest lie of all—The Choosing doesn't exist to give people freedom; it exists to make humanity predictable. Something vital is lost during clone transfers, something that makes humans unpredictable, and that is the real reason Omnius makes his people choose. Omnius has never been able to accurately predict human behavior, nor can he permanently do so with those he resurrects.

"I was one of Omnius's lead researchers on the team investigating the phenomenon before I escaped and came here. These are the results of just some of our experiments—"

Hoff watched a series of brain scans with *before* and *after* *resurrection* labels flash up before his eyes. He wasn't surprised. Omnius had already revealed all of this to him, and he didn't need any convincing.

"We have disabled Omnius." Therius said once the parade of experimental data came to an end.

The vision of Origin returned, and Hoff's viewpoint turned skyward, soaring ever-higher and aiming for the hazy blue shadow of a venture-class cruiser. Stars pricked through the blue and Hoff saw a combined squadron of Shell Fighters and Novas roar by in front of him, flying in tandem wing pairs. *"He has no more power over you, but he is far from defeated. Now is your chance to be free. Join us! Fight! For freedom!"*

The vision vanished, and Hoff was left staring wide-eyed at the ceiling. Suddenly he understood Omnius's absence, and the reason for it was better than he'd even dared to hope.

"It was all a lie..." Destra began.

"Help me up," Hoff croaked.

Atta shook her head and bit her lip. "You need to lie down, Dad. I'm going to get the medkit. I'll be right back!"

Hoff was about to object, but another wave of nausea swept over him, causing his stomach to convulse painfully. He cried out, and spots danced before his eyes.

"Hoff!" Destra cried. Her hand found his in a white-knuckled grip, and he focused on taking short, gasping breaths.

"You're going to be okay," Destra said between sobs. "Shhh..." she said.

Hoff looked up at her and smiled. "You're going to have to... go without me."

Destra looked shocked. "Go where?"

Atta returned with a medkit, already holding a hypo between her teeth. Something for the pain? She injected him, and a welcome rush of warmth replaced the blazing fire pulsating in his ruined side.

Hoff sighed out a belated reply, "Anywhere but here... find a way to get away from Avilon before it's too late."

Atta looked confused. "You heard what Therius said, they're—"

"They're all going to die, Atta."

"What?"

Hoff rocked his head from side to side. "Whatever these

rebels think they've done to Omnius... it's not going to last. He's going to find a way to regain control, and when he does, I don't want you two to be here."

Atta set her jaw and shook her head. "We're not leaving you, Dad."

Hoff regarded his daughter with a smile. He felt the darkness closing in again. "Even if you don't leave, I will. You can't save me."

"No, you're wrong," Destra said. "You just lie down and rest. We're going to take good care of you."

Hoff tried to object, but the fight left him. His eyes narrowed to hazy slits, and then the darkness consumed him.

By the time he awoke once more, he felt much better. He was still lying on the floor, but now his side was patched, and a pair of EMTs attended him, one to either side.

"Where's my family?" he croaked.

"We're right here!" Destra said, hurrying into view.

Atta appeared over her mother's shoulder, looking hopeful. "You're going to be all right," she said.

Hoff shook his head. This hadn't been the plan. They should have gotten away! He wondered if Omnius was back online already. "How long was I out?" he asked.

Before Atta could answer, the front door *swished* open and Atton walked in. Hoff tried to sit up, and the EMTs helped him.

"Hello, Atton," Hoff said, smiling at the sight of his stepson.

"Hoff, we have to..." Atton trailed off, his head cocked and listening. Hoff heard it, too—the *clanking* footfalls of drones.

Valari Thardris came into the room next, followed by a squad of drones.

CHAPTER 42

Omnius saw it all play out in the blink of an eye. His awareness returned as the message from the rebels' *human* leader played through the minds of each and every one of his people. He saw their initial reactions to that message, the state of the battle, the locations of enemy forces... he even learned the nature of the jamming field; it was generated by a device called the *Eclipser*.

The jamming was deactivated for all of a minute, most of which Omnius spent fending off a cyber-attack. Even so he had more than enough time to send orders to his drones. First he ordered the fighters aboard the Icosahedron to launch, giving them basic orders to seek and destroy; then he sent updated nav data for his Facets to finish docking without further collisions. Finally, he worked on narrowing down the location of the quantum jammer.

It seemed that one of the rebel generals, Atta Heston of all people, had given the order for it to be disabled. Omnius didn't understand how Atta could be in two places at once, but he didn't have time to figure it out. Strategian Galan Rovik had witnessed her give the order to disable the jamming field. Omnius instructed Rovik to find the device and take it out.

The jamming field came back online and his awareness collapsed once more, leaving him with just his human brain and senses to rely on.

Therius! Omnius fumed, recalling the name of the Union leader. Omnius had killed him and turned him into a drone a long time ago. Yet here he was, claiming to have *escaped* Avilon!

Something didn't add up. Maybe this Therius was an impostor... but if he was, then that didn't explain how he knew what he did about Avilon. Even his vocal inflections and the words he used were familiar. This man was either Therius, or someone who'd known him very well.

But besides that mystery and the mystery of two Atta's, was the mystery of Origin, where Therius claimed to have come from. Was that the uncharted planet he'd found them orbiting just before the attack? He would have to go back there and investigate once the battle was over.

He couldn't believe that the planet had actually been found. He hadn't even really believed that it existed, but even *he* recognized it from the holo recordings in Therius's message, and that was the most curious part of all. How could he recognize a place that he'd never been to?

Omnius paced the deck, anxious for his awareness to return so he could begin solving those mysteries. Rovik would find and disable the Eclipser. He would just have to be patient until then.

* * *

Atton saw Therius's message, and he finally realized that Omnius's absence wasn't some kind of test, or even a trap to lure the invaders into a false sense of security.

Yet even before Therius had finished speaking, Omnius sent Atton a message of his own, proving that he was back—

Don't be a fool, Atton. I have Avilon surrounded. My drones outnumber the enemy a million to one. I will regain control of the planet soon, and when I do, you don't want to find yourself on the losing side of this war. Don't forget, I'm the only one who can bring Ceyla back. Bring Valari to the Icosahedron and meet me there. I'll be waiting.

After both Omnius's message and Therius's vision ended, Atton found himself lying on the floor, staring up at the ceiling of Valari's penthouse. The drink he'd been carrying lay overturned on the carpet beside him. He must have fallen over at some point during the transmission.

Omnius? he tried.

No answer.

He tested his mental connection to the Omninet, but it was down, too. Omnius had only come back online for a moment. Atton sat up to see his father staring at him. Ethan's features were slack with shock.

The sound of high heels striking the floor at a hurried pace drew their attention and they turned to see Valari striding into the living room.

"We need to go," she said. "Omnius is waiting for us in orbit."

"What are you talking about?" Ethan demanded, jumping to his feet. "We're the Resistance! We need to fight Omnius, not help him!"

Valari planted her hands on her hips and regarded him with a condescending look. "You can't be that naive. A few million rebels can't possibly defeat Omnius."

"They disabled him."

"Temporarily."

Atton saw Ethan's eyes narrow, but his father said nothing.

"Think about it. Omnius created the Sythians. That must

have taken considerable infrastructure, somewhere far from Avilon. That infrastructure is called *New Avilon*, an artificial planet many times the size of this one. It's so vast and so powerful that there's no way this rebellion can succeed."

Ethan looked skeptical. "If that's true, then I'm going to find my family and get away from this frekking planet once and for all. If you really love me, Valari, you'll let me go."

Valari's expression darkened. "Fine," she said. "Go."

Ethan turned to leave, and Atton saw the metallic glint of a palm-sized weapon drop from a voluminous sleeve into Valari's hand. Her arm came up—

And suddenly everything seemed to be moving in slow motion. "Dad!" Atton screamed as he lunged toward her. Ethan turned just in time for Valari to pull the trigger. There came a sharp *snap!* and a bright red needle of light burned a smoking hole in Ethan's chest. He fell over, his eyes wide and staring fixedly at the ceiling.

Atton reached Valari a split second later and gave her a violent shove. She went sprawling, and he followed her down, raining blows on her face. Valari fired at him, shooting straight through one of his hands. Atton screamed as his palm erupted with a searing, debilitating pain. That moment of distraction was all it took for Valari to shove him off and regain her footing.

"Enough!" she screamed, wiping a split and bleeding lip on her sleeve.

Atton sat clutching his injured hand and glaring up at her, his chest heaving with fury. "Go ahead, shoot me, too!"

"That would be too kind."

"You dumb sclut, you killed him!"

"Watch how you speak to me. And no, I didn't kill him. Haven't you learned? No one ever dies here. I'll have Omnius resurrect Ethan after this is all over, but right now we don't need him getting in our way."

"He'll never forgive you for making him a clone. He barely forgave me for becoming one."

Valari laughed. "He was *already* a clone."

Atton did a double take and turned to look at his father's body. Ethan looked the same as ever—fifty-something years old, not twenty-one as he should have been if he were a clone. Atton turned back to her and shook his head. "He's too old to be a clone."

"Omnius aged him so that he wouldn't figure it out. I knew there was a chance he'd kill himself after I tricked him into sleeping with me, and that's exactly what he did. We had to bring him back the next day and invite you over to keep him from doing anything stupid."

Atton shook his head, sickened by Valari's machinations. "What guarantee do I have that Ethan will be brought back?"

"Do you really think I'd go to all of this trouble to get him just to throw him away?"

Atton stumbled to his feet and glared at her, his hand still stinging fiercely. He recalled Omnius's plan to kill Valari, and he willed himself to be patient. All he had to do was get her to the Icosahedron and Omnius would do the rest. "We need to go," he said. "It's not safe on Avilon."

"Agreed."

"First, I'm going to find the rest of my family."

"And do what?"

"Convince them to go with us."

Valari's expression softened. "I'll go with you."

"I'm going alone."

Valari hesitated. "Of course. Take one of my couriers."

Atton was about to object, but Valari was already heading to her hangar. He followed her out and up to the pilot's side of a shiny black air car. Valari waved open the door and Atton jumped in.

"Be careful," she said. "The streets will be more dangerous than ever right now."

Atton nodded. "I'll see you on the Icosahedron." He shut the door in Valari's face and dialed up the grav lifts to hover off the deck. Rotating the car to face the shielded entrance of the hangar, Atton gunned the thrusters and raced out into the Null Zone.

Atton set course for Hoff's apartment, and began taking the most direct path there. As he dove down into the lower levels, Atton saw that Valari was right about the streets being dangerous.

Cars crisscrossed between buildings in every possible angle and direction, except for the legal ones, making flying more hazardous than ever. But the pedestrian streets looked even worse. Racing shadows darted into stores and darted back, their arms fully-laden with stolen goods. Atton could actually hear the security alarms screaming as his car roared by.

By the time Atton arrived at Hoff's apartment, his hands were shaking from the adrenaline of near misses with other cars. Atton rode up the lift tube from the building's guest parking, straight to Hoff's apartment on level twenty. He ran out of the lift and down the hall. Rounding the corner to Hoff's apartment, he found the door wide open. Fearing the worst, Atton slowed to a fast walk and drew his sidearm.

When he reached the open doorway, his eyes widened with horror and his aim faltered. To one side of the living room lay the charred and smoking skeleton of a Null guardian drone. To the other side lay Hoff with two EMTs attending him, and both Atton's mother and half-sister crowding around.

Hoff was the first one to notice him standing there. He sat

up and said, "Hello, Atton."

Atton felt relieved to see him sit up. "Hoff, we have to..." He trailed off as he heard something—the *clanking* footfalls of drones. His heart suddenly pounding, Atton spun around just in time to see Valari come racing down the hallway toward him, leading a squad of drones.

He blinked, shocked and angry to see her. She'd followed him here! Valari brushed by him in the doorway.

"Valari?" Hoff asked.

"What are you doing here?" Atton gritted out.

"Keeping you safe. It's a war zone out there," Valari replied. Then, to Hoff she said, "We need to get away from Avilon right now."

"You've turned against Omnius?" Hoff asked, his eyebrows arching.

Valari snorted. "What are you talking about? We need to leave Avilon because it's about to go up in smoke, and we don't want to get caught in the blaze. Are you coming with us or not?"

"With you where?"

"To New Avilon. It's already in orbit. We'll be safe there."

"Go frek yourself, Valari," Hoff replied.

Guardian drones came *clanking* into position to either side of Atton, occupying all the space in his peripheral vision.

Feeling suddenly apprehensive, Atton turned to his stepfather with an imploring look. "You can't win," he said.

"We can't take Omnius's side," Destra said.

Atta shook her head. "Atton, didn't you see the Union's transmission? Omnius is evil. Now we have proof. This is our only chance to defeat him—or at least escape!"

By now the EMTs had stopped working to listen to the exchange. They eyed the drones and each other nervously.

Hoff smiled and jerked his chin toward the drones. "Are

these my executioners?"

Atton swallowed thickly. He felt like he was going to be sick. This was spiraling out of control. "No, Hoff, listen—"

"Save your breath. I'd rather die than serve Omnius again."

"That can be arranged," Valari said.

"Wait!" Atton said.

Valari pointed to Hoff with one arm raised, her thumb pointing down. The drones recognized her unspoken command, and mechanical *clicking* sounds filled the air as weapons slid out of armored compartments. The EMTs dove for cover, and Hoff spread his arms wide, welcoming the end.

"No!" Atton roared.

"Dad!" Atta said.

Then came a crackling roar and a blinding tirade of laser fire. Hoff's body jittered and convulsed under fire; then he fell over backward, his clothes smoking. A noxious smell of burned meat and synthetic fibers drifted through the room. Destra threw herself over Hoff's body, sobbing, while Atta stood up and took aim with a weapon Atton hadn't realized she was holding.

Atton tried to shout a warning, but the drones shot her first. Her shot went wide, slashing a dark furrow in the ceiling above Valari's head, and then Atta hit the floor with a solid *thud.*

Destra belatedly noticed what had caused the sound. Then she screamed and cursed at them as she rushed to Atta's side. Valari pointed at her next, thumb turned down, and another barrage struck her down.

It all happened in a matter of seconds. Atton gaped at the scene before him. The EMTs fled, not even bothering to gather their equipment. This was all his fault. His entire family was dead, struck down in seconds. He never should have come.

Blood raged in Atton's veins, demanding justice, but a cooler, calmer side of him warned him not to do anything rash.

Omnius had already promised Valari would die. He just had to be patient.

Atton turned to Valari, his eyes cold and dark with fury. "You didn't have to kill them," he said quietly. "My mother wasn't even resisting."

Valari frowned. "Don't be so dramatic. I didn't kill them. They're just sleeping. They won't be the only ones Omnius has to bring back when all of this is over. And they were already clones, so what's the big deal?"

What's the big deal?

Atton turned back to look at them all lying there, smoke rising from their clothes.

The big deal is that they're my family.

CHAPTER 43

Ethan ran after the redheaded Etherian who'd agreed to help him find Alara's apartment. After what felt like a lifetime of charging down streets, cross streets, and alleys, they found Fairview Tower and rode the lift tubes down to level 20. Once there, Ethan raced down the hallway until he came to apartment 20G. He raised his hand to trigger the buzzer by the door, but then he hesitated.

Would Alara be happy to see him? Or would she tell him to go jump off the nearest rooftop?

"What are you waiting for?" the redhead standing behind him asked.

Ethan cast a grimace over his shoulder. "A miracle," he replied, and then he touched the buzzer.

Moments later the door swished open and Alara appeared, her violet eyes wide and shining. She was even more beautiful than he remembered her.

"Who are you?" Alara asked, her gaze flicking from Ethan to the redhead beside him and back again.

Ethan's jaw dropped. She didn't even remember him! What had Omnius done to her?!

"Don't you recognize me?" he asked. But then he realized

why. Therius had cloned him on Origin and in the process he'd turned the clock back by about thirty years. Alara hadn't met him as a young man, so she wouldn't recognize him now.

"Ethan?" Alara asked.

Or maybe she would...

Alara's eyes widened, and her ruby lips parted in a gasp. Her shock only lasted a moment, however, before her eyes narrowed to angry slits and her gaze settled on the redhead standing beside him. "Is this your new girlfriend?" she asked, thrusting out her chin. Tears sprang to her eyes, but it wasn't sadness Ethan saw shimmering there—it was hate.

"Let me explain—" Ethan said, taking a quick step forward and reaching for her hand.

"Don't touch me!" she said, recoiling from him and slapping his hands away.

"Alara, just listen!" He nodded sideways to indicate the redhead. "She's someone I met on the way over. She helped me find you!"

"Find me? You already know where I live. Or did you get drunk again and forget that, too? The first time you forgot you were married to me, and now you forgot where I live. Pretty soon you're going to forget you ever met me. Why did you come here, Ethan? Why transfer to a clone? Did you really think I would take you back after what you did?"

Ethan's brow furrowed. He was missing something. "Wait a minute," he said. "When did I come here?"

"The night after you cheated on me, you came to convince me that it had all been a drunken mistake, that you thought Valari was me. You really don't remember any of that? Wow... when you get drunk you don't mess around!"

"Mom?" a little girl's voice came from somewhere within the apartment. "Who is it?"

Ethan's heart jumped in his chest. *Trinity!*

Alara turned to address their daughter. "It's your father," she said, just as Trinity appeared.

"Trin," he whispered.

She looked uncertain, not recognizing him.

"Don't you remember me?" He tried a crooked smile, but it came out broken. His eyes burned with the threat of tears. His own daughter didn't recognize him!

But then Trinity's eyes widened and she gasped. "Dad!" she exclaimed. She ran toward him and crushed him in a desperate hug. "I missed you so much!"

"So did I, sweetheart," he replied, kissing the top of her head. "So did I."

Alara looked on. She bit her lip and shook her head. "Why did you do it, Ethan? You're here now, a clone. Despite all your objections to life in Etheria and Lifelink transfers, you decided to become a clone anyway. You could have followed us here rather than drink yourself senseless and end up cheating on me with another woman!"

Ethan grimaced, feeling those words stab him straight through the heart. "Alara, I didn't transfer... not the way you think, anyway. When I woke up in Valari's apartment and realized what I'd done, and then I thought about you and Trinity, both dead—at least, that's how it seemed to me at the time—it was all too much for me. I couldn't take it. I crashed an air car into the surface and died a Null, Alara."

"You what?" Alara frowned. "Then why did Omnius bring you back?"

"It wasn't him. I woke up in the Getties, on Origin. A man named Therius resurrected me. He said he intercepted my Lifelink data when I died, and he used it to clone me. He's been doing that for some time to recruit his army from Avilon. You saw his message, right?"

Alara's eyes widened. "Yes. You came with them?"

Ethan nodded. "We need to go now, while we still have a chance."

"Wait—you killed yourself before or after you came here to convince me to take you back?"

Ethan's brow furrowed. "I never came here, Alara."

"Yes, you did."

"If I did, then it wasn't me."

"You looked more like you than you do now. You were still old."

"That doesn't make any sense."

"Unless Omnius brought you back and aged your clone so that even you wouldn't know he'd resurrected you. Why go to all of that trouble?"

Ethan shook his head. "I don't know. I don't even know what you're talking about, but we can figure this out later. We need to go."

"Go where? Therius said he came to set Avilon free. Why leave now?"

"What he didn't tell you is that Omnius has a massive warship in orbit right now. It's not even right to call it a ship. It's a hollow shell five times the size of Avilon that Omnius calls *New Avilon*. Even crippled as he is, we're too badly outnumbered to win. Therius knows it, and he has a plan, but you don't want to be around to see him put that plan into action."

"What are you talking about?"

"The Union fleet is loaded with nanite bombs. Therius is going to drop them on Avilon if Omnius doesn't agree to back down."

"*What?* Why would he do that?"

Ethan shrugged. "I wish I knew."

"They're going to kill us?" a panicky voice interrupted.

Ethan turned to see the redhead who'd led him here backing away slowly, shaking her head. She had her arms wrapped around her shoulders, hugging herself.

"It's okay," Ethan said. "We're going to be long gone before that happens."

The redhead backed into a corner and sunk to the floor in a daze.

"Who is she?" Alara whispered.

"I don't know. I ran into her on the hover train on my way here," Ethan replied.

Alara watched the other woman for a moment before turning back to him. "If what you're saying is true, then we have to do something, Ethan."

"Yeah, run away and never look back. And we need to go *now*. We're running out of time." He reached for her arm, but she resisted. "Alara..."

"We can't abandon the entire human race, Ethan."

"What choice do we have?"

"We can't just stand by and watch trillions of people die!"

Ethan sighed. "If you have an idea, I'd love to hear it."

"You tell me. You came with them. Isn't there some way you can get to the bombs? Disable them somehow?"

Ethan shook his head. "We tried that."

"We?"

"Me and Atta."

"Atta Heston? She came with you?"

Ethan nodded. "The only way to stop those bombs from going off is to bring Omnius back online so that he can intercept them with planetary defenses, but we're never going to escape Avilon if we do that. No one will. The war will be over in seconds."

Alara grimaced. "Then we'll be back where we started."

"Yes."

"But what's worse? A life of slavery to a lying, manipulating AI is still better than no life at all."

Ethan arched an eyebrow. "Are you sure about that?"

"Let me put it another way: would you rather be alive on Avilon with me and Trinity, or dead and turned to free-floating atoms by a hungry swarm of nanites?"

"There's a third option. Run while we still can, and live free somewhere far from here."

Alara shook her head. "Even if we could, and Omnius never found us—which you and I both know is unlikely—could you live with trillions of deaths on your conscience, knowing that you could have done something to stop those people from dying?"

"Frek it!" Ethan pounded the wall with his fist, startling Trinity. Ethan saw her wide eyes and trembling lips and began rubbing her back. He went on in a calmer voice, "We don't even know if the bomb threat is real. What if it's just a bluff? And even if it's not, Therius might stop short of using the nanites."

"You met this Therius, didn't you?"

"Yes..."

"So what do you think? Would he use them?"

Ethan thought about that for a moment, remembering the Union leader's emphasis on faith and belief in a higher power. "I think he's a codice-thumping nut who'll blow us all to the netherworld if we give him half a chance."

"Then it's not an empty threat."

"No."

Alara stood there, staring at him for a long moment. "How do we bring Omnius back online?" she whispered.

Ethan grimaced. "We're going to have to disable the

Eclipser."

"The... ?"

"The device we used to take Omnius offline. It disrupts quantum technology."

"Do you know where it is?"

"Roughly."

"Then let's go," Alara said, turning and leaving her apartment.

"Hold on a second!" Ethan called after her, but she didn't turn around.

Cursing under his breath, Ethan took Trinity's hand and then glanced at the redhead who'd brought him this far. She was huddled on the floor in a fetal position, her eyes glazed. He couldn't leave her there. Grimacing, he walked over and offered his free hand to help her up.

"Let's go," he said.

She stared at his hand, as if she didn't know what to do with it.

"Come on!" he snapped.

She grabbed his hand and he yanked her to her feet. He turned and ran to catch up with his wife, dragging Trinity along. They arrived at the lift tubes together, and found Alara already waiting there with the call button lit.

"Alara, you're not coming with me."

"You bet your cheating ass I am," she replied.

"What about Trinity? This is going to be dangerous."

"We're clones, Ethan. We already died. What's the worst that could happen?"

"You could die again, and we could fail to bring Omnius back online. Then you're going to stay dead."

"Then let's make sure we don't fail. Besides, you just said we're all going to die anyway."

"We're all going to die?" Trinity whimpered.

"Not if we run," Ethan said.

"No one's running anywhere," Alara replied. Then she looked to Trinity and smiled. "And no one is going to die, sweetheart. Don't worry."

"Frek it..." Ethan muttered.

One of the lifts opened up and they all piled in. Ethan selected the highest street level available, level 225, and then leaned back against the far wall of the lift. The redhead came slinking in just as the doors were closing.

Alara eyed the other woman anew as the lift tube shot upward. "What's your name?" she asked.

"Jena Faros," the other woman replied.

"Alara Ortane. Nice to meet you. You don't have to go with us."

"I want to," Jena said, hugging herself again and backing into the farthest corner of the lift.

Ethan was busy reassuring Trinity, so he didn't notice what Jena was doing until it was too late. In one smooth motion she snatched his sidearm and pointed it at his head. He felt the weapon trembling in her hands, the barrel shivering against his scalp.

"I'm getting off Avilon," she said, "and you're going to fly me out of here."

CHAPTER 44

Ethan felt Jena's arm shaking, the stolen sidearm shivering and jumping against the side of his head, and he knew that she wasn't prepared to use it.

"You're going to shoot me in front of my family?" he asked, turning his head to place the barrel of the weapon between his eyes.

Jena Faros backed away from him. "I will if I have to."

Ethan took a step toward her.

"Stop!" she said.

Ethan froze. "If you shoot me, you won't have a pilot to fly you off Avilon."

"I can fly myself out of here."

"Then why don't you?"

"Because you have a ship that Omnius can't track or control. If he comes back online, he won't be able to interfere with my escape."

"But he can still track *you*."

"I'll deal with my Lifelink later."

"All right, so we escape Avilon, then what? You kill me for my trouble?"

"No, we find a planet far from Avilon and live out the rest of our lives free of Omnius's influence. Your wife is a fool if she thinks Omnius will be grateful that she brought him back online."

Ethan took another step.

"I said stop!"

Alara hit the emergency brakes on the lift, and it came to a sudden stop just a few floors from their destination. The lift's inertial management system kept them from feeling much, but a piercing alarm screamed inside the lift, stealing Jena's attention for a split second. That was all Ethan needed.

He lunged toward her and snatched the weapon from her hands. Retreating quickly, he aimed it at her chest. "You're going to have to go by yourself," he said. "My wife is right. We can't just leave everyone to die. We're going to save a lot of lives today."

Jena's expression twisted up in misery. "Save them for what? A life of slavery?" She shook her head and collapsed on the floor of the lift tube. "It's not worth it! He took everything from me!"

Alara walked over and went down on her haunches beside the other woman. "We've all lost a lot," Alara said.

"He killed my sister," Jena said, her eyes drifting out of focus, as if she were suddenly lost inside her head. "We were Peacekeepers. Partners. She... she jumped from a rooftop, and Omnius *let* her! He could have predicted it. He could have stopped her! Afterward, he claimed she was a Null Rebel, and everyone just *believed* him, like they'd somehow always known she was a traitor. She wasn't a traitor! She was just tired."

"I know," Alara said. "Listen, we're going to help a lot of people like your sister, people whose only crime is that they're *tired*. We could use your help to save them."

Jena looked up. "My help?"

"You're a Peacekeeper, aren't you?"

"I... yes, but I'm suspended."

"Can you get a suit of armor?"

"Why?"

Ethan was busy wondering the same thing.

"Because we don't need drones shooting at us, and if you look like a Peacekeeper, maybe you can convince them that we're on their side so that we can find the Union's jammer and destroy it before it's too late."

Ethan's eyes lit up with understanding, and he hurried over to the lift controls, setting it in motion again.

"I don't know..." Jena said, shaking her head.

"Your sister died. How did that make you feel?" Alara pressed.

Jena looked confused. "I just told you."

"You were devastated."

Jena nodded.

"If you really believe it's better to die than to live with Omnius, then you wouldn't have been sad to hear that your sister died. And if your sister's death was still a tragedy, then how much more of a tragedy will it be if *everyone* on Avilon dies?"

The lift reached level 225 and the doors swished open. "Let's go," Ethan said, gesturing ahead of him.

Alara offered a hand to help Jena up. "Lead the way."

Jena nodded and bounced to her feet with sudden enthusiasm. "This way," she said, running out and down the hallway beyond the lift tube.

They reached the street-level exit and Jena led them out into the middle of a war zone.

Ethan saw civilians looting stores and running every which way with stolen goods in their arms. Laser fire flashed and crackled in the distance. Smoke curled through the air. People's screams and the sounds of breaking glass filled the air. It was like someone had flicked a switch. Turn off Omnius, and suddenly everyone turned to their inner devlins for guidance. *So much for paradise*, Ethan thought.

"Come on," Jena said, turning and running in the opposite direction from the firefight. Ethan kept pace beside his wife and daughter. Trinity's violet eyes were wide and terrified. Ethan wanted to say something, but there wasn't much he could say to lessen the terror of what was going on around them.

They followed Jena down one street after another, ducking through alleys and hiding in alcoves and entrances to avoid being seen by either Peacekeepers or drones. That went on for a long time before Jena took them into one of the buildings. "I have spare armor and weapons in my apartment," Jena explained as they reached the lift tubes.

Alara nodded and turned to Ethan with a grim look. "I hope you can still find your way back to the jammer after this."

Ethan nodded, thinking about all the twists and turns he'd taken since abandoning his squad in the omni node. "So do I," he replied.

Once they reached Jena's apartment, she stepped up to the security scanner and waited for the door to open. When it did, they were greeted to the sight of a messy apartment. Jena clearly hadn't been in the mood to clean for the past... *couple of years,* Ethan decided, noting that dust had settled in a thick coat on every surface.

"I don't spend much time here," Jena explained while leading the way through her living room. "And I fired my servant drone after my sister died."

"That's all right," Alara said.

Ethan nodded, trying not to choke on the smells or trip over any of the clutter on the ground.

Jena took them down a hallway and then to a door with another security system guarding it. The scanner recognized Jena and the door *swished* open a moment later, revealing a room full of weapons and gleaming suits of armor.

"They let you keep the hardware when you're suspended?" Ethan asked.

"I was about to be reinstated. It's more convenient for Peacekeepers to have their equipment at home," Jena explained. "That way they have the quickest possible response time."

Jena activated a suit of armor and pieces began hovering down off the wall of their own accord, snapping into place over her calves, arms, chest, and legs.

Ethan took a pulse rifle off the wall.

"I'll take that," she said and slotted it into a magnetic holster on her back. She held out her hand and nodded to the sidearm strapped to his waist.

"No way," he said.

"If we're going to tell all the drones and Peacekeepers we meet that I'm in charge, and you've switched sides to help me to find and disable the jamming field, then you'd better not be armed."

"Disabling the Eclipser was our idea, not yours," Ethan said.

"But who's going to believe that?"

Ethan unbuckled his gun belt with a grimace. Jena took it from him and buckled it to her own waist. Nodding at that, she said, "Let's go."

Rather than take them back to the streets, she took them to her garage and they all piled into her patrol car. Ethan sat up front to give directions as she hovered up and out the static-shielded entrance of her garage.

"Where to?" she asked.

Ethan eyed the rising columns of buildings and shook his head. He didn't recognize any of them. "Where's the nearest omni-node?" he asked. "We were trying to get to the control center inside the node closest to the train station where I met you."

"That's about fifty blocks from here," Jena said. "Hang on."

Ethan was pinned to his seat as the car rocketed toward the nearest row of buildings, aiming for an alley between towers. Glittering lights rushed at them. Up ahead the alley appeared too narrow to fit their car. Ethan fumbled to buckle his seat restraints.

"You sure you know how to fly this thing?"

Jena shrugged. "Maybe. I'm used to having Omnius fly me around."

Ethan's eyes widened. The alley was just a thin black line between the buildings. "Jena..."

At the last possible second, she flipped the car up on its side and skated through the alley sideways. She ducked and wove around garbage chutes and emergency stairwells with practiced ease, and then they flew out and roared across the next chasm between rows of buildings.

Ethan let out a breath and turned to glare at the Peacekeeper. "You did that on purpose."

"Did what?" she asked.

"Pretended not to know how to fly."

"We all know how to fly, Ethan. We used to fly X-1's with the fleet, remember?"

"That was almost a decade ago!"

Jena shrugged. "It's just like riding a hover cycle."

Fifty blocks went by in a blur of colorful glass. Soon a tower Ethan recognized came into view. Here and there flames belched from broken windows. High above, the Celestial Wall gaped open and flaming debris tumbled through holes in the shield.

"This is it," Ethan said.

"Upper or lower levels?" Jena asked.

"Upper, I think..." A row of windows burst open and fire blew out in pressurized streams. Ethan pointed. "Over there."

"Hang on," Jena said. She flew them right up to the blaze and then drifted down the row of windows to a section that wasn't already on fire. Hovering there, she opened the driver's side window and aimed one arm out at the building. Lasers screeched from her palm and the side of the building burst open in glittering clouds of shattered glass. Jena flew through the hole she'd made, scraping the top and bottom of her car on the window frame. The car knocked over data towers and crushed them beneath its grav lifts. Jena landed on top of the debris, and they all spent a moment studying the swirling clouds of smoke inside the building. Ethan turned to Alara where she sat with Trinity on the back seat. "Stay here with Trin," he said.

She looked ready to object, but he stopped her. "There's too much smoke."

Jena opened the glove compartment and withdrew a set of translucent membranes. She passed them out. "Put these on. They'll help you breathe through the smoke."

Ethan accepted his filter and eyed it for a moment before placing it over his mouth and nose. It adhered to his face with wet sucking noises, as if it were a living thing.

"Let's go," Jena said, simultaneously activating the faceplate of her helmet and opening the driver's side door. She stepped out into the swirling smoke. "Follow my lead if we run into any drones," she called out in an amplified voice.

Ethan left the car, his eyes already burning and blurring with tears. The air filter kept the smoke out of his lungs, but did nothing for his eyes. He blinked away his tears, and turned to look around for his family. Alara and Trinity came out behind him, holding hands. He took Trinity's other hand and ran to catch up with Jena before she disappeared in the drifting clouds of smoke.

It wasn't long before they heard weapons fire, followed by the sound of mechanized footsteps. Jena told them to wait, and then she disappeared.

After just a few moments of waiting, the weapons' fire went silent, and not long after that, Jena returned.

"I found them," she said. "Let's go."

* * *

—30 Minutes Earlier—

Atta heard one of the Rictans come up behind her, armored boots *thunking* as they struck the floor. She turned toward the sound to see that it was Magnum.

"The Eclipser is hidden. Even if drones start breaking through our lines, there's no reason they should find it."

Atta frowned. "What about collateral damage? You put it somewhere safe, I hope?"

Magnum jerked his head to the far corner of the control room, where a broken wall and the associated debris camouflaged the device from immediate scrutiny. "There's only so many places we can hide it that won't draw attention."

The Eclipser was disguised as a broken chunk of castcrete, so they had to leave it somewhere that similar debris might logically be found.

Atta's gaze darted to the hole in the wall beside the device. The rest of the Rictans were on the other side helping Galan Rovik and his Peacekeepers guard the rear entrances.

"We need to carry the Eclipser deeper into the city," Atta

decided. "Even if no one finds it here, we're too close to the rooftops. A crashing ship could take us and the Eclipser out at any minute."

Magnum blew out an uneasy breath. "Gettin' to the lower levels ain't gonna be easy. We ran into hordes of drones down there. They've got the entire Second Battalion pinned down, and we don't have the numbers to break through."

Atta pursed her lips, about to suggest an alternate course of action that would work to get the Eclipser to safety.

Then a mighty *boom* shook the building and dust trickled down from the ceiling. Atta looked around quickly, eyes scanning her rear view and peripheral displays for the source of the explosion. "What was that?"

Ripper and laser cannons roared, and the comms lit up with exclamations from the Rictans. Magnum ran toward the commotion just as his squad came diving through the hole in the wall and into the control room.

"Report!" Magnum ordered, taking cover with them beside the opening.

Atta took cover opposite Magnum. Lasers came lancing through the hole in a crimson flurry, burning equipment in the control room to slag.

"That Peacekeeper turned on us!" one of the Rictans said, breathing heavily over the comms. "He dropped a grenade and ran to join the drones attacking us. He killed his own men."

"What?" Atta said, her voice barely loud enough to be heard over the sounds of laser fire.

Suddenly enemy fire ceased and they heard a gravelly voice say, "Tell me where the Eclipser is, and you will be shown mercy."

Atta switched to external helmet speakers and yelled back. "Frek you!"

"You will die here today, Miss Heston."

The enemy began firing again, and Atta gritted her teeth.

"What are your orders, General?" Magnum asked.

She was about to order them through the hole, to go out in a blaze of glory, when something caught her attention on her rear view display.

Squads of green friendlies were racing up behind them. Atta turned, hope swelling in her chest. Their armor was a glossy black, their eye-shaped visors glowing red. *Gors,* was her first thought, but the voice that announced them wasn't that of a Gor—

"Lookss like we arrive at a good time."

The voice belonged to a Sythian.

Atta blinked, confusion swirling through her thoughts. She didn't know there were Sythian ground teams. They were too cowardly to risk their necks like that. Yet here they were.

"Who are you?" she demanded.

The Sythian removed his helmet and revealed an ugly, but familiar countenance with translucent skin, gills flaring in his neck, and a bald head with a ridge of horns running down the vertex. He was the same sub-species as Shallah.

"I am High Lord Kaon," the Sythian said. He nodded to the dazzling stream of lasers still pouring into the room. "Where is the Eclipser? We must get it someplace safe! You hold this position while we take it to safety," Kaon suggested.

"Forget it! We're not going anywhere until we clear these space rats off our six. Get in position!" She waved the Sythians over and turned back to watching the entrance. "We're going to get them as they come through," Atta said. "Switch to melee, Rictans."

Energy blades sizzled out. Atta kept half an eye on the Sythians walking up behind them. She saw them fanning out, keeping the other entrances covered. Returning her attention to the fore, Atta watched the red outlines of enemy contacts growing larger on her HUD. Behind her she saw Sythians raising their palms in readiness. Their integrated weapons were charged, the apertures glowing bright red.

Kaon spoke once more, "Where is the Eclipser?"

"I told you, we need to clear our six before..." Atta trailed off, suddenly realizing that the Sythians weren't keeping the entrances covered. They were aiming their weapons at her and the Rictans.

Atta rounded on Kaon. "You frekking traitor! You're going to get all of us killed!"

"Perhaps, but Shallah will resurrect *us* if we die."

The first drones came bursting through the broken wall with weapons blazing. Magnum slashed two of them in half before Kaon called out, "Stop!" and fired a lavender-colored laser bolt at Magnum's feet. Speaking to the drones, Kaon said, "We are on your side!"

To Atta's surprise, the drones stopped shooting. The Rictans stood idly by, watching as over a hundred of them filed into the control room. Finally, a solitary Peacekeeper came in, his blue cape swirling behind him. His faceplate was deactivated, and Atta could see him smiling as he walked in.

It was Galan Rovik.

"What happened to the rest of you?" Atta asked, noting that he was the only Peacekeeper who came in.

"The truth is a burden that not everyone is prepared to carry, Miss Heston. I had to lighten their loads."

Atta shook her head. "You're insane."

Galan raised a finger to point at her. "No, what's insane is trying to fight a battle that you cannot win." The Peacekeeper turned to face Kaon next, and the Sythian gave a rubbery imitation of a smile. Galan frowned. "You people can't seem to make up your minds about whose side you're on."

Kaon inclined his head. "We were never on the humans' side."

Galan nodded. "I know." With that, he raised his arms and unleashed a dazzling stream of fire. Before the rest of the Sythians could react, the drones opened fire, too, and in seconds all of the Sythians lay motionless on the ground, their armor smoking from myriad holes. Atta watched, speechless, as Galan walked over to Kaon and stood over the Sythian's body.

Kaon hissed something, proving that he was still alive, and Atta's translator whispered into her helmet: *"Why?"*

"You said it yourself, you're not on humanity's side, but Omnius is, and he doesn't need your help. What he needs is for you to get out of the way."

Galan either had his own translator—which Atta doubted— or more disturbing still, he actually understood Sythian. Kaon hissed and Galan unleashed another stream of laser fire, reducing Kaon's head to a charred and smoking ruin.

Turning back to Atta, Galan smiled anew and said, "Now, where were we?" He raised his glowing palms in her direction and strode up to her. "I believe you were about to tell me where your jamming device is hidden."

Atta shook her head. "I'd sooner die."

"Yes, I can see that death doesn't frighten you. Someone else's death on the other hand..." He glanced meaningfully at the Rictans. "It would be better for everyone if you simply tell me what I need to know."

Atta set her teeth and thrust out her chin. "Go frek yourself."

Galan's palms changed directions and he aimed at the Rictan closest to her. Lasers *screeched*, and the man fell with a *clatter* of armor. The designation on his left breastplate marked him as

Rictan Three, *Hop.* Atta gaped at the blackened holes in his armor.

"You were saying?" Galan asked.

CHAPTER 45

Ethan wondered *who* Jena had found—Peacekeepers, drones, or Union forces?

They walked through aisle after aisle of ruined data towers. Bodies littered the ground. Bits and pieces of drones lay scattered through the rubble, some of them still twitching and sparking.

They passed a man without a face, and Trinity whimpered.

"Don't look," Alara said.

Then they came to a room with a gaping hole in the far wall, and this one was cluttered with the bodies of Peacekeepers, too. They followed Jena across the room and through the hole in the wall. On the other side they found at least a hundred drones standing in a circle around a huddled, kneeling group of Union soldiers. A lone Peacekeeper with a royal blue cape, a strategian, stood before them. The Union soldiers' helmets were off, and Ethan found he recognized them immediately. It was General Atta and the Rictans—what was left of them, anyway. One of the Rictans was crumpled on the floor with a smoking hole in his chest.

"It seems you have outlived your usefulness," the Peacekeeper said to Atta before turning to address the newcomers. "Peacekeeper Faros tells me you know where the Eclipser is."

"No, but I can find it," Ethan said.

Atta's eyes found him and abruptly widened. "We thought you were dead!" she exclaimed.

"I got cut off during the fighting," Ethan explained.

Atta appeared to notice Alara and Trinity, and a wry smile crawled onto her lips. "You sure you didn't run away?"

"I didn't run. You thought I was dead. Why do you think that is? My comm beacon dropped off your scanners. You couldn't see me any better than I could see you."

"You could have tried to find us."

"I did, but I ended up behind enemy lines."

"Well, looks like you had enough time to save your family. Good for you. Now you're going to bring Omnius back online. You're two for two."

"You frekkin' traitor!" Magnum roared, jumping to his feet.

The Peacekeeper standing guard over them raised both palms to fire. "Halt!" he said, and Magnum just stood there, his chest rising and falling quickly with barely-contained fury.

"This is the only way, Atta," Ethan explained, his voice muffled by the air filter he wore. "We can't win, but we *can* stop Therius from killing everyone out of spite."

Atta shook her head, speechless.

The Peacekeeper with the blue cape smiled and walked over to them. Ethan was startled to find he recognized the man. It was Galan Rovik, the Peacekeeper who'd guided them through their Choosing Ceremony when they'd first arrived on Avilon all those years ago.

"Rovik?" Ethan asked.

"I'm surprised you remember me," he replied.

This was the man who had relayed Omnius's warning that

he would cheat on his wife. Ethan shook his head. "I should have listened to you."

Galan cocked his head.

"Never mind. We need to disable the Eclipser."

"Yes," Galan replied. "I'm glad you've chosen the right side in this war, but I am curious... *why* are you helping us, Ethan? You were no fan of Omnius."

Ethan explained about the nanite bombs.

Rovik looked shaken. "If they drop those bombs before Omnius transfers the Lifelink data, then we're all going to die. Where is the Eclipser?" he demanded.

"It should be around here somewhere..." Ethan said, turning in a quick circle. "It was disguised to look like a piece of debris."

Galan gave orders for the drones to spread out, to look for any debris that didn't fit in. Moments later they found something, a large chunk of castcrete buried under a pile of self-healing bactcrete debris.

"That's it," Ethan confirmed.

"You're such a skriff, Ethan," Atta breathed.

He rounded on her. "Would you rather Therius kill us all?"

Atta clenched her jaw. "He hasn't made any threats yet. We don't even know—"

"That he'll use the nanites? Yes we do. You know Therius just as well as I do."

Atta scowled but said nothing, and Ethan turned his attention to the Eclipser. A pair of drones carried it between them and dropped it at Galan Rovik's feet. He went down on his haunches to study the device. "Clever camouflage. Are you sure this is it? Surely such a powerful device cannot be so tiny..."

"I'm sure," Ethan said.

"Think about what you're doing," Atta said, her eyes on the Peacekeeper. "You're going to bring Omnius back online. Is that really what you want?"

Galan looked up. "Why wouldn't I? Life has never been so sweet! We live forever, and we can get away with murder! There's no longer any need for us to worry about right and wrong. Our only guiding principle is to follow Omnius's will, and He is faithful to those who are faithful to Him. Our future as a species is secure! In the face of that, freedom is overrated, Miss Heston."

Galan rose from his haunches and backed away from the device. Once he reached a safe distance, he gestured to the device with his thumb pointing down. The drones turned and fired in unison with a blinding stream of crimson fire that left Ethan's ears ringing and his eyes seeing spots. When it was over, the Eclipser was a smoking ruin.

Galan turned to them with the symbol of Avilon glowing bright on his breastplate. "Omnius has something he'd like to say to all of you." The symbol flared brightly and a blinding light suddenly appeared in their midst.

"This insurrection has come to an end," a booming voice said. "Stop your fighting, and listen to your God! My fondest wish is for all of my children to be happy, but this invasion has brought to my attention that many of my people are actually unhappy. I cannot help but feel responsible for this. I have lied to you, yes, but only with the best of intentions. To prove that to you, I'm going to give everyone what they want. You're all going to be allowed to choose one last time. For anyone who wishes to be free from me, all you need to do is stay where you are and stop fighting. Avilon is yours. You win. For those who have lost loved ones in the fighting, rest assured they will all be returned to you just as they were.

"Yet for everyone who would rather spend eternity in paradise with me, simply tell me so, and I will come and get you. New Avilon is *here,* in orbit, and it is waiting for *you!* I have built an entire planet for you and your children to share eternity with me. It will grow as you grow, with infinite space to accommodate all of your children for countless generations to come. In New Avilon there will be no Null Zone, nor any need for one. Nothing will be hidden from you, and no one will be forced to stay, but for those who do—the whole universe shall be your birthright, and we will explore it and delve into its mysteries together."

Ethan frowned, his eyes watering against the dazzling brilliance of the light radiating from Galan Rovik's chest. Something about what Omnius said didn't add up. If he was suddenly loosening the reins, then why not do so sooner? And why spend years seeding the Getties with nanites to cover up all the evidence of his lies if he ultimately planned to reveal the truth anyway?

Omnius went on, "To prove that from now on I will not hide the truth from you, there is one final thing you should all know that not even this Therius, the so-called Redemptor, will tell you.

"The reason I seeded the Getties with nanites was not because I wished to erase the evidence that I had lied to you. It was always my plan to reveal the truth when the timing was right. The real reason I seeded the Getties with nanites is because your real enemy is still out there.

"The Great War took place in the Getties Cluster. History tells us your ancestors were fighting among themselves. A third of them died in the fighting, a third escaped, and a third remained behind.

But all of that is a simplification, an oral history told and retold by the survivors who came to the Adventa Galaxy and settled on Advistine.

"In order to make a small population more viable, your

ancestors spliced DNA from a local species of primates with their own, creating humanity. Forced to start over, you went through a period of tribalism and barbarism, and over time you forgot where you came from. It wasn't until you began noticing gaps in your evolution that you hypothesized humanity might have had an extra-planetary origin.

"The gaps in your evolution are filled by the species whose bones I found littering the Getties Cluster. Buried with them in the ruins of your lost civilization, I found quantum technologies and adapted them for our purposes. The people who possessed those technologies, your ancestors, are the ones the Codices call *Immortals*.

"They destroyed the entire Getties Cluster on a cosmological scale, making its worlds dark, cold, and uninhabitable. Then they left your ancestors there to die. Some of them escaped and came here, to the Adventa Galaxy, and you are their descendants. The ones who stayed behind eventually evolved into Gors and Sythians.

"But I suspect the ones who won the war also left the Getties Cluster. I seeded the Getties with nanites in my search for them, but I didn't find them. Now the entire cluster is teeming with self-replicating drones that will act as a buffer between us and the Immortals if they do someday return. Hopefully by then, I will be powerful enough to defeat them, but if not, perhaps they will encounter my nanites before they encounter us, and our enemy will be defeated before they even realize that a group of you escaped to the Adventa Galaxy.

"I was wrong to lie about all of this, and I hope that in time all of you can find a way to forgive me."

Ethan gaped at that explanation. It all made sense, but he was reluctant to trust Omnius after so many lies and so many betrayals.

"Now, the time of the final choosing is at hand," Omnius said. Please think carefully about your choice. If you wish to be free of me, all I ask is that you don't try to leave Avilon yet. There is still a war being fought, and I do not wish to see anyone else die today. But take heart! I have heard your cries for freedom, and you shall have what you desire."

The blinding light disappeared, and Ethan was left blinking spots from his eyes. It was too much for him to take in all at once. He couldn't decide what to make of it, but one thing was clear—they had to leave Avilon. The very fact that Omnius had told them not to was suspicious.

"What a load of krak!" Atta said.

Galan turned to her and shook his head. "I'm surprised that you are not embracing your newfound freedom."

"What freedom?" she challenged. "You still have a hundred drones watching over us, ready to shoot."

Galan smiled patiently. "You came here to cause death and destruction. If I let you go, will you not cause more of the same? You do not trust Omnius, therefore, I do not trust you." Turning to Ethan, Rovik nodded and said, "Or you."

"What?" Ethan blinked. "We were the ones who brought Omnius back online!"

"And he is grateful, but trying to escape now could get you killed. The time will come when it will be safe for you to leave Avilon, but not yet. Now, enough questions. It's time to go. Leave your weapons and armor behind."

No one made a move to follow that order.

"If you won't come willingly, I'll stun you all and have my drones carry you out," Galan said.

Ethan watched Jena draw the pulse rifle from the holster on her back and aim it at the Rictans. "You heard him!" she said.

Ethan gaped at her, wondering how she could change sides

so quickly. She'd been ready to abandon Omnius not so long ago. Maybe he'd convinced her with his speech about freedoms being restored.

Somehow Jena's order worked where Galan's hadn't. Atta and the Rictans began cracking out of their armor. A few of them glanced at their fallen squad mate as they did so.

"Everyone who died today will be resurrected. You have Omnius's word," Galan reminded them.

What's that worth? Ethan wondered.

"He didn't have a Lifelink," Atta said.

"Whose fault is that?" Galan countered. "But don't worry, that man is alive and well here on Avilon. Omnius resurrected all of you here years ago. You're just copies of copies."

Ethan exchanged glances with his wife, and Galan smiled.

"Makes you wonder which copy is the real one, doesn't it? Come. It's time for us to go."

CHAPTER 46

Farah woke up in a daze in the middle of complete chaos. People shouted; the ground trembled under her feet. *No, not the ground—the deck,* she realized, recognizing that she was aboard the bridge of a starship.

Then it all came rushing back: Therius, The Union, Avilon, the attack... and Drone 767 stunning her as she tried to incite a mutiny.

Farah eased off the deck, climbing unsteadily to her feet. Rigid hands helped her up. She was about to turn and thank the officer helping her when she realized that it was none other than the drone who'd shot her in the first place. She recoiled from him.

"I'm fine!" she snapped.

The drone withdrew, and Farah took in the scene around her. Out the viewports she saw the *Liberator* pouring blinding torrents of energy into a depthless void. Farah could have sworn they were flying through space, but the absence of stars was telling, and so was the faint golden glow shining through the shadowy carpet of clouds racing beneath them. Avilon had been cast into an artificial night by the shadow of Omnius's

Icosahedron.

Crimson light poured from the *Liberator's* laser cannons, drawing bright orange flares from the void as enemy fighters exploded all around them. Farah actually felt those explosions come rattling through the hull of the venture-class cruiser as supersonic shock waves of shrapnel went hissing off their shields. Alerts and alarms blared almost constantly. Shouts from bridge crew filled the air.

Farah rushed up to the captain's table to join Therius and see how the battle was going, putting aside for the moment that *he* was the one who had given the order to stun her.

But she didn't really need to see the tactical map to know they were losing the fight. Enemy fighters harried them to all sides, and the *Liberator* rocked with a near-constant roar of exploding ordinance.

It took Farah a moment to realize what that meant. Avilonian ordinance was all quantum-fired, teleported instantly to their targets, and if they were firing quantum weapons now, that meant that Omnius was back online.

Farah reached the captain's table, breathing hard not from exertion, but from sheer panic. "Therius! What happened? Why is the Eclipser offline?"

He turned and blinked pale blue eyes at her, a wan smile stretching his lips taut. He looked all-together too calm for her liking. "You're awake," he said. "Good. I wouldn't want you to miss this. It's time to initiate the Armageddon Protocol."

Suddenly all of the crew's frantic activity ceased. Silence rang. The finality of Therius's command seemed to echo from the walls, whispering death to anyone who would listen. They'd all heard the rumors about the nanite bomb plot.

"You can't!" Farah screamed. "What's the point of freedom if no one is alive to appreciate it?" The crew seemed to be in agreement with that. Farah assumed she'd missed the part where Therius had delivered his ultimatum.

"Omnius already surrendered," Lieutenant Devries said from the comms, revealing just how much Farah had really missed.

"And it's a trick," Therius said. "Humanity will never be free as long as Omnius is the one calling the shots. It's time to use the greatest weapon of all—ourselves. We're going to deprive Omnius of his people."

Farah gaped at Therius in disbelief. Omnius had surrendered! Therius had accomplished what he'd set out to do, but like a petulant child who'd gotten his way only to decide that it wasn't what he really wanted, he was going to drop the nanites and kill everyone anyway!

"No one is going to do it!" she said. Therius turned to her, his eyebrows raised, and she went on, "You're the only one crazy enough to advocate self-annihilation!"

Therius smiled. "Me and a whole army of Sythians. I anticipated resistance and had the nanites relocated to the Sythians' ships before we jumped here. Shallah thinks I don't know of his plans to betray us, but I have always known, and now I have given him the tools he needs to destroy humanity once and for all. By the looks of it, he has already begun to use them."

Therius nodded to the tactical map. Farah looked down and saw Sythian Command Ships racing down from the heights of Avilon's atmosphere, skimming low over Celesta. There was only one reason for them to get that close.

Bombing runs.

It was too late! Fury boiled up inside of her. "The entire point of the Armageddon protocol was to get Omnius to back down! He actually surrendered, and you're *still* going to kill everyone?"

Therius met her gaze unblinkingly. "*Trust* me, Miss Hale. I'm going to set humanity free."

"By *killing* them?" Farah shrieked. She turned in a dizzy circle to see that the rest of the crew was all equally shocked and outraged. Behind her, drone 767 came *clanking* down the gangway, his weapons trained on her, anticipating that she would make a move to attack Therius. Torv, the ship's Gor chief of security, remained at the doors to the bridge, silently watching the developing confrontation.

The rest of the crew was not so passive. Multiple officers rose to their feet and drew their sidearms. 767 wouldn't be able to defeat them all.

"Stand down, Seven Sixty Seven!" Therius called out. "I surrender," he said, raising his hands above his head.

Weapons remained trained on both Therius and his drone bodyguard. "Torv, arrest him!" Farah ordered, while watching 767 carefully. "And someone shut down that drone!" she added.

"Yes, ma'am," Lieutenant Devries said, abandoning the comms.

Farah turned to Torv. "I gave you an order, Sergeant."

The Gor hissed, but made no move to obey.

"Your people are on the ground, too, Torv. They're also going to die because of what Therius did."

That got through to him. Farah watched as the Gor strode down the gangway to the captain's table, steadily advancing on Therius.

"I have not betrayed your people, Torv," Therius said.

"We need him, Torv. If nothing else, so that we can bring him to justice later.

Hiss. Torv reached Therius and stopped within a hair's breadth of the man's face. The Gor glared at Therius for a long moment before producing a pair of stun cords from a compartment on his belt. Therius made no effort to resist; he even held his hands behind his back for Torv to tie with stun cords.

"You don't know what you're doing," he said, his eyes on Farah. "But it doesn't matter. I forgive you."

"You forgive *me*? If anyone should be sorry, it's you, you sick frek," Farah said. She turned to see that Devries had flipped open 767's access panel, and the drone's optical sensor was now dark. "Check him for weapons," she said, nodding to the Lieutenant.

Devries walked over and began patting the admiral down, but Therius wasn't even wearing a standard-issue sidearm. "He's clean ma'am," Devries said. "What should we do with him?"

"Let's keep him on deck, just in case he has anything else up his sleeve that we need to know about."

"Yes, ma'am."

"All right, everyone back to your stations!" Farah said, clapping her hands. "Devries, call a retreat. We need to get out of here before those nanites infect the entire planet and us along with it. Warn the Gors that the Sythians are now hostile."

"What about our people on the ground?" Devries asked.

Farah glanced at the tactical map just in time to see a Sythian command ship go crashing through the upper city of Celesta, knocking down dozens of monolithic towers as it went. She grimaced and shook her head.

"We can't risk bringing nanites aboard."

The deck shuddered violently underfoot and a *shields critical* alert shrieked through the bridge speakers.

"Aft shields are in the red!" engineering reported. "Equalizing."

"Gunnery! Keep those drone fighters away from us! We can't shoot their ordinance, but we *can* shoot them."

"Yes, ma'am. We're doing our best..."

A moment later, the gravidar officer called out. "Captain! We have multiple enemy contacts launching from Avilon! Epsilon class."

Epsilon class meant they were several kilometers long, at least. Farah eyed the tactical map, zooming in on one of the enemy contacts and toggling the map for a simulated 3D holo view rather than a bird's eye perspective.

She saw Celesta at night. Towers shone dazzlingly bright, like radiant columns in the sky. Urban parks sprawled between those columns, their pathways lit to a shadowy green by snaking rivers of streetlights. To one side blazed a massive inferno where the Sythian command ship had crashed, and in the middle distance a massive tower rose from the city.

No, not a tower—a ship, Farah realized as its thrusters cleared the rooftops of Celesta with a blinding flare of red light. She recognized the tower-ship immediately. It was one of the Trees of Life, the buildings where Omnius kept everyone's clones and Lifelink data.

Farah panned her viewpoint around, searching the city in all directions, and she saw no less than half a dozen identical towers racing up into the artificial night. The Trees of Life were all leaving Avilon.

Farah blinked, unable to believe it. All this time, those towers had been starships, not skyscrapers, and now Omnius was ordering them to leave. That could only mean one thing.

He was evacuating the planet.

CHAPTER 47

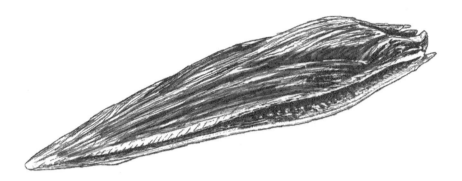

Shallah watched from his command chair as Lord Shondar's ship crashed into the surface of Avilon. "Have them detonate their nanites!" Shallah ordered. "We shall resurrect them all here after we jump out."

"Yes, master," the operator at the communications station said.

"We must leave the planet now, Supreme One," the nav operator warned.

"Yes. Tell the command ships to make orbit and jump away."

Even as Shallah ordered them to flee, the deck shuddered under their feet with a violent *roar* as Avilon's ground defenses battled once more against their shields.

"It isss unlikely that we all make it," Shallah's second in command, Queen Tavia said.

He turned to her. "We only need one ship to escape. From there we can resurrect all of our dead."

Tavia nodded. "Yes, master."

"The losses are regrettable, but is it not worth it? Look at them burn!" Shallah said, gesturing out the forward viewport to the raging inferno that Shondar's ship had caused. "Now, finally, we have our revenge, and Omnius is made to pay for casting us aside!"

"What is that?" Tavia asked, pointing out the main forward viewport.

Shallah saw a gargantuan tower rising from the burning planet, blasting away into the depthless black sky. "Sensors! What is that?" he demanded, his gills flaring with surprise.

"I do not know, My Lord!"

Shallah gaped at the sight, unable to decide what he was looking at. Then he saw more identical towers rising. He summoned a star map from his command chair and studied them with sensors. The towers were shielded, powered, and accelerating straight up at a rapid rate. They were also off the charts with lifeform readings. Maybe Omnius was evacuating some of his people? Shallah watched as those towers clawed for orbit. Yet there weren't enough ships to evacuate everyone, unless...

Omnius didn't have to evacuate the entire planet. He only needed to take the clones and their Lifelink data, and he would be able to bring them all back again. Shallah's eyes watered and itched with frustration.

Omnius had won! The only victory they could possibly hope for would be to escape so that they could fight another day. *Or just so that we can hide,* Shallah thought.

That was a more realistic goal, he decided, whilst furiously rubbing his lips together.

Suddenly a dazzling light suffused the deck, blinding him, and searing his eyes with its heat.

An explosion roared and Shallah screamed as he was catapulted out into the upper atmosphere. The cold air seared his skin. Wind whipped past his ears as he tumbled and fell, gasping for breath. His eyes bulged. Capillaries began bursting from decompression and Shallah saw red.

Twisting around, he caught a glimpse of his command ship above him. Fire leapt from a ragged tear in the ship's midsection. Debris and bodies gushed out. The behemoth was slowly cracking in half, its mighty engines still driving the back and ripping it free of the front.

Resistance is futile, Shallah realized.

Then a secondary explosion tore through his ship, shredding the back half with a blinding flash and a titanic *boom*. The shock wave hit him mere seconds later, debris punching his body full of holes. He died and his mind retreated to a purely digital existence within the next nearest command ship. But he only had a few seconds to recover before an explosion rocked that ship, too. The power failed, bringing with it an endless void as Shallah's awareness faded.

* * *

Ethan heard the immense, bone-rattling roar, long before he saw what caused it. His first thought was that the entire planet was caving in. He imagined all three of the world-spanning cities telescoping down on top of themselves and the ground under his feet opening up in a gaping maw.

Then he saw the black sky suddenly a turn bright, fiery gold as the flaming hull of a massive Sythian ship skimmed by low overhead. The next thing Ethan knew, he was flying. The air pocket carried by that thirty kilometer-long ship sent them skipping across the rooftops.

By the time they stopped tumbling they'd been carried at least a few hundred feet. Ethan stood on wobbly legs, surprised to find all of his limbs still attached to his body. He and Alara had both landed on top of a bridge over the shimmering blue sea that was the shield wall between Celesta and Etheria. Titanic *booms* sounded in the distance as the crashing warship hit kilometers-high skyscrapers, knocking them down with violent shrieks of rending alloy and shattering glass. As the debris fell, the bridge where they stood picked up the vibrations, jumping and skipping under their feet like a plucked string.

"Where's Trinity?" Alara asked suddenly.

Ethan whirled around, searching. Then he spotted her, a dozen feet away and struggling to stand up on the shield. He grimaced. She would have some nasty burns where her skin had touched that energy field.

"Trin!" he called.

"Dad!"

He barely heard her over the roar and rumble of crashing debris. In the distance, he saw Atta and a group of Rictans jump down onto the shield to help Trinity up. They half-carried and half-dragged her to the bridge where Ethan stood. Further away, Galan Rovik had also landed on the shield, but he appeared to be in no hurry to get off. The Peacekeeper stood watching as Celestial towers collapsed in the distance. Drones gathered on all sides of him, forming a protective circle around their human leader.

Atta and the Rictans reached the bridge and began pushing Trinity up. Looking away from the destruction, Ethan grabbed his daughter's hands to pull her up. She cried out in pain, and he almost dropped her.

"Careful!" Atta warned.

Trinity's hands were raw and bleeding with burns from the shield. Ethan felt sick. "Brave girl," he said, grabbing her behind her wrists instead.

Alara hurried over and helped him pull Trinity up. "We need to get off this bridge..." she said as it began vibrating again.

Atta grunted, giving Trinity a final shove before letting go.

"I've got you," Ethan said, pulling his little girl over the railing.

Rictan Six pulled himself up next, and Ethan realized from the man's curly blond hair that he was *Blades,* the squad medic. He was about to ask Blades to tend to Trinity's injuries, but the man was already opening his medkit.

The railing rattled, and Ethan turned to see the remaining Rictans lifting and pushing Atta up to the bridge. For a moment he wondered why she couldn't help herself up, but then he noticed how one of her shoulders hung well below the other one. It was either broken or dislocated — maybe both.

"Sorry," he said, reaching over the railing again to help her up.

Atta grabbed his hand with her good arm. "Thanks," she panted, her face contorted with pain.

Then the world flashed with a dazzling burst of light. A mighty *boom!* left Ethan's ears ringing, followed by a thundering roar. The shock wave hit, and the bridge twisted, tipping toward the shield. Atta's hand was wrenched free of his, and Ethan watched helplessly as she and the Rictans went tumbling across the shield, screaming and cursing wherever bare skin touched the energy field. The shock wave doubled Ethan over the railing, threatening to throw him face-first onto the shield and give him a few burns of his own, but he held on tight.

Then it was over. Ethan would have breathed a sigh of relief, but the wind had been knocked out of him. In the distance he saw Atta and the Rictans pick themselves off the shield, struggling to crawl out of a pile of drones. Off to one side, Galan Rovik did the same.

Ethan glanced behind him and saw *Blades* loosening his grip on Trinity and Alara. The Rictan had hooked his legs around the railings and his arms around Ethan's family to keep them from flying off the bridge. Ethan was just about to thank him when he heard a woman scream. He spun around in time to see the shield flickering dangerously.

Atta and the Rictans ran toward the bridge, but shields gave next to zero traction, and their feet slipped with every step. Atta threw her weight from side to side, using her momentum to skate, not run. She made faster progress like that, but she was still a long way off.

"Come on, Atta!"

Then the shield stopped flickering and failed completely. This time no one had a chance to scream. They fell like rocks.

"Atta!" Ethan roared, half-lunging over the railing as she disappeared amidst a glinting, tumbling rain of drones, Rictans, and one fluttering blue cape. The chasm below the bridge went straight down, almost 300 floors to the Null Zone. No one could survive that. Even the drones would be pulverized on impact. "Atta!" he called again, but he couldn't even see her now.

A hand gripped his shoulder.

"There'll be time to grieve our losses later." Ethan turned to Blades in a daze, and the Rictan shook him to snap him out of it. "Triage. We've got to focus on saving the ones we still can."

"Omnius can't bring them back," Ethan said. Atta was dead.

"No, he can't," Blades replied. "But at least that Peacekeeper and his drones went with them. That means *we* have a chance to escape, and we need to use it while we still can." The bridge shuddered, and the railing rattled once more. "Come on!" Blades said.

The Rictan took off at a run, and Ethan raced after him, grabbing Alara by the hand and Trinity by her forearm.

By the time they reached the end of the bridge, Ethan saw a pair of people running up to greet them. It was Magnum and Jena Faros.

"Where's everyone else?" Magnum asked as he drew near.

Blades shook his head. "They fell with the shield."

For a long moment no one said anything. Something flickered through Magnum's eyes, and then he nodded. "No guts, no glory."

"No guts, no glory," Blades agreed.

"What are you all standing around for?" Jena Faros said. "We need to go!"

Ethan shot her a dark look. "We just lost a lot of good people."

"And we'll lose the ones we have left if we don't leave *now*."

"Where?" Alara asked, her eyes glazed with shock.

"That depends... where's that ship of yours?"

Ethan recited the address for her.

"Heritage District..." Jena said, nodding. "That way," she said, pointing in the opposite direction from the crashed behemoth cruiser. She took off at a run. Magnum and Blades ran after her, while Ethan brought up the rear with his family.

Beside him, Alara whispered, "Omnius is telling us not to go. He's saying we should trust him."

Ethan frowned. He'd forgotten that Alara and Trinity were linked. So was Jena Faros. Only he and the Rictans weren't.

"Is he going to stop you?" Ethan asked.

"I told him about Atta, and I explained that it's not about trust, it's about getting to safety. He said he's sorry, and he understands, but he suggests that the safest place to be right now is the Icosahedron—if we can find a way to get there."

"We're not going to the Icosahedron."

"I know. I told him. He's wishing us luck."

Ethan snorted. "What kind of luck?"

Before Alara could reply, they heard another deafening *roar*. Ethan's heart jumped in his chest, afraid that another ship was about to come crashing down on top of them. Then he saw the source of the sound. Massive towers were blasting off, rising steadily from Celesta, their thrusters glowing bright red against the night.

"What the..." Magnum stopped running to stare up at them.

"The Trees of Life!" Jena exclaimed.

Ethan squinted against the blinding glare of the towers' thrusters. "They were starships?"

"I don't like this," Magnum said. "Why's *he* runnin' with his tail between his legs? He won!"

Ethan remembered the nanites, and his eyes grew round. "Therius must have dropped the bombs anyway." He shook his head. "Omnius is taking all the clones and leaving Avilon to its fate."

Magnum turned to look at him. "Then why's he tellin' everyone to stay here?"

Alara answered. "He says the ship that crashed was infected. He's going to sterilize the crash site from orbit, but he's withdrawing the Trees of Life just in case."

"How do we know that's true?" Ethan asked. "For all we know dozens of bombs made it and he's telling the people who didn't choose him to stay on Avilon so he has an excuse to get rid of them."

Alara shook her head. "Either way, we need to get out of here. Even if Avilon survives, it's going to be a dangerous place without Omnius to keep law and order."

"We're wasting time!" Jena said.

They ran again, and this time they didn't stop to gawk along the way. Ground-based beams crisscrossed the sky, and explosions roared both distant and near. Fighters raced, screeching with blazing streams of lasers. Sonic booms echoed by the dozen with every minute that passed, and the night turned to day as a deep, throbbing *hum* filled the air.

Whatever it was, the sound came from behind them. Ethan glanced over his shoulder to see a dozen blinding white beams converging from the sky on the crash site, making it look like an upside down maypole. Omnius really was trying to sterilize the crash site, but did that mean he was being honest about everything else, too?

A little bit of truth can cover up a whole lot of lies, he thought. The question was, *What's Omnius lying about now?*

CHAPTER 48

The bridge shuddered with a violent tremor. The *hum* and *roar* of energy being exchanged and dissipated by their shields was so loud that it actually set Farah's teeth on edge.

"Ventral shields critical! Equalizing..." the *Liberator's* chief engineer reported.

How much more of this can we take? Farah wondered. "What's our overall shield strength?"

"We're in the yellow, ma'am, almost red, with twenty eight percent."

They weren't even out of the atmosphere yet, and at this rate they weren't likely to get there. "Devries! Send a message on an open channel—we surrender! Tell Omnius all we want is to leave Avilon in peace. He can have his people. We won't try to stop the Trees of Life from reaching orbit."

A moment later Devries replied, shaking his head. "He's not going for it! He's accusing us of mass-murder. When that Sythian ship crashed it took out one of the Trees of Life. Those people are gone for good, Captain."

"What? You're telling me Omnius doesn't have backups of their data?"

"Apparently not."

Bullkrak, Farah thought.

"He says we need to be brought to justice, something he's calling Judgment Day. Isn't that from the Codices?"

Farah snorted and shook her head. This had to be a nightmare. The people they'd thought were their allies were actually their enemies, and now she and her crew were being blamed for a heinous crime that Therius had used the Sythians to commit.

Nightmare was too pleasant a term to describe what was happening.

"Helm! Plot a quantum jump out of here! I don't care where, just get us as far as you can, as fast as you can. As soon as we clear the atmosphere, punch it. Comms, make sure that order is relayed to the rest of the fleet, and don't bother sending them our jump coordinates. We don't need Omnius decrypting our message and following us. It's every ship for itself now."

"Yes, ma'am," both officers replied in unison.

The deck rocked again and *again,* and Damage alarms screamed one after another.

"Shields depleted, ma'am!"

"Shall I give the order to abandon ship, Captain?" Lieutenant Devries asked from the comms.

Farah's eyes darted around the bridge, taking in everything one last time—the pale, frightened faces of her crew, the triumphant look on Therius's face... smoke hissing into the bridge from broken coolant pipes, sparks sputtering from an open access panel in a buckled support beam, the spider's web of cracks in the main viewport...

"No," Farah said. "What for? So nanites can kill us slowly and painfully when our escape pods land on the surface? We're going down with the ship."

Farah was surprised that she'd even had that much time to contemplate their fate. By now they should have been hit by one final, killing beam. Instead, the constant roar of ordinance exploding and the periodic *hum* of beams hitting their hull abruptly vanished. Farah spent a moment listening to the sound of coolant *hissing* into the bridge and to the ship's mighty thrusters *roaring* as it fought to escape Avilon's gravity.

"Why aren't we dead yet?" she wondered aloud.

"Maybe Omnius doesn't want to shoot us down over Avilon..." the ship's chief engineer suggested. "If he waits for us to reach escape velocity, the debris won't crash into the planet and do further damage."

"That's not the reason," Therius replied, smiling faintly. "Why should he care if we cause more damage when he's already evacuated the planet?"

Farah resisted the urge to slap the smile off Therius's face. She settled for scowling at him instead. "What's the reason then?"

"He doesn't want to shoot us down at all. He wants to take us captive."

Farah gritted her teeth and focused on taking deep, calming breaths. "We should have attacked the Icosahedron with nanites while Omnius was being jammed. We could have defeated him!"

Therius shook his head. "We never would have gotten past the shields."

"Then we should have found a way to infiltrate it!"

Therius's smile suddenly blossomed into a full-blown grin. "What do you think we're doing now, Miss Hale?" he whispered.

"Escape velocity attained!" the officer at the helm announced.

"Jump away!" Farah ordered.

"We're not out of the atmosphere yet! The tidal forces could—"

Suddenly the deck shuddered once more, and every powered system died, plunging the ship into utter darkness and silence. Farah's stomach did a flip as artificial gravity failed. The only light they had to see by was the fake starlight shining down on them from the billions of viewports in the distant shell of New Avilon.

"Frek!" Farah said, and pounded the captain's table with her fists. The momentum of that movement sent her spinning up toward the ceiling.

"Have faith, Miss Hale," Therius said, kicking off the deck to join her. "They're going to take us aboard."

"And then what?" she asked, pushing off the ceiling as she drew near. "We don't have any nanites aboard... or do we?"

Therius smiled, and for a moment Farah dared to hope that defeating Omnius was still a possibility. Then he shook his head and said, "No, they will not allow us aboard with any weapons, and we will be thoroughly scanned to make sure of that."

Farah frowned. He was right, of course, but that meant there was no coming back from this catastrophe, and Therius's cryptic smiles were a symptom of his insanity, not some hidden genius. Avilon was infected with nanites, doomed to a slow but certain end; Omnius had evacuated the planet; and the Union no longer had any power to threaten him.

The battle was lost, and Omnius had won.

* * *

Jena Faros led Ethan and his family and the remaining Rictans under the golden dome of a quantum junction. She used the junction to jump them directly inside one of the History Towers. From there she led them through a museum full of human history.

Some of it Ethan recognized, exhibits of early species of humans from Advistine—hairy primates, mostly—including showcases of primitive tools, and fossilized bones to describe the different stages of human evolution. Then there were exhibits of architectural wonders created by the earliest civilizations, long before the advent of space flight. He saw pyramids, giant statues, temples...

Ethan marveled at it all.

"The History of Space Flight is this way," Jena said, as they began to linger.

"Where did Omnius get all of these artifacts?" Ethan asked, wondering if he'd somehow stolen them from museums on Advistine before he sent the Sythians to destroy the planet.

"They're mostly replicas," Jena explained.

Ethan snorted. "So there's no longer any *real* evidence to describe our past."

"I suppose not," Jena replied, slowing from a jog to a fast walk.

"That's convenient," Ethan said. "I guess he can rewrite history now."

They passed through increasingly modern exhibits until eventually Advistine's cities sprawled across the continents, covering most of the planetary surface. Space elevators soared, and orbital space stations became as common and as numerous as land-based hotels. Up ahead Ethan saw a pair of doors leading to the next exhibit. Above those doors was a rotating hologram depicting Advistine from space at the end of the terrestrial period. Dozens of space elevators climbed up to giant counter-weighting stations. Under the hologram Ethan read the caption, *Earth at the End of the Terrestrial Period.*

He frowned. "I thought this exhibit was about Advistine? I've never heard of a planet called Earth."

Jena glanced over her shoulder as she waved open the doors to the next exhibit. "*Earth* is what we used to call Advistine before the Galactic Period."

"How do you know that?" Alara asked, proving Ethan wasn't the only one in the dark.

"Omnius must have found a reference to it somewhere," Jena said.

Ethan nodded, noting that the next exhibit was the one they were looking for—The History of Space Flight. He was even more distracted by all of the different space ships and technologies that powered them. Some of the designs looked absurd, but all the more intriguing for their novelty.

Something outside the History Towers exploded with a terrific *bang!* and shook the building so hard that the walls and floor cracked.

Ethan lost his balance and fell against the railing of the nearest exhibit. "What the frek was that?"

"We better hurry!" Alara said.

"Let's go!" Jena added, yelling to be heard above the residual rumblings of the explosion. Ethan scooped up his daughter and sprinted down the aisle between showcases. So far the History Towers were deserted, which was just as well. Ethan wasn't sure if Omnius would try to stop them from leaving, but he didn't want to find out.

They came to the most recent part of the Galactic Period, and Ethan saw his ship gleaming in the distance, sitting on a landing pad in front of a vast wall of windows.

Ethan stopped to stare up at his pride and joy, a 40-meter-long seraphim-class corvette. His breath caught in his chest, and he was momentarily at a loss for words.

"The *Trinity*," he whispered.

"Hey, that's my name!" Trinity said, sending him an accusing look.

Ethan turned to her with a smile. "Where do you think you got it from?"

Another explosion *boomed* and *rumbled* through the floor. Then came a distant *shriek* of rending metal, and Ethan's eyes were drawn out the wall of glass behind his ship. There, in the distance, a massive tower was on fire, a chunk bitten out the side. As they watched, the top half of the tower began falling toward them.

"Take cover!" Magnum yelled just before the tower landed in a grassy green park at the base of the History Towers. There came a world-shattering *boom*, and then a roiling gray cloud of pulverized bactcrete burst out, knocking over trees and consuming everything in its path.

Ethan saw the rushing cloud of debris and he hit the floor, pulling Trinity down with him. He held her down firmly. Then the shock wave hit and the glass wall exploded. Trinity lifted her head to look just as a glittering rain of shattered glass came flying at them. She screamed.

"Head down!" Ethan yelled, feeling glass shards dig into his back and arms. Then it was over. Ethan's ears rang, and his back stung fiercely with embedded glass. He lifted his head to check how Trinity was doing, and the air left his lungs in a strangled cry.

A jagged wedge of glass protruded from Trinity's forehead with blood bubbling out around it.

She was conscious and crying, but he doubted it was from the pain. She had to be in shock.

"Medic!" Ethan yelled.

Alara reached them first. "What happened?" she demanded. "Oh no... Trinity..."

Rictan Six dropped to his haunches beside them. His gaze flicked to the chunk of glass in Trinity's head, and his cheeks turned gray.

Ethan wanted to pick the man up and shake him. "What are you waiting for? Fix her!"

Trinity's eyes rolled in her head, and she mumbled incoherently. Alara began sobbing. She held their daughter's head in her lap, stroking blood-matted hair away from her forehead, telling her that everything was going to be all right.

"I'm sorry," Blades whispered.

"We need to go!" Jena called out.

Ethan felt sick. He grabbed his daughter's hand and squeezed. "Trin," he said. Her eyes stopped rolling long enough to settle on him, and he gave her a strangled smile. "I love you, sweetheart."

Then he realized why her eyes had stopped rolling, and he burst into tears.

CHAPTER 49

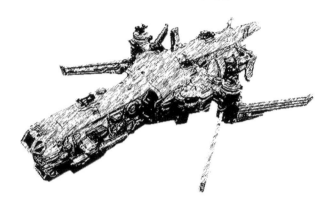

Jena and the Rictans did their best to drag them away from Trinity. Ethan didn't have the strength left to resist. He rose to his feet, backing away slowly, his heart broken.

"If we don't hurry, we could be next," Jena said, still trying to tear Alara away.

"Who cares?" Alara screamed.

Jena took a step back and shook her head, looking startled. "You don't have to go with us," she said, "but we're leaving Avilon. Maybe if you stay, Omnius will bring your daughter back."

Ethan walked up to his wife and placed his hands on her shoulders. "Alara—"

"Don't touch me!"

"Trust me," Ethan whispered through gritted teeth.

"I tried that, remember?" Alara's lips twisted into a bitter smile. "Look how that worked out. If you'd been in Etheria with us, this never would have happened."

Ethan winced. It wasn't fair to lay the blame for this on him, but Alara needed someone to blame, and right now her cheating husband was an easy target. He shook his head. "Look—we brought Omnius back online. That's got to count for something. If he doesn't repay the favor by resurrecting Trinity, I'll be very surprised."

Alara's expression took a hopeful turn. "You're right. We *did* bring him back, didn't we...?"

Ethan nodded.

"Fine, so you're staying, and we're going," Jena said. "Nice to meet you all..."

"Hold on!" Ethan caught her by the arm and yanked her up to within an inch of his face. "You can't fly *my* ship out of here without my launch codes, and we're not going to sit around here waiting for nanites to kill us. You're going to take us up to the Icosahedron so that we can speak with Omnius in person."

"Forget it."

"I'm not asking you," Ethan said. "I'm *telling* you. Now let's go."

Jena started to object, but Ethan silenced her with a venomous look. "She's my *daughter*. End of discussion."

Alara surprised him by slipping her hand into his.

She hadn't forgiven him yet, but it was a start.

Jena held Ethan's gaze for a long moment. Then she scowled and nodded. "Fine."

They ran to the *Trinity* and straight up the ramp. Ethan led the way to the cockpit and found the Rictans already there, trying to bypass his launch codes.

"Out of the way," Ethan said, yanking Magnum out of the pilot's chair. He sat down and entered the codes; then he ran a quick check on the ship's systems. To his amazement, all ship's systems were in the green, even after almost a decade of disuse. Feeling suddenly more positive, Ethan fired up the grav lifts and then the thrusters, cold-starting them both. The ship's only complaint was a mild shudder before it hovered up from the landing pad.

"Still purrs like a kitten," he said, and rotated the ship until it faced the shattered wall of glass. Alara sat in the copilot's seat beside him, and Jena Faros hovered over their shoulders.

"We're not going to board the Icosahedron," Jena said. "You can send a message to Omnius and then launch yourselves in an escape pod so he can pick you up."

"Sure," Ethan replied, and dialed the inertial management system back to eighty percent. Then he pushed the throttle up past the stops and rocketed out over Avilon. The ship's sudden acceleration pinned him and Alara both to their seats, while Jena Faros and the Rictans all went tumbling backward, screaming as they went. He heard someone cursing, and risked a glance over his shoulder to see Magnum clinging to the open hatch by his fingernails.

"Motherfrekker!" Magnum gritted out.

"Guess I forgot to warn you guys to strap in," Ethan said. Then he pulled up, adding the planet's gravity to accentuate their momentum. Magnum lost his grip with a curse and a shout, and Ethan sealed the cockpit from the pilot's station. Now that they were alone he brought inertial management up to 100%.

"Are they okay?" Alara asked.

"I don't know," Ethan said.

That uncertainty hung between them as the *Trinity* clawed for orbit in a near-vertical climb. Thousands of fighters danced above them, their thrusters tracing neon swirls behind the clouds—Nova blue, Shell fighter orange, and drone fighter red. The colors mingled and swirled together in buzzing swarms. Streams of red and purple lasers crisscrossed between the fighters, and explosions speckled the sky with fiery bursts of light.

Ethan keyed the comms and set them for an open channel, about to ask Omnius for permission to approach the Icosahedron and land, but Alara touched his hand and shook her head. For a split second he was afraid she'd had a change of heart about bringing Trinity back.

"I've already told him," she said. "Omnius knows we're coming. He's going to send a drone escort to get us there safely."

Ethan remembered her Lifelink implant, and he nodded. "Good."

They raced through the clouds and emerged in the middle of a dazzling firefight between a pair of Gor cruisers and a few thousand drone fighters.

One of the Gor ships exploded with a titanic *boom*, spraying their shields with supersonic debris, and Ethan grimaced as their forward shields went from blue to green. Laser fire flickered by them, so close that it actually made the corvette *shudder*. No, something else had to have caused that shudder. Lasers didn't impart kinetic energy with their passing. Ethan checked the threat detection system to identify their attackers, but there weren't any. Then the deck shuddered once more, and another dazzling flicker of laser light stole Ethan's attention. This time he noticed the source.

The lasers were coming from *them*.

"What the frek?" Ethan's hands flew over the controls as he hurried to shut down the ship's weapons systems.

"What is it?" Alara asked.

"Looks like our passengers are okay after all. They've found the turrets and they're using them to get some target practice."

"They're trying to shoot down drones? Are they crazy?"

Another flash of lasers streaked out from them. This time Ethan saw the lasers impact on the side of a nearby cruiser—a *Gor* cruiser. He gaped at that.

"Ethan?" Alara asked.

He braced himself for return fire. "They're not shooting at drones," he explained. "They're shooting at Gors!"

"Aren't the Gors their allies? Why would they shoot them?"

"To get us all killed! Why else?" Ethan finished shutting down the weapon systems and then keyed the intercom. "I hope you're happy, Magnum!"

Laughter rippled back over the intercom. "No guts, no glory, motherfrekker! And I'm gonna spill yours if it's the last thing I do."

The TDS screeched out a belated warning, and a blinding light suffused the deck. A muffed explosion sounded somewhere aft of the cockpit, and damage alerts screamed. Ethan threw the ship into an evasive pattern.

"Damn you, Magnum!" he breathed.

"What was that?" Alara asked.

Another explosion roared through the cockpit and the *Trinity* rocked violently once more.

"The Gors are firing at us!" he said.

The TDS chirped out a series of rapid fire warnings, and Ethan saw half a dozen Shell Fighters lining up behind them, vying for missile locks. That wasn't good. Evading energy-based Pirakla missiles came down to speed and sudden, last-minute changes in momentum, but they were still in atmosphere, clawing for orbit, and the *Trinity's* lack of aerodynamic properties made it a sitting duck.

"Ethan, if those fighters get missile locks on us—"

The chirping warnings from the TDS became solid tones, and Ethan's hands tingled with adrenaline, getting ready to throw them into a last-ditch maneuver.

"Hang on..." he warned, watching the grid for the warning flash of light as the Shell fighters pursuing them launched their missiles. That flash of light came, but not from the star map. It suffused the entire deck, washing everything a dazzling white and making all of their concerns moot.

* * *

Farah Hale lay pinned to the main forward viewport with the rest of her crew, held there by a mysterious force of deceleration that had gripped their ship as they drew near to the Icosahedron. Farah could only assume that Omnius was arresting their approach with some type of grav gun. Most of the crew was content to lie against the viewport and wait for the inevitable, but Farah had twisted around onto her belly so that she could watch. It took all of her strength just to keep her face from being smashed against the viewport.

She was rewarded for her effort with a breathtaking view of New Avilon. They were finally close enough to pick out details on the inner side of it. The most curious detail were the thousands of giant, bristling towers pointing down toward Avilon. They looked like the barrels of giant laser cannons.

Farah remembered that the Icosahedron was supposed to be capable of mining entire planets for resources, and she wondered if those towers were massive beam weapons. She estimated by the size and number of them that Omnius could have wiped out the entire Union fleet in seconds.

So why hasn't he?

Even as she was thinking that, one of those towers opened fire and a thick white beam shot by them to hit some unseen target coming up from the surface of Avilon. Farah blinked the spots from her eyes. Whatever that beam had hit, it was gone now, but Omnius had fired just one beam out of thousands. He was cherry-picking the targets he wished to destroy and capturing others. She wondered what criteria Omnius was using. Was he capturing only human ships, or Sythian and Gor ones, too?

Farah watched as one of the Trees of Life reached the Icosahedron. It had rotated to dock with its engines facing the inner side of the sphere. As soon as the bright red glow of its thrusters disappeared and it finished docking, that tower became just one more out of thousands already aimed at the surface of Avilon.

Farah blinked. All of those towers weren't just weapons emplacements. They were New Avilon's cloning facilities and Lifelink data centers.

"We've stopped moving," Therius whispered, announcing the fact just a split second before Farah realized that the crushing weight on her back had disappeared.

She pushed gently off the main forward viewport and turned to see her crew all drifting and tumbling through the bridge. "I thought you said Omnius was going to take us aboard?" she said, eager to poke a hole in Therius's smug insanity.

"He will, but first drones will board us, scan us, and carry us away in one of Omnius's ships. He would never trust us to come aboard in one of our own vessels."

Farah smirked. "Of course not. So what exactly *is* your plan? Or don't you have one anymore?"

"I plan to wait until we are captured."

"And then?"

"Then we're going to meet with Omnius face-to-face, and I'm going to speak with him one last time."

Farah snorted. "Going to beg for mercy? We should kill ourselves now before Omnius finds a more painful way to do it."

"I'm going to give him one last chance to back down," Therius replied.

Farah stared at him, unable to believe what he'd just said. He refused to admit defeat even while looking down the barrels of a thousand planet-mining beam weapons. That, she decided, was the very definition of insanity.

"Would you please cut my bonds and help me power up your uncle's drone?" Therius asked.

"Seven Sixty Seven? Why?"

"Trust me, Farah."

Farah eyed Therius through the darkness. His eyes shone with reflected light from the Icosahedron, making him look even more insane than usual. She took a deep breath and shook her head. "If you're planning some kind of last stand, you're going to have to count me out of it. I'm done."

"Very well," Therius said, sounding disappointed. He turned away from her, and Farah saw his gaze settle on Torv next. "I brought your people back from the brink of extinction. The Gors are an honorable people, and I promised your matriarch they would be rewarded. My promise stands, despite what you might think. Will you help me?"

Hissss.

Farah's translator spat out a single word. "No."

"What do you have to lose?"

"He dropped nanites on Avilon, Torv. There are millions of Gors on the surface, and now they're all going to die."

"Not everything here is what it seems, Miss Hale. Torv, you need to make up your mind for yourself. Will you trust me?"

Torv replied with a sibilant stream of hisses and used the grav guns in his boots to regain his footing on the deck below.

Farah's translator whispered in her ear. "I trust. But if you lie, I eat you alive."

"Torv..." Farah said, shaking her head.

She saw Therius smile. "I accept your terms."

Torv walked over to Therius and reached up to grab his ankle and pull him down.

"Take me to the drone," Therius instructed.

Torv dragged Therius over to 767, who was floating a few feet above the captain's table.

"Please cut my bonds, Torv."

The Gor cut them with a brief flash of light from his scythe-shaped energy blade.

"Thank you." Therius stood on Torv's shoulders and reached around the back of the drone's head to turn it on. A beam of crimson light shot out from 767's optical sensor and washed across the deck.

"Welcome back, Seven Sixty Seven. It's time for us to leave the bridge."

"Where are we going, Admiral?"

"I'll show you."

Therius wrapped his arms around the drone's neck and 767 powered his own grav guns to join Torv on the deck. Therius nodded to the Gor. "Thank you, my friend. Your part in this is over, but you will not be disappointed. Have faith."

Torv hissed once more. "I go with you."

"If you insist."

Farah's brow furrowed, and she watched as the three of them made their way down the gangway, walking by the crimson light of 767's optical sensor. The bridge doors swished open and then shut behind them. Farah scowled, hoping Torv would get a chance to make good on his threat to eat Therius alive, but she had a bad feeling that the Union leader would doublecross him before long. Gors were too trusting, particularly the males. Farah was sure that if Matriarch Shara had been aboard in Torv's stead, she would have ripped Therius's throat out by now. Of course, that was probably why she wasn't aboard. Farah wondered where Therius was headed.

Critical systems like doors were running in low-power mode on battery backups alone. That meant they would be able to reach the escape pods, but abandoning ship wouldn't get them anywhere. Omnius would see their escape pod and either vaporize them or pick them up.

Still, the thought of Therius running from the mess he'd created made Farah's blood boil.

This was all his fault! The entire attack had been a lie. He'd never planned to defeat Omnius. His idea of setting humanity free was to *kill* them. Farah spent the next fifteen minutes dwelling on that and imagining ways she could get revenge on Therius for what he'd done.

The bridge doors *swished* open once more and a squad of drones came *clanking* in. Their optical sensors cast bright red fans of light through the air as they scanned the surviving crew.

Seeing her chance, Farah called out to them, "Our leader escaped! Check the escape pods. If there aren't any missing, then he's still aboard."

The drones gave no verbal response, but a pair of them went *clanking* back the way they'd come, going to search the ship. Farah felt better, knowing that whatever fate awaited her and her crew, Therius wasn't about to escape it.

The air buzzed with the *crackling* report of energy weapons set to stun. Dazzling blue bolts snapped out with pinpoint accuracy. People screamed and a few belatedly tried to resist by firing back with their sidearms.

Farah shut her eyes, and allowed her thoughts to drift to her Uncle Bretton—the *real* one, not the drone. Bretton was dead and gone, but maybe just maybe he'd passed on to a better place.

Farah chose to believe that.

Then a stun bolt hit her, and her body convulsed. Darkness closed in around her, and she welcomed it.

CHAPTER 50

As the spots cleared from Ethan's eyes, he saw what had caused the blinding flash of light. All of the Shell fighters on their tail had simultaneously exploded.

Drone fighters appeared on all sides, and a pair raced out ahead, leading the way to the Icosahedron. Omnius's escort had arrived just in time to rescue them.

Ethan breathed out a shaky sigh. "That was close."

Alara nodded.

Avilon's atmosphere fell away and they gained a crystal-clear view of New Avilon. Its viewports shone down on them like a dense field of stars. Lasers flashed against that backdrop, and explosions flared almost continuously.

The battle wasn't going to last much longer. Union ships were being taken out just as fast as they could race into orbit, and there were at least a hundred red enemy contacts for every solitary green one. Enemy contacts were purely fighter-class, but with so *many* of them, it didn't matter that Omnius hadn't brought any heavier weapons to the fight.

"I guess now all we have to do is wait," Ethan said.

"I guess..." Alara's eyes were glazed and staring, her mind

somewhere far away.

Ethan didn't have to ask to know what she was thinking about. "Trinity was already a clone. Nothing's going to change when Omnius brings her back."

Alara shook her head. "That doesn't make watching her die any easier."

Bang!

Ethan's eyes flew to the TDS, then to the grid, but nothing was attacking them. "The frek...?"

Then the sound came again, and Ethan realized it was coming from the cockpit hatch. He turned to see the hatch sprinkled with fingertip-sized dents.

As he watched, there came another *bang,* and another sprinkling of dents appeared. The pattern exactly matched the spread of a sawed-off ripper rifle. Remembering the armory aboard his ship and the pair of elite commandos he'd left rattling around in the *Trinity's* aft sections, Ethan's eyes flew wide. He was shocked that those weapons hadn't been stripped from the *Trinity* before the ship had been made into a museum exhibit.

"They're going to punch a hole!" Alara said.

Bang!

Even as she said that, holes began shining through the hatch. Ethan saw a familiar brown eye appear in one of them.

"Omnius killed her," Magnum said. "Just thought you might want to know that before you delivered us all into his clutches."

"Killed who?" Ethan asked.

"That Peacekeeper woman. He pulled the plug on her like she was some kinda drone."

Alara replied, "He killed her because she was trying to get us killed by firing at Gors!"

"You locked us out of the cockpit and took us hostage to deliver to the enemy. It's kill or be killed, Motherfrekkers!"

Bang!

Ethan took cover behind the pilot's chair, his mind racing to come up with a way to defeat them. He remembered the trick he'd pulled earlier with the ship's inertial management system and sudden acceleration.

"Hang on," he told Alara, one hand poised over the throttle, the other picking a new setting for the IMS.

But he never had a chance to set it. The cockpit came alive with a gusting wind and a blinding light. Then the light faded and Ethan heard a *screech* of lasers firing, followed by a *thud*, a strangled cry, and another *thud*.

Clanking footsteps approached, drawing Ethan's attention to the rear. He watched as metallic claws reached through the shredded hatch, tearing it open like paper. A pair of drones came into the cockpit, their optical sensors scanning with crimson beams of light.

Omnius had quantum-jumped these two aboard to deal with the Rictans.

Ethan spotted the pair of commandos lying motionless in a spreading black pool of blood just beyond the hatch, and he grimaced. The drones' eyes settled on him, and he hesitated, suddenly afraid that he might be next.

"Thank you," he managed.

The drones gave no reply. They merely took up guard positions, one to either side of the ruined hatch.

Ethan went back to piloting the ship with his hands shaking on the flight controls. Omnius had just dispatched both of the remaining Rictans, and apparently, one of his own Peacekeepers.

"They would have killed us," Alara said, seeming to read his mind.

He pressed his lips into a thin line. "I guess Magnum was right. It's kill or be killed."

"Would you rather we be the ones lying on the deck in a pool of blood right now?"

"No, but Omnius didn't have to kill them. They're not coming back, you know. They didn't have Lifelinks. None of us did. Even if they had clones on Avilon, they weren't the same people, and they didn't share the same memories."

"They came to Avilon knowing there was a chance that they could die in the fighting."

"And that means their deaths don't mean anything?"

"Ethan, we saved Avilon, and now we're going to save our daughter. We did everything we could to prevent further loss of life."

"But what is Omnius doing to prevent further loss of life?"

"He's disabling Union ships, not destroying them," Alara said, nodding to the star map.

Ethan saw that Alara was right. One in every two Union ships had gone dark on the grid. Space was crowded with more derelict warships than debris.

Ethan was taken aback by that. Maybe Omnius wasn't the real enemy, after all. He'd agreed to give the Union what they wanted, and they'd *still* dropped nanites on Avilon.

But just because Therius's side was the wrong one didn't mean Omnius's was the right one. He was just as guilty of unnecessary bloodshed, if not more. After all, he'd created the Sythians and used them to start all the fighting in the first place.

The vast shell of the Icosahedron drew ever-nearer, and the drone fighters guiding them in banked suddenly to port. Ethan was about to match that maneuver, but his ship moved before he could.

"What the..."

"Omnius is guiding us in," Alara explained. "He wants you to shut down your engines."

Ethan hesitated for a second before killing thrust. "Now what?" he asked, sitting back in his chair with his hands folded in his lap.

"Now we wait to be brought aboard."

It was a short wait. Half an hour later they raced past an inverted city of lights and towers, the tallest of which looked identical to the Trees of Life they'd seen launching from Avilon.

Ethan marveled at the sheer size and scale of Omnius's creation. It was like someone had turned the cities of Avilon inside out and stretched them into a thin shell around the planet. Although, according to the *Trinity's* sensors that 'thin' shell was more than twenty kilometers thick.

"Where did Omnius get enough raw materials to create something like this?" Ethan wondered. "He must have mined a few planets into nonexistence."

"Maybe a few solar systems," Alara suggested.

Dead ahead Ethan saw a small blue rectangle appear. As they drew near, he realized it was a hangar bay, and it wasn't small. It could have berthed an entire fleet. The drones flying ahead of them disappeared through the hazy blue glow of the hangar's shields. Then the *Trinity* glided in after them with a faint *sizzle* of exchanging energy, and Ethan saw a vast, empty hangar deck with myriad glowing red circles to denote landing spaces. Without him having to touch the flight controls, the *Trinity* hovered down into the middle of a green-glowing circle, while their fighter escort settled down on matching circles around them.

A mechanical voice spoke, startling Ethan out of his thoughts. "Welcome to New Avilon. Please follow me."

Ethan turned to see the drones who'd been standing guard at the hatch come alive and go *clanking* out the cockpit, down the access corridor beyond.

Alara unbuckled her flight restraints. "Come on," she said, and hurried after the drones.

Ethan followed, grimacing as he was forced to step around the bloody mess that Omnius had made of the Rictans. Seeing Magnum's glazed and staring eyes gave him pause once more.

Everything that had happened since the Sythians invaded was all just a lot of senseless killing for the sake of killing. It was almost as if Omnius enjoyed the bloodshed.

It's time to get some answers, he thought.

CHAPTER 51

As the drones led them through the vast, echoing hangar bay, Ethan noticed all of the empty racks folded up along the walls and ceiling. They looked like gleaming black skeletons. Ethan realized they were meant to hold drone fighters, but they were empty now that all of the drones were out fighting the Union fleet.

Once they reached the far wall of the hangar, the drones led them down a broad corridor with a familiar, shiny golden dome at the end—a quantum junction.

The drones activated the junction, causing it to rise on four shimmering pillars of light, and Ethan and Alara hurried to the center of the green-glowing circle underneath. The drones came *clanking* into position and then one of them raised its hands to activate the junction.

Ethan shut his eyes as the dome fell and began glowing with a dazzling light. He fumbled for Alara's hand and laced his fingers through hers as wind gusted around inside the dome, tearing at their clothes and hair.

Then the light vanished and the wind died down. Ethan opened his eyes to see the dome rising once more.

He saw a small group of people standing in front of a

massive wraparound viewport. Beyond that, Avilon lay dark and whorled with the dendritic patterns of light from its cities. As the drones led them to the viewport, Ethan recognized the people standing there. One of them was Grand Overseer Thardris. The overseer turned and smiled. His eyes flickered bright silver in the light of his ARCs, making it all but impossible to see the whites of his eyes.

"It's good to see you, Ethan—and Alara," he said. "I would ask who resurrected you, Ethan, but I think I already know the answer to that. Therius will be joining us soon. Hopefully he can clear up the mystery for us."

Ethan was about to reply, but the next person who turned around was none other than Valari Thardris.

"Hello, Ethan," she said.

Ethan's expression darkened.

"What are you doing here?" Alara demanded, before he could ask. She withdrew her hand from his and crossed her arms over her chest.

Rather than reply, Valari walked straight up to them, and before either of them could react, she planted a kiss on Ethan's lips.

Ethan recoiled from her, trying to spit the taste of her out of his mouth.

Slap!

Valari reeled from Alara's blow and recovered with a girlish peal of laughter. Alara reared back to hit her again, this time with her fist. But Valari caught Alara's wrist in a white-knuckled fist.

"There's no need to be angry with me, dear!" she said, still laughing. "Your husband is the one who seduced *me!*"

Alara shot Ethan a venomous look, to which he could only shake his head and say, "I'm sorry. I don't remember."

"That's a fine defense," Valari scoffed. "Amnesia! You're beginning to hurt my feelings, Ethan. Am I that forgettable?"

"It's the truth. I thought you were my wife, and I thought we were in my apartment!" He reached out for Alara's hand. "Alara I—"

"Don't touch me!"

Valari sidled up to him and slipped an arm through his. "You see, Ethan? She'll never take you back. It's too late. You may as well lie in the bed you've defiled with me."

Ethan pushed her away. "I'd rather die."

"Yes, you tried that, didn't you?" Valari said, her bright turquoise eyes laughing at him.

"That's enough!" Grand Overseer Thardris boomed, his voice reverberating off the walls. "I won't have my moment of triumph turned into a petty circus."

"Your moment of triumph?" Ethan asked. "Don't you mean Omnius's?"

"I am Omnius."

Ethan blinked, only half shocked by that revelation. It made sense that the so-called Grand Overseer of Avilon was actually an avatar for its AI ruler.

Omnius went on, turning to a stranger standing beside him. "And this is Atton."

Ethan blinked, studying that stranger, but he wasn't a complete stranger. This was the taxi driver who'd taken him home the night he'd drunk himself senseless and cheated with Valari. "You drove me home..." Ethan said.

"Yes."

"You're not my son."

Suddenly the man's appearance shimmered, and back was a face that Ethan recognized, one with his own green eyes, *his* jaw and *his* dark, wavy hair.

Ethan shook his head. "I don't understand."

"It's a long story," Atton said. "I asked Omnius to resurrect me in another body for the woman that I love. For my wife."

"You're married?" Ethan asked, shocked and dismayed all at once. He'd missed so much... and all because he'd thought that clone transfers were impossible. Now that *he* was a clone transfer, it was suddenly much harder to argue with the process.

"You don't remember any of this," Atton said, "but your clone does. He already met me, and he'd be here with us now, but Valari killed him when he tried to join the fight against Omnius." Ethan saw Atton's eyes flick sideways to address Alara. "That clone is the one who went to Etheria to convince you to take him back."

Alara shook her head.

"I know it's all very confusing, but the only thing you really need to know is that Valari tricked Ethan."

"What?" Valari shrieked. "That's a lie!"

Atton ignored her. "She had me pick him up from the bus stop where he'd passed out drunk and deliver him to her penthouse, which she disguised to look like the apartment you and Ethan shared. She was wearing a bio-synthetic suit, like I am, and she looked and sounded just like you, Alara."

Ethan's hands balled into fists. His pulse thumped out a drumbeat in his ears. He turned to see Valari gaping accusingly at Omnius, her face a shade paler than usual.

"How could you?" she demanded. "Ethan was mine! You promised—"

"I promised I would help you to be with him, not that you would remain with him forever," Omnius replied.

Ethan's gut twisted. He felt like he was about to be sick. All the lies on Avilon had just reached him at a very personal level.

"You hateful thing!" Valari screamed. "I created you! You

wouldn't even exist if it weren't for me!"

"You might have created me, but I made you immortal, and you are only alive after all of these years because of *me*," Omnius said. "You lost your way. You spent all of your energy on petty, selfish pursuits. You thought you were the exception to all the rules, just because you were the first to imagine creating me. In exchange for that, I've put up with you for countless years, hoping you would grow out of your childish ways, but you only ever got worse, not better." Omnius turned to Ethan. "Go ahead. Kill her."

Ethan watched Valari slowly backing away from him, her eyes wide and full of fear. His fists tightened until his hands felt numb, but he remained where he was, frozen in shock.

Alara shot by him in a blur. "You frekking sclut!" she screamed and landed a blow under Valari's chin, shutting the other woman's mouth with a noisy *clack* of teeth. Valari fell over and hit the deck with a startled cry. Alara followed her down, her fists still flying. Valari defended herself, kicking and punching, but Alara was too furious to care.

Ethan hurried to his wife's defense and pulled Alara off Valari, receiving a few blows from both women for his trouble.

"Let me go!" Alara screamed. Her feet kicked his shins, and her chest heaved in his arms.

Ethan held her fast, his attention on Valari. She lay blinking up at him, shock and horror written on her face. "I *should* kill you," he said.

Valari managed a wry smile despite her split and bleeding lips. "But you can't, can you? Because you have feelings for me."

Ethan noticed Omnius walk up beside him. "Go ahead," he said and held out a shiny black sidearm. "Finish her."

"If you won't, I will!" Alara said, struggling anew to break free of his grasp.

Valari scuttled away from them, and Ethan eyed the weapon for a long moment.

At last, he tore his eyes away and shook his head. "There's been enough bloodshed today."

"Very well," Omnius said, but rather than re-holster the weapon, he aimed it at Valari's chest. She'd fetched up against the viewport and was unable to back away any further.

"Wait!" she screeched, holding up both hands to stop him.

"New Avilon will be different," Omnius said. "No more lies. No more exceptions to the rules. True perfection. Goodbye, my daughter." Omnius pulled the trigger and there came a loud *screech* and a bright flash of light. When the glare faded, Ethan saw Valari slumped against the viewport with a smoking hole in her chest.

He looked away, feeling sicker than ever. Omnius had just shot his own family, or the nearest equivalent that he had, anyway, and while part of Ethan was tempted to say *good riddance* another part of him realized that Omnius was equally to blame for tricking him—and for everything else that had happened.

Omnius holstered the sidearm and turned to them with a smile. "Now, justice has been done and we can all put the past behind us. Thank you for bringing me back online—both of you," he added, glancing at Alara. "To repay that kindness, I will of course be more than happy to resurrect your daughter, and you are all more than welcome to live with me in New Avilon."

"What if we'd rather be free?" Ethan asked.

Omnius's smile faded, and he shrugged. "Then I will let you go. I meant what I said. Everyone who wishes to be free will be free."

Ethan narrowed his eyes, but before he could reply,

someone else did—

"Haven't you grown tired of lying yet, Omnius?"

The voice was familiar, and it was accompanied by a full squad of drones, their feet *clanking* in a steady rhythm as they approached.

Ethan turned to see Therius being led from the quantum junction by a squad of drones. He came to a stop just a few feet away.

"Well, well," Omnius said. "I don't know how you've done all of this, Therius, but some congratulations are in order. Your plan almost worked."

Therius smiled. "Are you going to answer my question?"

"I'm not lying," Omnius replied.

Therius nodded out the viewport to the glowing orange ball of Avilon. "You can't stop the nanites."

"I don't need to. I have all the Lifelink data and clones safely aboard *New Avilon*. I'll resurrect everyone here."

"Everyone? Or just the ones who chose to be with you?"

Omnius shrugged. "People can't have it both ways. If they don't want to be with me, then they're going to die sooner or later. Besides, their deaths won't be on my conscience. They'll be on *yours*. You're the one who decided to infect Avilon with nanites."

Alara let out a strangled gasp, her eyes wide and blinking as she stared open-mouthed at Omnius. "You *are* evil!"

Ethan shook his head. "I was right... you didn't want everyone to stay on Avilon to keep them safe. You wanted them to stay so you could get rid of them!"

Omnius gave a bellowing laugh. "Therius is the one who wanted to kill everyone! And you say *I'm* evil? At least when I kill people, I bring them back."

Therius shook his head. "Not always. Making people into

drones isn't bringing them back, it's removing everything that's independent and free-acting about them. Humans were created to be free, and you've made them all prisoners."

"Correction, they made themselves prisoners. They created me and put me in charge. They were the ones who programmed me to replace the chaos of freedom with perfection. All I have ever done is work to fulfill that goal."

"I wonder if Ethan would agree that your involvement in his life has brought it closer to perfection. You know what your problem is, Omnius? You know the truth, but you refuse to believe it or even look at it too closely for fear that you might learn you're not as powerful as you think you are."

Omnius burst out laughing. "I know more than anyone has ever known in the history of the universe!"

"You repeatedly ignored the results of the Lazarus experiments, and you spent your time erasing the ruins in the Getties rather than studying them. What is it that makes humans unpredictable to you? You still don't know, do you?"

"It doesn't matter. In the future I'll resurrect people weekly if I have to. They'll never have a chance to become unpredictable again."

"So instead of solving the mystery, you'd rather bury all the evidence forever."

Omnius suddenly cocked his head to one side. "Speaking of mysteries, how did you escape Avilon, Therius?"

"Once you've broken into a prison, it's easy to break out."

"What are you talking about?"

Ethan was busy wondering the same thing.

"You found evidence of the war in the Getties, and the people who fought it," Therius replied. "You stole their technology, and you found the survivors of that war and used them to create the Sythian invasion. You found all of that, but if you had dug just a little deeper you would have found me, too."

Omnius's eyes suddenly widened and began darting around the room, as if searching for an escape.

"Is something wrong?"

"The Eclipser was destroyed!" Omnius shrieked. "How can you be jamming me again?"

"Did you really think I could jam all the quantum fields around Avilon with such a tiny device?"

"Kill him!" Omnius screamed, his eyes on his drones, but they made no move to obey. Omnius's eyes flashed, and his sidearm whipped into line with Therius's head. One of the drones standing beside Therius leapt in front of him just as Omnius fired, and the shot burned a glancing hole in the drone's armor. The drone lunged at Omnius, knocking the weapon out of his hand, and then he grabbed both of Omnius's arms and twisted them up behind his back.

"Thank you, 767," Therius said.

Omnius burst out laughing. "What are you going to do? Kill me? I'll come back in another body! You'll never escape. You'll have to fight through legions of drones just to get to the nearest hangar!"

"They don't seem to be doing very much fighting," Therius said. "They've all been deactivated."

"Impossible! I am in comppppleeete contrrrrol!"

"Really? You don't even seem to be in control of your own tongue right now," Therius replied. "The attack was a distraction, Omnius. The nanites were the bait. The real threat was *my* drones. Look at the one holding you. Can you tell him apart from the rest? All I needed to do was infiltrate the Trees of Life and then force you to withdraw them to New Avilon. Those towers were designed to keep out humans, not drones. And of course, you were being jammed at the time, so how could you possibly see them coming? As soon as the Trees of Life docked with New Avilon, my drones began infecting your systems with a virus, and now that the virus has taken hold, I've activated the jamming field so that you can't defend yourself."

"No virusss can def-f-feat m-m-mee. I am a su-per com-p-p-puter."

"A super computer with a stutter."

Ethan gaped at Therius, shocked to his core. "You *let* me overhear that conversation with Captain Hale."

Therius turned to him with a smile. "I knew you would take action, if not to save humanity, then at least to save your family. All I needed to do was put you in a position to know where the Eclipser would be, and make you desperate enough to disable it. Making you a full commander and putting you in charge of the Rictans raised a few eyebrows, but it worked. I needed you to disable the device so that I would have an excuse to stop jamming Omnius. As soon as you did, and I dropped the nanites, Omnius withdrew the Trees of Life to New Avilon, taking all of my drones with him."

"You could have just told me the truth," Ethan said.

"Omnius needed to think he was always one step ahead, and everyone needed to perform their parts flawlessly in order to convince him. If anyone had known the real plot, they might have given it away."

"You still took a big risk with me," Ethan said. "I could have run away with my family like I was planning. Alara was the one who convinced me to bring Omnius back."

"Omnius isn't the only one who can predict what people will do, Ethan."

"What if I died along the way?"

"Then I would have found an excuse to disable the Eclipser myself."

Omnius roared with frustration, drawing all of their attention to him.

"There's still a chance for you, Omnius," Therius said. "A human mind can't be affected by a computer virus. The stutter you are experiencing is coming from the parts of the virus that have spread to your Lifelink. Your implant can be purged and you'll be back to your usual self."

"I w-will be n-no be-better than a-a-a hu-*man!*

"You never were. That was the greatest lie of all—that you are god."

"I *am* God!"

Ethan saw Atton bend to pick something up off the deck. Then he caught a glimpse of black alloy glinting, and he realized what it was. "Atton, wait!"

Atton pulled the trigger, and Omnius's body jerked as the pistol burned a hole in his gut. His expression contorted with pain, and his eyebrows drew together in an almost comical look of betrayal.

"Atton? I d-didn't predict that..."

The flickering silver light went out of Omnius's eyes as his augmented reality contacts deactivated themselves. The drone holding him stepped away, allowing Omnius to crumple to the deck.

Atton stared at Omnius's body. "If you're god, then god is dead," he said.

"Atton, what have you done?" Ethan yelled, his chest heaving desperately. "We *needed* him! Trinity died! Now who's going to bring her back?"

Atton looked up, his eyes shimmering with tears. "My wife is dead, too."

"No one is dead," Therius interrupted. "Least of all me."

"What do you mean *you're* not dead?" Atton asked.

"You said God is dead, but I'm standing right here."

Ethan's jaw dropped. "Who are you?"

"I am Etherus."

CHAPTER 52

"**W**hat do you mean, you're *Etherus*?" Ethan asked. "You *created* us?"

Therius smiled. "I think it would be better if I showed you." Turning to the drone who had been holding Omnius, he said, "Seven Sixty Seven, take us to Ethan's ship, please."

Ethan watched the drone go *clanking* across the control room to the exit. Therius went next, and everyone followed close on his heels. Ethan studied the man more carefully now, trying but failing to see through his humanity. *There's no way he's Etherus. He's insane, that's what he is.*

In the corridor beyond the control room, there were dozens of drones standing frozen in mid-stride or toppled over on the deck. All of them were deactivated by the virus, just as Therius said.

Ethan tried to imagine the chaos on the surface of Avilon as millions of drone fighters rained from the sky.

"You said no one is really dead," Ethan said, walking up beside Therius. "I guess that means you're going to use the Trees of Life to bring them back?"

"The databanks are infected with the same virus that

corrupted Omnius's systems. All the data is unrecoverable."

"What?" Ethan's heart sank.

"Have *faith,* Ethan. How did I bring *you* back on Origin? How did *I* return after Omnius killed me on Avilon?"

"I'm still waiting for the answer."

"Then come."

Feeling suddenly apprehensive, Ethan stopped walking. Alara came up and grabbed his hand.

"What other choice do we have?" she whispered to him.

None. That was what scared him.

They spent the next hour walking down corridors and riding down lift tubes before they finally returned to the hangar bay where Ethan had left his ship. The Icosahedron had been designed with quantum junctions as the primary form of transport, but they were all offline now that the jamming field was back.

When they reached the *Trinity*, Therius stopped at the foot of the boarding ramp and waited. "Lead the way."

Ethan led the way to the cockpit. He grimaced once more as he was forced to walk around the Rictans' bodies.

"So much needless bloodshed..." Therius said as he came into the cockpit behind him and Alara.

"Those nanite bombs you dropped aren't exactly helping," Atton said.

Ethan sat in the pilot's chair and began spinning up the ship's reactors, while Alara ran systems' checks from the copilot's station.

"The nanites will deactivate themselves soon," Therius replied. "I built a kill switch into them."

Ethan fired up the engines and hovered the *Trinity* off the deck, turning it to face the hazy blue wall of static shields. He still hadn't decided whether or not to believe Therius. He had a terrible feeling the man was skriffy as a space rat, and no one who had died was ever coming back.

"Where are we going?" Ethan asked as he rocketed out of the hangar and into space.

"There." Therius pointed to the gravidar display, to a tear in the repetitive landscape of the Icosahedron. That jagged line ran straight through the otherwise perfectly spherical shell, providing a way out.

Ethan set course. Along the way a surviving Union ship hailed him.

"Unidentified corvette transport, please identify yourself!"

Ethan keyed the comm for a reply, but before he could say anything, Therius spoke over his shoulder.

"This is Admiral Therius. Omnius has been defeated. Spread the word to the rest of the fleet. Have them cancel their quantum jumps and board the Icosahedron to take control of it; there's no need to retreat anymore."

"Admiral Therius? Your ship was captured. We thought—"

"You're not the first person to accuse me of dying today," Therius said, sending Atton a wry smile. "But I assure you, I am very much alive. Send the message, Captain."

"Yes, sir."

The comms went silent, and Ethan guided them out through the ragged tear in the Icosahedron. The gap was surprisingly wide, and crowded with debris. To either side of them Ethan saw the internal structure of the Icosahedron laid bare, with thousands of decks torn open and slumping on top of each other.

"What happened here?" Ethan asked.

"When I first started jamming Omnius, his Facets were still coming together around Avilon. Without him to guide them in, they began colliding with each other."

"Where are you taking us?" Atton asked. "What could you

possibly have to show us that will support any of what you've said?"

"I'm taking you to Origin," Therius replied.

"That's in the Getties," Ethan said. "My ship doesn't have a quantum jump drive. I can't take us there."

"I know, which is why I've brought Origin to you."

"What?" Atton burst out. "You jumped an entire planet here? How is that possible?"

"You think Omnius is the only one who can create a planet? Why do you think Origin was never found? Because it kept moving."

"Why would you need to create an entire planet?" Alara asked.

"To guard a secret that's been hidden since the day we created humans in our image."

"*We?*" Ethan echoed. "We, who?"

"We, the Immortals."

* * *

Ethan was still reeling in shock by the time he saw Origin on sensors.

"How did you jump an entire planet into orbit around Avilon's sun without Omnius noticing?" Atton asked.

"Most of the time he was being jammed, and when the jamming field wasn't active, the planet's cloaking shield was. It would have taken an active scan for Omnius to find Origin, and his attention was elsewhere."

Ethan still didn't believe Therius. There was plenty of evidence to suggest that humans had evolved naturally, just like any other species. The best Therius could do would be to help them fill in the gaps in their evolution. He couldn't prove that he'd created them—whoever *he* really was.

Ethan clung to those rationalizations as he guided them down through Origin's atmosphere. Seeing clouds streak by the cockpit, he frowned. If Origin was an artificial planet, then why did it look so natural?

"Head for the fortress," Therius said.

Ethan set course for the only man-made structure on the surface besides the obelisk-shaped ruins. He remembered Atta had called those obelisks tombstones. He'd never had a chance to take a look at them, but he was far more curious about their destination. Therius wanted them to go to the fortress, and Ethan could think of only one reason for that. He thought back to the underground chamber he and the Rictans had stumbled into . . . the locked doors, one of them leading into a medical supply locker inside the fortress, the other one leading to who knew where.

What's behind door number two?

The ground peeked through the cloud cover in bright green scraps. Then the clouds parted altogether revealing a sprawling carpet of jungle and a distant ridge of mountains. In the distance lay the towering fortress where Therius had raised his army to fight Omnius. That fortress had come complete with cloning facilities, which Therius had used to bring him and thousands of others back to life after they'd died on Avilon. Ethan's brow furrowed as he thought about that. Those facilities could easily be used to do exactly what Therius claimed—to create humanity.

No, Ethan shook his head. That didn't make any sense. If they'd been created, then where had all of the fossils of early humans come from? The progression from one pre-human species to another was too clear to be refuted by a purely extra-terrestrial origin of the species.

"I've been here before..." Alara whispered.

"So have I," Atton said.

"Of course you have," Therius replied. "In many ways, you never left." Ethan shot him a look, and Therius just smiled. "Land on the rooftop," he said.

Ethan did as he was told, and then he and the others followed Therius through the echoing, now-empty halls of the fortress. They traveled down lift tubes and stair cases, all the while trading worried looks with one another.

Finally, they came to a familiar-looking medical storage room. The hole the Rictans had blown in the door had been repaired, but the welds were thick and lumpy.

Ethan watched Therius walk up to it and open it with a wave of his hand. Beyond was the empty castcrete chamber Ethan remembered, and at the end of that, the mysterious second door.

Therius led them straight up to that door and waved his hand at the lifeless sensor. The door came to life and *swished* open, revealing a long, well-lit corridor beyond. The walls gleamed with a strange, metallic glow.

Therius walked inside, and Ethan hurried after him with Alara and Atton close behind. The air on the other side of the door hit him like a bucket of ice water. It was freezing. Ethan ran his hands along the glowing walls. They were smooth and neither cold nor hot to the touch.

The door slid shut behind them with a muffled *boom,* and Ethan turned to look, his suspicions intensifying.

"I don't like this," Alara whispered beside his ear.

He grabbed her hand and squeezed. "Come on," he whispered back. "It's too late to go back now."

Up ahead Therius walked out onto a catwalk and stopped to lean on the railing. They joined him there, looking out into a vast chamber. The catwalk where they stood was just one of many, with subsequent levels visible through the metal grating under their feet and overhead. The catwalks ran between row upon row of glowing, transparent tubes, each of them frosted and marked with a glowing control panel.

"What is this place?" Ethan asked, afraid that he already knew the answer—the cold air, the transparent tubes and control panels, level upon level of walkways to access them... it was some kind of vast stasis room.

"This," Therius declared, "is a prison."

CHAPTER 53

"**A** prison?" Ethan's eyes widened. "Who are the prisoners?"

"You are."

A sharp stab of adrenaline went cascading through Ethan's body. "Are you trying to tell me you lured us down here to put us in one of those tanks?"

Therius shook his head. "No, I'm telling you that you are *already* in one of those tanks."

"Prove it."

"Very well."

Therius walked down the catwalk, turned, and started down an intersecting one. As they went, Ethan became aware of Alara's fingernails digging into his skin.

"Ethan..." she whispered. "We need to get out of here."

"Yeah, I'm starting to think that might be a good idea..." he whispered back.

"There's no need to be afraid," Therius said, proving that there was also no need to whisper. "I'll explain everything to you in just a minute." He led them past hundreds of tanks until they came to one in particular. Then he placed a hand against the glass and suddenly the frosted texture became clear. Ethan's heart pounded, and he wondered what they'd see inside that tank.

Therius stepped aside and nodded. "Take a look," he said.

Ethan walked up and peered inside. Alara gasped when she saw the face looking back at her, but Ethan frowned. It looked human enough—two eyes, nose, chin, ears, long dark hair... but the bone structure was unusual, more angular, and the face was longer than the average human's would be. The most striking and least human feature, however, was its pale, luminous white skin.

"That's not even human," Ethan realized. He wasn't sure whether to be relieved or more shocked than ever. He knocked on the glass to see if the woman would react, but she was sleeping too deeply.

"Let me help you wake her," Therius said. He reached for the glowing control panel beside the tank, and Ethan took a hasty step back.

"I'm not sure that's a good idea..." he said.

But it was too late. Bright *violet* eyes snapped open behind the glass. Those eyes found him and flew suddenly wider.

Ethan stumbled back against the railing behind him, shaking his head. "Who is that?" he demanded, watching as Alara stepped up to the tank and placed a palm against the glass. The alien inside the tank mimicked her gesture, placing a hand with longer, more dexterous fingers against the inside of the tank.

"Those are my eyes..." Alara whispered.

"The eyes are the windows to the soul," Therius said. "Never a truer word spoken."

Ethan blinked. "There's no such thing as souls."

Therius turned to him with a wan smile. "Really? What do you think you are looking at right now?"

Alara turned to him, her cheeks slack with shock. "I remember... I remember *everything*, Ethan."

He shook his head. "What are you talking about? Remember *what?*"

"She's *me,* and I'm her..." Alara turned back to face the tank. "Somehow... we're linked to each other. I can *hear* her inside of my head."

Therius reached for the control panel once more, and Ethan watched as those alien eyes—*Alara's* eyes—slipped behind luminous eyelids once more.

"What the frek is going on, Therius?" Ethan demanded, his legs trembling violently.

"I told you, my name is Etherus."

"All right, Etherus, then. I need some answers."

"We all do," Atton added.

Etherus spread his hands. "That is why I brought you here."

"I'm listening," Ethan said.

"You call this world Origin. We call it the Garden of Etheria. We created the first humans here, but we didn't want humanity to realize that they had been created, so we took a species from Advistine—*or Earth,* as it used to be called—and we spliced genes from that species with our own. It appeared to you as though your species had evolved naturally from the primates we spliced our genes to; the only evidence leading back to us was in the form of a few mysterious gaps in your evolution."

Ethan shook his head. "Our ancestors left the Getties and settled on Advistine. They spliced their *own* genes with a local species to create humanity," Ethan repeated all of that before he remembered the source.

"Omnius told you that when he came back online, and even though he lied about many things, he truly believed that was what had happened. Like you, he was left with a lot of mysterious clues and forced to draw conclusions from them. The conclusions he drew, however, were incorrect."

"Let's assume we believe you," Atton said. "That explains how you created us, but it doesn't explain why we're linked to aliens that you call *souls* in this place that you say is a *prison*. What did we do to deserve imprisonment?"

"The link to your soul is passed down from your mother at birth. That link is broken when you're resurrected as clones. That's why Omnius was able to predict your behavior after Lifelink transfers. It takes time for souls to find their resurrected bodies, which is why Omnius discovered that as time went by, even resurrected clones became unpredictable again."

Ethan chewed his lower lip. "So we're in some type of symbiotic relationship with these aliens."

"No, you and your souls are one and the same. As you saw with Alara, if I were to wake your souls, you would suddenly find your minds flooded with a much greater awareness of who and what you really are."

Ethan glanced at Alara, but she was still staring into the stasis tube.

"That answers *how* we're linked," Atton said, walking straight up to Etherus. "But you haven't told us *why*."

"All of you remember Origin because you were awake when you first came here. You walked into these stasis tubes willingly. Most of your souls' memories are repressed while they're sleeping here, but we allowed you to retain a few memories of Origin to help you realize that there's a bigger picture to your existence. That bigger picture is Etheria, the galaxy where the Immortals live. The Getties Cluster used to be Etheria, but it was made uninhabitable by the *First Great War*, the one you mistakenly call *the Great War of Origin*. The truth is, that war had nothing to do with this planet, immortality, or with your origin as a species."

"So the ruins on the surface, the obelisks that Atta said were tombstones... they're memorials from that war?"

"They serve many purposes. They're the quantum transmitters that keep souls linked to their human bodies, and they're also what's used to generate the jamming field that defeated Omnius. They are the real Eclipser. And yes, they are also memorials. The bones found there are real, recovered from Immortals who actually died in the war. We piled those bones on top of your heads as a symbolic gesture, to represent the weight you carry on your consciences. Even though the dead were ultimately brought back to life, all the suffering you caused while fighting for your cause was real."

"What cause?" Atton asked.

"Freedom," Alara breathed, finally turning away from the stasis tube where her soul rested.

Etherus nodded. "Humans were created in order to give you all a taste of true freedom."

Ethan's brow furrowed. "Freedom from what?"

"You are made in our image, but we are not the same. Immortals are never tempted to do something that they know is wrong. Humans, however, were made to be curious. You want to *know* everything, to *try* everything, to *do* everything—even the bad things. That is what it means to be free, to be able to choose between good and evil. Humanity's very first field test was conducted here.

"Once the test confirmed that humans were truly free, we put all of the rebels into stasis and sent the original pair to Earth to begin testing. Your sentence here was only ever meant to last as long as your human lives, but cloning and Omnius undid all of that."

"What were you testing?" Atton asked.

"Your human lives serve to show you and us whether or not you really *want* to be free. Some people see the chaos that freedom brings, and they *regret* their mistakes. Those people are the ones that are both worthy and capable of living in Etheria once more. Then there are others who look back on their lives and see it all, even the mistakes, as a grand unfolding adventure. All they wish for at the end is more time to continue it. Do you know what we do with those people?"

"You send them to the Netherworld?" Ethan guessed.

"Do you know what the Netherworld is? Or where?" Therius asked.

Ethan hesitated. "No..."

"It's here, all around you. Why do you think early depictions showed it *under* the Earth? In the distant recesses of your minds you still recalled that the Netherworld is what we called the underground prison complex where you were imprisoned. But we don't have to send people here, Ethan; they are *already* here."

Alara came to stand beside Ethan. She took his hand, and he felt her skin cold and clammy against his own. She was scared. He couldn't blame her.

Ethan shook his head. "Why tell us all of this now?"

"Because the tests are over. They were over years ago already, but we wanted to be sure, so we left things running."

"You ran out of souls," Atton said.

Etherus nodded. "We stopped giving souls to new-born Avilonians long ago."

Ethan blinked. He felt sick, afraid to ask the question that had just occurred to him, and unsure that he even wanted to know the answer.

"Do *we* have souls?" Atton said, asking the question for him.

"Everyone who came from the Imperium has a soul, but not everyone who was born on Avilon does."

Etherus's eyes settled on Ethan with a meaningful weight, and suddenly he understood. "Trinity..." he whispered.

Etherus began nodding. "Yes."

"She can't follow us to Etheria," Alara said.

"She would have to go as a human, and that would inject unwelcome chaos to our way of life."

"But you're Etherus!" Alara said. "You created us! You can fix her!"

"I could, but there's another way. I never answered your question, Ethan, about what we do with the souls who decide that they still want their freedom. The answer is, we left them here sleeping until now. Now we're going to use Omnius's Icosahedron to bring all of them back as immortal humans, just as Omnius did with everyone on Avilon. The difference is, he could only bring back *one* generation, but we have them all— minus the ones who went back to Etheria, of course."

"What about our previous lives?" Alara asked. "The ones we lived in Etheria... all of our memories... ?"

"What do you remember?" Etherus asked.

Alara shook her head. "As soon as my soul went back to sleep, I began to forget. Now it's all very vague. It feels like a dream that I can't quite remember."

"And that is how it will remain. It wouldn't be fair to leave you to live as humans, yet undermine that life by injecting memories of a previous one. Your souls will be incorporated into you, but your memories of Etheria will be repressed just as they've always been. You will be able to access them, if you wish, by focusing on your past life, but for most of you, looking back will be an unsettling experience that you won't wish to repeat, and the memories you recover will fade away soon after you have remembered them."

"So paradise isn't for us," Atton said. "We'd rather live in chaos. That's what you're saying?"

"Those who enjoy freedom will likely call it *exciting* rather than *chaotic,* and there will be rules to live by, just as there have always been. Undesirable outcomes will be mitigated by laws given to you by your ruler—me."

"Aren't you the ruler of Etheria?" Alara asked.

"That, too."

"So... we're all going to live on New Avilon and you're going to be our... king?"

"Let's rather call it New Earth, but yes, and for those who wish to be free even from my laws, they will be allowed to leave the Icosahedron and settle the Adventa Galaxy once more. For now, though, there's more than enough room on the Icosahedron for everyone we're going to resurrect."

Ethan felt the first stirrings of excitement. This could be everything that Avilon should have been! Eternal life in paradise, but without Omnius's lies and suppression of freedoms.

"What about the souls that returned to Etheria?" Atton asked.

"Only the ones that we've chosen will leave, and choosing them is about knowing who really *wants* to go. After all, if you don't want to be in Etheria, you might just start another Great War, and we can't have that."

"So families are going to be separated again, just like they were with Omnius," Atton said.

"Your loved ones will visit you. For now, since so many people have already returned to Etheria, we're going to take the Icosahedron there to facilitate reunions."

Suddenly Ethan realized what he was missing, and fear gripped him. What if Alara wanted to go to Etheria? He turned to his wife, wondering what he could say to convince her not to go. Why had Etherus brought them to see *Alara's* soul? Why not some random person's soul? His heart pounded in his chest, and his palms began to sweat.

"Don't leave me," he said.

Alara turned to him, and he looked deep into her violet eyes, trying to see what she was thinking—or what her *soul* was thinking. Her lips parted to say something, but he kissed her before she could. He poured all of his pent-up fears and desperation into that kiss. She leaned into it and kissed him back, making his head swim. He just hoped she wasn't kissing him goodbye.

"Ethan..." she murmured against his lips.

He withdrew by a fraction of an inch. "You'll be leaving Trinity, too," he said, still trying to convince her.

"I'm staying," she replied, her eyes bright and shining as she smiled. "And you're enough reason for me to stay all by yourself."

"I woke your wife's soul for a reason, Ethan," Etherus said. "I did it to put you both out of your misery. Even now that she vaguely recalls what it was like to live in Etheria, she would still rather stay with you in this life. Don't you remember my promise to you?"

Ethan's brow furrowed as he struggled to recall.

"I promised that you wouldn't be parted from your family."

"But how could you know what Alara would choose?"

"Like Omnius, it's my business to know what my people will do before they do it, but unlike him, I don't use my predictions to rob them of their freedom."

Ethan let out a long, shuddering breath. "Thank you."

"Thank your wife. She's the one who chose to stay."

"We all have families..." Ethan said, his brow furrowing once more. "Who would choose to leave them behind?"

"I would," Atton said, turning from Etherus to face them.

Ethan blinked. "Son..."

"She went to Etheria, Dad. I know she did."

"Who did?"

"My wife, Ceyla." Atton turned back to Etherus. "She did, didn't she?"

"Yes, and you're going to follow her."

CHAPTER 54

Atton couldn't contain himself. He couldn't even bring himself to sit down. Instead he stood in the cockpit, watching over his father's shoulder as Ethan flew the *Trinity* back to the Icosahedron. He was going to join Ceyla as one of the Immortals in the real Etheria!

It seemed too good to be true, but there was a catch. Ceyla hadn't forgiven him before she died. Would she forgive him now, in Etheria?

"She already has," Etherus said, interrupting Atton's thoughts, and proving that like Omnius, he could read people's minds.

Atton frowned. This seemingly normal man standing beside him was *Etherus.* But what was he really? If Etherus could read his thoughts, then Atton supposed there was no point keeping them to himself.

"You created us, but did you also create the universe?" he asked. "What are you? You said you're an Immortal?"

"When you get to Etheria, you'll already know all the answers to those questions."

Atton shook his head at the non-answer and went back to

gazing out the forward viewport. The Icosahedron shone as bright as a mirror reflecting the sun. Twenty flat, angular sides faced out in an approximation of a sphere, collecting solar energy from Avilon's sun. With no frame of reference it was easy to forget how large that spheroid was, but Atton could just barely see Avilon peeking through the *tear* in that artificial shell. The planetary surface appeared as a river of lights, glowing orange like magma, the Icosahedron the crust.

Atton remembered the battle raging over Avilon and suddenly he wondered if that orange light came from the cities or the blazing infernos now consuming them.

What had happened to all the drone fighters when they'd been disabled? Had they simply fallen from the sky? And what about the Gors, humans, and Sythians who'd come to conquer Avilon?

"The Sythians are gone," Etherus said. "Omnius killed them all before they could escape. The drones were disabled, but the virus recalled their fighters to the Icosahedron via autopilot."

"And the Gors?"

"Most of them died, too."

"Did any of them have souls? The Sythians or the Gors?" Alara asked, turning from the copilot's station.

"They were the instigators of the Great War, and their punishment was to go on living in the galaxy they destroyed. They were neither imprisoned nor linked. Over time they evolved into what they are now as a consequence of the worlds they lived on."

"What will happen to them now?" Atton asked.

"Some of them redeemed themselves by joining the fight against Omnius, and they will be coming to live with you all on the New Earth."

Atton saw his father cast a worried look over his shoulder.

"There are going to be Sythians and Gors living with us?"

"Only the good ones."

"They mass-murdered us!" Ethan said.

"There is a difference between being forced to do something because of circumstances, and doing something because you want to. War makes everyone do terrible things."

Atton grimaced, thinking about some of the terrible things he'd been made to do because of circumstances. "What about the drones?"

"They are not sentient. The humans they once were have either returned to Etheria or they're waiting to be resurrected now."

Just two options. Alive in Etheria or soon to be ressurected on the New Earth. Suddenly Atton realized what that meant. "So no one is really dead? They're all coming back? Mass-murderers and warmongers alike?"

"I believe in redemption, Atton. That is why I am called the Redemptor, but for those who are beyond rehabilitation, there are plenty of Nightstalkers and other beasts to link them to."

Atton saw his father abruptly turn from piloting to face them. "Nightstalkers? They have souls?"

Etherus nodded. "Some of them, yes."

That's why they took us to that chamber. They remembered where the entrance to the Netherworld was."

"Nightstalkers are relatively unintelligent, but in retrospect I believe they were trying to dig a way into the Netherworld and free themselves. In taking you there they may have hoped you would open the door for them."

That got Atton wondering about something. "What about Omnius? He must have been sentient. You told him there was still a chance for him, right before I shot him."

"Don't tell me that he's coming back..." Ethan said.

"I was giving him a chance so he could be brought to justice, and take responsibility for his actions, but I knew he wouldn't take it. I also knew that Atton would redeem himself when he realized Omnius might be allowed to live. He shot Omnius even before he realized who I was and that I could bring Ceyla back, too. That proved he was only ever on Omnius's side because he didn't think he had a choice. It was a test for Atton's benefit, to ease his conscience after everything he did and allowed to happen."

Atton nodded to himself, watching as the Icosahedron drew near. Shooting Omnius definitely had made him feel better.

"Did he have a soul?" Atton asked.

"He used to, back when he was known as Kain Markonis."

"Kain Markonis?" Ethan asked.

"They never told you. It would have done too much to undermine Omnius's claims to deity if anyone knew, but the controlling mind in the collective was actually Neona's father. He was executed for murder in the old Avilonian Empire. It was illegal to resurrect him under those circumstances, so Neona used as much of him as she could and brought him back as Omnius. She assumed she'd successfully removed the murderer in him, but all she did was bury it deeper. They planned to rule Avilon together, with him as the overt ruler and her as his covert accomplice. Their intentions were initially good, albeit misguided, but they used the ends to justify the means so often that eventually nothing seemed wrong to them anymore."

"Wow..." Alara breathed.

Atton shook his head. "No wonder Omnius did all the things that he did. He was always a killer." Turning to Etherus, he asked, "When will I get to see Ceyla?"

"As soon as everyone else has learned the truth."

Atton tried to imagine how long it would take Etherus to

explain to trillions of people everything that he'd explained to them. The answer he came up with was disheartening at best.

"You might be surprised," Etherus said. "While we were on Origin, I disabled the jamming field, and in just a moment I'm going to wake *all* of the souls. When I do, everyone will know everything. After that, all that will be left is for people to see the Netherworld with their own eyes, but those pilgrimages will take a lot of time, and they need not happen before people are taken to Etheria."

"So..."

"So you should say goodbye now."

Atton blinked, shocked and suddenly at a loss for words. He hadn't been given enough warning. Ethan and Alara both turned to him, and he smiled. "I guess I'll see you when you visit Etheria, then."

Ethan rose from the pilot's chair and enfolded him in a backslapping hug. "You're sure about this?" he asked as he withdrew.

Atton nodded. "Yes."

Ethan regarded him a moment longer. His eyes were hard and full of concern. "Good luck," he said, his voice hoarse.

"This isn't goodbye," Etherus reminded them. "It's just farewell for now, until we've resurrected everyone and we can make the jump to Etheria."

Atton nodded and then Alara rose and gave him a hug, too. "Say hello to your wife for us," she whispered. She withdrew to an arm's length, her expression suddenly serious. "And I expect a proper introduction when we get to Etheria."

Atton smiled. "You'll get one." He wiped a warm trickle of moisture from his cheek and sighed. Finally, he turned to Etherus. "I'm ready." His heart thumped eagerly, threatening to leap right out of his chest.

Etherus nodded, and Atton felt his whole body grow warm and pleasantly numb. His pounding heart slowed and his vision narrowed to a pair of dark tunnels. Then his heart—

Stopped.

Atton felt his eyes roll up in his head, and the twin tunnels he was looking down merged into one. He felt himself go racing down that tunnel toward a bright light, and as he emerged in that light, a familiar voice whispered, "Welcome home, Atton."

Blinking the spots from his eyes, Atton turned to find Ceyla sitting beside him, staring at him with big, vibrant blue eyes.

How had he gotten here? Shouldn't he be waking up in a stasis tube on Origin? Suddenly he knew the answer. He hadn't awoken on Origin because the stasis tube where he'd lain sleeping had quantum-jumped his body home even before he could wake up. Now that he was awake, he found himself reeling in a rushing stream of memory. There were so many memories that it was difficult fitting the pieces together. "Ceyla, I'm so sor—"

"Shhh." Ceyla placed a long, dexterous finger to his lips. That finger was luminous, and so was she. "I know," she said, and then she kissed him.

Suddenly all of the pieces snapped into place. As he drifted away from that kiss, Atton turned to see that they were sitting in a luxurious home beside a sparkling lavender lake, overlooking a breathtaking view of white and azure trees sloping down to ivory shores. The sun painted the sky purple as it slipped below the horizon, and in the middle distance a giant rainbow splashed the sky with variegated color, arcing clear from one shore of the lake to the other. A glittering city lay to one side, looking like it was made entirely of glass.

Atton turned back to his wife and shook his head. Ceyla was just as he remembered her, but not as he remembered her from their human lives, rather from their Immortal ones. Somehow, after all this time, it all still seemed like yesterday—Etheria, the war, imprisonment...

"Hello, Atton," another woman said.

He turned and saw three familiar faces. His gaze flicked from one to the other, unable to believe his eyes. Hoff, Destra, Atta... they were all there! He rose to his feet, a smile bursting to his lips. Then they all rushed forward and enfolded him in a hug.

Atton remembered watching all of them die on Avilon, and he grimaced. "I thought..."

"So did we," Hoff said, whispering beside his ear.

Atton blinked tears from his eyes, unable to believe it all. His thoughts returned to the family he'd left behind, and he felt a pang of sadness, but he knew he would see them all again soon.

"I'm still having trouble making sense of all this," Atton said.

Atta snorted. "You're lucky. At least there weren't two of you. You only have one set of human memories."

Atton frowned at that, wondering how Etherus dealt with multiple copies. As they withdrew from each other, Destra explained, "Atta and I were alive on Avilon, *and* in the Getties. We went with the Union to attack Avilon, and we died *twice* during the fighting. Etherus integrated all of our human memories, so now it feels like we lived two separate lives."

"That must have been confusing," Atton said.

"It still is," Atta replied.

Atton sighed and turned back to look at the view. He recognized the planet, but not the house he was in. "Whose home is this?" he asked.

"It's yours and Ceyla's," Hoff replied. "Ours is down the road."

Atton shook his head. "If it's mine, why don't I remember it?"

"Because it's new. Your old home was destroyed in the war."

"The war that we caused."

Hoff nodded.

"Makes you wonder if we deserve to be here," Atton said.

Ceyla took his hand and squeezed it, getting his attention. "Everyone deserves a second chance," she said.

"Then I guess we'd better not waste this one."

"We won't," Ceyla said. "This time we won't take paradise for granted."

Atton smiled and nodded, watching as the sun sank behind a distant line of white and blue trees.

No, we won't, he thought. *Never again.*

CHAPTER 55

Farah Hale's eyes fluttered open. The transparent cover of the stasis tank where Omnius's drones had taken her for confinement hissed open. Clouds of moisture billowed around her as the cold air inside the tank rushed out to meet the warmer, more humid air of the stasis room.

Farah shivered violently and stepped out of the tank just as soon as she could. She expected to see drones waiting for her—or Peacekeepers—but what she saw instead was a Union soldier with a lieutenant's chevrons. He saluted and quickly averted his eyes, staring over her head. "Captain," he said.

People entered stasis naked, and apparently Omnius's version of it was no different, but Farah didn't have time for modesty. She returned the man's salute and nodded to him. "At ease, Lieutenant. Give me an update."

He went on staring at the wall above her head, not daring to make eye contact with her. "Ma'am, we have taken control of the Icosahedron."

"You *what?* How did that happen? Omnius—"

"He's dead, ma'am. Admiral Therius ordered us to board, and we found all of the drones disabled. Omnius's human body was found dead in his control room, along with an unidentified woman. The drone fighters are returning to their hangars on autopilot, but the drones aren't even trying to leave their cockpits. They're all powered down."

Farah shook her head. "How?" Therius must have had a plan after all. She recalled him telling her to have faith, and she frowned. "What about Avilon? Is it a total loss? Do we know where nanites were dropped and where it might be safe to begin evacuating the population?"

"Preliminary reports show that nanite activity ceased as soon as the quantum jamming field returned."

"The jamming *returned*?" Farah blinked twice quickly. "The Eclipser was destroyed, Lieutenant."

"I don't understand it either, ma'am. We are attempting to make contact with Therius to ask him about it."

"Where is he?"

"He left the inner sphere of the Icosahedron. Our last contact showed him approaching another planet in this system's habitable zone.

"What other planet? There's only one in this system's habitable zone and that's Avilon."

The lieutenant shook his head. "Ma'am I'm not qualified to answer that. I'm with the ground forces."

"Of course you are. Carry on, Lieutenant." Farah brushed by him, crossing the stasis room to the nearest set of lockers. Along the way she saw more stasis tubes hissing open with swirling clouds of vapor, her crew stepping out to be greeted by drones.

"Lieutenant!" she roared.

He hurried up beside her. "Ma'am?"

"I thought you said the drones were all powered down?" she said.

"They are. These are our drones, Ma'am. Therius somehow

infiltrated the Icosahedron with them and infected the entire thing with a virus. The drones are helping us to access restricted systems, but it's going to take some time to secure the entire vessel."

Farah shot the man a look. "*Some* time? The Icosahedron is five times the diameter of Avilon, and it's twenty klicks thick. We're not going to secure it without a whole lot more manpower than what we brought. We need to focus on securing key areas."

"Matriarch Shara is working on that, ma'am. Her people are landing as we speak."

"The Gors? How many of them survived?"

"Ten percent, maybe twenty. They didn't fare as well as we did. Omnius wasn't trying to capture their ships."

"What about the Sythians?"

"All dead as far as we can tell. Omnius hit them the hardest."

Farah snorted. "Good." She heard *clanking* footsteps approaching and turned to see one of the drones walking up to her with a bundle of clothes.

"Would you like your uniform, Captain Hale?" the drone asked.

That voice was vaguely familiar. Her eyes narrowed to slits, searching for some distinguishing mark.

"Bretton?" Farah asked.

"My designation is 767, ma'am."

Farah frowned and made a *gimme* gesture, to which 767 handed over her uniform. By the time she was half dressed and bending down to put on her socks, a bright light flashed before her eyes, and she stumbled, falling against the wall of lockers beside her.

Farah was suddenly painfully *aware*. She *knew* things, remembered things—things that until now she'd forgotten. The war, Etheria, the Immortals, Etherus, the Netherworld... It all coalesced in one horrible instant.

She gasped and turned to look around the room. Her crew wasn't faring any better. The lieutenant who'd greeted her when she'd emerged from stasis lay belly up and staring at the ceiling.

"Are you all right, ma'am?" Drone 767 asked, his optical sensor glowing momentarily brighter as he scanned her. "Your life signs are fluctuating in a manner consistent with extreme distress or excitement. Are you distressed or excited, Captain?"

Farah shook her head. She turned to the drone with a smile. "You're alive."

"I am a drone, Ma'am. I am either powered on or off, never alive nor dead."

Farah shook her head. "No, I mean, Bretton Hale is alive!"

She ran from the stasis room without even bothering to finish getting dressed. She knew where Therius—*Etherus*—was coming aboard. She was going to beg him to resurrect Bretton now. She had to see her uncle. But Bretton wasn't really her uncle at all. She *remembered,* and now she finally understood her feelings. She knew *why* she loved him.

She loved him because they'd been together in Etheria. Farah smiled as she pounded down the corridors of the Icosahedron to the nearest quantum junction. As she ran, specific memories went drifting away, but the key points remained. She knew to expect that. Etherus had already explained everything to all of them. That was how she knew that Bretton was coming back. His soul hadn't gone to Etheria, and it wasn't going there now. He was going to live out his human life with her in the New Earth.

Farah reached the nearest quantum junction and tried activating it, but it wouldn't respond to either her gestures or verbal commands. Then she remembered what the lieutenant had said about the Union's drones helping them to access key systems aboard the Icosahedron.

Farah kicked the junction and winced as pain radiated from her big toe. She'd forgotten to put on her boots. While she was still hopping on one leg and cursing her own foolishness, she heard the *clanking* footfalls of a drone racing down the corridor toward her. Farah turned and the drone chasing her slowed to a fast walk. It stopped in front of her and said, "May I assist you, Captain?" It was 767 again. He'd followed her like a lost puppy.

Farah grimaced and nodded to the junction. "Hangar bay 17, deck five hundred." That was where Etherus was going to land.

"Of course." The drone gestured to the junction and it rose on four shimmering pillars of light.

Farah watched that drone curiously, wondering what would become of him. "What am I to you?" she asked as she stepped under the dome of the junction with 767.

"You are Captain Hale."

"And that's all?"

The drone's optical sensor brightened once more, as if he was scanning her again. "You are... familiar," he said. "I know things about you that I do not know about other humans."

"And what does that tell you?"

"I have data locked in archives that I am not permitted to access. Based on what I am told about the man named Bretton Hale and my relation to him, it is likely that those data archives belong to him, and accessing them would interfere with my primary programming."

Farah nodded, thinking how ironic that was. Omnius turning rebellious humans into drones and archiving their human memories was a parallel of what Etherus and the Immortals had done with prisoners from the Great War.

"When this is all over, we'll see what we can do about

unlocking those archives for you, Seven Sixty Seven."

"Thank you, Captain Hale. I believe I would like that."

"No problem. Let's go meet Etherus."

"Yes, ma'am."

Farah blinked, surprised that the drone hadn't asked who she was talking about. "You knew who Therius was?" she asked.

"I was programmed to know my creator, ma'am. Why would he hide his identity from me?"

"I meant that you know Therius is Etherus."

"In my records Therius is spelled with an '*e.*' Ther-e-us. It is an anagram of Etherus. My programming instructs me to refer to him by that anagram."

Farah snorted and shook her head. "Well, let's go meet your maker." *Our maker*, she thought, correcting herself.

"Yes, ma'am." Seven Sixty Seven dropped his hands and the junction fell around them with a *boom*.

When the junction rose once more, and Farah exited into hangar bay 17, she saw Etherus already striding across the deck to greet her. She recognized the man walking beside him as Commander Ortane of Rictan Squadron, but the woman was a complete stranger to her.

Etherus stopped a few feet away and flashed her a broad smile. His pale blue eyes were somehow brighter and livelier than she remembered. "I told you to have faith, Farah," he said.

"I'm sorry that I didn't. It all makes sense now."

Etherus placed his hands on her shoulders. Looking her straight in the eye, he said, "I forgive you. Now come, and follow me."

Etherus continued on, back to the quantum junction she'd just left. The others followed, and Commander Ortane nodded to her as he walked by.

"Captain," he said.

Farah lingered a moment longer. "Where are we going?" she asked, her eyes on Etherus.

He cast her a backward glance and smiled. "Trust me," was all he said.

And this time, she did.

EPILOGUE

—One Month Later—

Farah watched as a pair of drones pulled Bretton Hale up out of his clone tank—his was just one out of thousands on this floor of Tree of Life 10,976. The deck disappeared almost endlessly to all sides, with glowing hexagonal clone tanks making the floor look like a giant, blue-tinted honeycomb. Everywhere Farah looked people stood in huddled groups, waiting for their loved ones to be awakened. It was a bizarre way to have a reunion—not the dramatic show Omnius had put on for newcomers to Avilon. But somehow it was better this way. *More real,* Farah decided.

She smiled, watching as Bretton's clone stood naked and shivering before her. Nutrient water dripped from all the angles and edges of his body to the floor. His eyelids fluttered, and he muttered something about being blind. The drones holding him released his arms so he could wipe the smeary liquid from his eyes. His gaze found her, and he went abruptly still, staring at her for a long, silent moment.

His soul's memories had already been incorporated with his

human ones, so there was no need for her to explain anything. Farah walked up to him with a towel. Bretton used it to dry himself, and then wrapped it around his waist and regarded her with a grim smile. "Is this a dream?" he asked.

Farah shook her head. "The dream is what you woke from. This is real. You have a lot of catching up to do," she said. He might know where he came from and why he was here now in a human body, but he had yet to learn about his new home.

"I can't believe you were right there in front of me all those years. I think maybe I felt something, but..." Bretton trailed off. "I didn't know what it was."

"Our hearts don't know how to forget. They just know how to beat."

Something in Bretton's eyes flickered, and suddenly he took her face in his hands and kissed her. Farah kissed him back, pouring years of pent-up longing into that kiss.

"There's one thing I still don't remember," Bretton murmured as he withdrew.

Floating on a cloud, Farah asked dreamily, "What's that?"

"What did I ever do to deserve a woman like you?"

Farah smiled and took his hand in hers. "You always knew the right thing to say. We should get out of here. I'm dying to show you where we live."

Bretton nodded. "All right, but no dying, please. I think we've all had enough of that."

Farah turned to address one of the drones that had helped Bretton out of his tank. "Seven Sixty Seven—"

"Yes, ma'am?"

"It's time to go home."

"Home, ma'am?"

"Etherus didn't tell you? You've been reassigned. You're going to live with us."

"That is good news. I would like to get to know my old self."

"His old self?" Bretton echoed, regarding the drone with a furrowed brow.

Apparently Etherus had left some things for her to explain. Farah took Bretton's arm and began guiding him to the nearest exit. "While you were sleeping, Omnius copied some parts of you to a drone."

"So he's me."

"He's Seven Sixty Seven, but you can think of him as your digital son."

"The son I never had..." Bretton mused.

"We could change that," Farah said.

"We're still able to have children? I thought there weren't any souls left to put in bodies."

"There aren't, but that doesn't mean we can't create new ones. A soul is just a prior state of existence. Anyone born from now on will be born the same as us, but without any past to reconcile before they can move on to their futures. They'll be the lucky ones, Bret."

"And what if they take this world for granted the way we did with Etheria? What if they start another war? They haven't been through everything we have. They might not appreciate that with freedom comes the responsibility to choose wisely."

"So we'll teach them."

"And if we fail?"

"Then I'm sure Etherus will have a plan to rehabilitate them, too."

"Another Netherworld," Bretton suggested.

"Maybe."

Bretton sighed. "Sounds risky to me."

"I think that's the point," Farah added as they reached the nearest quantum junction. She raised her arms and the junction hovered up. "Life's an adventure. It's what we wanted. The uncertainty is half the fun."

"True," Bretton said, nodding as they stepped into the glowing green circle in the center of the junction.

"So what do you say?" Farah asked.

Bretton turned to regard her with a wry grin. "I say, let the adventure begin."

* * *

Ethan hovered the *Trinity* down for a landing beside his new home. It was a mansion, much bigger than the 40-meter-long corvette that he was landing beside it. Omnius had spared no expense building his new world.

At twenty kilometers thick, there was more than enough room for five kilometers of air and artificial sky for the biosphere. The landscape looked so natural and real that it was easy to forget where they really were.

Forests, lakes, rivers, mountains, and fields all ran boundlessly around the Icosahedron. When docked, individual Facets opened up to share their air and living space. Each of the twenty flat, triangular faces of the Icosahedron were self-contained with their own unique climate, wildlife, vegetation, culture, living accommodations, and inhabitants—be they Gors, Sythians, or humans.

Ethan was still trying to get used to the idea of living beside a creche full of Gors, but that's what he got for picking the relatively cold and mountainous side of the Icosahedron. This face of the New Earth was the one that most reminded him of his old home in the Imperium, back on Roka IV.

A subtle jolt came through the deck as the *Trinity* touched down, and then his daughter bounced up from the copilot's seat and said, "When can we go again?"

Trinity's violet eyes were wide and full of wonder from their most recent flight over the New Earth. For her, everything that had happened was not as close and personal as it was for him and Alara. Trinity had been born without any prior existence to weigh her down. She hadn't taken part in the Great War that he and Alara had fought on the wrong side of all those years ago.

"We'll go again after dinner," Ethan said as he rose from the pilot's chair. "Maybe your mother can join us this time."

"Yay!" Trinity squealed.

But after dinner everyone was too tired to go touring. They took fermented tea and a hot chocolate for Trinity up to the rooftop to watch an artificial sunset. They lay on a reclining couch, bundled up under thermal blankets, watching stars prick through a deep indigo sky as the sun sank below the distant, craggy line of the Crystal Mountains.

Trinity recounted the day's adventures for her mother's benefit, but soon her bubbling conversation lapsed into rhythmic breathing, and Ethan had to take her cup away before she spilled hot chocolate all over herself. He looked on with a smile as she nodded off.

Three days ago they'd welcomed Trinity into this new world. They had a month's head start on her, but it was still just as fun seeing everything for the first time through their daughter's eyes. They went out with her every day, discovering new things, exploring new places, and meeting people they'd once known who now lived close by—Alara's parents, Ethan's mother... Magnum.

Meeting the former lieutenant of the Rictans had been tense, but Magnum had chosen to take the high road.

"Water under the bridge," he'd said. "You did what you had to do to save your family. I would've done the same. No guts, no glory, remember?"

Ethan smiled at the memory. He was glad that Magnum wasn't holding any grudges, particularly now that they were neighbors.

Alara laid her head on Ethan's shoulder and sighed. "This is a dream."

"No, the dream is what we woke up from. I'm pretty sure this is real."

"That's not what I meant."

Ethan smiled. "I know. I was just being a wise ass."

"Always were."

Ethan snorted and shook his head. "There's still something I don't get. If Etherus created us, did he create everything else, too?"

"I'm not sure, but something tells me we're not going to get all of the answers unless we go to Etheria, and we've already been there. We didn't like it."

"Well, we're going to visit. Maybe I'll ask a few Immortals while we're there."

"What makes you think they'll tell you? Besides, we used to live in Etheria. Having all the answers wasn't good enough for us then, and it won't be good enough for us now."

Ethan nodded, pursing his lips. "Maybe you're right."

"Of course I am. I'm always right."

Ethan shot her a skeptical look. "Really?"

"I was right about marrying you, wasn't I?"

"Good answer."

"We were meant to be together."

"You're talking about destiny. What about people who had other partners as Immortals? What if those were the people they should be with, rather than the ones they're with now? How's that fit in with destiny?"

Alara withdrew from him. "Are you trying to tell me something?"

"I'm just trying to figure things out. I don't think we have a destiny. Not anymore. I'm with you because of free will and circumstance."

"Sounds romantic," Alara said.

Ethan grinned. "And love. Did I mention that?" he asked, leaning in for a kiss.

Alara leaned away. "No, you didn't."

"Well, I was thinking it," he said, and used the arm around her shoulders to pull her in for the kiss she was desperately trying to evade.

"That's better," she said as they withdrew.

Ethan took a sip of his fermented tea. "What do you remember from Etheria?"

"Not much, why?"

"It makes me wonder if things were actually better there. What if staying here, as humans, isn't what we wanted? What if we didn't walk into those stasis tubes willingly and this is actually some kind of punishment for failing Etherus's test? Maybe the reason we don't remember everything anymore is just a way to keep us from figuring things out."

"Did you have those concerns when your soul woke up and suddenly you remembered everything?"

"No."

"Then don't worry about it. You're still thinking like we're living under Omnius's thumb. We're not. Etherus is everything Omnius pretended to be and more. We don't have to look over our shoulders anymore, Ethan. If you want to remember your life in Etheria you just have to concentrate and it'll come back to you. Etherus gave us new implants for a reason—to keep our old memories. They're not irrelevant, but they belong to the old us, and we're the new. Now we're mature enough to cope with freedom because we've learned how terrible it can be."

Ethan frowned. "I'm sorry. You're right. It's hard to stop doubting things when you have a lifetime of practice. It's a defense mechanism, I guess."

Alara rubbed his knee. "I know, but it's okay. We're safe. You can relax."

Ethan sighed again and took another sip of his tea. "Yeah, I guess we are. What do you think Atton is doing right now?"

"The same thing as us—" Alara replied, smiling. "—wondering where we go from here."

"Onwards and upwards," Ethan suggested, looking up at the sky as the last blotch of color faded with the sun. As the sky finally disrobed, a multitude of stars came out in a glittering field that took Ethan's breath away. Unlike the sky and the sun, which were artificial, those stars were real and recorded from visual feeds on the outside of the Icosahedron. Ethan's eyes skipped between those brilliant points of light, wondering what else was out there that they didn't know about.

"What's the first thing you're going to do when we get to Etheria?" Alara asked.

Ethan smiled wistfully as his gaze found a particularly bright point of light, one that he'd been told was actually the Immortals' galaxy—Etheria.

"I'm going to find my son," he decided. It was bittersweet to think of Atton being so far away, but the distance didn't seem so vast when he considered they had quantum jump drives that could travel from one side of the universe to another in the blink of an eye.

"Ethan..."

"Yeah?"

"I have something to tell you."

He turned from stargazing to look at her. "What is it?"

"I'm pregnant."

Ethan blinked; then his eyes flew wide and he shook his head. "How... I mean... we've only been together again for a month!"

"And before that, we were together for years."

"But you died!"

"I know."

Ethan gaped at her. He remembered losing his wife, and now he realized that in that moment he'd lost his wife and their unborn baby.

"Omnius cloned me with the fetus," Alara explained.

"Why didn't you tell me sooner?"

"Because we were barely getting by as it was, and I was looking for the right moment. Then it was time for Trinity's Choosing Ceremony, and I thought if we went to Etheria—the one on Avilon—maybe it wouldn't be such a problem anymore. I kept trying to convince you to go, but it didn't work."

Ethan pulled Alara into a hug. "I'm so sorry," he whispered beside her ear.

"It's okay. You didn't know."

Trinity stirred on the other side of him. "Mom?" she asked, sounding confused.

"I'm right here, darling," Alara said, leaning around Ethan to speak to her. "You're going to have a little brother!" she exclaimed.

"I am?"

"It's a boy?" Ethan burst out. "Wait—Trinity doesn't know yet?"

"I didn't think it would be right to tell her without telling you first. And after you... well, after I thought you cheated on me, I was too distracted. I think telling her without you around would have meant admitting to myself that we were over."

Ethan stroked Alara's cheek. "I'm sorry you had to go through all of that." Then something occurred to him. "Wait a minute—we've been here for a month already! You could have told me weeks ago."

"We've both been so busy, and I wanted to wait until I could tell you and Trinity together. Can you forgive me?" Alara whispered, pressing her forehead to his. Her lips were tantalizing close.

"Hmmm..."

"What's his name?" Trinity asked, interrupting them before they could kiss again.

"We don't have a name yet, sweetheart," Alara replied.

"What about... Lucien," Ethan suggested.

"Why Lucien?" Alara asked.

"Because it means *light*, and I think we've all had enough of the darkness. We spent years hiding from the Sythians in Dark Space, and then years hiding from Omnius in the Null Zone, but this life and this world are going to be different. They're going to be full of light, and Lucien will be one of the first to be born into it. That's his birthright—an unending kingdom of light."

Alara nodded. "Lucien it is."

"Now I have two sons that I'm waiting to see," he said, patting Alara's stomach. He couldn't feel her showing yet, so at least he knew she hadn't waited too long to tell him. "I'll see you soon, Lucien," he said.

Looking back up to the stars, he found that bright point of light once more and nodded to it. *See you soon, Atton.*

WHAT'S NEXT

EXCELSIOR

Coming December 2015!

To get a **FREE** digital copy of *Excelsior* when it's released, please
post an honest review of this book and send it to me here
(http://files.jaspertscott.com/excelsiorfree.html)

Remember, your feedback is important to me and to helping other readers
find the books they like!

EXCELSIOR SYNOPSIS

The year is 2790 AD, and this is the Second Cold War. The lines are drawn, with the communist Confederacy in the East, and the free citizens of the First World Alliance in the West. With space elevators and giant orbital fleets hovering over Earth, open war looks inevitable, and people are anxious to get away.

In hopes of finding a refuge from the looming war, the Alliance is sending Captain Alexander de Leon to explore an Earth-type planet, code-named *Wonderland,* but at the last minute before launch, a Confederate fleet leaves orbit on a trajectory that threatens both the mission and Alliance sovereignty. The resulting power struggle will determine not only the fate of Alexander's mission, but the fate of the entire human race.

FOREWORD

My name is Captain Alexander. I live in a world where people are genetically-engineered to perfection, never to age and never to die—all for the right price. We call them Geners. They call us *de-gener-ates*. They live in the Northern States, while the underprivileged degenerates or *natural-borns* are relegated to the South. Geners and degeners don't mix on any level of society. That might sound like discrimination, and it is, but it's legal, and it's actually enforced by the government. Degeners are overly aggressive, we have impulse-control problems, mental problems, and a host of other issues. We also score low on empathy and collective interest tests, which makes us bad citizens. But worst of all, we eventually *die* of old age. The only way to jump state lines from a degener state to a gener one is to take the retroactive therapies and implants to become like them. Problem is, that's a hell of an expensive way to go, and who has that kind of cash?

Thankfully, there's a war on; it's a *cold* war, but people still die, and Geners don't like risking their immortal necks *para nada*. Before you ask, we all speak English, but I grew up in the *barrio*, met my wife there, and got married there. I probably would have died there, too, but then I started contemplating eternity. The Alliance has this deal. They need pilots and crew to go up the space elevator and guard their half of the planet from orbit. In exchange, the Alliance promised to make us Geners. One four year term of service to buy one set of treatments and a passport to the heavenly North. I took two terms, one for myself and one for my wife. It seemed like a fair trade at the time.

But I was wrong.

They're sending me away, *far* away, and now I'm never going to have a chance to enjoy eternity with my wife. Those kids we always said we'd have—she's going to have them with someone else while I'm gone. When life gives you shit, you sure as hell can't make lemonade.

Usually you just step in it.

PREVIOUS BOOKS
IN THE DARK SPACE SERIES

Dark Space I: Humanity is Defeated
(http://smarturl.it/darkspace1amz)

HUMANITY IS DEFEATED

Ten years ago the Sythians invaded the galaxy with one goal: to wipe out the human race.

THEY ARE HIDING

Now the survivors are hiding in the last human sector of the galaxy: Dark Space—once a place of exile for criminals, now the last refuge of mankind.

THEY ARE ISOLATED

The once galaxy-spanning Imperium of Star Systems is left guarding the gate which is the only way in or out of Dark Space—but not everyone is satisfied with their governance.

AND THEY ARE KILLING EACH OTHER

Freelancer and ex-convict Ethan Ortane is on the run. He owes crime lord Alec Brondi 10,000 sols, and his ship is badly damaged. When Brondi catches up with him, he makes an offer Ethan can't refuse. Ethan must infiltrate and sabotage the Valiant, the Imperial Star Systems Fleet carrier which stands guarding the entrance of Dark Space, and then his debt will be cleared. While Ethan is still undecided about what he will do, he realizes that the Imperium has been lying and putting all of Dark Space at risk. Now Brondi's plan is starting to look like a necessary evil, but before Ethan can act on it, he discovers that the real plan was much more sinister than what he was told, and he will be lucky to escape the Valiant alive. . . .
Buy it Now (http://smarturl.it/darkspace1amz)

Dark Space II: The Invisible War
(http://smarturl.it/darkspace2amz)

THEIR SHIP IS DAMAGED

Ethan Ortane has just met his long lost son, Atton, but the circumstances could have been better. After a devastating bio-attack and the ensuing battle, they've fled Dark Space aboard the Defiant to get away from the crime lord, Alec Brondi, who has just stolen the most powerful vessel left in the Imperial Star Systems' Fleet—the Valiant, a five-kilometer-long gladiator-class carrier.

THEY ARE LOW ON FUEL

They need reinforcements to face Brondi, but beyond Dark Space the comm relays are all down, meaning that they must cross Sythian Space to contact the rest of the fleet. Making matters worse, they are low on fuel, so they can't jump straight there. They'll have to travel on the space lanes to save fuel, but the lanes are controlled by Sythians now, and they are fraught with entire fleets of cloaked alien ships.

AND THERE IS NO WAY OUT

With Brondi behind them, they can't go back, and they can't afford to leave the last human sector in the galaxy to the crime lords, so they must cross through enemy territory in the Defiant, a damaged, badly undermanned cruiser with no cloaking device. Making matter worse, trouble is brewing aboard the cruiser, dropping their chances of survival from slim . . . to none.

Buy it Now **(http://smarturl.it/darkspace2amz)**

Dark Space III: Origin
(http://smarturl.it/darkspace3amz)

THE DEFIANT IS STRANDED

Ethan and his son, Atton, have been arrested for high treason and conspiracy, crimes which will surely mean the death sentence, but it's beginning to look like theirs aren't the only lives in jeopardy—the Defiant is stranded in Sythian Space, and the vessel which Commander Caldin sent to get help has used all its fuel to get to Obsidian Station, only to find out that the station has been destroyed. Now the Defiant's last hope for a rescue is gone, and everyone on board is about to die a cold, dark death.

HUMANITY IS STILL FIGHTING ITSELF

Meanwhile, the notorious crime lord, Alec Brondi, is plotting to capture the remnants of Admiral Hoff's fleet, just as he captured the Valiant, but Hoff's men are on to him, and Brondi is about to get a lot more than he bargained for, forcing him to flee to the one place he knows will be safe—Dark Space.

AND A NEW INVASION IS ABOUT TO BEGIN

But Dark Space is only safe because the alien invaders don't know exactly where it is, and now they have a plan to find it which will threaten not only Dark Space, but the entire human race.

Buy it Now **(http://smarturl.it/darkspace3amz)**

Or Get All Three for a Special Price
(http://smarturl.it/darkspace1-3amz)

Dark Space IV: Revenge
(http://smarturl.it/darkspace4amz)

DARK SPACE WON THE BATTLE

Humanity has just won a major victory against the invading Sythians--the first victory in the history of the war. The savage Gors have joined forces with Dark Space, and now for the first time since the invasion, it looks like the tide is turning. But the Sythians weren't defeated. Humanity just bloodied their noses. Now they know where Dark Space is, and they are coming back for revenge.

THE WAR STILL RAGES

Admiral Hoff Heston is secretly terrified of what's coming, but he's lulling people into a false sense of security. He needs to buy time. The people of Dark Space are not as alone as they think.

AND EVERYTHING IS ABOUT TO CHANGE

Avilon, a lost sector of humans, has remained hidden and untouched by the Sythian invasion. No one knew they even existed, except for Admiral Heston. Now he must send a mission to contact them and get help, but what humanity finds there will change more than just the course of the war against the alien invaders . . . it will change the very nature of their existence.

   Buy it Now (http://smarturl.it/darkspace4amz)

Dark Space V: Avilon (http://smarturl.it/darkspace5amz)

THE SYTHIANS INVADED AGAIN

Dark Space, the last refuge of humanity, is overrun; its citizens are either enslaved or dead. The relentless Sythians have slaughtered humanity wherever they could find them, and now only a few hundred survivors remain. Desperate to escape, these few chase rumors of a lost sector of humanity and end up on Avilon, a planet covered with a vast, kilometers-high city that lies hidden and shielded from the rest of the galaxy by its impossibly advanced technology and its benevolent ruler-- Omnius, the Artificial Intelligence who would be god to his human creators.

HUMANITY FOUND REFUGE ON AVILON

Omnius reveals that no one really died in the war--he couldn't save them from the Sythians, but he did find a way to record the contents of their brains and resurrect them all in the bodies of immortal clones. Omnius keeps a record of everyone's mind in order to make predictions about the future and prevent people from making mistakes. The result is a perfect paradise where you can be assured of a happy, successful life for the rest of eternity--just so long as you are willing to give up your freedom and submit to Omnius's will. If you refuse, you can live in the Null Zone, a city that lies cloaked in shadows below the immortal paradise where Omnius reigns supreme. In the Null Zone humanity has its freedom, but the result is chaos, death, and forced separation from everyone living in the Upper Cities of Avilon.

PARADISE FOR SOME IS A PRISON FOR OTHERS

To Ethan Ortane, who spent years exiled on a prison world in Dark Space, Avilon and its utter lack of freedom is the

Netherworld incarnate, and Omnius the Devlin himself. His son, Atton, is not so sure--it's hard to argue with Omnius's governance when death and suffering have become just a distant memory. Even better, it looks like Avilon with all of its advanced technology might finally be able to put an end to the Sythians. Omnius is sending his Peacekeepers to Dark Space to rescue the human slaves and take the fight to the invaders....

THE ROAD TO THE NETHERWORLD IS PAVED WITH GOOD INTENTIONS...

Despite the Sythian apocalypse, Omnius knows that humanity's worst enemy has always been itself. Darkness lies in the human heart and if paradise is to be maintained, that darkness must be contained. For Omnius the rightness or wrongness of an action is determined by a mathematical equation: the choice with maximal benefit for humanity and minimal detriment is always the right one. And with his ability to predict the future, who could be better suited to making those judgments? But when the looming detriment defies the very purpose of Omnius's existence, the benefit that outweighs it depends very much on one's point of view....

Buy it Now (http://smarturl.it/darkspace5amz)

KEEP IN TOUCH

SUBSCRIBE to my Mailing List and Stay Informed about
Upcoming Books and Discounts!
(http://files.jaspertscott.com/mailinglist.html)

Follow me on Twitter:
@JasperTscott

Look me up on Facebook:
Jasper T. Scott

Check out my website:
www.JasperTscott.com

Or send me an e-mail:
JasperTscott@gmail.com

ABOUT THE AUTHOR

Jasper T. Scott is the USA TODAY best-selling author of more than thirteen novels, written across various genres. As an avid fan of Star Wars and Lord of the Rings, Jasper Scott aspires to create his own worlds to someday capture the hearts and minds of his readers as thoroughly as these franchises have.

Jasper spent years living as a starving artist before finally quitting his various jobs to become a full-time writer. In his spare time he enjoys reading, traveling, going to the gym, and spending time with his family.

Made in the USA
Middletown, DE
07 December 2015